Barkley Sound Secrets

A

"J" Team Novel

by

Jonathan McCormick

for

First responders whose dedication, expertise and humanitarianism have saved the lives of countless survivors of sexual and domestic abuse

You are heroes.

"Your hands and feet are your tools.
Your mind is your weapon."

Jessica Fukishura

Barkley Sound Secrets is a work of fiction. Characters are the author's creation. Names, characters, places and incidents are of the author's imagination or used with the permission of the owner. Any resemblance to actual events, locales, or persons, living or dead, is coincidental.

"Don't mistake kindness for weakness. Sometimes the kindest women are the fiercest warriors."

"Women hold only five percent of the CEO positions because of the old boys' club, networking organizations and brotherhood maintain the status quo."

Entity Magazine/Academy Los Angeles

Jonathan McCormick

Vancouver Secrets portrays educated, articulate and driven women living in an age of *Me To* and *Times Up* movements. As individuals, they long ago gave up on the concept of marriage and family, deciding instead to forgo having to care for a man incapable of managing his own life.

All have a deep-rooted dislike of men; Jessica's stemming from her mother sharing the atrocity of the 1989 massacre of fourteen women at Montreal's École Polytechnique and the fact that men left the women to die.

In the process, the "J" Team women's careers flourish while encountering, overcoming and in many instances, destroying workplace harassment, misogyny and sexual assault.

Vancouver Secrets embraces sex, love, mystery, suspense, martial arts, fashion and cuisine blending them with a well-researched plot of money laundering in Canada and the United States.

Cuisine and fashion enhance the readers' identification with the protagonists as the agents dine in some of the country's finest restaurants in Toronto, Vancouver, BC, Las Vegas, Los Angeles and shop the latest fashions from Nordstrom, Toronto's Holt Renfrew and specialty boutiques from coast to coast.

Jessica, Rebecca, Penelope and Elisabeth encourage readers; to leave abusive situations, to change their environment and to accomplish their goals and dreams.

Along with their male law enforcement partners, the women hope readers will find encouragement, support and reject violence and control as givens.

Praise

For

The "J" Team Series

"I liked Santa Barbara Secrets a lot. You have cut out your own turf and are sticking to it. As far as I know, no one has staked out this turf as you have.

The luxury life is your beat. The men hopelessly shopping for summer togs was quite funny. Also, the detective agency opens up lots of interesting avenues for sub- and parallel plots.

The ladies' shit-kicking men remain my fave scenes. I think we need them to meet a foe whose skills match their own in hand-to-hand.

And, gotta love them kitties.

Good work, my friend, and I look forward to the next installment."

Les Wiseman Royal Roads University

"What a treat for me to receive your book! Thank you so much for sending it and remembering me. Made my heart feel very good. I had no idea you were as 'dangerous' as you are... Heh!"

Dr. Barrie Bennett University of Toronto

“If you like to read, try this book, a very good read and hard to put down.”

Curtis Leithead Corrections Officer

“I hope by now your Jessica has found a literary agent worthy of her exploits. Be well! Write on!”

Harley Jane Kozak Author

“The author was my former high school English teacher and a few years later was my instructor in a self-defense program. He certainly knows the subject matter, which is evident by the rich detail in this story. Only someone with his training and experience could add the necessary realism to this kind of story. I look forward to the next instalment of these characters and their exploits.”

Kris Patterson

Thank you SO much for *Santa Barbara Secrets*!! I look forward to finding out more about Jessica and who she is taking down! When I first opened the book, it fell to page 272 (a scene with Tom and Karen) HAHA! I thought.... "this is going to be interesting!”

I love the cover by the way...very appealing.

Michelle Kamloops, British Columbia

"Jonathan McCormick has just released his second book in the "J" Team series. It is called *30,000 Secrets*. It totally rocks. McCormick's books (the first being *Wyoming Secrets*) take the side of women as heroes/heroines and enables women with strategies and tactics to help themselves with self-defense maneuvers.

A black belt in a number of self-defense arts, McCormick donates 100 percent of book royalties to support abused women. If you like a team of good gals against the contemporary ills of the world then this is the book for you. If you dig Brad Thor, Stephen Hunter, Tess Gerritsen, Andrew Vachss, Patricia Cornwell, John Connolly, Elizabeth George, or David Morrell, you want to add McCormick to your reading list."

Les Wiseman Royal Roads University

Prologue

The Chica de Oro slipped back into Cojo Bay off the tip of Point Concepción just north of Santa Barbara, after unloading her million-dollar cargo and headed south.

Her retreat was to have been executed covertly; the crew was ignorant their departure was observed from the cliffs. The watchers recorded the cylindrical vessel slide through the surf and disappear into the choppy waters; her exodus shrouded by the late-night coastal fog. She left much as she arrived, minus her cargo but with the addition of two, six-inch long cylinders magnetically attached to her hull, their presence unknown to the operators.

The cargo submarine was the proud development of Adrian Achterberg, the son of a WWII German boatwright who gained fame within the Nazi regime for his U Boat designs. Adrian had learned the trade quickly under his father's tutelage, acquiring his own notoriety within the boat industry for his steel fabrication brilliancy.

Never considering himself a Colombian, in spite of his Medellin birthplace, Achterberg harbored considerable resentment against western powers for what he felt was an unfair treatment of his father who fled Nazi Germany on the tail of the Nuremberg Trials, fearing reprisal for his role in the development of the deadly submarines which killed hundreds of allied sailors, destroyed millions in cargo and a wealth in lost vessels.

"The only thing that ever really frightened me during the war was the U-boat peril."

Winston Churchill

When the cartel approached Achterberg at his shipyard with the request to design and build a twenty-meter submarine capable of carrying a thirty-metric-ton payload and four crew members, capable of thirty-knots submerged and an air supply for ten days, he asked few questions, taking delight in the opportunity to retaliate against the Canadians and Americans whom he blamed for his father's decades of anguish, while reaping several million dollars for his efforts.

His creation was pure marine genius and so eclectic in appearance, few would have made a connection between the sub and its use in nefarious activities. It didn't have a coning tower of a traditional submarine, nor did it have any of the outer fittings usually associated with subs. The surface was smooth, almost glass-like to the eye and touch. The exterior was coated with photonic crystal, an acoustically tuned material off which sonar waves bounce, or more accurately, bend off the hull, to loop back around to the vessel's surface again and again, never returning to the source of the sonic pulse, thereby creating the impression the ping did not meet a solid object, as in contacting a submarine. The cargo space was generously spread throughout to provide adequate balance, particularly during submersing and surfacing.

Power was created with lithium batteries, designed by a British Columbia firm, which were less than half the size of conventional power supplies and rechargeable from a diesel engine, so quiet that it was undetectable by Coast Guard hydrophones. The hybrid system was designed jointly by Ontario and Nova Scotia firms created for commercial, law-abiding vessels.

Achterberg borrowed NASA and International Space Station technology to design a system to recycle crew urine, sweat and breath to create a water source and the electrolysis of water to generate oxygen, the power for the process provided by the lithium batteries. In the case of an air supply failure the sub would rise just below the surface and extend a tubular air intake, just long enough to absorb a twelve-hour air supply.

Back-up emergency air supply with autonomous breathing devices was available for each crew member, along with a vessel escape hatch from which they could surface while scuttling the vessel and cargo in case of a total system failure. The sub lacked radar to detect patrolling ships and planes, so their reconnaissance was strictly visual, necessitating as short a surface time as possible.

The cartel lost millions from a recent joint operation involving the Canadian HMCS Saskatoon and the US Coast Guard Hamilton off the coast of Central America. The drug financiers were committed to eliminating the catastrophic losses.

The twenty-meter/sixty-five-foot submarine was protected from interdiction from Canadian and American Navy by the Germanischer Lloyd. The two-person, mini submarine was equipped with fixed pontoon tanks on each side and a raised glass bubble conning tower. The interior remained unlighted for the entire length of the voyage save for the few control switches and buttons which created an eerie perspective of the stealth, low-profile vessel.

The scout sub carried four mini torpedoes to be deployed if, by unforeseen circumstances, a Canadian or American naval vessel became aware of the Golden Girl, the English translation of her name, the Chica de Oro.

The mini sub had state-of-the-art maneuverability and with its speed could advance, retreat or hide in an underwater cavern on an encroaching enforcement ship, then sneak up behind it once it passed the cavern.

"I must confess that my imagination refuses to see any sort of submarine doing anything but suffocating its crew and floundering at sea."

H.G. Wells

Chapter ONE

Jessica Fukishura sat in her Santa Barbara law office reflecting on the last few days of inactivity. For the first time in her lengthy Secret Service career she was unable to contribute to an operation, having left the coordination to Agent Elisabeth Peltowski who was working from Rebecca Simpson's Santa Barbara home.

She relaxed in the high-back leather chair, one leg crossed over the other, sipping her black, holding the white mug in both hands, musing the last operation.

Peltowski and her colleagues, Jason Spencer and Jackson Pennington, had been involved in the investigation of the Christians for a Better America's attempt to eliminate hundreds of Democratic candidates, sitting senators and congressmen and congresswomen by sabotaging a Mahalo Airline flight from Minneapolis to Los Angeles, carrying the Democratic dignitaries to a Marina del Rey convention, forcing the Boeing 737 into the Pacific just west of the international airport.

Once the bodies were identified at the convention center and arrests made in Denver, Colorado and Minneapolis, the trio were deployed to assist Jessica in locating the source of the political currency and cocaine.

The three were now working out of the most luxurious setting of their careers, retired Secret Service Agent, Rebecca and her life/business partner, Dr. Penelope Barker's ranch in the foothills above Santa Barbara.

Rebecca had owned the ranch for many years, having obtained it on the advice of Alane Auberée of Birdcage Investments, her financial advisor for the past two decades. Auberée put her into Warren Bates' Berkshire Hathaway Investments immediately upon taking her as a client, investing her entire monthly salary in Hathaway. He invested six thousand dollars for six shares on the date of Berkshire's IPO, initial public offering. The stock split fifty to one a year later, then every month for the last twenty years he invested her monthly salary. At retirement she was earning one-hundred and twenty thousand plus undercover bonuses with the Secret Service.

Early in her career, Rebecca knew she didn't want a White House or protection detail and acknowledged that working out of embassies would force her to leave the service out of boredom, which was why she jumped at the opportunity for permanent undercover.

It didn't take much effort on her part to become a minimalist; renting furnished apartments for several months, then leaving without a trace. But she did miss horses, the aroma of their hair, the essence of their bodies as she groomed, curried and saddled for a few hour's ride into the back hills…somewhere. She couldn't return to Montana for her R&R since every sheriff's deputy within the state's boundaries, and a few outside of them, knew her on sight, which would invite too many questions.

When the California housing market collapsed, Auberée took a loan out on Rebecca's portfolio, which produced an interest a fraction of what she was earning on her investments. His astute planning allowed her to avoid qualifying for a mortgage, a move that would have revealed too much of her covert activities.

The spectacular Mediterranean estate with a dual gated entrance and four car-garage, was a two-story, fifty-two-hundred square feet, five bedrooms, five baths, family room and a one-thousand square foot pool and guest house next to the

Olympic size swimming pool. It was previously owned by a hedge fund manager who found himself heavily in debt with two mortgages on the estate when the market disaster hit. The two banks foreclosed and with zero buyer initiative it sat empty for several years.

Auberée purchased the property in Rebecca's name and she signed the documents in StoneHead while working undercover against the Citizens for a Better America. Jessica, having passed the California bar exam upon graduation, could act as a notary and certified Rebecca's signature.

Alejandro, their neighbor and retired Beverly Hills landscaper, arranged to have the house cleaned before one of Rebecca's last visits. It took his team several days to make the house a pristine home. Alejandro renovated the exterior, replacing dead trees and bushes with drought tolerant varieties, creating a breathtaking garden.

Rebecca and Penelope set the agents up in their own bedrooms with on-suite bathrooms and the three made themselves at home with their hosts and their critters…six kittens which Pen and Rebecca adopted from the local animal shelter. The agents grew attached to the felines immediately, Jason more so than Elisabeth and Jackson.

With a full gym, indoor shooting range, massive gun safe and the Olympic size pool, the agents were hoping the current assignment would be indefinite.

"If your home environment is good, peaceful and easy, your life is better and easier."

Lori Greiner

Chapter TWO

Jessica had been directed by Secret Service Protection Detail Supervisor Sorento to infiltrate the Santa Barbara legal profession, collaborate with retired agent Rebecca and her partner Penelope to discover how and why American currency was moving through the Los Angeles drug business to a Caribbean financial institution and back to Santa Barbara.

Hundreds of millions of dollars were processed in and out of the Southern California area and given to the Christians for a Better America right-wing political candidates.

Jessica obtained a position with Katrina Barbados' law firm, her curriculum vitae enhanced by counterfeit University of California Berkley law degree credentials, a Washington, DC work history as a para-legal and a fictitious former partner whom she punched and threw out of their apartment after he became violent.

Barbados was expanding and needed an aggressive attorney to match the volatility of many of her criminal clients, some who had threatened staff with physical violence when they were found guilty of the crimes they committed.

Day one, Barbados assigned Fukishura to collaborate with colleague Marianna Gutierrez, who had three recently arrested clients sitting in LAPD lock-up. Gutierrez needed to separate the representation and hired Barbados' firm, which brought Jessica to the Santa Barbara Airport to join Gutierrez on a chopper flight to the LA courthouse to free the top lieutenant for the Hermanos de Wall Street cartel, The Brothers of Wall Street.

The cartel was one of the largest biker gangs in the state, albeit unknown to most. Organized during the tumultuous seventies by greedy San Francisco lawyers disbarred for their manipulation of clients' portfolios, they struck back at society with highly organized and profitable operations which created a wealth far beyond their law school dreams and more than they could ever steal from clients.

Their biking was as recreational now as it had ever been. Their criminal status didn't motivate them to ride with outlaw bikers or patronize their bars. They had their own drinking establishments. Private of course, and only open when they would be riding through. A phone-call a couple of days before their arrival would set in motion a lavish lunch, sans alcohol, and their enjoyment of partying with their fellow Hermanos de Wall Street members. Conversations could be open, honest, unobserved and unrecorded, as their security team scanned the facilities for electronic devices before their arrival, then left.

The Bar, if one wanted to be so crude as to call it that, was more in keeping with a high-end San Francisco or Vancouver hotel lounge, where sushi and seafood towers complimented handcrafted cocktails. Each of their lounges was unique with classy English-style décor, complete with tapestries and mahogany furniture.

Jessica did free the top lieutenant, to the astonishment of the senior attorney who had expected her to obtain a continuance and bail, not release him with the charges dropped.

Neither Gutierrez, nor her client, Julio Fernández were aware that Fukishura had met previously with the LAPD Drug Squad and arranged for detectives to violate Fernández's rights by not having a search warrant for the currency storage facility where Julio was arrested.

Fernández walked away from the arrest with several million dollars from street sales, which he would hand-deliver to Santa Barbara accountant, Anthony Henderson, the cartel's primary financial officer.

Unknown to the arrestees, Fukishura had arranged with the LAPD detectives to place GPS tracker chips in the arrestee's belts (which they had relinquished upon booking) and bug their cell phones, allowing Elisabeth to record all texts and conversations in and out of the suspects' phones.

The issue of civil rights and whether these actions violated those of the suspects was addressed, in writing, by the Secret Service, which received prior approval by a federal judge on the grounds of national security, the Christians for a Better America remaining a threat to the president.

Taking another sip of her black, Jessica turned slightly to enjoy the westerly view of the Pacific Ocean and mused how the operation had ended.

The street dealers, lieutenants, Henderson and Fernández were arrested and the Golden Girl's shipment of cocaine was transported to LAPD lock-up by LA County Jail Special Squad with ground and air support and housed in a jail section off limits to everyone during renovations.

"Together, we will defeat this epidemic. It's a true epidemic, as one people, one family, and one magnificent under God."

Donald Trump

The President claimed in March 2019, that in 2018 the southern ports of entry seized enough fentanyl to kill 90 million Americans.

The Department of Justice stated that between 2017 and 2019 more than 16,000 kilograms of heroin and 5,000 kilos of fentanyl were seized in America.

Within hours of the detainment of her clients, Marianna Gutierrez received two phone calls. The first was expected, Julio Fernández had been arrested…again. The extent of that conversation put her on the verge of panic when he cryptically shared the reason for his detention. The cartel owed their Colombian supplier the four hundred plus million for the cocaine, which sat in the LAPD vault along with the cash Henderson brought from the cocaine drop at a winery north of Santa Barbara.

The second call was from her contact within the Santa Barbara Police Department, sharing the confidential information that terrorism charges were eminent against her from a federal prosecutor in Los Angeles.

She wasn't terribly concerned about the financial loss as Hermanos would not experience a set-back. Her anguish stemmed from the possible ramifications and reverberations to the expanding Canadian market, which Hermanos had financially backed at Marianna's request.

The prospect of being charged was more annoying than troublesome and she racked her brain wondering what evidence they had that would warrant such an aggressive move.

She had never needed an attorney to be extricated from her transgressions with the LAPD but being an advocate of "*a lawyer who defended herself has a fool for a client*", she put in a call to Katrina Barbados.

Chapter THREE

Marianna was well known by the Southern California one-percent social sphere for her fund-raising acumen, amassing millions for various political candidates in Canada and America through $5,000 a-plate-dinners. Covertly, she orchestrated the distribution of millions to Christians for a Better America candidates and to the extremists' nefarious activities.

Gutierrez was a founding member of Hermanos de Wall Street. She was one of only two non-disbarred attorneys in the organization whose forensic accountants were experts at risk management and manipulating accounts and funds. They take the millions raised at various political functions, deposit them to a legitimate American business account, then send that same money around the world electronically through various VPNs-virtual, private networks, which are securely encrypted, guaranteeing anonymity.

They falsely report the millions raised, infuse the drug funds, contribute a portion to political parties and invest the remainder. Any government agency attempting to follow the transfers would be bogged down in the encryption and the funds bouncing from one country to another, landing in an obscure account, totally undetected.

In addition to the political funds' investments, once a month, the group sends an associate from Los Angeles or Vancouver, British Columbia, in a private jet, with cash from drug revenue on the pretense of a reward for the most billable hours. The employee enjoys a week on the islands at the firm's luxury condo, not knowing that the Lear jet landed in a foreign country with millions hidden within the plane's opulent interior.

The pilots and crew are treated similarly on another part of the island, leaving the plane unattended, albeit within the confines of the hanger, to be visited furtively by a messenger who retrieves the cash, then deposits it in the offshore account…no questions asked.

The attorneys owned various businesses into which part of the drug currency was filtered. One such company was the Central California Road Maintenance, a firm with multi-million-dollar fluid contracts. Fluid in the sense that many contracts activated their cost override clauses, adding hundreds of thousands to an already bloated project.

The complexity of Hermanos' financial empire was controlled and shaped by Anthony Henderson, whose current incarceration was puzzling to Marianna. There had been no communication between her and Henderson, ever. And Henderson didn't communicate with the team who moved the product from Point Concepción to the distribution location in Santa Ynez.

Gutierrez was unaware of Elisabeth Peltowski monitoring Henderson's phones or the tracking devices in Fernández's clothing and phone.

Chapter FOUR

Jessica continued musing her future, weighing the pros and cons of retiring from the Secret Service. She had been shocked to see what Rebecca could afford and although it was too late for her to amass a fortune matching Rebecca's, she could invest her monthly retirement check and supplement the investment from her Barbados medium six figure salary.

But would the service allow her to retire? Their policy required an agent to be at least fifty years old with twenty years' service. The latter she had, the former? She wasn't even close, at least that is what she told herself in front of the mirror daily.

Her gross monthly salary from the government was ten thousand, five hundred plus thirteen-hundred undercover bonus. The additional she'd been paid monthly for her law degree and multilingualism (French, Japanese and English) brought her to thirteen thousand, eight hundred dollars. She was earning twenty-five thousand monthly from Barbados.

Adding a complexity to her quandary was her desire to take down Marianna and her network. *Was that too lofty an ambition and did she need to be an agent to accomplish this goal?* she asked herself.

Christians for a Better America, which Marianna and Hermanos financed, had their criminal tentacles wrapped so strongly around the political movement they considered themselves impervious to indictment. At least they did until the arrests and trials which shocked thc world. She knew eliminating CFBA was impossible but cutting off the California financial wing? That was doable and she wanted to spearhead the operation.

She needed to speak with Rebecca and Penelope and see if she could work for Barbados in retirement as well as work as an attorney for R&P Investigations. Rebecca and Penelope had opened the private investigations company in Santa Barbara the year prior. Then she had to put out feelers at the White House to see what kind of a retirement deal she could arrange.

The last question to which she needed an answer was if she should or needed to tell Katrina the truth.

"Yes", she said loudly, making her decision, slapping her right hand on the desk, sliding out of the chair, grabbing her briefcase and heading to meet Gutierrez, either in a holding cell or in Margarite's office.

"There's nothing like biting off more than you can chew, and then chewing anyway."

Mark Burnett

Chapter FIVE

Five. Wide awake. Force of habit. Twenty plus years of living covertly, always on edge wondering if the truth had been discovered. Sleeping with a 9 mm. under the sheets. The smell of cordite.

No longer.

Rebecca turned slightly, hoping Penelope was awake but knowing full well she was not. All she could see next to her was an elongated lump under the light cream duvet with spring birds and flowers, which thwarted the fifty-five-degree mountain night temperature having slipped quietly into their bedroom through a slightly open security window.

Normally she would wake Pen from her rem sleep by snuggling and sliding her hands down her body, creating sensuousness, culminating in sumptuous sex. But this morning all she could do was inhale Penelope's scent, smile and slowly, gently extricate herself from the queen and shuffle to the bathroom, every muscle in her body aching from yesterday's long and intensive operation.

Her stiff and painful muscles weren't caused by the physical and mental stress of participating in the recent joint police operation. She had years of similar experiences, some back-to-back over much longer periods than this joint LAPD, SBPD and Secret Service undertaking. No, today's discomfort was generated primarily by the stress of R&P Investigations.

When she proposed the idea to Penelope, the concept was more of something to do. A vehicle to contribute to the community. To be part of something bigger. Their first emphasis was to develop *Refugio Seguro, Safe Haven* for homeless female teens.

They had a five-year plan to renovate an existing building and have it staffed but that prospect was fast forwarded to possibly a year, if not sooner. The dinner party they'd held for Santa Barbara's movers and shakers was more of a success than they could have dreamed. City council members, the chief of police and several philanthropists came forward to provide not only financial backing, which they hadn't wanted, but a location without charge and contractors to renovate.

Unbeknownst to either Rebecca or Penelope, their neighbor Alejandro was one of Santa Barbara's financial elite and with his encouragement, numerous others stepped forward to participate. Alane Auberée took on the responsibility of coordinating the project, relieving the women to concentrate on their business concept.

Rebecca had visited Santa Barbara regularly over several decades but didn't interact with the community given her Secret Service status, so she was an unknown factor at the dinner party. But once Alane introduced her and retired veterinarian Penelope Barker, numerous business leaders approached them throughout the night asking for their help. R&P Investigations was born and hit adulthood all in one evening.

Rebecca donned her Cobalt blue robe, the twin to Penelope's, with matching slippers and made her way into the kitchen. She stopped at the entry and took a moment to appreciate the good fortune Alane had provided. She admired the amber toned oak paneled cabinets above and below the sink which wrapped around the L-shaped kitchen, meeting a stainless-steel Miele built-in convection oven with a matching microwave above. The countertop was quartz with swirls of cream and copper tones with a matching backsplash. The theme repeated for the six by eight-foot island, which hosted a six-burner gas stove top with a wine refrigerator hidden behind one of the eight amber storage cabinets.

Smiling to herself, she prepared coffee, removed two large white mugs from the cupboard, placed a couple of frozen croissants into the convection oven, then stepped through the French doors to a covered patio and sat to wait for the coffee and pastries.

Slipping one leg over the other, she ran her fingers through her short blonde ‘do that was spiky over her ears. Not coincidently, Pen’s style was similar but short buzzed on the sides and long and overlaid on top.

As the coffee’s aroma drifted through the screen door, she glanced out on the semi-desert landscape Alejandro had created and mused how blessed she had become since moving to Santa Barbara.

Retirement hadn’t entered her thoughts until a magical weekend shopping with Penelope in Denver, Colorado. They had become friends interacting with the colts Rebecca was training and Penelope was treating. The relationship grew over many entertaining evenings at Cassandra’s, a local pub with music and dancing. It was late in the day at the Denver hotel while changing into their newly purchased swimsuits…when a spark ignited between them.

The rest of the weekend passed in a blur of love making, shopping and enjoying Denver’s fine cuisine. Upon their return to StoneHead, Rebecca knew she couldn’t maintain a deceptive relationship and shared her retirement plans with Jessica.

Her boss was directing the investigation of CFBA from StoneHead Ranch’s security center. While in office, then President Bakus maintained a western White House with plans to host a G7 summit meeting. It was during his reelection campaign that CFBA escalated their crusade against his liberal views and him personally.

Jessica not only gave Rebecca her unwavering support but arranged for full retirement benefits even though Rebecca didn't qualify. Jessica's argument with Sorento was the Service owed it to Simpson for her years of undercover work.

Rebecca was a key component in the take-down of two senior CFBA terrorists at an Idaho mountain-top hideaway and agreed to postpone her departure until the operation's conclusion.

Jessica arranged for a retirement party at the Ranch and offered to explain or rather unveil, the real Rebecca Simpson to Penelope since Pen believed Rebecca to be a horse trainer taking a break from teaching, a career with which she had become disenchanted.

Bakus' Executive Chef, Marc Stucki, created a culinary masterpiece for the event and served each course himself, delighting in the happiness of his friend of many years.

To her dismay, Penelope wasn't surprised, explaining that she began wondering the first time she removed Rebecca's blouse and saw the small pistol strapped under her bra. Pen said she really started pondering when Rebecca was groped by a guy at the hotel pool, knocked him out and broke the arm of his buddy. Her inquisitiveness hit with red lights flashing when the police arrived, and the lead officer called the station to run Pen and Rebecca's identification and promptly gave the phone to Rebecca.

With the truth revealed, Rebecca's anxiety vanished and she thought she and Penelope might have a chance at a life together.

Enjoying Marc's culinary delights and chardonnay, the dinner chatter moved to more normal discussions, each woman sharing her background and career choices. Several times Penelope laughed to herself, prompting the others to inquire as to the humor and Pen would share a memory of one incident or another where Rebecca had been involved in a fight.

The one that brought laughter to everyone was the night Pen and Rebecca were dining with friends at Cassandra's in StoneHead when two guys pestered them to dance. Rebecca rebuffed them numerous times and they left, only to try again in the parking lot. Rebecca broke one guy's leg and the nose of the other with Pen asking, "Shouldn't we have run?"

Rebecca replied, "I don't run".

Rebecca was jolted from her reverie by Penelope opening the sliding screen door. She smiled warmly at the sight of Pen wearing the matching Cobalt Blue bathrobe and slippers, gliding sleepy-eyed toward her.

Rebecca jumped up and took one step to meet Pen and enveloped her in a passionate hug, snuggling her face into Pen's neck and nibbling on her ear. "Good morning sleepy head. Are you as exhausted as I am?"

"Good morning to you too," Pen replied, kissing Rebecca's nose then brushing her lips and tongue slowly across Rebecca's, moving her tongue lustfully around Rebecca's lips.

Enjoying the tranquility but knowing she didn't have the energy to take the affection into the living room, Rebecca returned the kiss while caressing Penelope's butt, then moved back slightly while running her hands down Pen's arms, asked, "How about coffee and a croissant and we can figure out what we are up to today?"

Rebecca stepped around Pen, sliding her hand down her back, stopping at her right cheek, moving with her through the sliding door into the kitchen.

Rebecca had trained Penelope in the use of firearms; handguns, shotguns, fully automatic rifles and Tasers while the state of California instructed Pen on the nuances of being a private detective. Pen had received her PI license and concealed carry permit just days before joining the Secret Service and SB Police in taking down the cocaine smugglers.

Penelope removed the pastries from the oven while Rebecca poured their coffee, then sat at the kitchen table just as Pen joined her.

Clinking mugs, Rebecca began, "What are your thoughts on the last few days, regarding R&P? I thought the business would grow slowly, not take off like a gazelle. I am stressed out trying to figure how we can handle all the business."

Penelope thought for a moment as she broke her pastry into small pieces and ate one. Clearing her throat, she replied, "I have given it some thought as well, but just briefly after I woke this morning. I'm not stressed though. I mean, we are both retired, don't really have to work, so we can pick and choose the jobs we take?"

Taking a sip of her black, Rebecca said, "True, but we also want to move forward with the housing project and leave time for us as well. I've been tossing around the idea of a staff but don't want the hassle of the government paperwork."

Penelope replied, "I can attest to the hassle of taxes and records from my practice and I was a sole proprietor. There has to be a way to manage without the hassle. How about we ask Elisabeth, Jason and Jackson when they get up and also Alane, between the four of them they might have some suggestions."

"Sounds good to me. I'm not up for a gym workout or run today. Are you interested in a swim, then breakfast in town and see our first client?"

"Okay. Let's do it. Do you want to go skinny dipping?" Pen replied with a lecherous grin as she put her dishes in the dishwasher and headed upstairs.

Rebecca was right behind her, put her dishes away and said, "I am not that brave yet but maybe someday," as she quickened her pace to get right behind Pen as she ascended the stairs and cupped both her butt cheeks, then climbed the stairs beside her.

"Lesbianism, politically organized, is the greatest threat that exists to male supremacy."

Rita Mae Brown

Chapter SIX

RCMP Staff Sgt. Karen Winthrop had been seconded from her RCMP Corporal position as an Air Marshal to CSIS, Canadian Security Intelligence Service, Canada's spy agency, during the theft of cesium from a Manitoba mine that was used to bring down the Mahalo Airliner.

She and Toronto Police Service Sgt. Tom Hortonn had worked with the Costa Rican government to find and control Brian Sawyer, the Albertan drug producer who had received the cesium from the thieves and hid it in a secret compartment under a Canadian Pacific rail car.

The CP railcar was on a side-track waiting to move its cargo into Idaho. The radio-active material was picked up by two Idaho First Nations drug runners. They in turn placed the cesium under a corpse from a funeral home and sent it to Minneapolis where it was transferred to the LAX bound flight.

Since returning from Costa Rica where they were confident the Costa Rican agents were monitoring Sawyer 24/7, their CSIS supervisor, David Kopas, sent them to Vancouver, BC.

They had already engaged in preliminary meetings with the RCMP's anti-terrorism unit and CSIS agents, with the Force agreeing to Winthrop and Hortonn taking the lead on the burgeoning cocaine industry, which the RCMP believed was being spearheaded out of Vancouver, directed by Stan, who orchestrated the cesium theft and supervised Sawyer's drug operation. Stan had been under RCMP physical and electronic surveillance 24/7 for weeks.

Edmonton RCMP detectives wanted to track Stan Loblinski's phone activity but even with the Stingray technology, often referred to as Mobile Device Identifiers (MDIs) which requires a court order prior to implementation to track phone calls and texts, they were unsuccessful. They needed to make physical contact with their suspect, and once fruitful, Karen and Tom would be tasked with discovering with whom he was communicating.

They were once again operating covertly as a vacationing Toronto couple, scrutinizing Vancouver as a possible future home. Their morning runs, daily hotel gym routines coupled with dining habits unique to health-conscious Vancouverites, created transparency.

Home for Karen and Tom for the foreseeable future, was the L'Océan, French for "The Ocean" on W. Waterfront Road in Vancouver.

The L'Océan afforded guests a spectacular view of the Lion's Gate Bridge which spanned the Vancouver Harbour and joined the city to West Vancouver, and it provided a thirty-minute walk to Stanley Park and the acclaimed Seawall running/walking trail circling the park.

Their suite offered vertical gold and cream stripped wallpaper, a cranberry couch with an accent chair in a cranberry and gold pattern, square, red oak end tables, topped with intricate wrought iron lamps and warm cream shades. Numerous French Impressionist art pieces blended with four off-white sconces and the ubiquitous large screen television atop a six-foot tall credenza.

Off the sitting room was an ample bedroom with a queen bed, a high-boy and mirrored dresser, the décor of which was an extension of the drawing room.

Tom woke to the sound of rain thrashing against their suite's bay window and the seventy-kilometer wind trying its best to toss sidewalk café furniture across Waterfront Street.

He slipped on his bathrobe and walked slowly around the bed, groping the wall trying not to bump into something or wake Karen. Making it to the bathroom, he quietly closed the door, turned on a blinding light, used the facilities, shut the light off, unplugged his phone and used the flashlight feature to make his way past the bed, closed the door and into the sitting room.

He drank the complimentary five-hundred milliliter bottle of water and made a pot of Spirit Bear *Eagle*, a medium roast from Spirit Bear Coffee in Coquitlam, British Columbia, using the second bottle of water, retrieved the Globe and Mail and Vancouver Sun newspapers from the hallway, salvaged his doggy bag from last night's dinner and settled on the sofa to peruse the printed news and review yesterday's investigation notes.

The front page of each paper exhibited a half-page photo of Canada's Prime Minister Justin Trudeau as he addressed the nation regarding the scandal surrounding Members of Parliament, Jody Wilson-Raybould and Jane Philpott who resigned from Cabinet, sighting a loss of confidence in the prime minister's leadership.

He didn't bother to read the story in either paper, his emotions already saturated with the television coverage. He skimmed through various stories seeking anything regarding local drug arrests or incidents linking distributors or suppliers.

Nothing.

As he imagined, the Vancouver Police were concentrating their efforts on contraband being smuggled in shipping containers through the Port of Vancouver, a source Hortonn and Winthrop knew was not germane to their investigation since none of the containers were from Colombia, the center of their criminal probe.

Setting the papers aside, he filled his mug with more *Eagle* from the cafetière on the credenza, then walked to the bay window and pulled back the curtains, hoping to see a sunrise.

None.

The rain continued to pound against the window, but this observation brought a smile, not a frown. A physical response of which he was unaware other than a slight emotional exuberance.

Returning to the sofa, he took a sip of his *Eagle*, then began reading through yesterday's notes.

Law enforcers world-wide are territorial, sometimes within departments, but most often between agencies. Karen had been spared that unprofessional behavior as a Sky Marshal, operating independently from the RCMP. But now as a CSIS agent, even though technically still a Staff Sergeant in the Force, she had to deal with aloofness.

Tom had not experienced interagency conflict up to this point in his career. Being a Toronto Police Service Sergeant, he had worked exclusively with his own department and periodically the Transit Police and Ontario Provincial Police. His interaction with CSIS and the RCMP was new and his experience and common sense told him to follow Karen's lead regarding communicating with the Force and CSIS.

He read his notes briefly, then let his mind wander, enjoying the comfort of the hotel suite and Karen's company. They had met at the University of Ottawa what seemed like ages ago, then lost touch over the years until the surprise phone call which brought them to this point.

Karen had been on a flight from Washington, DC as the Air Canada Sky Marshall and had to clear Secret Service Agent Jessica Fukishura of her firearm and in doing so, the women became friends, dining in Toronto, engaging in morning runs in the park and defensive tactics techniques at the TPS Training Centre.

It was the latter which brought Karen and Tom together with Karen calling Tom asking permission to train at the exclusive facility.

The defensive training experience was unique with officers exchanging offensive-defensive positions, each learning from the other.

Nearing their allotted time, they were challenged by a misogynistic TPS officer who was late entering the twenty-first century and had zero respect for female officers. Jessica put the brakes on his ego and bigotry, sending him to Toronto General Hospital at the end of a challenge.

Smiling to himself, Tom remembered his nervousness calling Karen the next day to ask her out. Wasted emotions, it turned out. She accepted and they dined that night at the Calgary Steak House, whose GM was former classmate Soul Train, AKA Craig Stevenson.

Soul Train acquired his moniker as a bartender, his part-time gig while at the university, often dressing as a Mexican bandit with crisscross bandoleros holding shooter glasses of tequila. He made his way up the career ladder, operating upscale restaurants like the Calgary.

Hearing the bathroom functioning, he snapped out of his reverie, crossed to the credenza, poured a cup of black from the cafetière, then leaned against the wall, arms crossed with the Eagle in one hand as Karen emerged from the bathroom in her matching hotel robe.

Smiling wickedly, Karen moved cat-like across the cranberry carpet, slipping her fingers through her short bob and when she reached Tom, slipped her arms through his robe's opening, around his back and kissed him passionately.

Returning the kiss, he stood, arms fully engaged, holding the coffee with one hand and the front of his robe the other.

Karen broke the mood with, "Mr. Hortonn, do I detect a slight interest in something other than coffee?" as she slid her hand across his stomach, pulling the robe open.

"You do Ms. Winthrop, but if I give into my desires, we will miss the other action this morning," Tom replied, smiling, now holding both arms out to his sides, waiting to see what Karen had planned.

Karen took the black from him as he re-tied his robe, and offered, with a lift in her voice, "Okay. But I won't let you forget the offer you just turned down…all day."

Tom slid his arm around her waist and guided her over to the sofa and his array of notes, while trying to control his raised heart rate. As they sat, Tom began the review, beginning with, "I think we made a wise decision to stay clear of the division's headquarters and take the offer at the University of British Columbia's detachment. We are escaping the grueling commute and what we figured would be the constant overview of the Deputy Commissioner and her staff."

"Agreed," replied Karen, taking a sip of her black and a bite of Tom's pastrami sandwich on a hoagie bun. Wiping her lips, she continued, "That sandwich is better the second day. Thanks for sharing," she smirked. She glanced down at their notes and said, pointing to the names on the notepad,

“We have made an excellent breakthrough with the Edmonton detectives tracing Stan’s short text to Brosman and Snow LLP and Kuznetsov Chartered Accountants here in Vancouver. *Loblinski,* tapping the notepad acknowledging Stan’s last name. “This will help tremendously. It would be interesting to know how this information was unveiled to the Edmonton detectives. Something tells me their physical surveillance team used a Stingray,”

Tom slid into the corner of the sofa, lifted one leg over the other, exhibiting somewhat of a smirk, being careful not to expose too much and risk Karen pouncing on him. He took a sip of black and replied, “They could have used a Stingray for sure, but what about CHAP? It is possible they contacted Elisabeth who tapped into Bumblehive and have both throwaways monitored?”

Hortonn was referring to the 1.5 billion-dollar Utah electronic monitoring facility, Bumblehive, which was capable of capturing every key stroke, phone number and targeted conversation and maintaining the data in the system’s five zettabytes storage capacity.

The system processes private emails, cell phone calls, and Internet searches as well as personal data trails; parking receipts, travel itineraries, and store purchases. Bumblehive is synced with another NSA program, PRISM which collects Internet communications obtained from American Internet companies.

The 1.5 million square foot complex is capable of sharing information with any authorized agency, primarily American, but under special circumstances, theoretically any agency, anywhere.

Tom's comment about CHAP was in relation to a system devised by U.S. Navy Commander Cheryl Chapman, a former SEAL who had been seconded by former president John Bakus to tie all agencies into a common electronic thread.

Chapman was a SEAL, the U.S. Navy's special operations force (Sea, Air and Land). The United States Navy did not have female SEALs. That was the rule, not the policy. The rule. No women. The service offered a litany of reasons to the media; women are too weak and too sensitive.

But Chapman was a decorated Navy SEAL along with several platoons of other accomplished strong, insensitive sailors who were trained secretly thousands of miles from the male SEAL's training center in California.

The Big Boggy National Wildlife Refuge, 6 hours southwest of Houston, Texas, was home to thousands of migratory birds; geese, ducks and brown pelicans, in a 4,500-square mile marshland that opened to the Gulf of Mexico. The refuge was closed to the public and basically closed to the U.S. Fish and Wildlife staff too since the SEAL compound was in the most isolated and remote section which Fish and Wildlife employees were too glad to ignore.

Code named *JARC,* for Joan of Arc, who led French troops into battle against the English, the SEAL teams were housed in an abandoned farmhouse and outbuildings just east of The Boggy where their firearms, intelligence, counterterrorism and martial arts training were covertly conducted.

The Pentagon had used one of its many Black Accounts - money allotted to a legitimate government fund, then transferred from one account to another…somewhat like the con shell game where a pea is under one of three cups and the sucker must choose the pea's location.

JARC was the back-up team to SEAL Team Six which took out Osama bin Laden. The coalition forces created an interesting diversion for *JARC*.

The team was aboard the Canadian Destroyer *Athabaskan* patrolling the Gulf of Oman as their normal duty. The team had been choppered aboard the ship during the desert blackness, team members faces covered and were housed in separate quarters for the attack's duration. When one of Team Six's choppers went down, *JARC* was mustered and airborne within minutes, heading to Islamabad for a rescue, if needed.

Team Six regrouped and escaped with bin Laden's body so *JARC* returned to the ship to await their stand-down orders, which came 24 hours later.

Team Six members were later killed by Afghan insurgents using rocket propelled grenades, destroying the Chinook helicopter Extortion 17 as the Team was entering the Tangi Valley in eastern Afghanistan to back-up an Army Ranger strike force seeking an enemy combatant.

Cheryl Chapman had risen through the ranks, rejected all of the Navy's attempts to promote her to management and fought fiercely to maintain her qualifications, year after year. But age and nature were catching up to her and Bakus was positive he could make her an offer she couldn't refuse.

The system she'd devised, CHAP, was used extensively in monitoring the various suspects in the cesium theft and the ultimate unravelling of the circumstances of the Mahalo Airlines downed 737 off the coast of Los Angeles.

CHAP tied all approved agencies together, allowing on-going investigations to cross state, provincial or international boundaries and to link their efforts and expedite arrests and convictions more efficiently than each agency did previously on their own.

Edmonton RCMP detectives discovered Brian Sawyer's Costa Rica's general location using CHAP and his fingerprints off the quad he used to transport the radio-active material. Karen and Tom had been dispatched to the Central American country to locate and turn him to produce information for CSIS on cocaine smuggling routes/personnel from Colombia.

They were successful.

Karen and Tom batted the concepts around, making sure they understood their assignment and who was involved; both suspects and their law enforcement partners. Karen broke their concentration with, "Okay, we're good to go?"

"I think so. I'll go get ready."

"Not so fast Mr. Hortonn," she replied with a grin, jumping up and straight arming him. "I am going to have the pleasure of waiting for you to get ready this time," she quipped running into the bathroom. As she closed the door, she stuck her head around the doorframe, saw him looking, smiling and blew him a kiss, then closed the door.

Tom shook his head as he picked up his mug, walked over to the credenza, added more black then pulled the drapes back, hoping once again for the weather to have cleared.

Still no change..

He stood there, glancing down, appreciating the twinkling white lights lining Water Street, marveling how similar but yet different Toronto and Vancouver were.

His gaze moved upward to the murky mist of the Vancouver Harbour; the silhouette of several anchored freighters blurred by the pounding rain.

The massive ships would proceed inland to unload shortly, to be replaced by a never-ending flotilla, some carrying legitimate merchandise, others, contraband.

Tom smiled to himself, thankful the integrity of container traffic wasn't his responsibility.

He closed the drapes and returned to the sofa, listening to Karen's shower running, musing his fortune of reconnecting with her, remembering a quote from a writer Karen asked him to read:

"Seriously, what does 'having it all' even mean? 'All' is subjective. Not every woman's vision of a perfect future looks the same. Not every woman wants kids. Not every woman wants to get married.

Not every woman wants a house in the suburbs. Not every woman wants a career. Not every woman is attracted to men in the first place. Why and how did dudes become the key to our perfect future?"

Iliza Shlesinger *Girl Logic*

Tom thought, *I haven't a clue, but I sure as hell better find out before this relationship advances. And how do I do that?*

As he realized how ignorant that last thought was, his encrypted phone vibrated. Elisabeth.

Chapter SEVEN

The Chica de Oro reduced her speed and rounded the Isla Gorgonilla, a Colombian National Park. It had been a maximum-security prison until 1983 but now, two and a half hours from the mainland tourists observe Humpback whales in their breeding habitat.

Clearing the park, she headed south-east to a fiord south of the little town of Tumaco and slowed her approach, surfacing just a few meters from the dock and slipped into its mooring at midnight.

The southwestern corner of Colombia provided an ideal location for the Golden Girl with a hot, humid, often rainy and overcast climate.

These conditions, coupled with 2,300 millimeters-90 inches (Seattle, Washington receives 1,016 mm, while Wrangler, Alaska averages 2,667 ml or 105 inches yearly) present a discouraging environment for locals to explore or become curious about the surrounding jungle.

The two-hundred thousand local population shied away from going beyond the city limits for fear of the Fuerzas Armadas Revolucionarias de Colombia, Revolutionary Armed Forces of Colombia or FARC, the guerilla force which had been fighting the government since 1964 and now the criminal gangs which had infiltrated the vacuum left by the FARC.

Over 200,000 thousand Colombians died during the decades of violence, with America providing a billion dollars toward the peace process.

The group laid down their weapons in 2017 and its current leader Rodrigo Londoño, aka Timochenko, ran for president in 2018 but had to withdraw for health reasons with attorney Iván Duque Márquez being elected.

Whether Londoño could have controlled the cartels or if Márquez can, time will tell. In the meantime, the cartels continue to export their product by land and sea, the latter most notably in the Chica de Oro.

The retired U.S. Navy submariners were met by cartel drivers who transported them to the Flughafen Tumaco Airport and from there to Mexico City where each departed to various American cities.

The Golden Girl's crew was unaware that their voyage from California's Point Concepción had been monitored by Canadian Naval ship HMCS Toronto, recently reassigned from anti-terrorism duty in the Indian Ocean to track the submarine.

The Chica de Oro had traveled almost the entire distance submerged to twenty meters. For the crew, that was sufficiently deep to extend the air snorkel periodically without fear of detection. For the naval trackers, it was a perfect depth to monitor their signal.

As the vessel's final destination became obvious to the Canadians, they generated a radio beam to the magnetic GPS trackers breaking the connection, causing the trackers to drop into the ocean.

Santa Barbara Police Department SWAT team had affixed the trackers after she had unloaded her cargo. The devices fell one-hundred and twenty meters into the silt on the ocean's bottom.

Once the uncoupling was confirmed, the HMCS Toronto's captain deployed Canada's Special Forces' Joint Task Force 2 team, JTF2. The six members traveled half the distance to the Columbian shoreline in an inflatable Zodiac, then swam the remaining distance underwater, leaving the inflatable with a GPS to be recovered post-operation.

Rebreather scuba tanks created an undetectable approach, allowing them to breathe their own air repeatedly, producing no surface bubbles. The system removed carbon dioxide and replenished the oxygen using multiple computer-controlled sensors and a pure oxygen supplement tank.

The stealth team split into two groups as they approached the wharf, going left and right, breaking the surface simultaneously, their Colt C7 silenced assault rifles shouldered, while the remaining three agents adhered tracking devices on the bottom of the Chica de Oro, totally undetectable and permanent.

The assault team was unable to obtain intelligence regarding the possibility of cartel security for the multimillion-dollar vessel. Consequently, the squad scanned the sub and shoreline with ultra-light night vision goggles, searching for any movement or unidentifiable shapes, a task made almost impossible by the overcast sky and weathered buildings, and prepared to eliminate any threat.

The Colombian drug cartels had become overly brazen of late with their product being shipped undetected through a vast number of routes. Bolstering their entrepreneurial ego was the reality of little or no threat from law enforcement or military intervention.

Although the prospect of life in Colombia was brighter than that in Argentina, refugees escaping economic hardship and a collapsing government crossed the frontier borders with nothing and were prone to steal cocaine ready for shipment in the remote production camps.

Several million Argentinians had already crossed into Colombia with the number of refugees expected to hit four million by 2021.

All available Colombian law enforcers and soldiers were guarding border entries and registering refugees while cartel sentinels were deployed to guard inland production facilitie.

The day after her arrival, the Chica de Oro was refueled, refitted and loaded with its next shipment. The new crew of retired American submariners arrived on day two, familiarized themselves with the vessel, performed systems checks and sailed at the midnight-high tide.

"Of all the branches of men in the forces there is none which shows more devotion and faces grimmer perils than the submariners."

Winston Churchill

The drug cartel would find Sir Winston Churchill's WW2 analysis humorous given the crew's motivation was strictly financial.

The massive wealth the retired American sailors would make on this one trip was so overwhelming, any disgrace they might have felt for shaming their country and branch of service was insignificant.

Chapter EIGHT

Brian Sawyer maintained his weekly encrypted texts to Winthrop and Hortonn but had dismissed their threat of being arrested for terrorism and doing jail time in Canada, deducing their absence equated to freedom. He provided what he considered tidbits of information, gossip really, nothing worthy of further investigation by CSIS or whatever Costa Rica agents were involved. His lifestyle remained unchanged; enjoying the beauty and serenity of his coastal cove home, the interior walls of which held millions in American and Canadian currency and his friends and neighbors who continued to believe he was a retired Alberta oil worker.

With the stress of CSIS removed, he quickly reverted to the joy of the drug trade with frequent retrieval of the cartel's bait cocaine packages from the cove south of Limón. Money never being an issue, it was the adrenaline rush of getting away with an illegal activity, identical to what he experienced for years in Alberta which motivated him.

Brian had been drinking with his friends at the Cuir Ó dhoras, when CNN reported the story of the Port Authority of New York & New Jersey seizing four hundred kilos of cocaine worth a street value of ten-million and smiled to himself, knowing that he was part of that operation. The US Drug Enforcement Agency spokesperson interviewed by CNN exhibited great pride in explaining to the reporter that it was the container's latch pin which appeared to have been tampered with that clued them into something amiss.

The real shipment, on its way to the UK after the brief American stop, was what Brian had orchestrated. Twice the seized quantity of cocaine was packed with Costa Rican bananas, the odor of which prevented drug sniffing dogs from detecting the product.

The cartel knew that giving the drug agents such a huge quantity would leave the law enforcers so jubilant they would not inspect the ship further.

So much contraband passed through world-wide ports daily that it was impossible to interdict much, plus the tarantulas Brian inserted into every banana box tended to discourage a thorough investigation by DEA agents.

Unfortunately for the American drug interdiction branches, the front-line agents were unaware of the intricacies of the Puerta Rican and Colombian smugglers. And they didn't know fruit. Numerous banana shipments arrived at New Jersey and New York ports in refrigerated containers.

These were decoy shipments.

Bananas are never refrigerated, particularly the fruit picked green to ripen en route.

Sawyer remained unaware of the Costa Rican agents following him 24/7 and the video feed from the hidden cameras inside his quaint beach house, placed there by Winthrop prior to confronting Brian with his ultimatum.

Brian's belief that he had outsmarted the Canadian spies would have been shattered had he known that every shipment to which he contributed which sailed from Limón to Europe was confiscated in Tilbury, east of London, by the National Crime Agency-NCA-the UK's lead agency against organized crime: human, weapon and drug trafficking.

The NCA waited until the banana shipment had been retrieved from the docks and delivered to a fruit distribution outlet. Covert surveillance provided the intelligence necessary to identify those separating the bananas from the ten kilo cocaine packages, then transported the drugs to a warehouse outside of the main shipping terminal.

Heavily armed and armored officers descended upon the warehouse, confiscating the forty million in pure cocaine and arresting the low-level dealers.

Accompanying the NCA agents were several arachnology and entomology professors from prestigious London universities who removed the spiders before the agents extracted the cocaine. The educators were delighted to participate in the volunteer activity…they kept the spiders.

Subsequent investigations resulted in several of the original arrestees receiving a reduced sentence for reliable information on the major drug characters. NCA and Scotland Yard were linked to CHAP allowing the RCMP, CSIS and Elisabeth to have the investigative details immediately.

"Federal authorities do not have the manpower or the resources to protect America's international borders."

John Culberson

Houston is 5 miles/8 kilometers from the Mexican border where crossing the Rio Grande River is an everyday occurrence with hundreds of undocumented immigrants seeking financial relief. While scores are captured by the U.S. Customs and Border Protection agents, twice as many establish permanent, albeit illegal, residence in the border states. Many make their way to California where identification is readily available in the form of a driver's license. The license provides a bona fide legality to their residency.

The U.S Border Agents have apprehended suspected members of Somalia's al-Shabaab, Lebanon's Hezbollah, Pakistani Taliban, ISIS and Tamil Tigers. More are suspected to have entered either via the 3,200 kilometer/2,000-mile unguarded ranch property which runs through both countries, or across the Rio Grande River.

Chapter NINE

Francesco Loblinski was loading a full lift of red cedar two-by-fours destined for Japan's gazebo and outdoor furniture market. He lifted the three-thousand pound/thirteen-hundred and sixty-kilogram load, swung the forklift to his right and moved slowly to the end of the holding shed, rounded the corner and headed for the waiting railcar. As he approached the tracks, the forklift's right wheel dug into a pothole Francesco thought he had skirted. He tried desperately to correct the steering by turning the wheel sharply to his left, but it was too late.

The load shifted, throwing the lift on its side. Within seconds, Loblinski had been driven down toward the pavement just as the load landed. He instinctively threw his right arm out to brace his fall just as the load landed. His right arm was pinned.

British Columbia Ambulance Service in Port Alberni was at the scene within four minutes, quickly stabilizing Francesco's arm after his co-workers righted the machine and removed the lumber. Paramedics inserted an IV in his uninjured arm and started two lines; ringer's lactate: calcium, potassium, lactate, sodium, and chloride in addition to morphine, to stabilize the injury caused by the high energy trauma.

Paramedics placed their patient on a stretcher, slid him into the ambulance and spirited him to West Coast General Hospital, seven minutes away.

The ambulance made a right on Harbour Road, left on Dunbar and left on Third while the paramedic caring for the patient made the call to the West Coast emergency staff on their incoming patient. By the time the ambulance hit the Port

Alberni Highway, nurse Paul Manhas and his colleagues were at the emergency entry with a gurney.

Francesco Loblinski hadn't regained consciousness after passing out from shock. The morphine created a euphoric, dream like state taking him back to his small Italian village where he and his friends were playing in the street while his mother and sister prepared mafaldine, a ribbon pasta. He could smell the simmering red sauce and frequently glanced at his home hoping to see his sister beckoning him to dinner.

His family had immigrated to Canada fifty years ago, settling in Port Alberni with his dad finding mill employment immediately. Port Alberni was a port city sitting at the end of Barkley Sound, the longest inlet/fiord on Vancouver Island, just west of British Columbia's largest city, Vancouver.

The city was named for Spanish explorer Don Pedro de Alberni who commanded Fort San Miguel at Nootka Sound, north of Tofino on the island's west coast, from 1790-1792. The area saw the Spanish attempt to dominate as early at 1774, trading with members of the Nuu-chah-nulth. For decades the British, Spanish, Russians and French jockeyed for control of the area.

Explorers eventually found the remoteness of Nootka unattractive and concentrated on the deep-water port of Alberni for trade and development.

The first sawmill opened in 1860 and within one-hundred years loggers had stripped the forest surrounding the city, leaving an unappealing and ugly landscape of bald hills dotted with stumps. It took decades for the natural growth to recover while mills went further inland for their raw material.

By 2019 there were hundreds of acres back in the hills which were never replanted and remained moonscapes, barren of any marketable trees.

Alberni developed an impressive tourist trade, taking some pressure off the declining lumber industry throughout the mid-twentieth century, with salmon fishing, kayaking in the inlet and summer cottages springing up at nearby Sproat Lake.

Campbell River, which was just north of Qualicum Beach on Vancouver Island's east coast and Port Alberni had an on-going rivalry of which city was the Salmon Capital of the World with Alberni hosting an annual Salmon Fishing Derby sponsored by the local Kiwanis club featuring their "secret recipe" for salmon fillets.

American Cruise ships would visit Port three times during the summer with each ship carrying anywhere from 900 to 2600 affluent passengers who availed themselves of the numerous activities offered in the area and in Barkley Sound.

Times were good and within the first two years of arriving to Port Alberni, Francesco Loblinski's family had their own house above the Harbour Quay. Loblinski attended the junior secondary school two blocks from his house and the local high school of equal distance.

Many of his friends dropped out of school in grade nine to take a lucrative, albeit menial job at the mill but his parents insisted he graduate. Neither of his parents finished school in Italy and it was their dream that their children would enjoy the opportunities their adopted country afforded.

He did.

Life was good for many years until a downturn in the forest industry closed several mills, taking his high paying job.

His seniority created the fork-lift position, a minimum skill that he hoped to segue into retirement in a few years.

Francesco was saddened by the many negative social changes he had observed over the years, many having to do with cocaine addiction.

The opiate had been around for decades as a recreational drug. Addictions were seldom, but now overdoses were seen almost daily somewhere in town. He was thankful his son had left when he did to avoid the temptation of big money and recreational drugs.

He'd often see young employees leaving the restroom stall, talkative with flushed skin…the former always strange in a men's restroom. Some of the young men would exit a stall trying to stifle a nosebleed.

Loblinski was constantly torn between doing what he felt was his civic responsibility; turn the addicts in and call the Mounties on the dealers he saw selling in the wood stacks or saving the jobs of these young men with families.

His mind had drifted back to his house on the hill, inherited from his folks, with the aroma of parmesan, red sauce and spicy sausage, when the faint distant sound of a siren shook him from his reverie. The noise grew with intensity as pain began to consume his body, little by little until he was wide awake, staring at the ambulance's ceiling, strapped to a gurney, a mask over his face and what he learned later were two large bore IVs in his uninjured arm.

The paramedic, seeing his patient's fearful look, increased the morphine drip slightly to take the edge off the pain just as the double doors flew open with nurse Manhas and staff preparing to receive the gurney and dispatched Francesco into emergency.

The trauma team transferred Loblinski to their gurney, quickly wheeling him into the emergency ward where Ativan was added to his IV to reduce his anxiety.

A physical examination revealed his blood pressure to be 80/40 mm Hg with a heart rate of 130 bpm. He had sustained a ten-centimeter long laceration in the left axillary fossa. His forearm had suffered crushed flexor muscles with the fractured bone ends protruding.

Loblinski remained in the emergency ward until his blood pressure and heart rate were stabilized, received a unit of blood (525 ml), then he was transferred to Vancouver General Hospital. The staff were ready for him and he was immediately moved into an operating room where surgeons fused the bones using stainless steel screws, removed damaged tissue and sutured the laceration. He would later be fitted with a plaster cast to immobilize the arm during the healing process.

Four days later, Loblinski was back at West Coast General for a cast fitting, then discharged. Manhas was back on shift with Francesco as one of his primary patients. Francisco was eating, walking and would be well on his way to recovery, albeit after extensive physiotherapy with full recovery of his arm expected.

Both men being locals, it was natural for them to chat periodically about the city and their youth. Manhas shared that the hospital was experiencing a continuing rise in drug related injuries and overdoses, many of the latter being from Fentanyl, a synthetic cocaine. The men shared a common interest in having sons. Manhas' was attending university and sadly, Loblinski hadn't seen or heard from Stan in over a decade, having rejected Alberni for a richer, brighter future…somewhere.

Manhas' patient revealed how he had seen several of his colleagues using needles between the wood piles and in the washrooms.

Both patient and nurse found it disheartening that neither of them could affect a change in the opioid crisis.

The greatest artificial threat to human life was fentanyl, seen as law enforcement's primary objective, given the hundreds of deaths attributed to the toxic and controversial drug. Their focus left the recreational cocaine consumers unabated, much to the financial pleasure of Stan Loblinski.

"Despite our wonders and greatness, we are a society that has experienced so much social regression, so much decadence, in so short a period of time, that in many parts of America we have become the kind of place to which civilized countries used to send missionaries."

William Bennett

Chapter TEN

Fukishura was musing Bennett's philosophy while driving to Gutierrez's office, wondering if America would ever solve their drug problem. Reagan's War on Drugs spent billions providing funding to local and national agencies, creating educational programs for school districts and deploying CIA and Delta Force teams into Colombia attempting to stem the cocaine flow, all to no avail given the millions the "J" Team and LAPD had just processed.

"Sheepdogs can be male or female."

Jessica Fukishura

Arriving at Gutierrez's office building, she parked, locked and did her 360, spinning on her left toe, instinctively in Condition Orange-high alert, of the Color Code of Awareness, the psychological emotional mechanism of every apprised law enforcement officer.

She felt confident in a bay coral CeCe Ruffle Halter-Neck, sleeveless jumpsuit with tie sash. She had paired the suit with Bibbiana's taupe ankle booties with a two-inch heel and side zipper.

Her client's law office was an upscale version of Katrina Barbados' with what appeared to be original oil paintings of local landscapes hung artistically on a red-brick wall which ran the full length of the open concept agency.

The décor was somewhat edgy with a four-foot dark oak spindle railing running left and right across the office. Seated directly behind the courtroom replica was a Latino male receptionist whose upper body rose well above the railing revealing his height to be over six feet.

Observing the staffer's demeanor, Jessica's instinct screamed, *Gun*.

Setting aside the need to pull her firearm, she addressed her potential adversary with, "Good morning. I am Jessica Fukishura, here to meet with Ms. Gutierrez. She is expecting me," Jessica offered, extending her business card to the staffer.

"Certainly Ms. Fukishura. I will let Ms. Gutierrez know of your arrival. May I offer you a coffee, espresso or latte?"

"Black coffee would be appreciated. Thank you."

"I will have that for you momentarily. Please, have a seat," he replied, sweeping his left arm in an arc, gesturing to an elegant seating arrangement to her right.

The receptionist spoke briefly into his headset and just as she was about to enjoy the luxury of the black leather, nine-foot sofa, she spotted Marianna descending four steps from the slightly elevated second level, heading toward her.

Gutierrez looked stunningly professional in a thrill-pink Luxe single button, blazer jacket with long sleeves and notched lapels. She wore it over a cream Boston Proper three-quarter sleeve sweater with peekaboo trim across the bateau neckline. The matching straight leg, high-waisted pants draped perfectly above her Massimo Matteo Rojo Patent leather pointy toe pumps with a three-inch heel.

Hearing his boss approach from behind him, the receptionist left his seat smoothly and opened the railing gate, allowing Jessica to enter and greet her client. As he released the portal, he offered,

"Your coffee is waiting for you in Ms. Gutierrez's office ma'am."

"Thank you for your kindness. I appreciate the warm greeting." She wanted to add; *I hope you have low velocity rounds in your pistol.*

"Jessica, delightful to see you. Welcome to our humble establishment. Thank you for coming on such short notice. I appreciate your understanding the need to meet here."

"Of course, Ms. Gutierrez. It is my pleasure," Jessica replied, as she accepted her extended hand, then followed Marianna across the office floor and up the short flight of stairs.

As Jessica's left hand instinctively reached for the railing she glanced to her right, noticing the two female paralegals concentrating on their tasks, while the other male staffer followed her movements discreetly, feigning attention to his computer monitor.

Stepping on the landing and walking forward, Jessica thought, *two armed guards in a law office and I am employed by an attorney whose receptionist is enclosed behind bullet proof plastic. The local police department doesn't exhibit this security level.*

Marianna opened the door to her office, stepped back to allow Jessica's entry, closed the door and turned a deadbolt. Not surprising, her client's desk was neither to her left, right or in front of her, but behind and to her left.

Straight ahead was a seating area of three sofas, identical to those in reception with the addition of three ten-foot long, black rubbed, Brazilian wood coffee tables with wrought iron edging.

Highlighting one end of a table was a fourteen-inch circular, black metal serving tray with black tubular handles, hosting two black mugs, presumably the offered coffee.

Accompanying the coffee were several filo pastries adorned with drizzled chocolate.

Accepting the offer to sit, Jessica noted several portraits of female judges above her, the largest of which was of Renata Florez, California's first Latina judge. On opposing walls were matching bay windows, one decorated with throw cushions and the other various flowering succulents.

Once seated, Fukishura noticed her client's desk against the furthest wall. It was obvious the placement was a security measure to link with the bolted door and armed guards. Again, not surprising to Jessica, given Gutierrez's client list.

The desk matched the coffee tables except for clear glass rather than the black wood top. It too had to be ten-feet long with files, phone and two side-by-side brass lamps atop the glass.

"So, here we are, attorney representing attorney. Where to begin?" she offered, taking a sip of coffee, then settling back into the rich leather folds. "I never ask my clients if they are guilty and I suspect you were taught that as well at Berkley, so let's begin with the presumption of my innocence."

"That won't work for me Marianna," Jessica replied quickly needing to establish her assertiveness. "Yes, Berkley professors attempted to convince me of the presumption of innocence but as you know I entered the profession as somewhat of a mature student of human nature. What you are guilty of, as you implied, may not be immediately germane, but you are guilty of something and that is what I intend to explore and throw up barriers to prosecutors to save your reputation and freedom."

Marianna's expression remained stoical. She didn't know whether to be insulted, shocked or pleased with her new attorney's impertinence. She quickly thought back to meeting Jessica, how the freshman attorney dressed down the Los Angeles prosecutor and had Gutierrez's client released immediately and how, after their beach-side dinner defended them from a knife wielding assailant.

Fukishura pulled a pistol, struck and broke his arm, then pivoted on one foot and delivered a knock-out blow to his head.

She chose to be pleased to have a barracuda between her and a lengthy jail sentence, reached over for her coffee, smiled and said, "Let us proceed."

Gutierrez continued, "What I believe is strictly conjecture, information offered from a third party. The client you represented on my behalf in LA recently, Julio Fernández, was arrested along with a number of others, some of whom are also my clients, north of here in a massive drug bust. From what I hear, Santa Barbara Police, the LAPD and Secret Service executed the raid, seizing several thousand kilos of Colombian cocaine and hundreds of millions in American currency.

"Los Angeles county prosecutors are using a text from Fernández to me as a connection to the drug smuggling. The pivotal point of their case is the timing of the text. It was before the arrest."

"I'm following. Do you care to share the context of the text?"

"Certainly. The text was one word. *Now*. Nothing else."

Marianna knew full well to what the text referred. The Chica de Oro had landed and Julio was en route to retrieve the drug shipment and money from his street dealers. Full disclosure to Jessica had its limits. Client/attorney privilege aside, there was no way she was going to betray the Hermanos by revealing the entire truth.

"I can see how they are connecting the dots with a straight line to you, but I suspect their actions are motivated by revenge more than executing the law. This is pay-back time for them. A first-year law student could blast holes through their weak argument. However, I suspect they will convene the criminal grand jury and embellish their case. Of course, not having to offer evidence, the presentation will be a slam dunk of an indictment.

"If all they have on you is the text, it would be obvious to all that their motivation was political, and they would drop the charges after a few months of embarrassment to you. I want to get out in front of this immediately with a visit to the district attorney. Any suggestions on the approach?"

Gutierrez shifted on the couch, took a sip of coffee and offered, "I guarantee you do not want to play to her gender, ethnicity or workload. The first two are no brainers given you are presenting your argument from an Asian to a Latina. Avoid the latter as well, since she leads over one-thousand lawyers supported by three-hundred investigators. I believe you can make your case to drop the investigation by appealing to the overall acceptance of cocaine in Southern California as a recreational drug and lean away from the criminal and financial element."

"What do you mean, acceptance?"

Marianna explained the Los Angeles Cocaine Legalization Act of 2004, California's Proposition 47 and that possession of cocaine for personal use was a misdemeanor with either a small fine and/or one year in jail if the user had no record. In other words, the courts could consider the issue a health problem, not criminal."

Jessica leaned into the supple leather with mug in hand and replied, "All this is, as you noted, conjecture, so why don't I take a quick trip and chat with the lead prosecutor and find out what they have in evidence and we go from there?"

"Okay. Good. We must get ahead of this before the grand jury is convened or we could be months, if not years, in and out of court. That character defamation would be financially devastating. My clients will flee like rats from a sinking ship."

Jessica rose, extended her hand to Marianna and said, "I will chopper there this morning and hopefully have a meeting with the D.A and information for you later today."

Gutierrez accepted the handshake and replied, "Thanks Jessica. I hope you are as successful today as you were with Julio Fernández."

"Me too," countered Jessica as she turned and let herself out of her client's office. As she made her way down the short flight of stairs, the receptionist greeted her half-way to the railing, smiling as though he just sold her a pair of twelve-hundred-dollar Gianni Versace shoes and opened the rail-gate and wished her a safe and profitable day.

Exiting the building, she stepped to the off side of the door, sat her briefcase down, leaned against the wall, one foot up behind, bracing her body as she scanned the street looking for anyone sitting in a car, doorway or attempting a casual walk-by.

She was still a neophyte to the Southern California justice system and unlikely to have made enemies or created suspicion but the recent experience of being tailed to Rebecca's, her making the guy as he sped away, gave her reason for caution.

Seeing nothing out of the ordinary, she walked quickly to her vehicle, locked the doors, texted Katrina, then headed for the airport.

"Life is like riding a bicycle. To keep your balance, you must keep moving."

Albert Einstein.

And keep her balance was what she must do. She knew she was entering the proverbial lion's den, or in this case, the lioness', given the humiliation she caused the assistant district attorney who had planned on prosecuting Julio Fernández for drug trafficking. Julio had been videotaped accepting massive quantities of currency from known street dealers and transporting it to a storage unit.

The detectives neglected to read him his rights, so all the evidence collected would never be presented in court. Fernández was unaware the officers had set him up so the "J" Team could take him down later with the millions in cocaine.

"That which does not kill us makes us stronger."

Friedrich Nietzsche

California, notably in Los Angeles, is faced with the proverbial catch-22, dealing with a vast movement to decriminalize drugs as Portugal did in 2001. Many European Countries have enacted similar legislation reducing the criminalization of personal use.

Vancouver, British Columbia and Toronto, Ontario, two of Canada's major cities have called on the federal government to decriminalize all drugs as they did with cannabis in 2018.

Jessica wondered if the federal government's approach to controlling cocaine by interdiction was another waste of money and personnel given the massive movement to legalize all drugs.

The Chica de Oro set sail for its next northern destination at midnight at high tide, submerging immediately after leaving port. The Colombian cartel was unaware their last shipment sat unused in an LAPD vault. The California cartel paid for the shipment, not sharing details of the cocaine's demise, concerned the Colombians would cancel future deliveries and question their security.

The mini-sub and the Golden Girl were passing Clipperton Island, a 6 square kilometer, French territory, twenty-four-hundred-kilometers west of Nicaragua at the depth of one-hundred meters. They were communicating using cutting edge quantum key distribution (QKD), secure transmissions at the highest level of security available at rates of 170 kilobytes a second, which is 600 times more bandwidth than the Very Low Frequency (VLF) the U.S. Navy submarine fleet currently uses.

Chapter ELEVEN

Stan Loblinski sat in the furthest booth from the front door of his favorite Edmonton, Alberta coffee shop, a tactical move he learned from observing law enforcement. Every officer sat facing the front door and away from windows.

The top of Loblinski's head was all that was visible above his laptop's screen as he made encrypted notes regarding the expansion of his cocaine network in western Canada.

Since his orchestrating the cesium theft from the Manitoba mine and it subsequently being used to down the Mahalo Airline into the Pacific Ocean just off the coast of LAX, Stan had met with Marianna Gutierrez in a Colorado airport lounge, accepting her challenge and offer to expand her drug empire into Canada.

He absentmindedly reached for his white coffee mug with the iconic large red T emblazoned on the side and lifted it to his mouth. Realizing it was empty, he slid out of the booth, closed his computer, engaging the password protection feature, knowing it was impossible to steal anyway given the metal cable attached to the booth's leg, and walked to the counter to obtain a refill.

There were several customers ahead of him, so he stood, third in line, holding his mug, glancing aimlessly around the coffee shop trying not to lose his concentration of his previous task. He was unaware of another customer who approached from behind with her smartphone in her right hand, presumably reading the screen.

What the female Mountie was actually doing was getting her phone close to Stan's in his right rear pocket and pairing it with hers, a technique used frequently by the RCMP to track suspects.

The officer moved slightly, glancing aimlessly out the window as she dropped her right hand so her phone slightly touched Stan's device.

Stan moved to the counter, slid his mug toward the barista and asked for a refill, while the fellow customer returned to reading her phone...having forwarded the pairing data to the Edmonton RCMP detachment's detective squad.

Elisabeth Peltowski, Jason Spencer and Jackson Pennington continued to enjoy Rebecca and Penelope's hospitality for several days following their participation in the historic cocaine bust, appreciating the Olympic size pool, the house's impeccable ambiance and the daily meals provided by Conception's Catering service, thoughtfully paid for by the Secret Service.

Since Elisabeth's initial monitoring of Julio Fernández and his lieutenants' phones, she continually posted her findings on CHAP, working from her exquisitely furnished bedroom at Rebecca and Penelope's ranch.

There hadn't been any outgoing activity on either phone since the suspects' arrest, but a number of calls came into Anthony Henderson's phone, his family having not been notified of his whereabouts.

It was during this slack time when posting to CHAP that she saw the Edmonton detective's information about Stan's phone. She immediately retrieved the link and found several calls made to Vancouver, BC cell phones. She checked the service providers for the area and found no accounts matching the numbers.

Burners.

Peltowski lived on adrenaline, as did her colleagues and the downtime was bothering her immensely. Once she closed the service providers' screens she jumped up, pumped her fist in the air, ran out of the room, down to the kitchen, grabbed an egg and sausage burrito left over from breakfast, a soft drink and ran back to her computers, jumping up and down with excitement.

A couple of bites, a swallow and she put them aside to concentrate. She drew up a software program she had designed, inserted each of the phone numbers and found they were all active, turned on. Presumably not wanting to miss a text from Stan.

She was so excited to be making another major break in discovering for whom Henderson was working that her hands were shaking.

She pushed herself away from the computers, grabbed the burrito, cola and walked back downstairs and sat at the kitchen table, forcing herself to be calm. She finished her snack, then slowly returned to her bedroom.

Moving the mouse, she brought up the software program and clicked the icon beside all three phone numbers activating the speakers to record all voice dialog and all phone calls and texts to and from the phones.

Elisabeth had her mojo back and felt the energy flow through her body as the excitement almost overwhelmed her. She quickly logged on to CHAP and recorded her actions, visualizing the RCMP detectives sharing her joy.

Lastly, she sent an encrypted text to Karen and Tom with a GPS link to the suspect's phones, advising the agents how she was monitoring the Vancouverites' actions.

Chapter TWELVE

Jessica's flight was quick, the pilot not having to fight a Santa Ana headwind, and landed on the roof of the Hall of Justice on west Temple in Los Angeles. The pilot was on various flights around LA all day and said she could text him directly when she was ready to return to Santa Barbara.

During the flight she reminisced how she had changed, personally and professionally the past year. She had a well-earned reputation as being uncooperative and antagonistic, particularly with male colleagues. When she was recruiting the "J" Team from their respective posts around the world, she was concerned her reputation would score against her. But to her delight, none of the agents had ever heard of her and all were anxious for an assignment change and jumped at the opportunity.

Her negative attitude toward men stemmed from the shootings at the École Polytechnique in Montreal in 1989 where Marc Lépine used a Ruger Mini-14 to murder 14 women. Her mother knew several of the victims and as a Toronto teenager, Jessica was angry that none of the men who were permitted to leave the engineering class tried to stop him.

The anger stayed with her through the University of California and law school and affected every attempted relationship. Her aggressive personality coupled with her career choice resulted in few second dates: guys don't like dating women with guns.

It was when the investigation into the Christians for a Better America hit a wall that she accepted the reality, plus orders from Sorento, she had to extend the harmonious relationship she had with the "J" Team to the county sheriff and StoneHead chief of police. It was that collegiality which proved successful, and on which she relied during her first meeting with Detective Elise Pelfini of the Santa Barbara Police Dept. and the LAPD drug squad.

The pilot's voice advising of their impending landing brought her out of her reverie and she glanced out the side window as her transportation settled on the landing pad.

Exiting the helicopter, she had her action plan memorized and entered the building determined to be successful. Failure was not an option.

Jessica was confident the district attorney herself would meet her to discuss Gutierrez's fate.

As Fukishura left the elevator on the DA's floor, she spotted the team sitting beside a large, brass plaque, ANASTASIA ZINKTON, DISTRICT ATTORNEY COUNTY OF LOS ANGELES and her confidence sored.

She shook hands with all three colleagues, then lead the way into Zinkton's office, introduced herself to a receptionist and produced her identification.

The staffer quickly checked her boss' schedule on her screen, not having recognized Jessica's name from her earlier schedule perusal. Not hiding her surprise, she picked up a phone, hit a button, listened, exhibited a quizzical expression, rose and ushered the four quests into the hall of justice's inner sanctum where they were met by the DA's personal assistant.

Within moments, they stood face to face with Los Angeles County's top prosecutor in a petal pink, Etienette B Good wool suit; one button closure, peak lapels, four button cuffs, front flap-welt pockets and back vent. She paired the stunning suit with a light camel charmeuse silk top with Mother-of-Pearl buttons. Her short, black spiky 'do completed the image of power and influence.

Before her stood Detective Jenny Wong, Detective Teresa Vasquez, Captain Ortega of the LAPD Drug Apprehension Squad and Jessica Fukishura.

Sensing the DA's confusion as to who was who and why she wasn't informed her meeting was with four instead of one, Jessica stepped forward, extended her hand, introduced herself, then the others. Jessica then purposely walked to a seating area away from the prosecutor's desk so the bureaucrat couldn't control the conversation from behind it.

"Ms. Fukishura, I only agreed to meet with you on such short notice because of the magnitude of the pending case, but I do so as a courtesy and expect a clarification of your involvement first and foremost," she offered, obviously annoyed that her guest was taking control.

The three officers were aware of Jessica's identity and her role in the apprehension of Julio Fernández and the confiscation of the cocaine and currency. They collectively felt it in their best interest to read Zinkton into the former operation to gain her approval for the current scheme.

Once seated, Captain Ortega began, "Ms. Zinkton, you know who we three are from the LAPD and Ms. Fukishura is with the Secret Service with information we wish to share and obtain your assistance."

The district attorney's facial expression spoke of her confusion since she was expecting to speak with an attorney from Santa Barbara representing Marianna Gutierrez. While she composed herself, Jessica reached into her jumpsuit pocket, retrieved her identification and handed it to her potential colleague.

Zinkton glanced at the document, then up at Jessica, over to Ortega, then gave the ID wallet back and said, "I am not in the habit of being blindsided like this, Ms. Fukishura and Captain. Please explain yourselves before I have you thrown out of my office."

Ortega had anticipated the response. He, Fukishura and his detectives had rehearsed their delivery and he began as planned, "Ms. District Attorney, our squad has monitored changes in the cocaine supply for months and compared the quality with that found in New York, Chicago, San Francisco and Seattle. The product is identical, and we suspected it arrives in Southern California for distribution.

"The Secret Service is involved because they believe the recipients of the drug money are the Christians for a Better America and their candidates for Congress. Agent Fukishura devised the operation with a federal warrant. We have had eyes and ears on several known lieutenants for months and when the street supply slowed, we knew another delivery was eminent.

"One of those first arrested was Julio Fernández whom my detectives arrested, purposely without a warrant to search a storage shed. While in our short custody, we bugged his phone and belt buckle. Within hours of his release he received a short signal we traced to a vessel two-hundred kilometers off our coast. He then texted two people with one word, "Now." One of the recipients was attorney Marianna Gutierrez and the other Santa Barbara accountant Anthony Henderson.

Ortega waited a moment to see if Zinkton had any questions. Hearing none, he continued, "The Santa Barbara SWAT team observed thousands of kilos of cocaine being off-loaded from a submarine at Point Concepción and transported east of Solvang. We followed Fernández and the Secret Service shadowed Henderson from Los Angeles to an abandoned vineyard near Solvang where they planned to distribute the cocaine.

"We have Henderson, Fernández and several street dealers in secret custody and the currency in a LAPD vault."

The district attorney didn't conceal her shock and sat back in the chair, arms crossed, composing her reply. When she spoke, her hostile demeanor had vanished, being replaced with a litany of questions of the who, what, where and why of the operation but primarily what other agencies were involved.

Her four guests alternated answering her questions, the major one of which was why the DEA was not involved. Jessica responded to the best of her ability, purposely omitting CHAP and suggested she obtain clarification from Sorento.

Anastasia's expression remained perplexed, but the antagonistic flare had dissipated, and she said, "I can appreciate the Secret Service shutting out the DEA. We have had our share of run-ins with their attorneys and never appreciate their desire to run an operation in our jurisdiction solo. I like your attitude. So, now that I have the background, what is phase two of this operation and how does my office fit in?"

Jessica offered her input, "Ma'am, just as we scammed Fernández which lead us to Henderson, we'd like to replicate that operation with Gutierrez. She received the same text as Henderson but she never left her house. We had her under 24/7 surveillance physically and digitally. No phone calls or texts in or out, save the one from Fernández. She suspects you are in the process of taking a case to the criminal grand jury for prosecution. We are here to ask you to put that on hold and allow us to work our way up her cartel's hierarchy.

"The confiscated millions we believe were destined for an Orange County conservative congressional candidate as well as others across several electoral jurisdictions. Gutierrez knows me as an employee of Katrina Barbados, which I am, undercover for the Secret Service. Katrina is unaware of my cover and I need that to remain so for the foreseeable future.

"If we leave here today with an agreement from you that there will not be an indictment until we have a solid case against her and the cartel network, Marianna will be sure to either hire me or retain my services with Barbados. In doing so, I can get very close to the network.

"My team is stationed in Santa Barbara and participated in the last cocaine bust. They will assist in surveillance and monitoring with the authority of the valid federal warrant. This is a win-win for you and your office, ma'am."

Zinkton was unfazed by Jessica's assertiveness. She uncrossed her legs, leaned forward and offered, "We'll see. I need further background, but I can get that in the coming weeks. What is the status of the submarine? What is its port of call? Which agency is claiming the currency, or better phrased, which will receive it? Do we proceed with the charges against Fernández, Henderson and the others? For now, you can advise your client that we will not be convening the grand jury but reserve that opportunity if we obtain additional evidence.

Does that work for you four?"

Ortega, Wong and Vasquez, neither of whom had spoken during this recent exchange, glanced at Jessica and nodded, a gesture not missed by their adversary. Jessica replied, "It does Ms. Zinkton. Gutierrez believes the only evidence against her is the text from Fernández before his arrest. With your agreement, I will tell her that I was successful in convincing you there was no case and to politicize the issue, then lose will be detrimental to your career, particularly being reelected."

"Fukishura, you have one fucking nerve coming in here and making demands. Your arrogance and presumptiveness piss me off." She got up and walked over to her desk, turned and sat on the edge facing the group, arms behind supporting on the desk, then continued, "That goes for you three LAPD detectives as well," waving a finger at the detectives, "But I respect your audacity," she replied with a smirk, on the verge of a smile. "Something tells me that if I make a few phone calls, one to Sorento for sure, I will find out you have made a career of pissing off people and are probably successful at it.

"Okay, I have a thick skin but no press. I do not, and I emphasize, emphatically, do not want to read about this meeting and agreement in the press."

Jessica and the others rose and said in unison, "What meeting?" then shook Zinkton's hand and left.

Chapter THIRTEEN

In 2015, the Vancouver Sun published an exposé on the Vancouver Port Authority in which they revealed that at least twenty-seven Hells Angels and associates worked as longshoremen on the docks.

Similarly, they noted that the National Port Enforcement Team's budget was cut by almost a half-million and staff was reduced from thirteen officers to nine. By comparison, Seattle Port Authority, which processes similar volume, had one-hundred-and-ten officers.

The insufficient law enforcement presence on the docks had forced the RCMP to draw personnel from other investigations in an attempt to fill the void. As well, the British Columbia Ferry Services were not policed, allowing the free movement of contraband and drugs between Vancouver Island and the mainland. A fact of which the criminal element was well aware.

This was the reality with which Karen and Tom had to function and they knew the task was greater than could be handled by two investigators.

Having arrived at the University of British Columbia detachment around eight, they were in the spacious office normally occupied by an inspector, but which was currently vacant, the last occupant having been transferred. They were musing the complexity of their task, organizing their plan over coffee they brought with them, not wanting to trust that of the detachment, which was often either burned, weak or both.

Karen set her pen on the table, sat back in the chair, put one leg over the other, rested her hands on her lap and said, "I know we share the same thought, that of adding another body here, but I don't want to have to explain the operation and frankly, I don't know if we could find someone who shares our enthusiasm…this not just a job."

"I agree. I don't know anyone in CSIS other than David and can't think of a person at TPS with drug interdiction experience."

"I didn't have any collegial interaction when I was flying with Air Canada but let me think." She looked out the office window briefly, then continued, "There was a member with whom I trained at Depot (referring to the RCMP national training center in Regina, Saskatchewan). I could try and find her, see what she is up to. Maybe Kimberly would be interested in a change."

"Who is she exactly?"

"Kimberly Breyman. I heard she was working here in BC on the lower mainland. How about I make a few calls and see what's what?"

"Sure. Fine by me. I presume she shares your attitude toward criminality, apprehension and tactics?"

Karen smiled, looking up at him but remained mute, giving Tom her, *Duh* look. She picked up the phone and placed a call to personnel at "E" Division in Surrey, headquarters for the province's seven-thousand police officers and support staff.

Tom sat silently drinking his coffee, listening to the one-sided conversation, realizing what a dumb comment he made and wondering when he will learn to curb his attempts at small talk.

Karen provided her RCMP Identification number, explained her query, was transferred to a data base staffer and within minutes had a phone number and extension.

As Karen disconnected and dialed, Tom said, "I'm heading to the restroom while you chat with Kimberly. You don't need me here," as he turned and headed out of the office, hoping to return with his brain fully functioning.

Karen made connection, and replied, "Okay, but hurry back. If Kimberly is interested, we need to meet with her stat."

Hortonn returned in ten but found Karen still on the phone. Her animation told him the conversation was catch-up time and it would be awhile. He wisely left the detachment and wandered the campus, people watching, making sure his observation was casual not to draw attention to himself in the current climate of sexual assaults.

Forty-five minutes later he peeked into the office and saw Karen was off the phone, so he entered to find her in an exceptionally good mood as she erupted with information.

Tom's return had included coffee refills, one of which he placed in front of Karen, then took a seat to listen. When she concluded, Hortonn had a good idea who was to be their additional investigator.

Kimberly Breyman was of the same age group as Karen and Tom, having been a member for fifteen years. Although Kimberly was enjoying her current assignment, the idea of working with Karen was an opportunity she couldn't pass up. Assuming she could be relieved of her current duty, whether she is seconded by David Kopas or joined the operation as a Member would be David's call. They agreed that it would have to be the former as David would not tolerate a joint operation.

"We need women at all levels, including the top, to change the dynamic, reshape the conversation, to make sure women's voices are heard and heeded, not overlooked and ignored."

Sheryl Sandberg

Tom was about to receive a crash course in the power of strong, assertive women.

Chapter FOURTEEN

Rebecca and Penelope chose the least conspicuous items in their wardrobe for the task ahead. Penelope having been a country veterinarian and Rebecca a horse trainer, albeit undercover, they had little difficulty hauling a few items out of the back of their joint walk-in closet. Thankfully it was massive, more than sufficient for two women who loved fashion.

They knew there might be this one opportunity to make an impression with a wary audience, so they made sure their attire reflected conservativism with muted style.

They chose stone washed jeans with rips in the thighs because they were too comfortable to discard. They didn't purchase them distressed; the tears were earned. Penelope paired hers with well-worn tan work boots and a button-down pink, blue and yellow striped blouse, untucked. Rebecca found her thrashed Tony Lama boots with the duck-tape covering a tear in one of the toes and a white peasant blouse with flared bell sleeves and blue lace insets.

They finished dressing, then checked themselves in the twelve by seven, bedroom mirror, smiled at each other, bumped butts, high fived, then headed for the garage and breakfast at *The Toast*.

They found a parking spot for their new Honda on the main drag and walked holding hands to the restaurant. Open from seven-thirty until three daily, *The Toast* offered breakfast and lunch with a few well known and appreciated specialties: *The Everything Omelet*; sun dried tomatoes, spinach, mushrooms, banana peppers, red onion, black beans, cumin and Swiss cheese, and *Green Eggs & Ham*; two scrambled eggs with pesto and Swiss cheese, grilled smoked ham and a slice of multi-grain toast. Their greatest attraction was their signature potatoes; roasted baby reds tossed with the chef's guarded secret herbs and served with every dish.

Admiring the eclectic offerings, the item they both chose was *Cayenne in the Rain*; two scrambled eggs, signature reds, sautéed red onions, sundried tomatoes, spinach, melted cheddar, feta, dill sauce, cayenne pepper and salsa served with a slice of multi-grain toast.

Their server Christie remembered them from when they were introduced by Alane and arrived quickly with two black coffees, menus and a comment that she would return shortly for their order.

They were perusing the offerings when a forty something woman entered and walked to their table. Gabriela Gomez was dressed for her role as a street advocate, wearing khaki cargo pants, a pale blue button-down blouse untucked and well-worn hiking boots with robins-egg blue laces. Gomez wore her one-hundred and thirty pounds on a five-foot, seven-inch frame well with an accompanying demeanor which screamed, *Don't*.

Rebecca, with her seat facing the door, stood when the Women's Center director approached and shook her hand. Penelope, taken somewhat by surprise even though she knew Gomez was expected, jumped slightly, regained her composure, stood and greeted Gabriela with a handshake.

"So, what's good here?" Gomez asked as she took a seat beside Penelope. "In all the years I've lived here, I have never had the pleasure."

Rebecca passed her a menu, then mentioned they were having the *Cayenne in the Rain.* Gabriela scanned the menu, then offered, "Let's make that three," just as Christie arrived with her pad.

The director gave their order, then said, "Do you mind if we quickly review our approach, so I have it fresh in my mind?" she asked as she turned to Penelope for a response. Receiving a nod, she continued. "We are concentrating on homeless female teens who, although they may smoke marijuana, are not substance abusers. Our objective is to offer them a leg-up, so to speak, with a place to live, meals, safety, education and clothes. How am I doing so far?"

Penelope responded, "We think that covers most of it, Gabriela. It is difficult for us to get our heads around the fact that the majority are from here and yet are homeless."

"Sadly, it is true in too many cases. There are numerous shelters here in Santa Barbara with accompanying services such as meals, showers and medical treatment but most teens shy away, stating they feel safer living on the streets, which may be true, yet their hygiene and nutrition suffer.

"As you can imagine, some citizens object to their presence in our parks, the libraries and sleeping on the streets, under the freeway etc... The city claims they spend five million yearly dealing with the problem, either directly or in financial aid to charity resources. There is the added expense of cleaning creeks and riverbeds, public restrooms, and homeless camps plus the added expense of law enforcement and fire & rescue services, but the city is supportive and that is massive.

Seventy-five percent of homeless are female with almost forty percent identifying as Gay, Lesbian, Bisexual or Transgender. Almost fifty percent report being sexually or emotionally abused by a family member and almost all of them have dropped out of school. Many are former foster children who were mistreated in the system.

Some teens become separated from their homeless unit due to the shelter's inability to accommodate families, while others failed to manage grief, whether it be a family divorce or a lost loved one and they turned to drugs to mask the pain, eventually being turned out from their family home due to their destructive behavior.

Most of the teens panhandle for drug money and often share needles which could land them in a hospital. But often the girls shun medical treatment fearing being apprehended by social services."

Just then Christie arrived with their orders bringing happiness to an otherwise dreary discussion.

Accepting the meals, they thanked their server and began eating, leaving the conversation for after breakfast.

Twenty later, the three were finished with Christie having removed their plates and refilled their black while Gabriela took up the conversation, "Enough of the negative. We are excited about your ideas, enthusiasm and the financial interest you have generated from the movers and shakers.

"We are heading to the park where the majority of the girls hang out and *Girl Power's Green Cuisine* truck will be there with a complimentary lunch. Do I have that correct?"

Rebecca was having difficulty concealing her excitement. She replied, "That's the plan. We thought providing at least one unsupervised meal might be a smooth segue to the rest of the program and these chefs don't provide the typical food truck offerings.

"We sincerely appreciate your approval Gabriela; the slow progression to new clothes, permanent housing, finishing high school and the opportunity to attend university or trade school."

"I speak for the directors and staff that we are delighted to be a part of the concept. Your recent donation certainly pointed to your commitment. I noticed on the way here that the remodeling of *Refugio Seguro* is well underway."

Penelope smiled and said, "We can't take all the credit Gabriela, the number of folks who have joined our vision has been beyond our wildest dreams."

Rebecca chimed in with, "I echo Penelope's sentiments. We shared our objectives with our friends and the next thing an offer of a motel was made, then all renovations were donated. A security firm offered to wire the building and patrol the area. We have a couple who will be live-in managers. He is a retired contractor and she retired as a military cook. There will be a doorman 24/7 to let the girls enter and deter any unwanted visitors. Each of the girls will have their own room and private bathroom.

"We have several accountants donating their expertise and attorneys who will help emancipate any of the girls as needed."

"I am flabbergasted," responded Gabriela taking a sip of her black. "And to top all of that, the center is receiving donations of previously unseen amounts.

"We can't thank you enough," she added as she held her mug with both hands and continued, "This is going to change the lives of these girls forever."

Forty-five later they were stuffed, coffeed-out and ready to hit the park and experience the teen's reactions.

"Most homeless kids are on the streets because they have been forced by circumstances that cause them to think that they are safer there than in any home they once knew."

Jewel

Chapter FIFTEEN

Edmonton's downtown core community and the various neighborhoods throughout the city were resplendent with hanging baskets and large, well-cared for flower beds. Each Friday morning one of the local television stations highlighted a business for their participation in *Edmonton the Beautiful* campaign. One restaurant was reflected more than others.

The Horsemen was an iconic Edmonton, Alberta pub which caters to first responders, but primarily it is a social house for RCMP Mounties, their families and friends.

Often referred to as Horsemen or Rainbow Warriors for the mounted officer and rainbow stripes on their patrol vehicles, RCMP officers socialize primarily with their own, very much as health care professionals and others do in careers which deal directly with the public. Fraternizing among themselves is far less stressful than having to interact with those not in their profession.

The Horsemen was like that. Shop talk may enter conversations, discussing a particularly difficult case or arrest but most of the time when the Rainbow Warriors patronized *The Horsemen* it was with their spouses, partners and/or friends and none had to defend their actions.

The establishment's irony was, Members are of both genders, but the law enforcement agency's sobriquet had been around for so long, it was accepted by female Members with no ill will.

The Horsemen's location blended with the uniqueness of the name. It is the primary business in a neighborhood mall, partnered with an upscale barbershop and law offices, both of which sent their clients to *The Horsemen*.

Although there wasn't a membership, secret handshake or code, any potential patron is recognized by his/her demeanor as being law enforcement; the way they carry themselves, their heads in perpetual motion, scanning their surroundings, psychologically in the state of Yellow of the Color Code of Awareness and sitting with their backs to a wall facing the entry.

Roy Davidson saw that in his clientele and often greeted each with a welcoming handshake and menus, while personally seeing them to a table.

Davidson was a thirty-year veteran of the Force, having served in isolated communities in the early days of his career then specializing in traffic safety.

He wanted the interior to speak to the conviviality and authenticity of Mountie culture and generate camaraderie and friendship. He began by capturing every patron's attention with a massive three-meter, faux, buffalo head hanging from the rear wall.

The buffalo or bison's significance, dates back to 1873 when the North-West Mounted Police patrolled the prairies and depended upon the behemoth for food, fuel and clothing. Many current-day detachments have these in their foyers.

Patrons' attention was drawn next to the ambiance, accomplished with steel grey walls throughout and behind the curved cherrywood bar to the left as one entered. The floor completed the mood, pairing the walls with light grey stained planks.

The bar was absent of stools as no law enforcement officer would leave her or his back exposed. Imbedded into the bar surface were six, evenly spaced beer spigots delivering several varieties of local craft beer, the most popular being Grizzly Paw Brewery's Beavertail Raspberry Ale. National and international varieties were available in bottles, but the fresh keg beer outsold the other by fifty to one. *The Horsemen's* brew never had foam thanks to the diligent weekly cleaning of the delivery lines.

The welcoming, cozy atmosphere was enhanced by end to end, triple pane windows which began twelve-feet from the floor and rose to the twenty-foot textured ceiling, home to eight circulating, paddle fans aiding the controlled temperature.

Across from the bar, under the windows, were several seating arrangements with tables turned at an angle so no guest was with his or her back to the entry.

The one-hundred and twenty seat arrangement was accomplished primarily with sets of four or six weathered grey finished tables with pedestal bases. Adding to the monochromatic color scheme were matching grey, hardwood chairs with a neutral beige hue, cotton and polyester blend upholstery. The furnishings were rescued from an establishment consumed by an expanding condominium village and refurbished.

The bar's back wall was accentuated by steel grey wood panels staggered between photos of officers of the North West Mounted Police, the RCMP's predecessor organization and shelves of various world renown whiskies, gins, bourbons and vodkas.

Moving further into the pub, the space branched off to the left with a twenty-foot long gas fireplace and light grey mantle with two sixty-inch flat-screen televisions, side-by-side. Muted but with closed caption. The tables were set such that any guest could view either screen, which on most nights were tuned to hockey.

From any angle all patrons were aware of a conversation area at the far end of the restaurant with several groupings of leather, steel-grey couches, coffee tables and accent chairs. The furnishings were enhanced by a large, cherrywood wall-plaque with the following adhered in brass, *Maintiens le droit*, French for *Defending the law*. Surrounding the plaque were the photos of seventy-eight Members who lost their lives fulfilling that motto.

Below the dedication wall was another, identical, twenty-foot long, centered, gas fireplace, highlighting the social groupings.

Every patron visiting the tribute stood silently as they read the brief caption under each photo with many saluting. The first photos to be honored were most often those of Cst. Fabrice Gevauden, 45, Cst. David Ross, 32 and Cst. Douglas Larch, 40, and all who lost their lives at the hands of deranged Moncton shooter Justin Bourque, 24, now serving a seventy-five-year sentence for murder.

The deaths of these Members were particularly difficult to understand because they were outgunned by their attacker who was firing a rifle while Members were limited in their response by their short-range service pistol. The Force had approved the purchase, training and distribution of carbines several years previously but the then commissioner, for reasons only he is aware, denied them.

In Mayerthorpe, Alberta in 2005, four Members were murdered. They too, were outgunned by an assailant with a rifle.

The Wall didn't reflect the many Members who were injured in the line of duty, or those suffering from Post-Traumatic Stress Disorder, created by the many horrors they witnessed over the years and injustices from senior RCMP management.

Mountie culture meant quality dishes. *The Horsemen's* menu boasted some of Edmonton's finest recipes, attractively plated and priced to appreciate a Mountie's income.

Their specialty was Alberta grass-fed beef and locally grown, when in season, greens. At the top of the list of patron favorites was an Irish corn beef, slow cooked with Guinness beer, then baked for thirty minutes using the cooking liquid to prepare a glaze. The savory dish was served with pan roasted red potatoes, marinated red cabbage and a harvest salad with aged Irish whiskey cheddar.

Top Sirloin served with grilled asparagus and a baked Prince Edward Island Russet potato was the favorite steak with Blue Cheese Filet a strong second. The latter was wrapped in bacon, topped with blue cheese curds, served with roasted red, green and yellow peppers and baby red potatoes.

Rounding out the steak offerings were New York, Filet Mignon and Peppercorn New York.

Their poultry contribution to the menu was a chicken breast stuffed with sun-dried tomatoes and goat cheese served with a dilled cucumber and tomato salad and cumin-citrus roasted carrots. Second in line, but equally enjoyed, was their chicken potpie, served with an artichoke and tomato basil salad.

Completing their menu was slow cooked beef ribs with Prince Edward Island wedged fries, shaved beef with fried onions on a chipotle bun, French fries, white cheddar cheese curds with gravy, or the French word, poutine, as it was more routinely called here, and several twists on the traditional hamburger, utilizing a chorizo and beef mixture on a spicy chipotle bun with *The Horsemen* sauce and all the trimmings.

Stan Loblinski was arrogant in his criminality. Primarily a loner, he characterized himself as a hedge fund manager if his occupation ever became the topic of social discussion.

He dined out or ordered in frequently and it was in that routine on a late Friday afternoon after monitoring the Golden Girl's progress that he viewed the television station highlighting a unique business...*The Horsemen.*

He knew the name's origin and in his confidence of evading investigation for more than a decade, he made a decision motivated by audaciousness, not rationalization.

Larry Baird was a Calgary iron worker whose primary job sites consisted of building structures where he operated at eight-hundred and ten feet/two hundred and forty-seven meters or fifty-six stories. His company seconded him to an Edmonton project at which he would be working for several weeks. The company housed him in one of Edmonton's finer hotels where Baird ate most of his meals.

He was enjoying a well-earned end of the week drink as a guest of his host when he noticed the week's *Edmonton the Beautiful* business featured on a screen above the bar.

Baird needed a distraction, some place new to excite his taste buds and the overview of the winner was enticing. He made a quick detour to his room, showered, changed clothes and taxied to *The Horsemen.*

Chapter SIXTEEN

Right after Karen filled Tom in on Kimberly's current assignment and Tom reciprocated by showing her Elisabeth's encrypted text, Karen used her enciphered CSIS phone and called David Kopas direct.

Kopas' responded with a succinct reply, "Got it. Expect her to arrive by noon," and hung up.

Karen turned to Tom, smiled and pumped her fist in the air, "I fuckin' love this assignment. No bullshit. No having to talk the shit out of everything. No having to discuss the request with superiors. How long did that take? One minute...maybe?"

Tom returned her jubilation with a high-five and said, "Let's have a little fun. I'll order lunch for three, to be delivered at 12:30. It's 11 now. We take ninety-minutes and lay out the plan and see if she is here by 12:30?"

"Terrific. I like it. Given David's track record with us, I suspect Kimberly is already packing her desk. First things first, what do you want for lunch?"

Tom replied, "Better yet. There is a Jewish deli on Oak...and they deliver. I'll print off the menu, invite the detachment staff and do a 'Welcome to Us' lunch?"

"Count me in for a pastrami on rye with yellow mustard and plenty of dill pickles please. I'll find the site and get the menu to the staff. I remember Kimberly loves turkey, cranberry sauce on the side. Oh, and a side salad for each of us."

Tom asked her to order him a corned beef on rye and a coffee, then began scribbling notes for when Kimberly arrived.

Karen looked up from her computer with a puzzled facial expression, not sure she heard Tom correctly, then seeing the grin on his face, she knew he was teasing. Shaking her head and smiling at his mischievousness, she returned to her task at hand. He would place the order, even though he was being a butthead about it.

The Chica de Oro was passing the Farallon Islands, 48 kilometers west of San Francisco submerged at 110 meters. The pilot steered well clear of this small chain of Americana, known by indigenous mainland residents as the Devil's Teeth Islands.

In keeping with its name, the US created a nuclear waste dump off their shores. 47,500 containers were scuttled there between 1946 and 1970, many of them having deteriorated, spewing toxicity onto California's beaches. In 1951, the radioactive hull of the USS Independence which was used during the development of the atomic bomb as target practice, was sunk in the same area.

American sealers decimated the population in the early 1800's taking at least 30,000 skins during one count. In the mid-1850's, San Francisco food markets collected and sold millions of bird eggs to the tune of 500,000 monthly, reducing the bird population immensely.

President Theodore Roosevelt named the islands a wildlife refuge in 1909. The status protects a huge seabird colony of western gulls, pelagic cormorants, double-crested cormorants, the tufted puffin and scores of other species.

In addition, seals have rebounded with a 2016 count of 1,100 pups up from 100 in 2006. This increase has drawn great white sharks to the area. Their five-meter, 1,100-kilogram presence has been spotted frequently by research teams documenting the wildlife refuge activity.

Tom had followed through and ordered for everyone. They were eating with the detachment staff in their lunchroom when the receptionist stepped through the open door and announced, "Tom, Karen, you have a visitor," then stepped aside, allowing Kimberly Breyman to enter.

Karen smiled, glanced at her watch, noting it was 12:40, looked at Tom, pointed to her watch and smiled.

Kimberly entered and saw Karen's quizzical expression and said, "What?"

Karen responded with, "Oh, just a little wager Tom and I had on how long it would take CSIS to facilitate your transfer. We were off by ten minutes".

Kimberly was ready for the assignment in a mint-green Calvin Klein, stretch-twill, double-breasted blazer with peak lapels, flap pockets and matching pants. She paired it with a cowl neck, white T shirt and a latte nubuck, Eileen Fisher Billie Bootie with wrap-around, rivet hardware closure. The blazer allowed for her 9 without detracting from style or fashion.

Karen and Kimberly were about the same stature with similar pixie hair styles & color. Karen was admiring Kimberly's booties, musing how easy they would be to run and kick in with when she stepped forward and gave Kimberly a hug.

Karen introduced Kimberly to the detachment staff and then Tom, who responded with a handshake, then nodded to a sandwich and soft drink on the table for her.

Kimberly accepted the gesture and was waiting for the sexist punchline…but it never arrived. Tom raised his soda can and said, "Welcome to UBC, Agent Breyman."

The three Members/CSIC agents, enjoyed a leisurely lunch, chatting with the detachment staff, hoping to develop a camaraderie that would make working for another agency, but using their facilities, more comfortable for all.

Post lunch, the three agents returned to their borrowed office where Karen and Tom provided an overview of the assignment, paying particular attention to Stan's suspected involvement, explaining how he supplied the cesium which took down the Mahalo Airliner, their Costa Rica assignment and where Brian Sawyer fit into the investigation.

Kimberly had several questions, the primary one being how Elisabeth made the connection between Stan and the burner phones in Vancouver, the owners of which were to be tomorrow's agenda.

Karen took particular delight in sharing this with a fellow Mountie and explained how one of their female colleagues from the Edmonton detachment had cloned Stan's phone while he stood in line at a coffee shop. That information was sent to Elisabeth who would identify the phone's locations and owners.

Detectives were able to access Stan's information and saw the numerous back and forth texts between him and the Vancouver recipients. Although the succinct language was coded gibberish, the contact was made, and the recipients' identification would be known in the next few days.

They introduced her to CHAP, provided her with an access code, an office key, safe combination and an agency encrypted phone with preset numbers for investigators.

The trio spent the afternoon reviewing all the data which Elisabeth had provided and worked well into the evening before calling it quits and agreeing to meet at the coffee house on Howe Street across from Brosman & Snow Law Firm at seven in the morning.

Chapter SEVENTEEN

Rebecca, Penelope and Gabriela were successful in meeting a number of teens in the park around 10 with coffee, tea and carrot muffins from *The Toast*. The latter was Gabriela's idea, knowing from experience the girls were perpetually hungry, usually not taking advantage of the food service available for the homeless for fear of being harassed.

The girls, probably fifteen in total, knew Gomez and responded with a respectful nod, but they were leery of Penelope and Rebecca who, even in their kickaround clothes had the air of law enforcement or authority.

The girls all appeared healthy, albeit disheveled with hair that hadn't seen a brush in some time and clothes which had seen better days. They all appeared to be around fourteen to sixteen years old and of various ethnic heritage.

Gabriela introduced them to Rebecca and Penelope. The women responded by extending an arm to shake hands. Most of the girls reciprocated while others stood back with arms folded across their chests, staring, challenging.

Gomez, quickly assessing the mood, took the lead and explained the project and its objectives. All the girls had seen the motel renovations to which Gabriela referred. The teen's reaction was a collective sigh, all having heard plans for homeless housing before which never materialized.

"I appreciate your skepticism," offered Gomez, "as I too have seen the broken promises over the years. I guarantee this project is going through with Rebecca and Penelope spearheading the effort. The old motel will be called *Refugio Seguro* and it will be opening soon. Each participant will have her own furnished room and private bathroom. There is a dining room where three, well- prepared meals will be offered in addition to a tea-time in the afternoon after school."

Gomez paused to gauge the effect of the last comment and it took only a second for a reply, "Yeah, right, we are going back to school! Why? So the city or county can swoop in and put us in the system? No way. Not for me."

Several other girls echoed their fear of social services and rightly so thought Gabriela, so she replied, "I get it, but come on girls, you all have been coming to the women's center for a long time and you have never met anyone from social services and we have never contacted them. There is no reason for you to distrust me, my staff or the center."

"It's not you we distrust Ms. Gomez, it's them two," haughtily replied one teen, pointing an accusatory finger at Pen and Rebecca. "What are you two doin' here anyway? What's in this for you? You sure as hell ain't never been homeless or wondering if you will make it through the day without being assaulted."

Rebecca was sitting on a picnic bench with her feet up on the seat, leaning forward with her arms on her thighs. She said quietly, "You are right. Neither one of us have been homeless or kicked out of the family home when we were teens but that doesn't mean our hearts don't go out to you seeing you live this way. We have the means and influence to help make life better for you.

"And yes, we know what it is like starting each day worried that some guy is going to grab your butt, make a sexist slur, leer at you or outright attack you for being female. When I was your age a guy grabbed my butt in the hallway. I hit him so hard, he fell down unconscious. It never happened again. I know what you are going through, but I didn't have to live with it 24/7."

Several girls screamed and said, "No frickin' way. Really? You hit a guy that hard? How did it feel to do that? Did you get kicked out of school?"

Now the entire group was interested in the strangers, so Rebecca capitalized on their enthusiasm by continuing, "It felt empowering. The bullies, both girls and boys, stood back fearful they would be next. I was suspended for a week and for the rest of my high school years no guy would date me and none of the girls liked me. When I got home after the incident, my folks already knew, met me at the front door grinning and gave me a hug. My Mom told me how proud of me she was for standing up against sexism and assault. My Dad hugged me too then told me to clean out the paddock."

One girl asked inquisitively, "That is so cool. What is a paddock?"

The other girls laughed as Rebecca answered, "It is a fenced area at a ranch where horses are kept between being out in pasture and in the barn for the night.

"That incident wasn't the last of the sexual harassment. I have received it for decades as have millions of other women, but I never accepted it and I fought back. In most cases I won the respect of my male coworkers but some remained my adversaries. I was okay with either, but it always annoyed me, and it does to this day, that women and teens have to deal with this behavior.

"Penelope and I want to help you with a leg up at school and in life. The school counselor is on board as is the city mayor, council members and police chief. Any problems you have at school or elsewhere will be addressed immediately. We want to teach you skills that will give you confidence to avoid or eliminate a physical encounter with boys and men."

One girl interrupted asking, "What do you mean by physical skills and eliminating a threat?"

"We are martial artists and can teach you."

"Really? You're not just bullshitting us, are you?"

Penelope joined the conversation saying, "Absolutely not. Let me tell you this. When Rebecca and I were dating, we were staying at a hotel and were by the pool. Three drunks came by and were hassling us and wouldn't leave. One grabbed Rebecca and she broke his arm. One of the others grabbed her as well and she flipped him and broke his shoulder."

"Oh, come on. You did that Rebecca? No shit? And you can teach us to do that as well? That would be so cool to be able to defend ourselves and not be afraid all the time? Penelope, you do this stuff too?"

"I do. Rebecca taught me and she is a great instructor. That is just one of the things we want to offer you. We want to get you outfitted with new clothes and when you move into *Refugio Seguro* you can decorate your rooms anyway you want."

"Clothes? What the fuck? Oh, sorry," said one of the girls putting her hand over her mouth. "I mean, what the heck? What we have on is what we own. I can't believe this is happening. There has to be a 'but' here somewhere. What do you want from us?"

Rebecca responded with, "Nothing. When you finish high school, university or technical school, there won't be any cost. You could even go to Santa Barbara City College or UCSB and live at *Refugio Seguro*, Gabriela and her staff have developed the plan and can't see any downside."

Just as Gabriela was going to join the conversation, a vehicle approached, and all heads turned to see the brightly colored *Girl Power* food truck pull up beside them.

Gomez said with a swoop of her arm, "Girls, may we introduce you to the most delicious food in Santa Barbara. Please, tell *Girl Power* your desires and take some for later too, if you like.

The teenagers approached the truck with considerable trepidation. They had no money and had never been able to purchase food like this before. As they got closer the vehicle's side panel opened and they were greeted by a 40-something woman with a LA Angels t-shirt and baseball hat on backwards saying, "Good morning girls, or I guess it is afternoon now. What can I make for you today?"

Several girls had the veggie wrap; a spinach tortilla with cucumber, avocado, pickled red cabbage, goat cheese and arugula. They also ordered Sista smoothies with dark chocolate, homemade peanut butter and almond milk. *Girl Power* choices were a cornucopia of delicacies including a veggie lasagna, stir fry, quinoa salad with tomatoes, cucumbers and a sunflower and almond dressing, veggie pizza and mac & cheese.

The women ordered as well and joined the girls around the picnic tables and continued the conversation with Gabriela saying, "We would like to see you girls off the streets as soon as you are interested. We have cots arranged in the women's center with *Girl Power* delivering meals every day until your new home is ready.

"Some of you may be thinking this all sounds like a cult and the sermons will start but that is not the case. If you think of the failed proposals of the past, this is a version of apartments for homeless folks with a twist. We not only want you off the streets, but we want you to be happy, productive citizens and succeed in life. No sermons.

"This is strictly voluntary on your part and you can leave any time you want, but of course we hope you will stay, enjoy your new home, your education and lifestyle and then move on when you are ready."

One girl tried talking with her mouth full and put her arm up to reserve her speaking spot, like a talking stick. Swallowing, she asked, "There have to be rules. What are they? And also, who is paying for all of this?"

"Excellent questions," offered Penelope. "No drugs, no alcohol, no males. The main door will be locked with a guard 24/7 with CTV cameras in the halls and outside for your safety, but you can come and go at your leisure. You will have your own bus to ride to and from school, cell phones - not smartphones - but if you have one, we will pay the service fee. Each of you will have a personal laptop and Wi-Fi. You'll each have a laundry bag with your name on it. The cleaners will pick up and deliver several times a week.

"As far as who is paying for all of this, it is primarily Rebecca, me and a lot of very successful people who have wanted to see this develop but didn't know how. Other than Gabriela and the women's center, there are no government agencies involved.

"Before you ask, we are retired; Rebecca from government and me as a veterinarian."

Penelope was surprised that none of the girls had a question about their former jobs, money or rules, so she continued, "I almost forgot, if you want to get started today, Gabriela will set you up with a cot at the center and you can order clothes online from local stores and they will deliver. If you want to go to Nordstrom or another department store, that's doable too. We both know," she pointed to Rebecca then back to herself," about the fun of trying on clothes.

"Por eso, este lugar de la calle se llama *Refugio Seguro?"* asked one of the girls.

Gabriela responded with, "Sí. Refugio Seguro le brinda un refugio seguro para que sus años de adolescencia crezcan, aprendan y se conviertan en mujeres saludables y felices. (Yes. Safe Haven, is providing you a secure sanctuary for your teen years to enable you to grow, learn and develop into healthy and happy women).

As the women prepared to leave, Gabriela said, "Thank you for your time and conversation. We look forward to more of both and that you will join us today at the center."

Rebecca slid off the picnic bench and reiterated Gabriela's comment, gave a little wave and started to walk away with Penelope when one of the girls walked up, gave each of them a hug and said, "I'm going with. Anything has to be better than the hell I am going through now."

Another girl walked up to their opposite side and said, "So Rebecca, when are you entering the UFC?" referring to the Ultimate Fighting Championship/Mixed Martial Arts/MMA, the first of which was won by Brazilian Jiu-jitsu martial artist Royce Gracie in 1993.

Pen, Rebecca and Gabriela were so taken aback by the off-handed comment, they started to laugh with the girls joining in. Soon all the teens were laughing at the humor.

They walked out of the park as the food truck closed down and prepared to head to their next client. Left behind were two teens, one of whom was the most skeptical of the group sitting on a picnic bench, her body language difficult to read; sullen, angry, perhaps rejected?

Gabriela took one last glance back before they turned the corner and walked back to her office with Rebecca and Penelope.

"You know what? Bitches get stuff done."

Tina Fey

"Every girl, no matter where she lives, deserves the opportunity to develop the promise inside of her."

Michelle Obama

"I close the door to the past, open the door to the future, take a deep breath, step on through and start a new chapter in my life."

Author Unknown

Chapter EIGHTEEN

Jessica and the LAPD detectives were elated with obtaining the LA County District Attorney's support in delaying prosecution of Gutierrez. Jessica wanted to tell the DA that she didn't have a hope in hell prosecuting on the basis of a phone call but of course verbalizing that would be absurd, and she kept it to herself.

The investigative quartet left the building separately and met at a nearby Cuban coffee bar and spent thirty minutes reviewing the next phase of the operation, then everyone went their separate ways, all to be looped by CHAP once Jessica had put the hook into Marianna.

Jessica texted the helicopter pilot as she left the coffee house, then made her way back to the county building. Just as she approached the main door, she heard the telltale sounds of chopper blades overhead and ran to the elevator.

She knew the pilot wouldn't leave without her or be annoyed if she were not there immediately, but she didn't want to set a precedent knowing she could be using this service frequently.

Jessica used the thirty-minute flight to make notes and memorize her oral presentation to Katrina. Gutierrez was her client and to contact Marianna directly would be violating protocol, which could lead to a kink in her deception.

Jessica suspected Marianna would try and recruit her after Katrina shared the news, but she felt staying with Barbados would allow her to manipulate Gutierrez from a distance, probably in a social context, rather than becoming embroiled in Marianna's legal business.

Detective Elise Pelfini of the Santa Barbara Police Department, who played a crucial role in the raid on the cocaine delivery, was lead investigator in conjunction with the LAPD Gang Squad in gathering evidence against Gutierrez.

Jessica had to remain focused on the cartel, while working cases Katrina assigned. And on a personal note, she was quite enjoying practicing law, a revelation she would never have anticipated twenty plus years ago at UC Berkeley.

When the helo landed, she had her presentation ready, was confident and excited to set the hook into the person whom she believed to be intricately involved in the multi-million-dollar Southern California drug trade.

Jessica thanked the pilot, acknowledged privately that the trip's two-thousand-dollar price tag would be a minuscule expense for Marianna, grabbed the first taxi and headed to Katrina's office with renewed exuberance.

Jessica texted Katrina during the short cab ride so her boss was waiting in the hallway as Fukishura entered the office. Katrina's questioning expression was exemplified by her aggressive waving, encouraging Jessica to hurry.

Katrina held the door open allowing Jessica to enter, then closed it and joined her new attorney on the couch and said with an unreadable facial expression, "How did you make out?"

"Do you want the good news first or the bad news?

"It's been a hectic day, so how about the good news first? Is the DA going to bring charges against Gutierrez?"

"No", Jessica blurted out, not trying to hide her delight.

Katrina's reaction was immediate as she jumped up, prompting Jessica to rise as well and the two embraced. "You continue to amaze me Jessica. I have been thinking of you all day, wondering how you would survive going head to head against one of the most powerful attorneys in Los Angeles and here you have walked away with a massive win. What happened?"

"I met her on her turf, on her terms. She was arrogant with misplaced self-confidence until I pointed out that being the recipient of a text to which Marianna did not reply would be a fool's errand if Zinkton prosecuted. I also reminded her that an election year was not the time to be dragged through the media on a case she couldn't win."

Jessica wasn't sure Katrina bought her explanation. Theoretically, Fukishura was a recent law school graduate, albeit a mature student and one with a testy class and courtroom reputation, but to take on a seasoned district attorney successfully might have been stretching the bounds of believability, so she reined in her enthusiasm slightly and continued, "I honestly questioned whether she would see me at all even though you had arranged the appointment.

"I knew I had to take an aggressive stand, or she would have had me for lunch. She did pay me an offhanded compliment when she told me I pissed her off with my arrogance, which was humorous coming from her.

"I do believe either her investigators or the LAPD fed her misinformation trying to relieve the pressure she created wanting a prosecution in such a high-profile case. I say this because when I mentioned the evidence, she had a pained expression as though I had caught her off guard by approaching her before discovery.

"I elaborated on the evidence and my interpretation and it was shortly thereafter that she agreed to stay the prosecution…for now."

Fukishura could see that Katrina was more comfortable with the situation since she expounded. Jessica was somewhat remorseful having to lie to her boss who had been so welcoming and supportive. But her only alliance was the Secret Service for now and when she retired after taking Gutierrez down, she would reveal everything to Katrina and hoped she would keep her on staff and not feel she had been duped…which of course she had.

"I appreciate the elaboration Jessica but don't sell yourself short, any experienced attorney would feel intimidated going against Zinkton, which points to not only your chutzpah but your formidable acumen.

"Now to call Marianna and share the good news. Something tells me she will want to celebrate the removal of this massive weight. Just out of curiosity and between us, do you think she is involved in something nefarious?"

Jessica had a nanosecond to respond. She knew that Elisabeth had made the connection between the offshore signal to Fernández and then his text to Marianna. One, two, three. Quickly regaining her thoughts, she said,

"It seems extreme that the DA would consider prosecuting on the basis of an unreturned text. They can't prove the phone belongs to Marianna, *but the Secret Service can, she thought to herself,* it had to be a burner but that is not illegal.

"She's a defense attorney with numerous LAPD detectives harboring vendettas. More importantly, during dinner, after the first trip to LA, I was impressed with her aggressiveness and knowledge but when we were attacked in the parking lot, she seemed aghast at my physical response. That wasn't the behavior of a criminal."

"I agree. It really doesn't make a difference; our practice is primarily to the guilty. To change the subject before I call Marianna, how are you doing finding a place to live? You must be anxious to get out of the hotel?"

"I am but I'm not excited about actually looking. I'm not interested in owning. I'm not really a homeowner type of person. I would love a beach front house if I could find one under $10,000 a month. Fully furnished preferably," she smiled with her arms out to her sides knowing such a place was impossible to find.

"The reason I'm asking, nosey as it may sound, friends have moved to DC and they don't want to sell, and they didn't want to move their furniture. It is on Shoreline, right on the beach with the living room and kitchen overlooking the Pacific. Interested so far?"

"Yes. Please go on," Jessica replied, moving to the edge of her seat with enthusiasm.

"It is a four-bedroom, three bath rancher with a two-car garage about half-way into a gated community. I've been there socially numerous times. The grounds are fully landscaped, the weekly maintenance covered by the owners. Very private. The fourth bedroom is actually a guest studio with a separate entry, garden patio, kitchenette and washer/dryer. The master suite is light and airy with cream walls and a light oak hardwood floor. There are two area rugs with a cream and tan swirl pattern. Double French doors lead to the gardens, a slate walkway to the beach, an outdoor shower for rinsing off and a hot tub, the service cost covered by the owners.

"The extensive kitchen is elegant with its light-yellow walls. It faces the ocean with skylights and two glass and black steel, side by side lights above the island to enhance stainless-steel Miele appliances; six-burner gas stove with matching hood, double ovens to one side. The microwave and wine fridge are set into an eight-foot Aspen white granite island with a farm sink, matte black single handle faucet with six stools with black matte finished backs and light grey leather seats.

"The 3 x 8" Gainesboro grey backsplash tile is paired with silver grey cabinets which rise to the pale-yellow stippled eight-foot beamed ceiling. The farm sink with matte black single handle pull-down faucet is in front of a bay window overlooking the garden and several gardenia bushes.

"The living-room boasts a fifty-inch plasma screen TV with paid for cable, above a gas fireplace. Bookcases were built in on either side. The furniture is quite exquisite with two smoky grey leather couches and ottomans centrally located on vintage grey laminate flooring which extend into the open concept kitchen.

"What do you think?"

Jessica laughed and said, "Were you a realtor in another life? No, seriously. It sounds exactly like what I am seeking. When might I have a walk through?"

"With the house being empty and all their personal belongings gone, and me having the key…", she paused slightly to gauge Jessica's reaction. Observing a positive expression, she continued,

"How about this? Let me call Marianna and give her the news and see if she is interested in meeting us there, I'll order dinner and drinks delivered and we celebrate your accomplishment while you tour your new home?"

"Deal! This is alluring Katrina and I sincerely appreciate your invaluable help. What time?"

"It is my pleasure Jessica. You have brought a passion to the practice and I am delighted to help you get settled. If you can be done here by 4, I can as well, and we can meet there at 4:30? How does that work for you?"

"That works for me. I will head out a little early back to the hotel, change and meet you there at 4:30."

The two rose simultaneously with Katrina saying, "Deal. I'll head home and change as well. Let's hope Marianna can clear her schedule and meet us there."

Smiling broadly, Jessica hugged Katrina, grabbed her briefcase and headed to her office where she checked her schedule, then left for the hotel. In the car. Locked the doors. Started it. Turned on the air. Texted Alane.

She wasn't out of the parking lot when her phone chimed. Looking at the dashboard display, she noted it was from Alane.

Pulling into a parking spot, she retrieved the message, smiled to herself and texted Katrina that something came up and she would have to take a rain check for the same time tomorrow. Instantly Katrina replied, "No problem. I hadn't called Marianna yet. I will do so now and set it up for tomorrow night. See you in the morning."

Katrina couldn't contain her enthusiasm of helping Jessica get settled in her own place. She purposely didn't tell her that the owners were amenable to an offer to purchase at some point during the lease.

Gabriella, Rebecca, Penelope and most of the girls were walking past several businesses on their way to the women's center when first, one man, then another burst out the front door of *Doobella's* jewelry store brandishing handguns and carrying plastic bags. They sprinted towards the women and teens, waving their firearms, threatening bystanders to move. The incident occurred so rapidly, everyone froze…except Penelope and Rebecca.

The lead suspect stared at Rebecca as he barreled down on her, expecting his menacing glare to force her to move. She didn't.

He was at her in a nanosecond. Rebecca stepped to her left and thrust her right fist into his throat. He collapsed instantly. She grabbed his handgun, placed it in the small of her back, then pulled her own nine-millimeter, went to one knee and levelled it at the storefront anticipating a third felon.

The second thief was right behind his accomplice but didn't see Penelope.

Poor omission.

Penelope propelled herself into him, using her right shoulder, pivoted on her left foot, grabbed him around the waist and flipped him over her hip to the ground. A right-hand heel smash to his face knocked him out. She twisted the firearm out of his hand and stuck it in her pants waistband, pulled her own semi-automatic handgun and joined Rebecca as the two raced the short distance to the store.

Bystanders were in shock. Nobody moved. They looked at the two unconscious men then to the two women running into the store and back again to the sidewalk.

Rebecca quickly retrieved her identification, showed it to the unharmed proprietor, asked him to call 9-1-1, told him the suspects were down, then returned to the thieves.

Gabriela and the girls had pressed themselves against the cement wall of a nearby business, hands over their mouths in shock staring at Penelope and Rebecca as though to say, *who are these two?*

Penelope and Rebecca returned their firearms to their holsters and smiled at Gabriela and the teenagers, shrugged their shoulders in unison as though to say, *no big deal*, then approached the speechless teens.

The scene was eerily quiet with men, women, children and the teenagers riveted, as their attention on the surreal scene until the silence was broken by the ubiquitous sirens approaching, followed by a slow clapping initiated by one of the teens, with others joining her in joyous appreciation as officers arrived.

"Don't mistake kindness for weakness. Sometimes the kindest women are the fiercest warriors."

Entity Magazine

"11 years ago, I had my final marriage counseling appointment. From that appointment I emerged a different woman. I began a new single life full of tears, fears, smiles, depression, accomplishments, more tears, and hope. I found a voice, used it, got knocked down, dusted off and got back up, got challenged, cried some more, found new strength, fought back, got pushed down, fought harder back, found myself, believed in myself, thrived at being myself, loved being myself and am still growing. There are those out there who continue to challenge, fight, push and knock me, but I am Teflon...try as you may, I am strong, confident full of love and can no longer be broken by you or anyone else. THIS IS ME."

Ms. Janis Joseph, British Columbia *Warrior Woman*

Chapter NINETEEN

Jason Spencer and Jackson Pennington had spent the last few days on the phone, separately, with little to no progress, discovering if they could retire early and what their benefits might be.

Elisabeth was maintaining vigilance of the three Vancouver phones to ensure the users were in the building when Karen, Tom and Kimberly would take up surveillance.

On this particular late afternoon, the three were chatting by the pool, sharing a bottle of chardonnay. Jason and Jackson were expressing their frustration when Elisabeth chimed in with her decision to retire as well. She shared her colleagues' exhaustion with living out of a suitcase but confessed she couldn't give up the adrenaline rush she experienced with her computer skills.

Jason said, "I can relate somewhat Elisabeth. Not with your specific skills but those we all share. That last operation wasn't as much of an adrenaline rush as the airliner but close to it. And quite frankly I haven't been on a date for so long, I question whether I'd know how to conduct myself," he quipped throwing his hands in the air, hitting the overhead umbrella.

"I hear ya, Jason," offered Jackson. "The part of the Mahalo Airline operation of almost catching the bomber, before he took a header off the balcony, was exhilarating. I miss that and the challenge. This back and forth on the phone with Washington is a nightmare trying to find out our benefits. What do you think about asking Jessica to intercede on our behalf? She is still our boss, albeit incommunicado so to speak."

Elisabeth responded, “It’s worth a try. But we can’t call or text her because we have no idea with whom she is at any given moment. How about I call her hotel, leave a message to call us and we arrange for a dinner here? She can’t be seen with any of us, so just as before, she can make her way here in a round-about fashion to ensure she isn’t being followed. We don’t want a repeat of the last time she was tailed. What do you guys think?”

Both men nodded in agreement, and while Jackson refilled all their glasses, Elisabeth texted Rebecca and Penelope with their idea.

The Chica de Oro was passing Fort Bragg, California, submerged at 110 meters, in international waters, 20 nautical miles west, well beyond the international 12 nautical mile (22.2 km/13.8 mi) limit. The American submariners may have been aware of the town’s historical significance…if they were, their callous, mercenary character would reject any emotions to the destruction of the Pomo indigenous people by disease between 1830 and 1850 by Mexican settlers and the establishment of a military settlement.

The “J” Team trio were polishing off their second bottle of chardonnay, enjoying the last of the afternoon sun as it made its way towards the Pacific when Elisabeth’s private cell chimed with a text; *Be ready by 6. Dinner. Tell boys to get dressed” with several smiley faces. Rebecca.*

Elisabeth finished reading the brief text, passed it to Jason as she got up and gathered the empty bottles and glasses. Jason smiled, shook his head and shared the text with Jackson, whose response was identical.

The men rose and took the empties from Elisabeth and headed inside with Jason quipping that he didn't have anything to wear. Elisabeth shook her head, smiling and responded, "You guys! I will see you in an hour."

Jackson replied, "We will be in the living room sampling a bottle of San Leon Manzanilla sherry in twenty," a reply both men knew would irk their colleague knowing they could both shower and be dressed in less time than she took.

True to their word, the men were sitting in the living room with Chet Baker on trumpet performing softly through the myriad of hidden speakers and glasses of sherry. Before sitting down, Jason checked on the litter boxes in the laundry room, emptied and topped off the litter, dropped the waste in the kitchen garbage, then filled the kittens' water and food dish. As he headed for the living room he stopped, quietly caught Jackson's attention and pointed to the six kittens curled up together on one of the accent chairs.

Elisabeth arrived momentarily wearing an Elisa J blush and cream floral print wrap chiffon dress paired with Sam Edelman Ariella ankle strap sandals with two-inch heels.

Jackson rose and handed her a glass of the San Leon. Accepting the sherry, Elisabeth sipped, then used her lifted glass, sweeping her arm in an arc to comment on her colleagues' attire, "Very sharp guys. I like the look." Jackson wore a ruby Peter Millar one button blazer with a white button-down short-sleeve shirt, white pocket square, tan slacks and brown tassel loafers. Jason was ready for the evening with a sky-blue blazer by Topman, a navy pocket square, a navy open collar long sleeve shirt with navy blue slacks and blue woven loafers.

As Elisabeth sat down, she commented rhetorically, wondering how Rebecca and Penelope made out with the teenagers earlier. Neither Jason nor Jackson had a clue about teenagers and were about to say so when the driveway intruder alarm chimed and all three rose to meet whomever.

Elisabeth led the way out the front door as a mini caravan swung into the driveway with Rebecca and Penelope coming in first through the electronically controlled gates.

The three agents stood at the front door with raised sherry glasses in hand, toasting the arrival of their hostesses. Rebecca was first out of the SUV passenger side with Penelope quickly joining her with almost identical comments about her three colleagues' attire, "You guys look fantastic. What's the occasion? Should we change or can we drink looking like this?"

Jackson and Jason turned to Elisabeth acquiescing to her for an explanation. Just as she was about to respond and before Rebecca fobbed the gates closed, Alane drove in and Alejandro appeared from the corner of the house, having walked from his adjoining acreage.

As Alane exited his vehicle with a flurry of enthusiasm, a white, one-ton van with *Marc Stucki's Quintessential Dinning Experience* emblazoned on the side panels pulled in with the driver waving, then bypassed everyone and drove to the rear of the house.

Right behind them was yet another vehicle.

Marc Stucki.

"I heard there was a dinner party I didn't want to miss, so I invited myself and brought the meal," he shouted from his open car window as he slowly followed his staff to the rear of the house.

Everyone was expressing their delight of having Marc join the group, commenting to each other how this event was planned when another vehicle entered through the wrought iron gates.

Fukishura.

Rebecca and Penelope walked quickly to her car and embraced her as she exited, delighted to see their elusive boss after so long a period of just receiving orders through texts.

Alane and Alejandro moved in from behind to join in the welcoming hugs, then all headed for the front door as Penelope fobbed the gates closed.

Congregating in the kitchen, Penelope retrieved wine glasses, Rebecca acquired two bottles of Cabrillo Vineyards' chardonnay and all gathered around the massive island and chatted with Marc as he supervised his staff in setting the dining-room table and laying out numerous heated serving trays for family-style dining.

No one asked how the restaurant was doing as everyone there and probably all of Santa Barbara's dining crowd knew the community's reception was beyond enormous.

Marc had moved to Santa Barbara after losing his job as President Bakus' executive chef when Bakus lost the election. Unbeknown to Marc at that time, Rebecca, Penelope, Alane, Alejandro and numerous other movers and shakers planned to invest in Marc's talents and back a restaurant which all culminated shortly after he arrived.

The investors were Democrats and knew the "J" Team had prevented the disaster the Christians for a Better America had planned; destruction of the Marina del Rey Convention Center and the death of two hundred political delegates by downing their airplane in the Pacific Ocean. It was an easy choice for them to join the investment group in appreciation for the prevention of a major disaster.

Alane had made many of the investors extremely wealthy and they followed his lead in the investment knowing it was payback time for their success.

Marc Stucki's was located beside an old train station a few blocks from the beach. Marc decided to maintain the former establishment's dark paneling, mahogany tables and chairs, adding recessed lighting to create a more family atmosphere while maintaining a sophisticated ambiance.

He liked the twenty-foot slate wall with a centered gas fireplace, so he kept that but added a massive television screen showing feed from numerous beach web cams situated from Sycamore Creek to the south and north to Santa Barbara Point.

Rebecca and Penelope handled the remodeling and created the railroad theme by positioning period train pieces throughout, which paired well with staff attired in white jackets, black slacks and black bowties.

The menu featured Wyoming beef from former President Bakus' ranch. In addition, a massive salt-water tank in the entry featured Dungeness Crab caught each morning by a retired crab fisher friend of Alejandro's.

Jessica was circulating among her team when Marc announced that dinner was served and ushered guests into the dining room where his staff had just finished placing the last dish.

Alejandro and Alane held chairs for the women, then the men sat, and all were greeted by a plate of baby artichokes, crispy with a semolina coating, with lemon aioli and a little gem salad - a combination of butter and romaine lettuces with warm cannellini beans, smoked tomato with a lemon and garlic vinaigrette.

Penelope had brought several additional bottles of chardonnay and cabernet sauvignon and placed them strategically around the table so everyone could help themselves.

The group self-served two chafing dishes; ravioli with fresh ricotta cheese, roasted tomato sauce, heirloom cherry tomatoes and basil. The second dish was gnocchi served with rock shrimp, dried tomato, fava bean, roasted garlic and black truffle butter.

There was little discussion during dinner, as was the group's custom; everyone wanted to enjoy Marc's cuisine and leave the chat until later.

Twenty later, Rebecca noticed folks nearing the end of their meal, so she slipped away and retrieved ice cream from Julia's Creamery in Santa Barbara.

Pumpkin spice with whipped cream swirls.

Dishes all around and the four-liter tub, set into a cut-glass serving dish was passed among the diners.

Oohs and aahs from everyone as the delicacy disappeared, Alane scrapping the last from the tub.

Rebecca initiated self-bussing with the dish washer filling quickly. Marc rinsed the chafing dishes, then left them on the counter for his staff to retrieve in the morning.

The group retired to the living room with Penelope pouring the sherry Jason and Jackson had started, setting the mood to relax and prepare to listen to whatever or whomever initiated the impromptu dinner.

Elisabeth stood and said, "I'm retiring."

Jason followed with, "I'm retiring".

Jackson was next with, "I'm retiring."

By now the group was smiling and attempting to discern if there was a zinger approaching.

While they were contemplating the next move by those standing, Jessica stood and said, "I'm retiring".

With that, the room erupted in joyous pandemonium with Alejandro jumping to the occasion with congratulatory hugs to all four, with the rest mingling, sharing their enthusiasm of the news.

Marc was the first to renew the conversation with, "Sherry anyone?" as he gestured with the bottle of San Leon Manzanilla.

That broke everyone up as they presented their wine glasses for Marc, then returned to their seats to hear everyone's retirement story.

Jason lead the conversation with, "Several things have led to my decision and I probably speak for my colleagues as well. I have been a federal agent for a very long time and prior to that with the LAPD. The years in North Africa took more of a toll on me mentally than I ever cared to admit. I have never stopped 'to smell the roses,' so to speak, always moving from one operation to another and it wasn't until now, here, with all of you, that I realize what I have been missing. Friends.

"Also, it has been years since I spent any time with my mom. Actually, it has been since I left home to attend UCLA and now that she is up there in years, I want to make life more comfortable and spend time with her. She sacrificed so much for me growing up, it is time for me to give back. I am going to get my own place here in Santa Barbara", he glanced at Rebecca and Penelope and smiled and added, "and leave this glorious hacienda and the wonderful hospitality and hopefully find a little place for my Mom here in town."

Jessica interjected with, "I have just the place for her," and left the comment hanging, intending to complete the thought when it was her turn to explain.

"Alane, I will call your office tomorrow and arrange a time for us to get together, if that works for you."

Alane responded with, "Certainly Jason. Any time."

Jason continued, "There is one hitch, and this applies to all of us. We are not eligible for retirement from the federal government. Jessica, is it possible for you, as our boss, to enquire on our behalf and see what an early pension might look like?"

Jessica was quick to respond. "I spoke with Sorento the other day for myself and he authorized a full pension if I stay until we finish the current operation." She knew that Alejandro and Alane might be cognizant of the operation, but she wasn't going to chance it.

She continued, "I am confident Sorento will approve early retirement with full benefits for the Team with one proviso, we remain as a team and subcontract to the Secret Service for any assignment relating to drug trafficking, financial and computer crimes. It is purely conjecture on my part Elisabeth, but I believe the Service wants you on the west coast which will work in our factor.

"There is no doubt, Jason and Jackson that your track records speak for themselves, and Sorento will use those to make his case. Considering what we have accomplished for the Service, I would be astonished if it wasn't granted.

"To reiterate, the projected deal is that we are available for Secret Service assignments. My problem is; I have been enjoying practicing law and I hope I can explain sufficiently to Katrina to stay on with her. If not, Rebecca and Pen, could you guys use an attorney with R&P?" she quipped, smiling and emptying her sherry.

"I have a lot to evaluate," she concluded walking over to Marc for a sherry refill, noticing a strange whispering between Rebecca and Penelope.

Elisabeth picked up the conversation with, "I appreciate the confidence Jessica; I hope it comes to fruition. I'm looking forward to living in Santa Barbara. If I get my full pension, I should be okay financially and would need the work from Sorento for my mental health. I can't leave law enforcement, not yet anyway.

Jackson was the only one left to offer his input, and as he was about to stand, Penelope rose and quickly said, "I think we may have a solution that would solve all of our problems. Sorento is basically saying you can retire early if you agree to work for him as needed. That could be a lot or none, either way, it is a stipulation. We have been kept busy from day one with R&P Investigations and have been turning clients away. Might you be interested in joining us?"

Rebecca stood beside Pen and placed an arm around her waist and added, "We can change the name if you like. Actually, the more we think of it, *"J" Team Investigations* sounds pretty impressive. What do you guys think? Doable?"

Jackson was the first to respond. He sprinted out of his chair with his sherry glass raised and said with exuberance, "Here's to the "J" Team Investigations!"

There was no discussion. The rest of the Team rose as one and joined Jackson in the salutation with Elisabeth adding, "Here's to us!"

Penelope was quick with an addendum, "Before we forget, the new company will be all of us as equal partners. Alane, might we impose upon you to arrange the legal and financial particulars?"

Alane was already standing, toasting with the others, the joy of his friends' success palpable as he replied, "It would be my delight. Consider it done."

"Terrific Alane," said Rebecca, smiling broadly with her arms spread wide, "And Jessica, if Katrina doesn't fire you and accepts your apology, Barbados Inc. could handle our legal business."

That comment bent everyone over laughing, Alane and Alejandro as well, at the thought of Jessica, Ms. Legal herself, ever getting fired. They were unaware of her years of riding the fine line of employment with the Secret Service or how much lying she had done to affect her under cover persona.

While the Team was chatting and sharing their enthusiasm, Rebecca and Penelope raised their voices slightly, clinked glasses and Rebecca shared, "Just a quick comment if you will. We spent this morning with about sixteen teenage girls and believe we convinced the majority to leave the streets and join *Refugio Seguro,* which we are told will be completed in the next week or so. They are staying at the women's resource center until then. Thank you for your tremendous support. This is going to happen, and your participation is changing lives."

Alejandro added, "I am doing the landscaping next week and they are already placing the new furniture in the remodeled rooms," as he raised his glass to the new movers and shakers of Santa Barbara. "These are very exciting times, Penelope and Rebecca, for which the community will be forever grateful."

“We think poverty is only being hungry, naked and homeless. It is also being unwanted, unloved and uncared.”

Mother Teresa

“Poverty is not an accident. Like slavery and apartheid, it is man-made and can be removed by the actions of human beings.”

Nelson Mandela

Penelope and Rebecca didn’t want to rain on the retirement party, so they chose to keep the attempted robbery incident off the evening’s agenda, knowing everyone would learn of their involvement shortly.

The Golden Girl rose just enough for her antenna to extend above the surging two-meter waves engulfed in darkness. As the aerial broke the surface, the captain executed a five second burst of energy on the National Information radio band of two-hundred and fifty GHz to a Santa Barbara receiver.

The cocaine barons chose that frequency because the citizen band’s heavy traffic made it impossible to detect their short burst.

Once the signal was delivered, the aerial retracted, the Golden Girl submerged and continued her journey north, undetected…except by Peltowski.

Elisabeth saved the recording, then posted her analysis on CHAP, isolating the recipients to just the Edmonton RCMP detachment investigators and CSIS’s David Kopas.

Chapter TWENTY

Kimberly, Karen and Tom arrived separately at the *Innocent 'Till Proven Guilty* coffee house, ignored each other's presence, ordered coffee, a muffin and found single seats with their backs to a wall, facing the high-rise, the top three floors, which housed the law offices of Brosman & Snow.

The agents had downloaded Elisabeth's app yesterday, which connected them to a cell phone in the law offices. Each of their screens showed their location on Howe Street and each floor of the building across the street – particularly noteworthy was a red dot stationary on the fortieth floor.

Tom appeared the epitome of the financial district's entrepreneur in a blue pinstriped suit, a pale blue button down, long sleeve shirt, a blue and white striped tie and blue tassel loafers. The University of Ottawa lapel pin completed his outfit, which had been modified by CSIS technicians to house a miniature camera in the *O* of the emblem.

Kimberly sipped a black coffee in a signature mug emblazoned with the word, *Evidence*. Pretending to scroll her encrypted smartphone, she watched the red dot intently, prepared to follow the phone user whenever they left the building.

She blended with the business crowd in her Lisueyne wine, striped business suit with lapel collar, double button closure, front flap pockets and high waisted pants. The blazer was cut to conceal her 9. She paired the suit with a white, pointed collar, long sleeve blouse and narrow, wine and white scarf. Her booties were Canobie's with a 1 ½ inch heel, back zip closure, with a perforations in the leather upper in caramel leather.

Her taupe handbag sat on the bench beside her.

Empty.

The white pearl scarf clasp disguised a camera which transmitted real-time visual to her smartphone. A click of the phone's volume control snapped and stored the image.

Karen sat similarly at the far end of the coffee house behaving in the same manner in a Brooks Brothers, Zac Posen's powder blue, striped, stretch cotton seersucker one-button jacket with notched lapels, slanted convertible flap-welt pockets and center back vent.

An ivory turtleneck was accented with a gold airplane pendant on a gold chain. One wing tip held her miniature camera which functioned identically to those of her colleagues.

The suit pants had a set-on waistband with belt loops, concealed hook-and-bar closure, zip fly and front slant pockets. She paired the outfit with a Treasure & Bond lace-up, ivory leather bootie with a back zipper and 1 ½ inch heel. Complimenting her ensemble was a medium ivory, leather tote bag by Madewell.

It was not empty.

The agents were banking on the phone's owner to emerge to energize with fresh air and caffeine, presumably having arrived earlier that morning, with the other billable hour masters, probably around four am.

They weren't disappointed.

The red dot was moving.

Kimberly was the first to get into action, lifting her empty handbag onto her left shoulder, sliding the smartphone into her right blazer pocket, slipping out from behind the table and bussing her empty mug. She crossed Howe and entered the professional building's lobby.

Tom and Karen left moments later, each heading in opposite directions on Howe. They timed their movements to arrive at the next corner, cross Howe and head back on the opposite side.

Kimberly stood in the lobby feigning interest in her phone while watching the red dot slowly drop from floor to floor stopping at the lobby.

Six people exited the elevator. Without an ability to discern who was carrying the phone she walked toward the group and, using her broach, snapped photos of each.

She noted that only two of the six were interacting. These two men continued their conversation as they exited the building and turned left, heading north-east right toward Tom.

Snapping continually, Tom passed the men, maintained his direction and disappeared into the crowd.

Kimberly caught the next elevator up and exited on the fortieth floor. Exhibiting familiarity with the layout she found the women's restroom, entered and locked herself in a stall.

Sitting on the toilet seat, she activated the phone's encryption component allowing the device to connect with Elisabeth, then sent the photos. While Elisabeth ran them through her North American and International facial recognition software, Kimberly went online to the law firm's web site and found four of the six whose photos she took, listed. One was a paralegal and three were attorneys. The two men who were conversing while exiting the building were listed as partners.

Tom continued on Howe turning left on Canada Place, stopped at the convention center, settled into a coffee shop and completed the same task that Kimberly had just done.

Karen followed the exiting crowd until it thinned, and she could single out the person carrying the phone. Following the two men around the corner onto Cordova Street, she observed them enter the Cordova House coffee shop.

Karen continued her journey, walked by the coffee house glancing down the street as she did so, then ducked into a store alcove.

She emerged moments later wearing a cream, short brimmed straw Jazz hat by Baldwin and a full-length stone, Burberry grommet cotton gabardine, double-breasted trench coat, belt tied in the back with press-stud grommet closure. Her left hand held an empty coffee take-out with lid.

The tote.

She lingered by the store's entrance, presumably reading her phone waiting for the suspects to depart the coffee shop. That occurred moments later and as they both looked to their left to ensure they were not going to bump into someone on the busy sidewalk, Karen snapped several full front photos, then followed them back to the office building.

She was immediately behind the men as they entered an empty elevator. She was seemingly preoccupied with reading her phone as she ducked into the elevator just as the doors were about to close. Turning her head slightly as she entered, the suspects were unable to see her face, on the chance they had taken a moment from their conversation.

Karen stood behind and slightly to the left of the phone's owner and hit record.

As the men chatted nonchalantly about their joint pending court case, they were unaware that their voices were being recorded, to be analyzed by Elisabeth to create a voice comparison with the many calls she had intercepted from the law office's switchboard.

Building their case.

Officers from the Santa Barbara Police Department arrived on the attempted robbery scene, weapons drawn and found two men prone on the sidewalk a short distance from the alleged victim's store. The men had their hands and feet bound and what looked like masking tape across their mouths. Surveying the scene, they saw two women with their backs to a store front's wall with one leg up behind them pressed against the wall, the director of the women's center and a group of obviously excited teenage girls.

Addressing Gabriela, whom they knew, Sgt. Alfonso asked agitatedly, "Ms. Gomez, what happened here?"

Gabriela did her best to respond to the officer's questions, attempting to simplify the encounter by giving credit for the take-down to responsible citizens. Her attempts were futile given the inability of the teenagers to control their vociferousness.

The girls were talking all at once and Rebecca could see the sergeant's eyeballs rising, reflecting his growing anger in trying to figure out how to shut them up so he could get the information.

The girls were forced to take a deep breath when another officer entered the fray with the store owner in tow. He bent close to the sergeant and spoke softly while looking directly at Penelope and Rebecca.

Tipping his head in their direction, the sergeant followed his nod and approached Rebecca and Penelope saying, "Good day ladies. I understand you were involved in this incident. May I see some identification please?

Rebecca produced hers first, flipping the leather folder such that the officer could read her private detective license emblazoned with the Secret Service Logo in the bottom corner.

"Really? Secret Service? Are you armed ma'am?

"Yes, Sergeant. I am," as she flipped the leather folder to another plastic case revealing her license.

The sergeant. turned to Penelope and asked sarcastically, "What are you? Retired FBI?"

Penelope couldn't help smiling at this blatant demonstration of misogyny. Her smirk irked the officer, which he expressed by snapping his fingers saying, "ID smartass."

Penelope pulled her folder from her inside pocket, flipped it open to reveal her private detective license and firearms permit. She maintained the disdainful smirk.

Before the sergeant could continue with his impertinence, the store owner stepped forward and offered, "Sergeant, I can provide you with all the information you need to arrest these two," pointing to the two prone suspects.

"That will be fine," he replied, as he turned to his officers, gave them instructions to obtain identifications and statements from everyone, then said curtly to Rebecca and Penelope, "Tomorrow morning. Police station. Statements," then left.

"Enemies are so stimulating."

Katharine Hepburn

Chapter TWENTY-ONE

Larry was watching the Edmonton Eskimos and the Calgary Stampeders' football game on television while enjoying Beavertail Raspberry from Grizzly Paw brewery when Stan slid into the chair next to him.

Larry glanced to his right as the stranger sat and said, "Edmonton is leading by two touchdowns. Welcome to the *Horseman* and sports reality TV," with a chuckling, raising his mug in saluting the screen.

Sticking out his hand, Larry continued, "Larry Baird from Calgary."

Stan was taken aback by his fellow football fan and had fully intended to wander around the *Horseman* sipping a beer, maybe order some wings, take in the décor, expecting the experience to give him joy, being in the house of his adversaries.

Against his better judgement, Stan felt himself relax as he unintentionally placed one leg over the other, sipped his beer, shook Larry's hand, replying, "Stan Loblinski from Edmonton but I just enjoy a good game regardless of which team wins." Stan learned years earlier to be anonymous, that rooting for one team or another generates interest from other fans. He didn't need that.

During a commercial break Larry commented, "When I was a kid growing up in Port Alberni, I dreamed of living in a city where I could watch professional sports live. I see the Calgary Flames and Stampeders numerous times during their seasons and love it."

Stan looked at Larry incredulously, having lost all apprehension of socializing and responded, "Son-of-a-bitch, you're from Port? I am too. You go to ADSS?" referring to Alberni District Secondary School.

"Yeah, I did," and the men spent commercial times recollecting, sharing teen stories and finding several mutual friends.

Stan was drinking two to Larry's one and by the end of the game he was quite inebriated, a behavior in which he hadn't indulged since before he became a drug entrepreneur in his early twenties. And even with the numerous snacks, he was hammered.

Larry not only had to drive back to the hotel, but he was working on the eightieth floor the next day and he needed one hundred percent of his motor skills, hence his nursing three beers.

The former school mates decided to call it a night and as they were leaving, from behind the bar, Davidson asked if they wanted a cab. Larry replied that he had called one and was seeing that Stan got home safely.

The cab was waiting under the *Horsemen's* portico. Larry helped Stan into the back of the vehicle, shook his hand saying, "We have to do this again Stan. Give me a call. I'm in town for a number of weeks," then place his personal card in Stan's jacket pocket, closed the door, tapping the roof twice, then stood back as the cab departed.

As Larry Jr. left *The Horsemen* and put Stan into a cab he was filmed and his conversation with Stan was recorded with a parabolic voice amplifier.

The next morning while he was waiting for his coffee to brew in his hotel room, Larry texted his dad, Larry Sr. in Port Alberni, sharing with him last night's small world encounter.

Chapter TWENTY-TWO

Jessica arrived at her office the next morning at eight and spent the majority of the day on cases Katrina had assigned, pausing periodically to muse her retirement plans. She planned to ask one additional favor of Sorento during her chat later in the day.

Jessica ordered a salad and iced tea from a local bodega and ate lunch at her desk hoping to be ready to leave early. While eating and perusing depositions, Katrina knocked at her door, stuck her head in and said, “We are all set for 6 at your new home. Does that work for you?” she offered with a huge smile.

“It does Katrina. Thanks. I will be ready. I want to change beforehand so I will meet you there at six.”

“Terrific. See you then,” Katrina replied and closed the door.

Jessica waited purposefully until three to call Sorento to ensure he was done with his day (the time change being after six in Washington) and could best concentrate on the conversation.

Placing the call on her encrypted smartphone, she reached him on the second ring, exchanged pleasantries and updated him on the case against Marianna. Doing so was somewhat superfluous given she had posted everything on CHAP, but she needed to commence the interaction with a positive.

Using the notes she had prepared during breakfast at her hotel, she laid out her plan, or proposition, providing considerable detail to ensure as much of a success as possible. She was banking on *making him an offer he couldn't refuse*, to quote Mario Puzo's Don Vito Corleone in *The Godfather*.

Sorento asked numerous questions, the answers of which he knew FERS, the Federal Employees Retirement System, would require. He ended the conversation expressing both his regret that the Team was retiring and his joy that they would continue to function as an investigative unit. Although he told her nothing could be promised, he shared that he would do everything in his power to make it happen.

He adjourned the conversation with a warm comment that he planned to take his vacation in Santa Barbara the coming summer to visit with the Team he hadn't seen in years.

Jessica sighed heavily after disconnecting with Sorento, drained from the intense conversation. She pushed herself back into the chair's supple leather, put her feet on the desk and mused the evening's encounter with Gutierrez, formatting a plan that would allow her access to Marianna's inner circle.

Leaving the office at five, she made the short drive to her hotel, showered and dressed in a sleeveless, ankle length, yellow jump suit by Astr The Label with a twist detail in front, V-neck and elastic waist. She paired the suit with matching yellow Tory Burch Metal Miller open heel flats.

She was out the door and on her way to Shoreline by five-forty-five, ready to enter the inner-circle of one of America's wealthiest and most secretive cocaine cartels.

Jessica had little difficulty locating the house in which Katrina thought she would be interested. The street was right on the beach, literally. She would take note of the high retaining walls protecting the million-dollar properties later when she explored the beach.

Approaching the front door, the female voices from the patio were unmistakable. Acknowledging that the owners were absent, she ignored protocol and circled through the array of yellow and orange vireya rhododendrons, announcing her presence to avoid startling Marianna into pulling a firearm from her handbag, a maneuver Jessica was convinced would be the norm.

Rounding the corner of the house she found Marianna and Katrina enjoying the sun and a huge pitcher of margaritas. The attorneys were attired in what Jessica guessed were Calvin Klein khaki shorts, pastel tops and open toed sandals.

As she approached, Katrina rose and gave her a hug while Marianna poured a margarita and gestured for her to join them.

Feeling slightly overdressed but delighted it wasn't reversed so she would feel conspicuous, she took a seat and saluted her companions clinking glasses and taking a sip.

Katrina started the conversation with, "Jessica, I haven't shared the news with Marianna, thinking you wanted the honors. Go ahead."

Jessica knew introducing this information was not as simple as one, two and three. She had to explain what transpired and how she was able to convince the district attorney of the county of Los Angeles not to prosecute.

Yet her explanation couldn't be drawn out, so she began with, "LAPD isn't charging you with anything."

Gutiérrez's reaction was instant as she jumped from her seat saying, "Come here you. I have to give you a hug, demonstrative though I am not."

Jessica rose and accepted the emotional gesture. Marianna then stepped back, reached for her drink and offered a toast to Katrina and Jessica saying,

"Details. I need details please. I didn't know what to expect with you going head to head with Zinkton and I must know how you did it."

Jessica sat down and offered, "First off I don't think I would have gotten to Zinkton's inner sanctum without Katrina greasing the wheel.

"But I did and wow, she has quite a cutting tongue even when not provoked. I also appreciated you giving me a heads-up on her personality Katrina, otherwise she could have cut me off quickly.

"Anyway, I laid out the case her assistant district attorney had prepared which she had not perused. It appeared that Zinkton, as anxious as she was to use you as a springboard to the next election, left the case development to an underling.

"When confronted with the facts, she exploded…on me. I so much wanted to respond, but I let her vent. She did however do her due diligence and knew a little about me, being quite sarcastic in the process. Something about my having the audacity to challenge her integrity. Not that I intended to do anything related to that, but she was obviously using me to vent against the staffer who, it appeared, planned to build the case against you as he went. Which of course makes zero sense, either common or legal.

"She pretty much threw me out of her office, figuratively of course, but ejected I was…with the agreement that, and I quote her, 'I hope we meet in a courtroom someday Fukishura so I can kick your ass'."

Marianna was so delighted to hear the details of her inexperienced, or so she thought, lawyer go head to head with the Los Angeles District Attorney and win, she spent a few minutes showering Jessica with accolades until she was interrupted with the caterer's arrival at the front door.

Katrina was first to rise, grab her drink and head indoors saying, "I am starving. I hope you two will enjoy the delicious choices these folks have made. I preset the dining room table, so we just have to plate and eat."

"Sounds good to me, Katrina."

"Me too," echoed Jessica as she followed Marianna through the French Doors.

Katrina welcomed the catering team at the front door and guided them to the kitchen where they deposited the evening's fare and departed, Katrina having paid previously.

What the diners discovered was a smorgasbord of small, individual entrées warm and already plated; filet mignon with a mushroom brandy sauce, almond crusted Mexican bass topped with a lemon garlic sauce, white claw wild crab cakes with avocado, coleslaw and a chipotle sauce.

"Isn't this delightful," commented Katrina as she grabbed a plate in each hand and gave them to her guests. After Jessica and Marianna accepted the plates, Katrina took the last one and followed the women into the dining room which was already set for three with long stem wine glasses and two bottles of Giordano Winery's Pinot Noir.

As the women chose a seat and placed their plates on the table, Katrina uncorked a bottle of the Giordano, poured each a glass and raised a toast, "To Jessica for thwarting a prominent DA on Marianna's behalf," then stifling a laugh she continued, "and for many more years of thwarting, not necessarily Zinkton."

Her friends and colleagues accepted the toast, smiling at her attempted humor, then sat down with Jessica thinking, *I am going to feel like shit when I leave, and she discovers the truth.*

Marianna, satisfied with Jessica's explanation of her encounter with the LA district attorney abandoned the subject and they enjoyed the dinner time together chatting about Jessica's opportunity with the house and Santa Barbara gossip,

Katrina was first to remove her plate to the caterer's bins with Marianna and Jessica following. Marianna opened the second bottle of wine, filled their glasses then followed Katrina out of the kitchen for the tour.

Jessica anticipated a spectacular house from Katrina's pitch yesterday but was overwhelmed by what lay before her. The décor was far more elaborate than could be explained in dialogue and she was instantly convinced that this house was her home.

Barely able to contain her excitement, she tagged along with the duo enjoying their camaraderie, albeit misplaced given the circumstances. Jessica was anxious to conclude the tour and check-out of the hotel.

The tour concluded at the front door with all three exiting simultaneously. Katrina stopped on the porch to ask Jessica what she thought of the house.

"If you have the lease with you, I'd like to move in tonight," Jessica replied cracking a huge smile.

Katrina was delighted to have been able to help her friends find a trusted tenant and more so for Jessica and said, "Fabulous! Here is the key and we can sign the lease tomorrow at the office. Welcome, officially, Ms. Fukishura to Santa Barbara."

Jessica offered a slight curtsy, gave Katrina a hug as she accepted the key and all three moved toward their vehicles. Katrina reached her car first, said goodbye and drove away.

As Jessica reached her vehicle, Marianna stopped, hugged Jessica again and said, “You have no idea how much I appreciate what you did for me. I feared I was going to be embroiled in a contrived legal battle and end up losing my practice.

“I am fascinated by you Jessica and I would like the opportunity to get to know you better, on a personal level if that is okay with you. How about dinner at my place this Friday night?”

“I would be delighted Marianna. Thank you. What time?”

“6ish?”

“Terrific. I am looking forward to it.”

“I am too. You are a legal enigma Ms. Fukishura and I think we can become good friends,” responded Gutierrez as she walked to her car turning slightly to wave goodbye.

It is starting, thought Jessica as she pulled away from the curb, smiling, waving one more time to her client and heading to her hotel to pack, check out and move into her new home.

She hoped she could be friends with Katrina eventually and knew Marianna would probably put her on a hit list for the deception.

"He who permits himself to tell a lie once, finds it much easier to do it a second and third time till at length it becomes habitual."

Thomas Jefferson

"It's not about supplication, it's about power. It's not about asking, it's about demanding. It's not about convincing those who are currently in power, it's about changing the very face of power itself."

Kimberlé Crenshaw

Jessica was determined to change the face of the cartel by eliminating Marianna Gutierrez.

Chapter TWENTY-THREE

Penelope and Rebecca planned their approach to Sgt. Alfonso, ignoring their recent association with his co-workers Detective Pelfini and Chief O'Connor, knowing from experience that using a relationship as a buffer was a poor tactic.

Their attire during the robbery attempt was coordinated specifically to interact with the teenagers. Today they needed to approach the task in a totally different direction, choosing outfits that spoke of strength and power.

Rebecca chose a Lulus royal blue halter jumpsuit with a high mock neck, halter bodice, fitted waist with hidden seam pants pockets and wide cut legs. She paired the suit with a cobalt blue blazer also by Lulus with skinny tuxedo-style lapels, padded shoulders with angled, welted pockets. Her sandals were Majorca Cutout in black, natural yarn upper and a two-inch heel.

Penelope chose a power outfit as well, also by Lulus-their Night Out black, wide-leg jumpsuit with a high rounded neckline, sleeveless bodice, princess seams, high fitted waist with a cutout back. Her blazer was by Sander Lak and featured an icon green, wrap-front, one button closure, peaked lapels and a chest besom pocket in which she wore a black silk hankie.

She paired the outfit with Franco Sarto black sandals with one wide, adjustable strap, buckle closure and a two-inch heel.

The detectives, knowing Alfonso's disdain for either females in general or women officers specifically, purposely didn't make an appointment, wanting to blindside him.

Arriving at the police station they noted the stark white building with its red tile roof was what one would expect in a city of Spanish architecture dating back to the sixteen-hundreds.

Its exterior palette blended with the multitude of accompanying buildings, capturing the Mediterranean flavor and heritage with its numerous rotundas and massive, arched, entry way and front door.

The duo made their way under the arch, through the front door and were met by stately twenty-foot ceilings and more curved archways leading to hallways and offices. The interior was a combination of stucco and brick walls and six by six wooden beams, with those in the ceiling being colossal and at least twelve by twelve.

What Rebecca found immediately interesting and in contrast to the majority of police departments she had visited, was the lack of bullet-proof glass across the Information Area. Instead, it was adorned with a highly polished ornate wooden front and countertop.

Penelope asked for Sgt. Alfonso and mentioned that he had asked them to make a statement.

The staffer placed a call and moments later Alfonso was seen approaching from the end of the hallway. Approaching was inaccurate. Strutting was more appropriate.

Rebecca and Penelope couldn't help scoffing at his masculine insecurities, Rebecca more so since she had seen the identical behavior in former colleagues for decades.

"Good morning girls. I am glad you could take time away from your crime busting duties to provide a statement regarding the turmoil you caused this department and the city. Follow me."

As the trio passed Chief O'Connor's office Rebecca knocked on the open door saying, "Good morning Chief O'Connor."

She prepared to continue down the corridor when O'Connor shouted, "Hold on Rebecca. Wait a minute," and jumped up from his desk, scurrying to the door with an outstretched hand, adding, "Congratulations detectives. Talk about being at the right place at the right time. As I said the other day, we welcome two additional detectives to our fair city and you two certainly landed on both feet."

The sergeant had stopped when he heard O'Connor's voice. He pivoted and walked to the chief's office.

"Alfonso. What's up?"

"Just following up on a statement from these fine citizens on their interference yesterday with the robbery."

O'Connor stepped closer and lowered his voice, "Are you fuckin' crazy sergeant.? Are you deaf too? I just congratulated these detectives for the job they did and you diss them? Do you have any idea who Simpson and Barker are? I'll take their statement. Back to work.

Changing his tone and manner, the chief continued, "Detectives," as he swept his arm indicating a welcome to his office.

"Have a seat and I'll take your statement and you can be on your way. I can't promise zero media coverage on yesterday's incident. With the size of the crowd there was bound to have been numerous photos and videos taken. Uploading, as you know, to YouTube or to the print or broadcast media, is instant. The robbery suspects are going before a judge this afternoon.

"But hey, it could mean free publicity," he added with a grin as he pulled a keyboard from under his desk and typed a several commands.

While he did so Penelope asked, "Chief, what is with Alfonso? We never met him before yesterday and right from the get-go he was snarky and condescending."

O'Connor looked up from his screen and replied, "I have no idea. He seems to get along with his colleagues here, male and female and I doubt it is a misogyny thing. I suspect he feels threatened somehow by your credentials and you're now operating on his turf, so to speak.

"If it becomes an issue let me know and I will intervene, but I think he will come around given the support you are getting from this office. The other thing is I believe his nose is bent because he missed out on busting the cocaine shipment, while you two were front and center."

"Give it some time and I think, based on his previous performances, he will support your work. Besides, he is only one and if he tried to share his opinion, he would find zero support."

"We appreciate the clarification Chief," replied Rebecca.

"Please call me Rodrigo unless you are yelling down the corridor," he offered as he turned briefly from the screen with a smile.

Just as he was about to take their statement, there was another knock at his door and, "Sorry for the interruption Chief. I heard Santa Barbara's newest detectives were in the building. Wow, don't you look sharp. If this is the new detective fashion, I have to step up my game," Detective Elise Pelfini said as she bounced into the office and gave Rebecca and Penelope hugs.

"Stop by my office before you leave. Nice work yesterday. Very smooth. You are rock stars in Santa Barbara. Well, among the honest citizens at least. Oh, and I heard *Refugio Seguro* is almost ready for the girls. Congratulations on convincing them to participate," she concluded with a thumbs up sign, turned and left the office.

"Let's get this done quickly before the media or the rest of my staff hear about your presence here," O'Connor quipped as he began keyboarding.

Their statement took very little time given the collaboration from other witnesses. Theirs was slightly more involved due to the physical confrontation, take-down and firearms involvement, albeit, not discharged.

When O'Conner had completed the statement, he handed Penelope and Rebecca tablets for their signatures. Each signed, then manipulated the device to send a copy to their business email address.

The administrative task complete, they popped in to see Elise, who was embroiled in the case file of yesterday's robbery.

Knocking on her open door, they stuck their heads around the door-jam to see if she was on the phone.

Not.

Looking up from her computer screen, Elise motioned, "Come on in you guys," came around from behind the desk and gave each of her friends and colleagues another hug.

"I'm preparing the charges from your incident yesterday. How in hell did you two find yourselves at the right place and the right time?"

Penelope shared their morning with Elise, then as the story reached the point of the robbery, Rebecca took over with considerable animation on how they took down the thieves.

Elise got a kick out of the reenactment of the event and her laughing attracted the attention of two female staffers who stopped in her doorway to watch.

When Rebecca concluded, the two uniformed officers and Elise applauded with one of the former offering, "You guys were amazing," with both offering their hand to shake. Each officer gave her business card and said, "Anytime. Anywhere," turned and left.

Elise responded to their departure with, "I have never seen that before."

"What?" replied Penelope.

"Female officers responding to a successful takedown. Never happens. Never. It is obvious to this seasoned detective that your presence in Santa Barbara is already motivating.

"Changing the subject, are you guys free for lunch today?"

Rebecca responded, "Sure. We are finalizing our business name change and setting up the office. Where?"

"How about the *Blue Lily* on State Street, noonish?"

"Sounds good. But, Elise, before we head out, are you saying that the incident yesterday motivated the officers who were just here?"

"I am. I'd like to think my gender and success sparked them, but it didn't. When I started, I was the only female uniformed officer and fought for acceptance. Now we have a number of females, but I am pretty much an administrator and not in the field. You two ooze motivation. Your confidence is infectious. Hell, I caught it and find I have a lift in my spirits, so I can relate to others.

"I just wish I had been with you yesterday for that adrenaline rush I miss so much."

Rebecca and Penelope laughed, replying, "If we happen to be in the right place at the right time again, we will call you."

"Yeah, right."

"No. Seriously. Give us your cell number. You never know and since working with you on that cocaine take-down, we'd be honored to do it again, anytime, anywhere. And, yes, we know you can't reciprocate."

Elise gave each of them her card with her cell number on the back saying, "Okay, here you go. I gotta get back to work or I won't make lunch. See you in a bit."

Penelope and Rebecca hugged Elise, turned and headed out of the building to Alane's.

"Women understand. We may share experiences, make jokes, paint pictures, and describe humiliations that mean nothing to men, but women understand. The odd thing about these deep and personal connections of women is that they often ignore barriers of age, economics, worldly experience, race, culture, all the barriers that, in male or mixed society, had seemed so difficult to cross."

Gloria Steinem

Chapter TWENTY-FOUR

Sgt. Major Curtis Leithead had been the non-commissioned officer at president Bakus' StoneHead Ranch during Bakus' term in office. Leithead was responsible for the ranch's security; supervising the detail under his command, the facility's electronic surveillance system and although he didn't vet ranch staff, he oversaw their security clearance.

When the U.S. Air Force chopper team captured the ranch's mole, it was Leithead who, along with Fukishura, interrogated him, revealing the names of those in the Christians for a Better America for whom Len Thiessen, the mole, was working.

When Bakus lost the election, the ranch's security was transferred to a private firm and Leithead and his team returned to Fort Benning, Georgia, for Airborne requalification. It was during one of his HALO (high altitude, low opening) drops that he suffered his injury.

HALO drops are critical to inserting troops and equipment undetected behind enemy lines and to avoid anti-aircraft cannons or rockets. Parachutists typically jump from 45,000 feet using special equipment to prevent freezing and provide oxygen.

The students participating in this particular HALO drop had completed their pre-breathing period of inhaling pure oxygen for forty-five minutes to flush nitrogen from their bloodstream and were dressed in polypropylene knit underwear to survive the -45-degree Celsius temperature. Leithead exited the plane at 35,000 feet and free fell to 3,000 feet before opening his parachute.

Landing should have been routine but once his feet hit the ground and he tucked his body into a horizontal position, his oxygen tank's strap broke, twisted under him with all his weight hitting it.

Leithead fractured his hip.

He was airlifted to the Dwight D. Eisenhower Army Medical Center in Fort Gordon, Georgia where he underwent hip surgery using screws for stabilization.

Leithead spent a week recovering from the surgery, then six weeks of physiotherapy. Given the extent of his injuries, returning to Airborne was unlikely and although he was pain free and could be reassigned, his rank and specialty prevented him from being slotted in to just any position. Rather than ask for his options, he chose to use the remainder of his post-op recovery time to consider his future. Possibly a vacation.

Chatting with his assigned military rehab social worker, he found few places where he could experience a new adventure that didn't require physical exertion.

The social worker suggested fishing, but lakes involved getting in and out of small boats with little stability for a man recovering from hip surgery. She suggested ocean fishing, possibly chartering a boat and staying in a nice hotel.

That idea appealed to Curtis, as he had not taken a real holiday in over a decade. Narrowing down his choices, he ruled out Mexico, Oregon or Washington and settled on Campbell River, British Columbia after perusing several web sites for the Vancouver Island, east coast community.

His physiotherapist knew that unless she helped Curtis plan the trip, he would procrastinate, so she sat with him while he researched flights. Non-stop from Atlanta, Georgia to Vancouver, BC, then a one-hour layover for a float plane direct to Campbell River.

The web site indicated that the charter provided all equipment and he figured there would be at least one store where he could purchase clothing which would be a necessity considering he had a miniscule wardrobe. So he packed a small carry-on, dressed in his civvies, caught an Uber to the airport and headed off to British Columbia.

Never having been in a civilian airport it took him some time to find the Air Canada kiosk, obtain his tickets and be processed through Canadian Customs, his military identification and passport quickly accepted.

He spent a short time in the Maple Leaf Lounge enjoying a complimentary coffee and muffin before his flight was called.

Processing through business class was quick, simple and pleasant. The Sergeant Major had been on many airplanes during his career but none like what he was experiencing. His therapist had suggested he fly business class which gave him a little more leg room and only two seats to a row rather than three.

He quickly found his seat, placed his carry-on in the overhead as directed by the flight attendant and settled in the dark blue leather seat, wiggling his rear end to find his comfort spot.

His first impression once the plane was airborne was the lack of vibration, an unpleasant experience for anyone flying on a military plane loaded with equipment.

Within fifteen minutes, the flight attendant appeared with a breakfast tray of a warm croissant with Georgia Peach jam, an individual egg and bacon quiche, two breakfast sausages, a bowl of sliced strawberries, yogurt and black coffee.

Curtis looked at the food, lowered his head to smell the aroma, shook his head thinking, *I could get used to this and retirement might just be for me.*

He enjoyed his meal while scanning the cloudless skies, appreciating the view never before seen on his hundreds of flights.

Once his tray was removed, he spent a couple of hours researching British Columbia and Campbell River on his smartphone, excitement growing with each viewed video of Vancouver Island and its east coast.

Having adjusted his watch to west coast time, it was noon when the flight attendant interrupted his viewing to serve braised beef short ribs with red wine sauce, parsnip puree and baby carrots and a half-bottle of Okanagan Pinot Noir.

Placing the tray in front of him, the server poured a taster of the red for his passenger's approval. Nodding such, the attendant poured the glass a quarter full. Thanking the attendant, Curtis picked up the wine glass, took a sip appreciating the taste and realizing he was drinking from real glass, not plastic.

Leithead enjoyed his meal watching America's Midwest pass under him, amazed at the vastness of the landscape which he had never seen traveling on military planes.

Curtis had never flown civilian and was taken aback by the service, but in fact, he was being treated as any guest in a fine dining restaurant.

He had just finished his meal and the last of the wine when the server appeared as though he had been watching him. Before him was a cart carrying a German chocolate cake with coconut-pecan frosting on a cake tray.

Curtis had not expected dessert but there it was, not a slice of cake, but the entire cake with a couple of slices removed.

The attendant removed his tray, slipped it on a shelf under the cake and said with a smile, “Sir, may I interest you in a slice of German chocolate cake and a cup of Kicking Horse coffee from British Columbia’s Kootenay region?”

Leithead accepted both, savoring the delicious chocolate, pecan and coconut with the tartness of the coffee. Draining the last of his coffee, he leaned back in the leather’s suppleness and thought, *if this is what retirement is like, I’m in.*

Curtis was using a calculator on his smartphone appraising his retirement benefits when the announcement was made of their decent into Vancouver. Pleased with what he had discovered, he put his phone away and glanced out the window, shocked at the beauty of his destination.

His seat afforded him a view of the approaching Coastal Mountain Range, Burrard Inlet with about ten ships waiting to unload, Stanley Park and numerous high rises marking the downtown area.

Curtis buckled his seatbelt and enjoyed the smooth landing and taxing to the terminal. Departure was simple given his limited baggage but once he was inside the terminal, he slowed his movements to enjoy its beauty. YVR airport received the prestigious award of the best airport in the world in Amsterdam in 2016 at the Aviation Awards.

Knowing he had a little wait for his next flight, Curtis wandered through the main section admiring the various bronze Spirit of Haida Gwaii, a Jade Canoe and Warriors and others so massive, he felt dwarfed by their imposing size.

He stopped at an information booth, learned the directions for his float plane boarding and realized he would need to take a taxi to the south terminal located on the Fraser River.

Abandoning his musing of his newfound freedom, he increased his pace to the main entrance, grabbed a taxi and arrived at the terminal with about twenty to spare.

Leithead was used to the friendliness of Georgia folks, on and off base, but the receptionist and waiting passengers were different, an experience he couldn't clarify.

People were chatting with one another, strangers really, finding out where each was from, where they were going.

He freely shared that information, a behavior in which he had never engaged…which surprised him.

Shortly after checking in, the pilot arrived, introduced herself saying, "Good day, folks. My name is Susan. Are you all ready for the trip of a lifetime?"

Everyone replied with a resounding, "Yes".

"Well let's get started then. Follow me."

The luggage was already stored, and a staffer helped passengers board, ensured their seatbelts were fastened, instructed the use of the headsets and shut the doors just as the pilot settled herself behind the yoke.

The pilot took a few moments to communicate with aviation control as she started the DHC-3 de Havilland Turbine Single Otter, then said over the interior com system, "Welcome aboard folks. This flight normally takes forty-five minutes but with this beautiful weather and knowing this is a first trip to Vancouver Island for everyone, we will do a little sightseeing. Hope that is okay."

She received thumbs-up from everyone as she acknowledged take-off approval and taxied into the river, gained speed with the 720-horsepower turbine and took flight.

Curtis thought the other trip was an exceptional view but what he was seeing now was beyond his expectations.

As the Otter flew across the Georgia Straight, the pilot offered a running commentary on the two massive BC Ferries below, then the southern tip of Valdes Island, across the middle of Galiano Island, Salt Springs Island where she said Canadian born Tommy Chong of the infamous pot smoking comic team of Cheech and Chong lives along with singer/songwriter Gordon Lightfoot.

Flying over the province's capital, Victoria, she pointed out the legislative buildings providing political background of the parties and a brief history of the buildings themselves.

As the Otter headed out over the Pacific Ocean Curtis was thrilled to see a pod of Orca whales leisurely heading north. Considerable distance away from the massive mammals, were several former fishing boats converted to sightseeing vessels. Boats must stay at least one-thousand meters/one kilometer from whales, a law strictly enforced by federal fisheries officers.

Since the decline of the fishing industry along with forestry, many fishers converted their boats for tourists installing seats and railings to the upper deck.

Some retained their commercial fishing license while engaging in drug smuggling.

Susan continued with her commentary as she followed Vancouver Island's coastline providing details of the many inhabited islands which dotted the Strait of Georgia. Flying over Nanaimo, she shared information of the massive ferries which moved thousands of cars and commercial vehicles back and forth from the mainland.

Several of the passengers asked questions about Lasqueti, Hornby and Denman Islands, having read that they were inhabited by American draft dodgers who sought asylum from the Vietnam War draft.

They read correctly. These islands and the community of Nelson in the Kootenays were destinations for draft dodgers.

They covered the remaining distance quickly with the Otter pushing out 219 km/hr. They approached Campbell River then circled over Quadra Island just east of the city of 35,000. Coming in from the north, they approached Dick Murphy Park at the end of a peninsula jutting out from the mouth of the river and landed at the commercial docks.

Curtis was the last to exit the Otter, stopping to extend his hand in appreciation to Susan saying, “Ma’am, I am a U.S. Army Paratrooper and have flown a great deal during my career but this flight has been the most spectacular experience I have ever had in the air. Thank you for a great time.”

Susan was somewhat taken aback by Leithead’s comment. She had received appreciative feedback many times but never from a paratrooper and never from someone who had flown thousands of miles. She quickly regained her composure replying, “You are most welcome, sir. What is your name?”

“Sir. I like that. I’m usually the one calling someone else that. Ma’am, I am Sgt. Major Curtis Leithead arriving at your glorious community from Atlanta, Georgia to recuperate from an injury and try my hand at salmon fishing.”

“Well, Sgt. Major Curtis Leithead, welcome to Campbell River, which claims to be the salmon capital of the world, a title disputed by Port Alberni just west of here,” she offered.

"I take it Hector on the dock there is waiting for you. Have a great time…sir, she said with a huge grin."

Leithead returned the smile, gave her a modified salute and exited the plane to be welcomed by, Susan was correct, Hector, his host for the next week.

Hector introduced himself, grabbed Curtis' bag, stored it in the *Albacore Resort* emblazoned late model van parked on the dock.

Hector's appearance was as though he stepped back in time to the 1960's and never left San Francisco's Haight Ashbury district and its counterculture.

He touted shoulder length blonde hair, parted in the middle. He carried his six feet on a two-hundred-pound frame well with his blue jeans, red and black check shirt and tan work boots.

Hector drove the short distance south to the marina where he parked the van and the two headed to a vessel with *Albacore* painted across the bow.

Their transportation across the inlet was a navy-blue Thunder 24 Pilot, 26-foot aluminum boat with a Mercury 350 XL Verado Phantom outboard engine. It boasted stone-grey leather interior seating in the heated seven-foot cabin.

Hector navigated the Pilot around the southern tip of Quadra Island and up the interior bay to the lodge's wharf, providing a brief history of the area.

"It was my dad who immigrated to Canada and settled in this area to avoid the draft. He loved it and when President Carter granted pardons for the evaders, Dad didn't want to return. He became a citizen decades ago, met Mom and here I am. I grew up with their counterculture philosophy which produced this," he swept a hand up and down his body referring to his attire.

"Anyway, the folks really identified with the Salish People and made many friends on these islands, became farmers and toyed with the idea of growing marijuana. But when it became known that the Mounties were scrutinizing Lasqueti Island for grow-ops, my folks decided not to draw attention to themselves and became farmers, selling vegetables in Campbell River.

"Captain George Vancouver arrived here in 1792 aboard the HMS Discovery, hence the name of the passage. Logging and fishing became the mainstay of the community and was sustainable for decades. Today, the economy centers mainly around tourism, fishing and mining. We have numerous fish hatcheries which support the fishing industry.

"The economy is sustained through the service industry, professional services, retirees, government offices and of course, tourists like yourself, who have such a good time, they tell their friends and return," he concluded turning to Curtis with a smile.

Hector reduced power as they rounded the point and Leithead saw the *Albacore Resort's* full brilliance, its illumination captivating guests, drawing them to the hospitality.

As they slowly motored toward the wharf, the scores of moored, identical vessels was evident. Curtis exited the cabin, walked around the structure and marveled at the architectural beauty before him.

The designers had maintained the curvature of the island's natural rock and flora, building among the trees and outcrop, creating numerous angles highlighted by recessed lighting.

Hector brought the Pilot alongside the dock, cut the motor quickly exited the cabin, jumped onto the wharf, secured the stern and bow with dock lines, then grabbed Curtis' luggage and invited him onto the wharf.

Hector led the way up several flights of red cedar stairs with dual railings passing a ten by ten-foot red cedar sign with a hand-carved tuna set in the center.

The Albacore.

Sculptured by a Kwakiutl Master Carver, the sign was the only distraction from the surrounding natural fauna.

Opening the main eight-foot carved red cedar door, Hector accompanied Curtis across luxurious deep pile chocolate carpet to Guest Services and introduced him to the receptionist, Bethany.

Hector shook Leithead's hand, welcomed him again to the resort saying, "I will see you in the morning Curtis, bright and early. I am your fishing guide for your adventure."

While Bethany processed his registration, Curtis admired the heavy stone walls rising to the red cedar cathedral ceiling. The Lobby was dotted by numerous seating areas adorned with light grey couches, accent chairs and black cast-iron, glass topped coffee tables. Off to one side was the *Long Fin,* (a pseudonym for Albacore) restaurant which served all meals and snacks. Adjacent was the *Quatsino Pub*, named after the sound, where schools of albacore are known to travel in groups two kilometers wide.

Curtis asked Bethany for several hundred dollars in Canadian currency, which was added to his bill, just as a staffer arrived, welcomed him to the *Albacore* and showed him to a room on the third floor overlooking the bay.

The staffer showed him around, opening the drapes to reveal a large deck with black, wrought iron patio furniture. The one-bedroom suite was styled with heavy, red cedar ceiling beams and cedar sheeting, stone, hearth to ceiling gas fireplace, kitchenette with a sink, under counter refrigerator and a black and cedar textured stone counter-top.

A seating arrangement of two maroon accent chairs, couch and solid red-cedar six-foot coffee table were grouped around the fireplace with a red cedar dining table and chairs set in the corner under a subdued six teardrop lighted chandelier.

Expressing his appreciation for the tour, Curtis thanked the steward, tipped him twenty dollars, then walked around admiring his new quarters, accommodations he had never experienced in his life.

As he walked through the kitchen, he stopped and opened the fridge to find two bottles of Iceberg Canadian Vodka, several bottles of Schweppes Tonic, a bowl of limes and two Manhattan glasses.

Leithead was so overcome by the contents, he flopped on the floor and stared inside the fridge. Finally accepting the reality of the situation, he grabbed a bottle of Iceberg, tonic and the limes.

Rising to his feet smiling at his good fortune, he prepared a drink and headed to the deck. Settling in a maroon, deep cushion wrought iron chair, he sipped his drink, admired the wall of black beyond the resort's lights, wondered how difficult it would be to navigate those waters at night.

Chapter TWENTY-FIVE

Larry Baird Sr. had been Port Alberni's International Longshoremen's union representative for decades so when he heard of the accident at the dock involving a union member, he called the hospital for details then went to Francesco Loblinski's home to ensure his family was okay and to enquire if their needs were being met.

After chatting with the Loblinski family, Larry Sr. checked in with the hospital hoping to see Francesco to advise that his family was well and that their needs would be taken care of, but Loblinski had already been airlifted to Vancouver for reconstructive surgery on his arm.

When Francesco returned to the Alberni hospital, Larry Sr. was there to greet him with several gifts of books, magazines and Loblinski's favorite Italian candy, Perugina Caramelle Rossana, a delicacy of hard exterior and soft inside of hazelnut and almond cream filling.

The men chatted for some time, discovering they had sons about the same age who attended Alberni Secondary School. Larry Jr. was an iron worker constructing high rises in Calgary while Francesco's son Stan hadn't been heard from since he left Alberni after high school, almost thirty years ago.

When Larry Sr. heard the sadness in Francesco's voice, he immediately shared the conversation he had recently with Larry in Edmonton and said, "Francesco, Larry says Stan looks good but he didn't ask him much about what he was doing for a living, as they were watching a football game at a pub. I'll call Larry this evening and see if he has had contact with Stan and get back to you."

The conversation turned to their union's labor dispute with the shipping industry until the physiotherapist arrived for Francesco's treatment.

As Larry Sr. left, he turned back and said with a grin, "Oh, and Francesco, the company fixed the pothole which put you in here," and waved over his shoulder as he left.

The Bairds chatted later that night with Sr. sharing Francesco's medical condition. Jr. didn't know the family but promised to get together with Stan in the next few days and let him know about his dad.

The two chatted for a while with Sr. bringing Jr. current on union negotiations but avoiding telling his son that he already knew Stan.

The Edmonton RCMP detectives monitoring Stan acted immediately when they observed Stan associating with someone new.

By the time Stan was dropped off and his apartment lights were turned off, detectives had uploaded the numerous photos of Larry Baird to CHAP.

The Members were perplexed about Baird's actions and how, or if, he was involved with Loblinski's criminal affairs. By all appearance, Baird was a law-abiding citizen working as a high-rise iron worker in Calgary, temporarily assigned to an Edmonton project.

However, no police investigation into a suspect was based on the brevity of the data they had on Baird, so the decision was made to monitor him electronically and physically.

Their dossier indicated Baird was staying at a moderate downtown hotel, ate all of his meals in the hotel restaurant or bar. However, based on his credit card records, Baird had deviated from that pattern to patronize *The Horsemen*. The detectives didn't believe in coincidences and needed to discover the connection between Baird and Loblinski.

Loblinski's criminal intentions were still unknown to the Mounties. So far, they had his relationship with Sawyer. They knew that Brian had orchestrated the cesium delivery and Members were connecting the dots to Stan. Loblinski's texting the Vancouver attorneys and accountant with encrypted messages was perplexing but they knew they would have answers soon from the CSIS agents..

Edmonton detectives approached *The Horseman's* owner, retired Cst. Roy Davidson who didn't hesitate to offer his establishment for their operation.

Early morning hours of the next day, several members of the Integrated Technological Crime Unit installed monitoring equipment that would allow the Force to capture voice and visual data in several seating areas of *The Horsemen* and transmit the information directly to the detachment.

Deputy Commissioner Samantha Benedetti insisted a Member oversee the operation in person. When either of the suspects appeared to be headed to Davidson's, an undercover Member would be dispatched.

Physical profiling enabled the undercover patrons to blend with Davidson's clientele. The task wasn't too difficult given the customers were primarily cops, paramedics or medical staff-all First Responders.

Benedetti chose two seasoned Members, one who had been with the Canadian Forces in Afghanistan as a medic and often trained other RCMP officers in field trauma techniques, while the other was a graduate of Simon Fraser University with a criminal justice degree.

Janis Simcoe and Roberta Wilkins.

The Canadian military and CSIS believed the Chica de Oro's next sailing would be as soon as a shipment could be loaded.

They were correct.

The Canadian Naval ship the HMCS Toronto, took up surveillance immediately when the attached GPS monitors indicated movement out of the hidden Colombian fiord.

Chapter TWENTY-SIX

Santiago Antúnez lived on a beautifully landscaped parcel, with a three-thousand square foot ranch house overlooking San Antonio Canyon Park off Camino del Rio Drive in the Santa Barbara hills.

The isolated property was listed on county tax records as belonging to a San Francisco real estate investment firm, an anonymous leg of the Hermanos de Wall Street empire.

Antúnez was not listed on any legal document connected to the property and the modest salary he collected as a professional driver was less than ten percent of his actual income. As far as the Internal Revenue Service was concerned, he was a forty-year old, single Latino male living a simple California life.

He had completed his duties for his employer around seven and was enjoying Chinese chicken salad with shredded chicken, leafy greens and pea pods, mandarin orange slices, crispy noodles and a sesame dressing, while watching the Los Angeles Lakers host the Toronto Raptors on a sixty-five-inch LG plasma screen, fastened to the wall of his spacious den.

Toronto had just scored again, bringing the embarrassment to Los Angeles with a score of 90-76 when he heard the familiar sound of his satellite monitoring system advise that he had a recording.

Setting down his salad on a black six-foot, glass top, wrought iron coffee table, Santiago casually rose from the navy blue nine-foot leather couch and sauntered into the equipment room.

Sitting at the desk, he utilized a few controls of the four channel DVB-5/S2 satellite audio receiver, listened to the message and smiled at the genius of the firm for which he worked.

He downloaded the message, then encrypted it and forwarded the data to his boss who had an identical system, albeit better hidden in her home than his. Once delivery was confirmed, he copied the message on a flash drive then placed behind the loose rock in his living room stone fireplace hearth.

Antúnez returned to the game and his take-out dinner. Sitting on the couch, he took a sip of his beer, picked up the bowl of food and leaned back in the supple leather thinking, *life is good. Life is very good.*

Santiago was unaware that staff at the NSA Bumblehive facility in Utah had also recorded the short burst, triangulated the location of the transmission and stored the data, leaving analysis to another department.

Elisabeth Peltowski's elaborate system housed in a bedroom of Rebecca and Penelope's ranch house also copied the transmission and triangulation. The massive difference was that Peltowski knew exactly who and what generated the short burst of information. She immediately analyzed the data and forwarded it to the Edmonton RCMP detectives, Detective Pelfini with the Santa Barbara Police Department and Jessica, via an isolated CHAP link.

I'm riding the wave, thought Elisabeth, smiling broadly, slapping her hand down on the desk. *These dumb fuckers have no idea who or what I am or that I am following their every move,* she mused.

With joy in her heart, she danced down the stairs into the kitchen, found left over taco salad from lunch, poured a tall glass of chardonnay and sat on the patio, savoring another success for the "J" Team. *I can't give this up for retirement*, she thought. *I just hope the Team maintains a connection with the Secret Service.*

Marianna Gutierrez was enjoying a late pitcher of margaritas on her private patio off her dining room when a smartphone app notified her of the satellite message's arrival.

Picking up her drink, she rose slowly, pleased with the knowledge the message brought. Stopping to tighten the sash of her pink, Lorie terry robe, she opened the sliding door, entered, closed and locked the door then ambled up the stairs to her elaborate office, a duplicate of her downtown suite.

Sitting down at her ten-foot long mahogany desk with four side drawers and ornate legs, she touched a button on the four channel DVB-5/S2 satellite audio receiver, listened to the recording, saved it to the receiver's hard drive, then sent it via text to Edmonton.

Elisabeth was scanning the numerous screens before her, having just returned from a brief respite with the taco salad and chardonnay when the screen to her far right flashed twice producing a small icon at the bottom.

Clicking on the small picture of a satellite, she opened the link, then sat back with immense pleasure, admiring the screen's image. She saved the data, then uploaded it to the restricted CHAP recipients knowing the Edmonton and Santa Barbara detectives must be delighted with back-to-back incriminating evidence.

"First rule of a gun fight. Bring a gun. Second rule, being friends with guns."

Richard Wolf

"On the eighth day God looked down on his planned Paradise and said, 'I need a protector'.

So he created police officers"

Author Unknown

"Women are hitting their stride in Criminal Justice. As the once male dominated field begins to answer the call for more complex, proactive form of policing."

King University

Chapter TWENTY-SEVEN

Stan Loblinski's part time job while in high school was on a clean-up crew at the waterfront mill storage and shipping facility. The night foreman assigned one section of the massive open warehouse for him to clean each evening. On weekends he was often assigned to sweep and vacuum around the giant saws. It was the union wages and accumulated weekly hours which enabled him to purchase a gently used Dodge diesel pick-up.

While most male teenagers preferred their trucks with an open bed, Loblinski chose a canopy to conceal the fruit of his nefarious activities.

Stan noticed quickly after taking the job in his grade ten year that many employees returned at night and filled their vehicles with company gas. Stan did likewise and found the theft saved him hundreds of dollars a month. The next step in his criminal development seemed a natural segue. He took a day off school and had a Nanaimo after- market store install a 100 gallon/378-liter fuel storage tank in the bed of his pick-up.

Just before shift end Loblinski would fill the tank from one of the numerous unmonitored, company pumps then meet several of his friends on a vacant forestry road where he would pump the stolen fuel into their vehicles.

Gas was selling for $1.20 a liter in town. Stan would sell it for $1.00 a liter, earning himself three-hundred and seventy dollars each night.

He knew the company operated on the honor system without security cameras. He was unaware that the union didn't share the company's trust and had a series of hidden cameras throughout the facility. The organization's objective was to have corroborating evidence for or against a member's disciplinary hearing.

Union member oversight was the responsibility of long-time representative Larry Baird Sr. who, during his daily perusal of the previous evening's digital data, witnessed Stan filling his truck with company gas.

Not being one to jump to conclusions, Larry Sr. saved the data over a week's time and never saw Loblinski leave a note by the pump or otherwise indicate he planned to pay for the fuel.

Baird Sr. saw an opportunity he couldn't ignore. That night he was waiting for Stan to complete his theft and stepped out of the darkness, confronting the teenager and offering to make him a deal he couldn't refuse.

Showing Loblinski the video proof, he offered to split his daily take of three hundred and seventy dollars in exchange for Stan's freedom.

It didn't take Stan long to agree to the deal. He knew that his arrest would be an embarrassment his parents would never live down. The decision was not difficult to make, a factor on which Baird Sr. counted.

That was the beginning of a lucrative arrangement for both thieves. As their relationship grew, Larry Sr. introduced Stan to a sling of two-hundred and ninety-two, two by fours. Larry Sr. would arrange for a sling on varied weekdays to be set aside in the freight car marshaling yard.

Stan would load them into the back of his pickup with a forklift, drive to an offloading spot on a forestry road where he would be met by a stranger with a five-ton van and an automatic dolly.

The transfer was made, Stan would be paid a thousand dollars which he would split with Larry Sr. Each eight-foot piece of lumber would retail for $3.00 in Vancouver. The middleman would sell the sling for thirteen hundred dollars.

Included in their thievery were numerous high-end chain saws waiting to be shipped to the manufacturers to be refurbished, miscellaneous woodworking equipment and heavy-duty mechanics' tools.

The lucrative partnership lasted through Stan's graduating summer, then abruptly ended with Loblinski leaving town without telling anyone, even his parents.

Stan felt it was only a matter of time before the company or union had him arrested and therefore disappearing was the best course of action.

The company from which he and Larry Sr. stole took several months to become suspicious when fuel and inventory didn't equate. Their investigation proved difficult because Larry Sr. had manipulated the inventory software to reflect an accurate count.

It took months of physically counting the inventory and computer analysis to ascertain with certainty that the discrepancies were the result of theft. By then the thefts had stopped.

Stan had graduated.

No connection was made between the two seemingly unrelated incidents.

Life returned to normal for Larry Sr. and remained so for a number of years, until Stan reached out to offer him a chance to make a great deal more money.

Larry Sr. admitted to himself that he missed the larcenous side of his lifestyle. He found manipulating the system, outsmarting law enforcement and the financial gains for his creativity, exhilarating.

He accepted.

"Each of us has a measure of criminality."

Ahmed Saadawi

"If only people knew how madly tiresome it is to be a criminal!"

Hermann Hesse

Chapter TWENTY-EIGHT

Jessica reviewed the evening with Marianna as she cleared her desk, locked files away and prepared for the weekend. The dinner would not be an extension of the celebration at her new residence, but it also was not a girl's night out.

Her former landlady had volunteered to pack her belongings and ship them to Santa Barbara, but they had yet to arrive, so when she got home Jessica's outfit selection was limited.

She chose a pair of simple burnt navy Bermuda shorts, and a Hinge, navy abstract floral print, lightweight, short sleeve top with a twenty-six-inch front length and twenty-eight back and a band collar.

She paired the outfit with Mykonos-Wig one-inch, wedge brandy sandals with wide instep and ankle straps.

Checking herself in the floor to ceiling six-foot wide mirror, she was confident her appearance was Santa Barbara professional, casually chic.

Running her fingers through her short 'do, she added lip gloss, eye shadow, grabbed her car keys, driver's license, headed to the garage and drove to Marianna's, almost within walking distance from her own residence on the ocean.

Pulling into Gutierrez's cement driveway, she parked to the far left of the two-car garage and activated the mini-microphone disguised as a button on her outfit. The conversation would be recorded on her encrypted smartphone without it being activated.

Elisabeth.

She exited her vehicle and stopped to admire her hostess' Spanish style, two-story home. The exterior was white stucco, the front adorned with two bay windows with two sun awnings matching the red tile roof.

Jessica walked the short distance to the arched porch with large black lanterns on corner stanchions beside an array of calliope dark red geraniums in long, red tile boxes under the bay windows.

Just as she reached for the door knocker, Marianna opened the door with a flourish, holding two appletini's, offering, "Welcome to my hacienda Jessica. Come in, come in. You can place your cell phone in that basket," pointing to an elaborate aboriginal woven artistry on an entry table without further explanation.

Jessica complied without hesitation accepting Gutierrez's need to dominate and control the evening.

Her host was wearing a floor length, paisley, rust and turquoise, loose fitting, Challis Culotte jumpsuit featuring a strappy back accent, spaghetti straps, V neck and high/low hems which fit her perfectly and set off her wind-blown, messy, layered, naturally grey, highlighted with white 'do.

Fukishura accepted the drink and the cheek peck form Marianna, then stepped into the foyer.

Once inside, she took a moment to admire the elegant living room with its Tuscany rubbed stucco walls, cream, floral couch and accent chairs, the apparent focal point of the three-point nine million home. Appreciating the decorative sense, she pondered whether Alane was responsible.

The ceilings throughout were vaulted with horizontal distressed oak boards, supported with matching six by six beams, spaced two feet apart. The brown tinted Tuscany décor enhanced every room with various furniture pieces and accents to highlight the wall tones.

The evening being somewhat chilly, Marianna chose to host her guest in the living room at the seating arrangement in front of the lit, gas fireplace, starting with the pitcher of appletinis and a plates of taquitos; cumin, oregano, chili powder, cayenne, shredded pork, cheese, cilantro and lime juice. She served the mixture in fresh flour tortillas with sides of guacamole, sour cream and salsa.

As Jessica sat in one of the chairs facing the fireplace, she offered, "You have a gorgeous home Marianna. Exquisite design," as she surveyed the living room with an appreciative eye, noting with a sway of her cocktail, the window dressings and numerous oil paintings of the Southern California coastline.

Gutierrez sat on the couch facing Jessica and replied, "Thank you, Jessica. I wish I could take credit, but the honor is not mine." She replicated Jessica's sweeping hand gesture, then added, "Portofino Interiors chose the furnishings and their drapery professional designed and made the window dressings. I love the hand rubbed walls. So unique and the color blends the décor.

Draining her drink, Marianna rose from the couch, picked up the pitcher, walked over to Jessica and refilled her glass saying, "Please help yourself to the appetizers. I have chicken mole in the oven with Spanish rice and these are a delicious segue to the entrée."

Gutierrez placed two on a plate, picked up a napkin, refilled her glass, then returned to the couch, savoring the taquitos.

Jessica enjoyed the Latin hors d'oeuvre, took a sip of her drink and said candidly, "I appreciate the invitation Marianna and if the chicken mole is anything like these taquitos, I agree to whatever prompted our solo time."

Gutierrez laughed so hard she leaned over the coffee table, practically spewed her drink, grabbed a napkin and said, "Fukishura, you are so fucking funny…and goddamn direct, it takes me by surprise every time."

Jessica remained mute, took a sip of her drink and waited.

"Well you are absolutely correct. I do have alternative a motive for getting together socially," Marianna began. Turning serious, she sat back in the couch, put one leg over the other, rested her appletini on her knee and continued, "Our numerous interactions over this brief period have ingratiated me with your persona."

Jessica started to reply but Marianna put her hand up saying, "Please, let me finish".

"I know I can't hire you away from Katrina and I respect that. I honor the loyalty you show her, but I am looking at something entirely different. Not attorney related.

"There are several layers of you that I don't understand and of course it is none of my business. However, if I am correct, you may be just the person I need as a lieutenant.

"Invoking client, attorney privilege, nothing I am about to share goes any further than this room. I know you are aware that my law practice deals almost one hundred percent with guilty clients, most of which are in the drug business in one form or another.

"They are but a small part of my professional activities. I am the principal of a Colombian drug cartel."

She stopped there waiting for Jessica to react.

She didn't.

Jessica sat calmly with one leg over the other, sipping her drink wearing a slight smirk.

"What's with the look?" asked Marianna.

"I am both amused and surprised," replied Jessica. "If you recall, when you hired Katrina, and by extension me, to represent you with the LA County DA, I told you at the time that you had to be guilty of something. I just wasn't prepared for something of this magnitude. I figured maybe money laundering, but not cocaine distribution. How much are we talking about here?"

"Whoa, not so fast Jessica. I need to know where we stand. I do not for a minute believe you are a recent Cal graduate and I doubt you were a para-legal in Washington. When I hired Barbados' firm to represent Julio Fernández, you had him out in ten minutes. The skill you employed in dealing with the DA, that take-down in the parking lot at dinner and the smooth firearm delivery tell me there is more to you than what has been shared.

"Either my suspicions are correct, or you are an undercover cop. Which is it?" she concluded spreading her arms wide with her drink in one hand and the other uplifted in a questioning manner.

It was Jessica's turn to snort her appletini out her nose. Grabbing a napkin she dabbed her nose, wiped her face, set her glass on the end table while uncrossing her legs and replied, "Marianna, I can assure you I am the former and not the latter," smiling as broadly as she could. "I did in fact graduate recently from UC Berkley but there is nothing nefarious in my demeaner. I was a para-legal for many years, helped prepare cases, interviewed clients and sat in court. The only aspect of the profession in which I didn't engage was representing a client in court or in documents.

"The weaponry was my way to survive my abusive ex-husband. After I threw him out, literally, and received a quick divorce thanks to my boss, he hounded me relentlessly and swore he was going to make me pay for 'humiliating' him.

"I took a lot of firearms lessons and learned how to use it as a weapon without discharging. So, what you see is what you get.

"I would think you should be more concerned about whether I have sufficient larceny in my character to join the business."

Marianna seemed unfazed by Jessica's explanation, making it impossible for Jessica to determine if she bought the story. Marianna replied, "What I think Fukishura is that you are fucking crazy," smiling broadly, apparently believing Jessica. "And crazy is what I need. Someone who has the audacity to stand up to the LA County District Attorney, to bust the head of an attacker and someone who can manipulate the law and stay on the right side. Oh, and also someone who can spot a tail and lose it," she concluded, leaning forward, refilling her martini glass, sitting back smugly, then putting her feet on the coffee table.

"I figured that was your guy and he wasn't very good."

"Actually, he is very good. He allowed you to spot him on my orders. I wanted to test your mettle and here we are enjoying these delicious taquitos," she offered putting her feet down, extending the plate to Jessica.

Jessica helped herself to another appetizer then offered, "What kind of money are we talking here Marianna? I am pulling in just below mid-six figures with Katrina without breaking a sweat. What's in this arrangement for me? I obviously don't need the money."

"It is not the money that will draw you to my organization Jessica, it is the adrenaline rush. When you turfed your husband, physically and then took defensive firearms lessons, it was not to protect yourself. You'd already proven that to yourself when you broke his nose. Yeah, I know about that.

"You enjoyed the rush. A feeling you haven't experienced previously. There is a certain danger that comes with this business, but you won't be dealing with that except in an existential way. I have Santiago Antúnez, the guy who tailed you, for that.

"I want you for your agresivo, or aggressiveness," she said, offering the Spanish term as emphasis to her Latin character, "combined with your intelligence. Think about it while we enjoy the chicken mole," she concluded rising from the couch and heading to the kitchen.

Jessica rose quickly, put her glass on the coffee table and followed her host as they entered a kitchen the elegance of which matched Jessica's.

Entry was through an eight-foot arch which led to a huge kitchen; light grey walls with granite counter tops and eight by six-foot island in a slightly darker grey. Appliances were stainless steel with glass cupboards beside a large arched stain-glass window in front of double farm sinks with stainless faucets.

Two eight-foot arched windows looked out onto a manicured lawn and white blossom chrysanthemums mixed with red rhododendrons.

A dining room table with a grey granite top and darker grey wooden legs, eight matching chairs, both colors duplicating the kitchen tones was through another arch and set for two. Several chrysanthemum blossoms were centered in a tall crystal vase accenting the sterling silver cutlery and bone white china.

Marianna retrieved a bottle of Jacobson Winery's chardonnay from the fridge, two glasses from the glass cabinet next to the sink and handed the bottle to Jessica asking her to open it, showing her the drawer with the corkscrew.

As Jessica opened the wine, Marianna removed the chicken from the oven as well as a casserole dish with a variety of root vegetables and Spanish rice and placed both on the dinning-room table on black trivets.

Marianna smiled conspiratorially as she returned to the kitchen for a green salad with olive oil and balsamic dressing and arrived at the dining table just as Jessica was pouring the chardonnay.

Marianna spooned a medium size chicken breast and sauce onto Jessica's plate, followed by several roasted potatoes, asparagus, carrots and rice, handed it to Jessica and then repeated the procedure for herself, while offering, "We need to set you up with a Caribbean account for automatic deposits. This will have to wait for a bit as our accountant has run into a bit of a personal problem."

Jessica controlled her reaction but thought to herself, *I would certainly call being arrested for drug trafficking and distributing hundreds of millions in drug money, a personal problem.*

Sitting down, Marianna continued, "Please enjoy. I often order dinner, but for this special occasion, I prepared the dishes myself. I hope you like the Latin flavor."

Jessica took a bite of the chicken and exclaimed, "Oh, this is delicious Marianna. I taste cumin, chipotle and is there a hint of chocolate?"

"You have a discerning palate Jessica. Yes, on all three counts. This is one of my go-to recipes I reserve for very special guests," she said, lifting her glass of chardonnay in a toast.

Jessica responded with, "Salute, Marianna. I believe you have yourself a new lieutenant."

"Excellent my dear. Excellent indeed. We will work out the details as we proceed. First and foremost, I will give you an encrypted cellphone at the conclusion of our evening."

Jessica smiled, sipped her chardonnay and thought, *Oh, great. Just what I need, another encrypted phone. I'm going to have to put ribbons on them.*

"You have to have confidence in your ability, and then be tough enough to follow through."

Rosalynn Carter

Chapter TWENTY-NINE

The Caribbean bank accounts which the Hermanos de Wall Street created for upper management personnel, required electronic transmission of the account holder's fingerprints and a name of their choice.

The disgraced California attorneys were unaware that the details of every account, old and new, were encrypted by an undercover Secret Service agent working in the bank and sent to Washington and Ottawa. This was the same agent who identified the American currency deposited into the secret accounts as being from Los Angeles, the circumstances which brought the "J" Team to Southern California.

Gutierrez was a founding member of Hermanos de Wall Street, the only non-disbarred attorney in the organization. She was well known by the one-percent social sphere for her fund-raising capabilities, amassing millions for various political candidates in Canada and America through $5,000 a-plate-dinners.

Hermanos de Wall Street forensic accountants were experts at risk management and manipulating accounts and funds. They took the millions raised at various political functions, deposited them into legitimate American business accounts, then sent that same money around the world electronically through various securely encrypted, virtual, private networks, guaranteeing anonymity. They falsely report the millions raised, infuse the drug funds, contribute a portion to political parties and invested the remainder. Any government agency's attempt to follow the transfers would be bogged down in the encryption and the funds bouncing from one country to another, landing in an obscure account, totally undetectable.

In addition to the political funds' investments, once a month, the group sends an associate from Los Angeles or Vancouver, British Columbia, in a private jet, with cash from drug revenue on the pretense of a reward for the most billable hours. The employee enjoys a week on the islands at the firm's luxury condo, not knowing that the Lear jet landed in a foreign country with millions hidden within the plane's opulent interior.

The pilots and crew are treated similarly on another part of the island, leaving the plane unattended, albeit within the confines of a hanger, to be visited covertly by a messenger who retrieves the cash, then deposits it in the offshore account...no questions asked.

The California attorneys were unaware that the currency serial numbers were recorded by the undercover American Secret Service agent and now with their fingerprints, the RCMP had connected them to the millions in each of their Caribbean bank accounts.

California, as many other states, was riddled with independent banks, many with local boards of directors with little or no financial acumen, the lack of which created a corporate atmosphere ripe for manipulation.

However, these banks were still regulated by the state of California and had to submit to an annual audit by state bank examiners. This oversight was not an issue with Hermanos since they had numerous lieutenants throughout the examiner's office and could control the outcome of any bank's audit.

The complexity of Hermanos' financial empire had been shaped and was controlled by Anthony Henderson, who had generated loyalty to the attorneys through years of dedication and expertise, amassing huge fortunes for the group.

The former lawyers regretted losing Henderson who had been arrested with the millions in currency and several thousand kilos of cocaine was awaiting trial in Los Angeles.

Law enforcement needed to connect the Caribbean bank accounts to their suspects and without their fingerprints, the task was impossible.

The LAPD, SBPD and the Secret Service were concerned that Henderson and Julio Fernández's participation in the half billion dollars and three thousand kilos of cocaine would result in their death.

As well, law enforcement had to prevent the cartel and Colombians from learning their delivery system was known and that the sub was under 24/7 surveillance.

If word got out of the cartel's loss, that knowledge would generate a drug war in Los Angeles with the Mexican cartels attempting to fill the void. To date the Hermanos did not resort to violence in controlling their massive territory, but that could change instantly if their competitors saw their weakness.

Law enforcement concerns prompted the LA District Attorney to file terrorism charges against Henderson and Julio Fernández.

Under a Federal court order and by the direction of the US Attorney General, the two suspects were provided a court appointed attorney, their employer refusing to acknowledge them and hence unwilling to pay for an attorney.

The evidence against them was overwhelming. LAPD and SBPD officers testified to the documentation against the two defendants and there was little the defense attorney had to counter the charges.

Guilty.

To their shock and dismay, they were transported to the Los Angeles Airport in an unmarked van, chained together and to the vehicle's metal braces, guarded by US Marshals and flown on a US Marshals' airplane to an air base in upper state New York. They were transported from there via helicopter to an isolated prison, dubbed, "Guantanamo of the North", guarded by US Army Military Police.

The prison was currently home to two former CIA operatives convicted of spying for the Soviet Union, the Unabomber, the Boston Marathon Bomber, the man responsible for the World Trade Center bombing in 1993 as well as violent prisoners serving life sentences transferred from other institutions.

Prisoners were isolated in single cells, electronically monitored. There were no rehabilitation programs or group sessions. They remained in their cells 24/7 with an hour exercise daily in an enclosed outdoor cage through a remotely controlled door at the end of their cell.

They neither saw, nor heard other inmates or the military staff. Their food was delivered robotically. Their cell was cleaned once a week while the prisoner was enclosed in the cage. Prisoners bathed in a sink. There were no blankets or pillows from which they could manufacture a suicide noose. Their bed was built into the cell's wall. There was no mattress.

Such was their fate.

Chapter THIRTY

The teenagers didn't actually move into *Refugio Seguro,* since they didn't have any belongings.

They just arrived.

At once.

All sixteen, the lone disgruntled teen having been convinced to give the arrangement a try.

Sabrina, the retired military cook and her husband met the girls, showed each of them their rooms and provided room keys. Diego, one of the retired police officers providing 24/7 security, introduced himself, explained his role in *Refugio Seguro,* then girls had about thirty to explore their rooms before meeting in the elegant dining room for snacks.

That afternoon, Rebecca and Penelope had taken the girls shopping. The stores were all within walking distance of *Refugio Seguro,* but the quantity of goods purchased was so overwhelming they needed several taxi vans to transport the boxes and bags.

At one point the girls were encouraged to slow the process to ensure they were getting what they wanted. There was no rush and there would be other shopping days, "Many more shopping days," advised Penelope as she watched the buying frenzy.

Although the girls had very definite tastes in styles and quality, a number asked R&P for advice and some actually took it.

Penelope and Rebecca had arranged to have the Magnum cosmetic staff spend several hours with the girls instructing them on makeup application, leaving each client with a year's supply of product.

Later the same day several hair stylists from

Alistar Films in Culver City, the CEO of which was a friend of Alane's, arrived. This was the longest process since the hair stylists took the time to discover the personalities of each of their clients and fashioned a style based on their findings.

The next few days were consumed with the girls being interviewed by Chumash High School counselors to affect their graduation programs. Some of the girls hadn't done well before they dropped out and rather than repeat courses, Rebecca and Penelope convinced the counselors that qualified tutors were available for any subject.

That gesture alone made the transition back to the life of a student more palatable than the girls had anticipated. Many were still skeptical of the guarantee that their parents would not interfere or try to gain custody or control, but even the skeptics were losing their convictions with every day's passing.

Rebecca and Penelope had been with the girls for most of every day since they had moved in, and the night before school started, Sabrina created a special dinner with an exotic non-alcoholic punch and had invited their benefactors to join them.

When Pen and Rebecca entered the dining room, the girls were already seated around the fireplace. Two massive round oak tables were adorned with white table clothes and center pieces of yellow bush poppies mixed with local greenery. The place settings were with Sagler flatware, baby blue Royal Doulton dishes and Williams Sonoma stemware.

As Rebecca and Penelope entered, the girls stood and gave them a round of applause. Each was dressed in one of their new outfits with recent hair- cuts, styling and makeup.

Sabrina approached, offering a brief menu for their perusal. Taking seats next to the girls, Pen and Rebecca attempted to make a selection but the girls were so excited about having them join them for dinner, they were non-stop chatter making it impossible for the women to glance at the menu.

Penelope and Rebecca respected Sabrina's expertise but they didn't want the girls to eat military style food, so they hired her with a proviso.

Sabrina readily accepted the challenge, having tired of thirty years of boring meal preparation in the military.

Sabrina spent several months working in *Marc Stucki's* kitchen, learning recipes and techniques, knowledge she was anxious to demonstrate.

The high-end restaurant taught her something interesting regarding patrons' eating habits; men and women were turning more and more to vegan choices, a concept she would offer at *Refugio Seguro.*

Sabrina had done an excellent job in consulting the girls regarding their favorite foods and produced an enticing menu with several bowl entrées; chicken with brown rice, black beans and guacamole, a vegan bowl of sofritas with brown rice, black beans, fresh tomato salsa and romaine lettuce and a paleo salad bowl with lamb barbacoa, guacamole, tomato and chili corn salsa and roasted vegetables.

Besides the bowls, she offered two entrées of chicken parmesan with a spicy marinara sauce and a traditional burrito with pulled pork, brown rice, corn, salsa, guacamole, cheese and sour cream.

While the girls chatted, Rebecca stole a quick glance at the menu, nudged Penelope pointing to an item. Pen nodded and they chose the burrito and side salad just as Sabrina arrived to take their order.

The original restaurant was far too spacious for their needs, so the contractor reduced the area by half to add more bedrooms and enlarge some of the smaller suites. The dining room boasted taupe stucco walls, chocolate brown décor with numerous cloth covered benches set up against the walls and beside the fireplace. Six large artificial flower arrangements were tastefully spread throughout the space to compliment the beige Italian tile floor and taupe walls. Lighting was provided by numerous copper chandeliers which muted the ambiance on the edge of romantic. But not.

Penelope and Rebecca enjoyed their meal and the girls' company for a couple of hours before the girls left to get ready for school the next day.

As they rose as one, Pen stood and asked, "Girls, before you leave, Rebecca and I were wondering if we might join you tomorrow morning for your first day. It might make the transition a little easier?"

The women were taken aback by the enthusiasm as the girls rushed over and gave them a hug, responding almost as one, "Would you?", "Really?" and "You're kidding."

Rebecca replied, "Of course. We'd be delighted to be a part of your big day. Thanks for allowing us."

The teens left, several turning to wave goodnight, then disappeared into the hallway leading to their respective rooms.

As the women left the building, Penelope put her arm around Rebecca, kissed her on the cheek and said, "This is going to be good."

Rebecca returned the kiss, replying, "Yes, it is. Very good," as they walked the short distance to their SUV.

"We can't undo what's been done by abuse in this country, but we can let these girls know they are loved, get them the help they need, and assure them that there is much light at the end of the tunnel."

Steven Tyler

"Every step toward the goal of justice requires sacrifice, suffering, and struggle; the tireless exertions and passionate concern of dedicated individuals."

Martin Luther King Jr.

Chapter THIRTY-ONE

By the end of the day, Kimberly, Karen and Tom had identified the two attorneys, taken their photos with the covert cameras and transmitted the information to Elisabeth. She in turn listed the names and photos on CHAP. Edmonton detectives found the lawyer's fingerprints from their application to practice law.

The next day the trio duplicated the previous day's activity to identify accountant, Aleksander Kuznetsov who was being primed to handle all financial arrangements for Stan.

Posting the information to CHAP, the Edmonton Mounties quickly identified Kuznetsova's fingerprints through his application to the BC Chartered Professional Accountants Association.

Edmonton pinged Elisabeth's computer, alerting her to a CHAP posting. Elisabeth copied the data regarding the fingerprints and sent it to the Secret Service agent in the Caribbean. She in turn identified the three accounts with low seven figures, an astounding amount given the cocaine flow had yet to begin.

The downside of the Caribbean agent's input was she couldn't identify the depositor. Wherever the money transfer began, it was lost in virtual, private networks which encrypted the transmissions so many times, bouncing from one country to another, tracing was impossible.

Hermanos de Wall Street used the generous deposits to prime their newest partners during the Canadian network's establishment.

Listing the information on CHAP, the Caribbean agent's evidence was noted by Detective Pelfini in Santa Barbara, Jessica Fukishura and the Edmonton RCMP.

Building their case.

A few days after his evening at *The Horsemen,* Larry texted Stan from work letting him know that he'd be at the pub that night to watch the Hamilton Tiger-Cats take on the BC Lions over dinner.

Larry didn't expect a reply, figuring Stan would either be there or not. After a quick shower, khaki slacks, short sleeve Van Heusen, blue floral print shirt and Mundo chocolate brown lace-up, chukka boots, he grabbed a cab and arrived at *The Horsemen* as the network was airing the pre-game intro.

Roy Davidson was behind the bar and remembered Baird, giving him a nod of welcome as Larry made his way through the crowd to the game area.

Glancing around he couldn't see Loblinski and there weren't any empty seats, so he ordered a Grizzly Paw ale and leaned against the far wall waiting for the game to begin.

Halfway through his draft, two staffers arrived with a slew of folding chairs which they placed in every available space from which a person could see the screens.

Larry sat.

He was just about to order dinner when he spotted Stan walking in his direction. Larry quickly placed his jacket on the chair beside him, saving it from the crowd, then stood to welcome Stan.

Loblinski's timing was perfect. He was positive Larry was his Port Alberni contact's son and had accepted his invitation, hoping to get a take on his character and personality.

Since the game was about to start, neither man looked at the menu but ordered beers, the filet wrapped in bacon, sprinkled with blue cheese, served with roasted red, green and yellow peppers and baby red potatoes.

Baird was a Lions fan and Stan had no preference, having never followed sports, so Larry could get excited and not have to contend with opposing backlash.

They were into their second Grizzly when their dinner arrived, complete with mobile tables; 19" x 13" x 24" high, solid, distressed wood top with four black tube legs and small wheels. The men were so taken aback by the display of customer service, all they could do was shake their heads at the two servers, thank them and enjoy their steaks.

During the first quarter patrons came and went, periodically leaving a table or front row seat quickly snagged by a newcomer so often Larry and Stan decided to stay put.

Although *The Horsemen* was considered either a couples' pub, single men/women or groups, tonight there was the odd group of women, particularly female RCMP officers socializing. Davidson knew them all so when he glanced up from washing beer glasses at the bar and saw Janis Simcoe and Roberta Wilkins enter arm-in-arm he ignored their entry, presuming correctly, that they were the undercover Members assigned to monitor Baird and Loblinski.

The Mounties were attired in distressed jeans and loafers. Simcoe wore a blue chambray top with a navy blue, one button J. Crew blazer. Her caramel, shoulder length hairdo, and the outfit created a classic look which was matched by Roberta, with a somewhat shorter hairstyle; natural ginger layered and cut just below her ears with eyebrow length bangs, attired in jeans, white, long sleeve, button down blouse and a chocolate brown Calvin Klein blazer.

The officers were already in a festive mood as they took a small table for two facing one of the platinum screens, two meters from their subjects.

Davidson's lead server, Joyce, had been present at the installation of the additional cameras and microphones early and made it a point to serve the officers to ensure their operation was devoid of any unpredictable hiccups.

Davidson had purchased a six-pack of non-alcoholic beer which Joyce now served in mugs identical to those from which the other patrons were drinking. She handed the women menus then left to serve other customers, trying to catch up before the next quarter.

Larry and Stan had finished their meal and were on their third Grizzly pint when, during half-time, the conversation turned to Port Alberni. Stan was positive the guy sitting next to him was the son of the union boss who busted him as a teenager.

At one point in the conversation Stan nodded toward the women sitting one table over, making a homophobic comment that grated Larry. Baird chose to ignore the slur and returned to the previous conversation. Stan had his answer. Baird Jr. would not fit into his operation.

While the men were engrossed in who remembered whom at their former high school, Joyce took the officers' order of the special of the night – grilled chicken and roasted cauliflower salad with baby kale, gala apple chunks, avocado, roasted pumpkin seeds and parmesan cheese with a lemon and avocado vinaigrette dressing.

Had any patron taken notice, they might question the behavior of the millennials not on their phones. Feigning interest in the football game, they were monitoring the conversation between Larry and Stan at the nearby table using the parabolic feature of their enhanced smartphones, courtesy of CSIS. Simply pointing the phone while it lay flat on the table allowed the men's conversation to be gathered by the microscopic reflective surface hidden inside the frame at the top of the phone.

Citing a need to use the restroom, Roberta excused herself and weaved her five-foot-two, lean frame through the enthusiastic fans as the Lions took the lead with their second touchdown.

She stopped midway to her destination to watch the replay, an action taken by several men at the table next to her as an invitation to demonstrate their pick-up lines.

Roberta was fully aware of their presence and by training was in Color Code of Awareness Orange which allowed instant body movement.

As the network completed its replay and the players prepared for the kick-off, one of the men grabbed Roberta's left wrist in an enquiring move to get her attention so he could deliver his line.

He didn't have that opportunity.

The forty-something, married fan, like so many other men, regardless of their age, never seem to learn.

Do not engage in unwanted touching of a woman.

His hand had just closed its grasp on Roberta's wrist when she spun on her left toe turning into him simultaneously wrapping her right arm over and under the groper's right, then grabbing her own bicep, trapping his arm.

She spun further on her left toe and leveraged her grip up and to her left, flipping him over backwards onto the floor, his chair flying out from under him.

As he landed on his back, Roberta maintained her hold and dropped quickly onto his chest with her right knee, knocking the air out of him. She could have broken his sternum, but chose not to, wanting to avoid the additional RCMP paperwork.

As the man laid on his back, stunned and embarrassed, Roberta grabbed his hair, pushed it backwards, forcing him to look up at her. She said quietly, "Don't ever touch me."

She was unaware that several patrons in the near vicinity were staring, aghast of what had just occurred. She rose from her kneeling position, adjusted her blazer, then turned to continue her route to the restroom, with numerous women and a few men providing her a standing ovation.

Baird was one of the men.

The incident was over so quickly that the bouncers and Davidson were unaware of the skirmish.

Ignoring the response, she completed her journey and ten later made her way back through the crowd of patrons, all of whom had heard of the encounter and everyone stood to applaud.

Brushing aside the attention, she weaved her way back through the crowd with several people purposely moving out of her way.

The man who had grabbed her wrist was nowhere to be seen, but it was obvious by his companions' demeanor that they wondered if they were next.

As Roberta sat, Janis controlled her desire to give her a high-five, choosing instead to bump her knee as Roberta settled into her seat, picked up her "draft" and returned to watching the football game.

"There are some people who still feel threatened by strong women. That's their problem. It's not mine."

Gloria Allred

Larry noticed her return, turned to Stan and quipped, "I suspect that asshole made a sexist comment he will never live down, either that, or he touched her."

Stan's sheepish expression was sufficient for Larry to see he made his point.

Baird's comment cemented Stan's evaluation of Larry's character and personality. Satisfied, he changed the conversation back to the football game to get Larry talking about his favorite team, the Lions.

"Football fans share a universal language that cuts across many cultures and many personality types."

Hunter S. Thompson

Loblinski was running the operation solo and it was only a matter of time, given the quantity of product to hit British Columbia, that he wouldn't be able to control its many tentacles by himself.

He needed help but Baird was not qualified to participate in Stan's operation.

Chapter THIRTY-TWO

Jessica was working on a case assigned by Katrina - a father whose son was arrested for drug trafficking with the son's statement that dad was his dealer.

The son was arrested by university police and turned over to SBPD for prosecution. While combing through the social worker and child services interviews her encrypted phone buzzed.

Her door being closed she didn't hesitate to remove the phone from her locked desk drawer, enter her code and answer, "Yes."

"Jessica. Good afternoon."

She didn't need an introduction to the man for whom she had worked for many years, so she replied, "Good afternoon, sir."

"Nice work getting into her inner circle. Your new adversary will be delighted, albeit still wanting a piece of your hide," offered her boss with a laugh, referring to the LA county district attorney objecting to what she considered was Fukishura's arrogance, her colluding with the LAPD and blind siding her with information which should have gone through channels.

"Should I say thanks boss?"

"Sure. It was a compliment. It is that attitude which has made you so successful and why I authorized your early retirement and that of your team."

Jessica was thrilled and started to reply when Sorento interrupted with, "Hold on. Not so quick with the appreciation. There is a proviso to the approval. Do you want to hear it?"

"Certainly sir."

"The Team is indentured to us for five years. No active cases assigned and no travel, just those cases in your area where we need the assistance."

Although both phones were encrypted, meaning their conversation and voices were filtered at both ends of the conversation in case another agency tried to pick up chatter between them, they were not using names and purposely vague regarding the conversation details.

"That is very generous sir. I know the team will accept those arrangements and be delighted in doing so."

"Glad to hear that. I made a strong case for them based on their years of undercover work and living out of a suitcase, but it was the CFBA takedown which sold the Federal Employees Retirement System on approving the applications. Full retirement and benefits starting on the first of the month.

"I will notify them immediately sir and thank you for all your time and effort to affect their future."

"No problem. Talk to you later and keep up the pressure."

He ended the call.

She didn't waste any time in communicating the extremely good news to her team. Initiating a conference encrypted call, she waited the few moments for all phones to be processed by the software. When she heard three clicks, she identified herself, shared the news, then waited for the whooping and hollering to subside.

"Have you three met with your financial advisor?" she asked, meaning Alane.

Collectively, all three answered in the affirmative. She didn't need to know the details, just that they had completed that task for their financial stability.

All three agents' salary had averaged one-hundred and fifty thousand for a number of years. They were G-15 on the federal salary scale with bonuses for undercover, location, military and law enforcement experience and education. They hadn't had expenses for over a decade, the government having paid a daily stipend for room and board, so they had quite a savings nest egg which Alane would maximize.

Jessica continued, "Good, now for the proviso attached to your early, full retirement."

Once she explained the terms, she said, "Jason and Jackson, I need you to be my lieutenants. Let's the five of us get together tomorrow night for a quick meeting and I will fill you in on the details."

"Sounds good to us," replied Jason, knowing he could speak confidently for all three.

"Tomorrow. Your place. 6 pm."

"Got it. See you then."

Call ended.

Jessica was delighted with the developments. She had been concerned about approaching the Team before Sorento approved their retirement. Now all was set. Gutierrez would provide them with all the contact information for street dealers to deliver their cash to Jason and Jackson while Elisabeth would record all conversations through their phones and a back-up microphone in their belt buckles.

Stan pondered his options now that Larry Jr. was out of consideration. He had but one choice given the operation's magnitude.

Brian Sawyer

He knew he was on the east coast of Costa Rica, probably a small village on the ocean, attempting to blend into the culture. That was the extent of Stan's knowledge of his whereabouts.

He mused his challenge. *Maybe he changed his name? Not likely, as there was no need. His participation in the Southern Alberta operation was an unknown factor by police, or anyone other than himself.*

I can't leave now to head to Costa Rica and search for him. I have neither the skills nor the time with the product arriving.

He figured his only option was to hire a private investigator. It would be expensive but there wasn't time to gain someone else's confidence, determine their trustworthiness and be ready for the delivery and distribution.

The next morning he did just that, hired an international firm, offered them the photo he had on his phone for identification and a healthy bonus if they were successful quickly.

The firm's only task was to locate Brian, provide him with the disposable cell phone Loblinski provided and Stan's number and stay with Brian while he made the call.

The Chica de Oro was passing Astoria, Oregon and the mouth of the Columbia River, staying several hundred kilometers west of the infamous region. It was estimated there are over two thousand wrecked ships at the ocean bottom, having been defeated by the rush of the Columbia River as it met the pounding Pacific Ocean surf.

Their next obstacle would be the American Trident Nuclear submarine base on the Washington coast west of Seattle.

The Golden Girl was on schedule.

Simcoe and Wilkins left *The Horsemen* immediately after the game, not wanting to be drawn into a discussion of Roberta's altercation. They had Larry and Stan's entire conversation recorded and would upload it to the Edmonton detachment once they were in their vehicle.

Walking past the bar on their way to the front door, Davidson was smiling broadly, nodding his appreciation for their 86ing an undesirable patron.

"I am too intelligent, too demanding and too resourceful for anyone to be able to take charge of me entirely."

Simone de Beauvoir

Chapter THIRTY-THREE

Jessica wanted the "J" Team meeting to be a quick event, so she called *Marc Stucki's* which prepared pastrami sandwiches with pickles and coleslaw. She arrived at six with dinner in tow. Jackson and Jason met her at the front door, took the bags of sandwiches and handed her a glass of Bourgogne Winery's 2016 Pinot Noir and followed her into the kitchen where Elisabeth, Rebecca and Penelope were already enjoying their second glass.

The Team exchanged hugs then gathered around the kitchen table to enjoy their casual meal and wine, everyone but Jessica on edge waiting to hear what their boss had to say.

After devouring her pastrami on rye with yellow mustard and a giant dill pickle, she began, "You are looking at Marianna Gutierrez's lieutenant and I need two henchmen to be my collectors."

She was stopped in her delivery by the confused expressions of her colleagues. Her opening line was intentional, now she backtracked and provided them with the history.

There were a number of questions, the overwhelming majority of which concerned her safety and whether the loss of the cocaine from Gutierrez's last shipment had created a vacuum which the Mexican cartels were filling.

Jason asked, "Won't the Mexicans be gunning for Gutierrez's crew trying to retake her market share?"

"Totally. There is no way the Mexican cartel is going to allow Gutierrez back into the market without a bloody fight and a lot of bodies. We are letting the LAPD handle the Mexicans while we work to put Gutierrez away. That will leave one cocaine supplier which is far easier to control than two, and Marianna being the greatest supplier, will mean an overall drop in cocaine use.

"The Mexican cartels smuggle their cocaine across our southern border. They do not, to our knowledge, have anything as sophisticated as the Colombians' delivery system.

"This is very short term while we put together our case against Gutierrez. If I didn't fill the gap, she would regroup from within her criminal element and we could be back to square one.

"I want to get this case done and over with soon so I can join you guys and move on with my life. I am so tired of undercover I could scream," she concluded by symbolically pulling her hair and making a screaming face.

"I get where you are coming from Jessica. I really do. So, we are in a countdown. Do you want us to touch base with LAPD Drug Squad detectives, discover who is left of Marianna's street dealers?" asked Jason.

"I suspect those dealers are already selling Mexican coke and have already forgotten about Gutierrez, considering she didn't come through with a product to sell."

Rebecca, Penelope and Elisabeth watched and listened to the conversation, offering nothing, drinking wine, wondering how the Team could move the case against Marianna along quicker. They asked.

Elisabeth interjected with, "Changing the subject somewhat, we have all kept current with CHAP but in case you haven't picked up the last day or so, we have solid identification of the Vancouver attorneys, accountants and their Caribbean bank accounts. We are working to identify the source of their income. So far, we can't make a connection to Gutierrez. In addition, from what you have noted Jessica, she isn't too concerned about the millions in cash and product lost, for which they still owe the cartel. I've been wondering, could she be a lieutenant herself?

"I would like to run her prints. If she isn't who she purports to be, that trail might lead us to whomever is operating the cartel, if not her."

"This could be a massive opportunity Jessica," offered Rebecca.

"What do you guys think?" asked Jessica of Jackson and Jason.

"Our case rests primarily on conjecture," replied Jason, leaning back in his chair, hands on the back of his head. "All we have are the texts, the content of which will not get her indicted. However, she had her prints taken for a license to practice. The California Bar Association just does a cursory background check. Let's get the prints and run a full National Crime Information Center check to determine if she is in fact, Marianna Gutierrez, and go from there."

Jackson nodded, pointing a positive finger to Jason. Jessica rejoined the conversation with, "This will be easy. Now don't laugh, but I haven't cleaned up after the dinner party Katrina had at my new place. I won't know which glass she used, so I will get all three to Pelfini and she can run the prints through the system.

"Sound good to everyone?"

Observing positive body language from the Team, and ignoring the smirks, she continued, "Where are we with Loblinski in Alberta? I haven't seen anything from the Edmonton RCMP."

Elisabeth responded with, "Karen, Tom and Kimberly Breyman, Karen's friend and a Member from the Surrey detachment, identified the attorneys and accountant in Vancouver with help from moi," she smiled and curtsied then continued, "The RCMP obtained their prints and sent them to me. I forwarded those to our Caribbean agent who identified hefty accounts for all three Vancouverites.

"Here is the sweet spot. The Mounties had brief texts from Stan to someone in Dallas, Texas back when they first started surveillance and hadn't made any connection. With the help of the FBI Special Agent in Charge, they obtained an American warrant, executed by the FBI on the recipient's cell phone. That connection lead them to another cell.

"Are you ready for this? This is sweet. Gutierrez." she concluded with a little dance.

Jackson jumped up, pumping his fist in the air, "No fuckin' way. Really? Shit. Remarkable."

Jessica, Rebecca and Jason were likewise excited, walking around, hands over their heads and running them through their hair.

Finally Jessica stopped pacing, turned to Elisabeth and gave her a hug saying, "You are so fucking incredible Elisabeth, so unfuckin' unbelievable, I am at a loss for words," and sat down, drank the rest of her Pinot, refilled her glass and put her sock feet on the table.

"You are most welcome my illustrious Team members," Elisabeth replied with a little bow. "More on Stan. The last communication the RCMP had with him is a text between him and a Larry Baird in Port Alberni. The text seemed to indicate that Stan was looking to add the son who lives in Calgary to his team. The father was adamantly against it, so much so that he threatened to back out of his participation. We have no idea what that could mean so the Port Alberni detachment is running the father through their local drug informants. So far, nothing.

"Even with the texts between Stan and the Vancouver connections, we don't have enough for a case. The Mounties will keep digging and let us know the connection between Stan and the father. In the meantime the sooner we can get those prints processed the better."

"Sounds good. I'm on it. Will one of you call Pelfini and let her know I will drop the glasses off tonight and tell her our objective?" asked Jessica.

"I will get that," offered Penelope.

"Great Pen. Thanks.

"Before everyone heads out, there is one more piece of the puzzle dropping into place," offered Elisabeth. "The Canadian Navy which has been tailing the submarine since it left Colombian waters, signaled that it continues a northerly route and just passed Astoria, Oregon. If we didn't have the GPS tracking devices, the sub would be undetectable. The ship's commander noted that the sub isn't being picked up by their sonar.

"With what we know about Stan, this guy Baird on Vancouver Island and the RCMP making the connection between Loblinski and Gutierrez, there is no doubt in my mind that the shipment is headed to British Columbia.

"There are a lot of moving pieces in the Canadian operation, but they are all being driven by the RCMP. Will they continue with the Secret Service's position to allow the product to be distributed, then arrest the participants, rather than arresting those at the port of delivery?"

"Good points, Elisabeth. I don't know how to approach that. I think it wise to pass it on to Sorento. I recall him having a relationship with the previous RCMP Commissioner and considered him an asshole for manipulating Mounties, denying them a union, long guns and training. From what I have read, the new commissioner is a woman and has already made changes in the organization. What do you guys think?"

"Wise decision Jessica. This is far above our ability, particularly when we are all leaving," offered Jackson.

The other agents nodded agreement.

"I will call him in the morning. I better get going. Hopefully Elise will have something for us in the next twenty-four hours on the fingerprints and we will have a direction."

With that she ate the last of her sandwich, downed the remainder of her Pinot Noir and left.

The Team cleaned up the kitchen then retreated to the living room to continue the discussion.

Inspector Lorne Wood of the Port Alberni, British Columbia detachment had been advised by Edmonton's Deputy Commissioner Benedetti of the developing events and detectives' speculation, introduced him to CHAP, a system he quickly embraced, and provided him Elisabeth's assigned access code.

Wood was a quick study and was up to speed on the investigation within a few hours, briefing his Members during the learning process.

Understanding that Loblinski, Baird Jr. and Baird Sr. were under digital surveillance, his first move was to configure his staffing schedule which currently stood at twenty-eight officers but with holidays and illness, his numbers were down considerably.

He had asked city council and the riding's member of parliament for two additional officers, which didn't appear to be plausible given the council's plan to reduce the numbers rather than increase. The cost of one officer was $175,000, which included salary, benefits, computer and vehicle expenses. Receiving a quarter of a million dollars was unlikely.

In addition, Wood was dealing with an additional twenty-six hundred tourists from a cruise ship. Although the travelers were a massive economic boost for businesses, their sightseeing around town and surrounding areas strained his already depleted force.

Based on the evidence at hand, Wood was debating whether to ask the deputy commissioner in Vancouver for personnel. His experience told him the answer would be a resounding 'no', so until he could present solid evidence that the Colombian submarine would disgorge its cargo in Port Alberni, he would have to maintain the status quo with the personnel he had.

Or would he?

Wood's key to success was his ability to interact with the citizens of the community for whose safety he was responsible. It was common for residents and business staff to see him walking the streets alone, in uniform, chatting with whomever he met, walking into stores, engaging in conversations or as he like to say, "showing the colors", meaning the rainbow on the RCMP's vehicles.

It was that philosophy which prompted him to make a call from the detachment's blind number and arrange a coffee chat at the marina.

Chapter THIRTY-FOUR

When CSIS lead investigator Kopas discovered that the Colombian vessel was about to enter Canadian waters he assigned the Vancouver law enforcement trio to expand their surveillance to include the suspects' vehicles, the identity of which Kimberly obtained through the provincial vehicle registration data base.

Kimberly, Karen and Tom had mounted surveillance on the attorneys and accountant, changing their clothing and unmarked cars frequently. David Kopas had obtained federal warrants for the suspects' additional communications, including both phone and internet transmissions at their homes and companies. Elisabeth was recording all digital interaction of the suspects in Vancouver, Edmonton and newly added, Port Alberni.

Kopas' orders were difficult to perform given the restrictive parking in the downtown financial district. They had three suspects to follow, made difficult with the readily identifiable law enforcement unmarked vehicles; dark colors, generic hub caps and a slew of communication roof aerials.

Tom, Karen and Kimberly chose rentals. Each day a different make, model and color but never the large SUV, always choosing a vehicle easy to park and maneuver through Vancouver traffic. Several rentals had a decal or a license plate holder with the company name. All were removed and placed in the trunk once the officers left the rental lot.

They located and identified the suspects' vehicles in a nearby commercial parking lot, possibly one retained by their respective firms.

Tom had borrowed a pair of overalls from the maintenance staffer at their hotel and quickly slipped them on one morning shortly after the suspects had parked and left for their offices. He slid under each vehicle, while his colleagues ensured he was not interrupted, and placed a GPS tracking device similar to that used on the Chica de Oro. Once installed, they notified Elisabeth who downloaded software to each agent's encrypted phone allowing them to follow any of the vehicles at a distance.

Three suspects.

Three agents.

Three vehicles.

Bottle neck traffic.

Each morning the detectives arrived separately and parked in spots previously reserved for VIPs or the owner of the parking lot; a man of swarthy complexion and overstimulated appetite, who succumbed to the enticement of one-thousand dollars for each vehicle. Cash. For a month's parking. All other tenants were paying three hundred.

Stan Loblinski hired the Samuel Jefferson Investigation Agency. Two agents were dispatched immediately, traveling directly from Edmonton to San José, Costa Rica, then a local flight to Limón on the west coast.

The male agents' task was made more complicated by their mutual gender. Their former law enforcement persona was evident to every person from whom they chose to seek information. Their approach was successful with the distribution of hundreds of American dollars, the black-market value of which was considerably higher than its worth in the U.S.

After several days tracking Sawyer from village to village south of Limón, their last stop was the small community at the end of the coastal road. A long and exhausting day. Choosing the only establishment which had any customers, they entered Mariscos Punta Manzanillo and spotted Sawyer sitting with a group of men watching international soccer.

Marianna Gutierrez planned to organize her Los Angeles street dealers to coordinate with Jessica, but her objectives went askew when she discovered they possessed no loyalty.

In defending a local smalltime thief and periodic dealer in LA, he had shared that all street dealers were now working for the Mexican cartels. They had divided the inner cities, West Los Angeles, Santa Monica and surrounding areas into districts, all of which were assigned to her former peddlers.

The dealer being the last client, she asked her assistant to prepare the necessary documents for the next day's court appearances, then rushed home to interact with Hermanos de Wall Street before the end of the day.

Gutierrez was angry with the current news. She refused to let the Mexicans take over her territory…at least not without a fight.

To conduct a turf war required Hermanos' approval and although they had the available firepower to engage their competition, such action would create far more police scrutiny than was economically wise. Knowing her partners' reluctance to confront the Mexicans, she had to temper her anger and argue intellectually to regain that business.

Arriving home in record time, she changed into a pair of floral print, high waisted Bermuda shorts with a turquoise, long-sleeve T, longer in the back than front. Going barefoot, she made her way from the master bedroom to the office and sent a quick communique to Hermanos in San Francisco.

Marianna had no qualms about using email to connect with her colleagues. She had the utmost confidence in her encrypted system and a virtual private network, VPN, the same system used to deliver funds to various right-wing political action support groups, Super PACs.

Gutierrez was unaware that Elisabeth had placed a filter on her internet service which sent copies of all her computer actions to the R&P ranch while allowing the transmissions to be completed.

Elisabeth was cocooned in her bedroom office when she saw the email enter her system.

Smiling to herself, she thought, *now all I have to do is wait for the recipient to open the email and I will identify to whom Marianna answers.*

Chapter THIRTY-FIVE

Francesco Loblinski's physiotherapy had progressed well, his mobility about seventy-five percent of his former self. Doctors told him the pain would subside with time, but for now he had to rely on pain medication.

But the pain got worse. Doctors refused to renew his opioid prescriptions and he began withdrawals.

Every movement was excruciating painful. Nights were worse. No position in bed brought him relief and he woke each morning as tired as when he went to bed.

His behavior changed dramatically with the withdrawal symptoms: sweating, hallucinations and seizures, causing tension and arguments with his wife.

During one visit by Larry Baird Sr. he confided in his union rep that his doctors refused to renew his pain medication prescription, leaving him in agony 24/7.

Baird Sr. felt obliged to help his union brother. He contacted a local drug dealer and obtained one-hundred and fifty Vicodin, Percocet and OxyContin of various dosages, enough to stem his pain for thirty days. Baird was unaware that the calls he made to locate the drugs were recorded by the RCMP and Elisabeth. He was also not cognizant of the police surveillance which videotaped the drug transactions and deliveries to Francesco.

Francesco's needs quickly rose to two hundred pills monthly, a thirty-plus percent increase. Larry never charged him for the narcotics or enquired about his rising needs. Francesco believed the drugs were compliments of the union, not procured illegally by Larry Sr.

Soon Loblinski's needs exceeded Baird's disposable retirement income and he became indebted to the dealer, his altruism now a financial burden.

The economic strain coincided with the initial contact from Stan. Although they hadn't spoken in years, their previous arrangement allowed a smooth segue into Larry Sr. being Stan's lieutenant and a promise of financial relief.

Jackson and Jason contacted LAPD Drug Squad Detectives Vasquez and Wong and quickly confirmed that the dealers the unit had been monitoring before the massive takedown outside of Santa Ynez were now selling for the El Serpiente Cartel, which took over from El Chapo who was being held in an American Supermax prison.

The Mexican Cartel controlled the illegal cocaine business in New York, Denver, Atlanta, Chicago, Dallas, Miami, San Diego, El Paso, Laredo and now, Los Angeles. El Serpiente's financial lieutenants quickly filled the void when it became apparent Hermanos de Wall Street could no longer deliver a product in a timely manner.

In addition to amalgamating Gutierrez's territory, they began cutting their Mexican cocaine and created a specialty market for cocaine laced with fentanyl, the latter having a nationwide tract record of hundreds of deaths.

Elisabeth was cognizant of all the transactions between the Mexican lieutenants and Marianna's former street dealers since she continued to monitor the dealers' phones.

Logging this information into CHAP, she found it interesting that LAPD Captain Ortega shared his concern whether taking the thousands of kilos of cocaine off the street and confiscating the nearly one-half a billion dollars in currency from the Santa Ynez operation, moved law enforcement forward or backward given the almost immediate infusion of Mexican cocaine into Los Angeles society.

Jessica monitored CHAP from her secure, encrypted laptop in her home office and deduced that it was only a matter of days, if not hours, before Marianna would learn the fate of her territory. Jessica had to be prepared with a plan B for her role as lieutenant now that there wasn't a market to supervise. She hoped that whoever was controlling Gutierrez didn't agree to retake the market by force. Doing so would leave bodies scattered throughout Los Angeles County; dealers and by-standers alike.

Chapter THIRTY-SIX

Penelope, Rebecca, Jason, Elisabeth and Jackson had chatted into the late evening after Jessica left. They knew they were engaged in a waiting game, although the stakes were far from a sporting event.

Penelope commented, "With the number of cases we are running at the agency and gathering evidence against Gutierrez and whomever, I don't know about you guys, but I am pretty strung out and could use a little distraction."

"What do you have in mind?" asked Rebecca.

"Nothing real hairy, just a little dinner together where we aren't talking shop. Maybe hitting up a sports bar and watch a few games…or something. It doesn't matter to me what. Just something other than technology and maybe, sorry guys, no offense, but just some girl time."

"No offense taken," replied Jason. "Why don't you guys go out for the evening. Invite Detective Pelfini too. She would probably enjoy getting to know you better. Jackson and I will find our way around town, maybe get into a little trouble. What do you say, Jackson?" smiling all the while.

"Sounds good to me. But honestly, I think I am well beyond the hell raising age. Maybe a nice steak and a couple of beers. How about we apartment hunt tomorrow. We have to meet with Alane regarding our portfolios, for what they are worth," Jackson responded, raising his eyes questioning. Continuing he added, "and see if he has any ideas?"

"That settles it then," injected Elisabeth. How about dinner at the Pelican Club tomorrow night. I will text Jessica and Elise?"

"We're in," responded Pen and Rebecca in unison, raising their hands as though volunteering for a grade school function.

With those decisions made, they turned in for the evening, Elisabeth checking her system one more time for news from Pelfini on the prints.

Nothing.

Sorento, in his capacity as head of the president's protection detail, called the RCMP commissioner in Ottawa on an encrypted line. Expecting to get a staff member, he was pleasantly surprised when, moments after the call was decrypted in Ottawa, she answered.

Sorento had followed her recent career move and the prime minister's directive to change the Force with attention to the history of harassment, workplace violence, gender parity with women and minorities better reflected in leadership. No small tasks as individual directives, but collectively, he was happy the task wasn't his.

The commissioner was current on the prospect of a massive influx of cocaine on the west coast investigation via CHAP and Deputy Commissioner Benedetti in Edmonton. She shared information regarding Stan, the Samuel Jefferson Investigation Agency, the Force's surveillance of Samuel Jefferson's staff and their current location in Costa Rica. She couldn't add new information regarding the Port Alberni connection, but expected that to materialize within days.

She anticipated an update from the Mounties who were in Costa Rica and would relay that information to Sorento personally rather than list it on CHAP at this time.

Sorento laid out what transpired with the cocaine shipment into Point Concepción, pronouncing with his New

Mexican dialect, rounding out the last four letters, *seeon*. He had prepared for this crucial conversation, making notes to ensure he provided all the details needed to convince the RCMP chief to allow the cocaine to be distributed, the submarine to return to Colombia, then apprehend Stan's lieutenants and street dealers.

His apprehension was unwarranted. The new commissioner rose through the ranks and knew the value of Sorento's plan. She agreed to allow the sub to leave Canadian waters and be tracked back to Colombia, to confiscate the cocaine and keep the currency.

The commissioner asked numerous questions, the answers of which Sorento had at his fingertips. Her primary concern dealt with British Columbia's lower mainland gangs and if they were involved. And if not, the prospect they would attempt to grab the massive shipment and thereby create a turf war. The RCMP was already dealing with several intergang warfare and didn't need another. In addition, the city of Surrey planned to cancel the RCMP policing contract and hire their own force, creating, in her mind, more policing problems than those which already existed.

Sorento assured her that the entire operation was controlled by Stan and his American connections, whom his team were tracking down. There wasn't a chance that news of this shipment would leak, given only three CSIS agents were involved, one of whom was sequestered from the Surrey Detachment. The scope of those needing to know was small and contained.

The commissioner replied, "This will be a coordinated effort between the RCMP and CSIS. I see no reason to include any of the lower mainland police departments."

"I envy Canada's streamlined law enforcement. We have so many agencies involved in drug enforcement, it makes operations very difficult to mount, maintain and process." he concluded.

"Yes, I gather that is the reason you stonewalled your DEA and FBI in the last operation and the current one."

Sorento could almost see the smile on her face as the truth was revealed by a foreign agency. He hadn't planned on this becoming an issue, hoping Jessica and the "J" Team contained any fall-out.

He replied, "I'm sure you can understand our reasoning for the decision. Had we not maintained anonymity it would have been an organizing nightmare and a feeding frenzy for the four-hundred million in seized currency. As well, I confess that I have developed a growing dislike for the FBI."

"That explains the protection detail being involved in cocaine smuggling," she laughed. "I presume you decided that since the fruit of the activity is funding a domestic terrorist organization, the president is threatened."

Here was the first indication that the commissioner was by far and wide a delightful change from her predecessor when she laughed, saying, "I shudder at the thought of organizing an operation with so many agencies involved."

Sorento listened to the head of Canada's federal police force with considerable interest. He had not gotten along with her predecessor, constantly wishing he could have some influence over the man's management style which had resulted in many officer deaths and low morale.

Listening to her elaborate, he smiled to himself, that he was embarking on a unique relationship; observing the rebuilding of the framework of a law enforcement organization steeped in tradition yet strangled by misogynist senior management.

They ended the call with brief pleasantries on how the commissioner was settling into her routine and initiating the changes she had been wanting for years.

Chapter THIRTY-SEVEN

When Jessica got home, she activated the alarm system, then headed to the kitchen. She was somewhat embarrassed that the room hadn't been cleaned after the party and vowed to hire a service.

This is just disgusting she thought as she made her way around the kitchen picking up the three wine glasses with a pair of tongs, placing each in separate plastic bags, then all three in a larger one, inserting her Secret Service business card with her personal cell number on the back. Lastly, she wrote *Detective Elise Pelfini* in bold letters across the seal.

Taking the bag into the bedroom, placing it on the nightstand, then removing her 9 mm from its shoulder holster and placing it next to the glasses, she was confident the evidence would be on the nightstand in the morning. Although she had told the Team the prints would be dropped off tonight, she didn't have the energy and felt nothing would be lost by waiting until the morning.

She was just exiting the bathroom, walking towards the bed, naked, when her personal cell chimed. Climbing over the bed to reach the phone, she slid the button to answer the call, not recognizing the number on call display, said, "Yes."

"Hey, don't sound so serious boss."

"Oh, hi Elisabeth. Sorry, I didn't recognize your number. What's up?"

"Tomorrow. Girls night out. All five of us! Six at the White Pelican. How about it? After all we have been through, we need a night out, just the girls. What do you think?"

Jessica was prepared mentally to crawl under the covers and be out so she was somewhat groggy. Hearing Elisabeth's effervescent invitation brought her out of her sleepy reverie, and she responded gleefully with, "Count me in! I know just what I am wearing. What about you?"

"I have this really cute, ankle length, short sleeve, round neck dress with a swirly pattern of yellow, turquoise, orange, black and cream. I have a sweet pair of flat sandals with a one-inch heel which will go perfectly, the toe and ankle strap have copper insets."

Wide awake now, Jessica sat cross-legged on the bed and shared her outfit; a knee length, red Rachel Parcell ruffle front tie dress with flouncy sleeves with a pair of taupe, one-inch open toe sandals.

They chatted briefly about nothing, both realizing the phone line was not encrypted, then ended the call, excited for a girls' night out.

The next day was exceptionally exciting for Penelope and Rebecca as they dressed California casual in light weight tan slacks and flat rainbow strapped sandals. Rebecca wore a short sleeve, blue and cream print peasant top that tied at the neck. Penelope chose an olive flowery print boho-inspired blouse with pin tucks and billowy sleeves.

Not wanting to wear blazers, they chose Seecamp, .25 caliber pistols in holsters across their stomachs concealed by their puffy blouses.

When the non-descript fifteen-passenger bus pulled into the school drop-off loop at seven-thirty, the girls exited the vehicle to see Rebecca and Penelope leaning against their SUV, one leg up behind, resting on the bumper, arms crossed in front.

Dropping their newly acquired fashionable backpacks, all sixteen teenagers rushed over to greet their benefactors with hugs and wonderment that they were there.

The arrival of a large group of teenage girls brought a swarm of interest from both genders. Some of their female friends came up to say hello, while others, undoubtedly the campus queens, stood back from the crowd with their arms folded, expressing their distain with sneers.

Pen elbowed Rebecca gently and nodded to the snobs saying, “High school hasn’t changed a bit has it, Rebecca?”

Rebecca looked in the direction of the girls attempting to outcast the new arrivals and replied, “Geez, one would think our gender had made some advances in social interaction, but it would appear social media has set us back decades.”

As the entourage headed to the front doors, a group of boys dressed for their appearance on the cover of GQ magazine, approached speaking loudly, “Well, if it isn’t the group of misfit, drop-out street sluts. What, you gave up on homelessness and being whores?” said the tallest.

Several of the other male teens bellowed equally disdainful epithets as they attempted to surround the girls milling about Rebecca and Penelope’s SUV.

Rebecca hesitated to get involved in solving what might be an ongoing problem with the girls fitting in, but her sense of morality was in overload as she eyed Penelope to gauge her reaction.

In the brief moment the women exchanged looks, another male teen stepped between the jeering crowd and in front of the loudest confronting him with, “Watch your mouth, Reeves.”

Reeves responded as do all bullies by shrugging his shoulders, balling his fists and stepping toward Dominic Laina, a six-foot junior with a reputation as a scholar and outstanding basketball player. “And what are you going to do about it Laina, if I don't stop calling these street whores what they are?"

"For a guy who has such nice parents, I can't believe you are this crude Reeves. Look around and see all the phones recording. Maybe you will be the homeless teen once your folks see this on the evening news."

That was too much for Reeves to channel intellectually. He moved on his left foot, brought his right arm back cocking it to punch Laina when suddenly, his opponent stepped to his left and executed a powerful front kick to Reeves' groin, dropping the attacker to his knees.

Laina unaffected by the encounter, took one more step with his left foot and drove his right palm into Reeve's nose, breaking it instantly.

Reeves fell over sideways as blood gushed onto his Persian Gol o Bolbol Print Shirt, while smartphones continued to record.

The crowd had expanded considerably in the short time it took for the physical altercation to run its course, everyone chanting, "Fight, fight, fight". Several of the jeering boys looked up from Reeves and started to move against Laina but were halted in their quest for revenge by sixteen determined girls stepping in front of Laina and walking slowly toward the now shocked students.

None of the girls spoke, but their facial expressions screamed their intent to take the boys down quickly with skills they learned surviving on the streets.

As the boys quickened their steps to leave, one found the need to have the last word. He turned to yell a final insult but found his forward motion stopped abruptly…his head jerked backward by Vanessa Henderson's firm grip on his hair. His eyes went wild as he attempted to free himself and relieve the pain. As his hands moved to grab Henderson, she twisted his head and jerked it backwards so he was thrown on his side. Henderson bent down and said, "Is there something you wanted to say prick?"

Last Word kid was speechless and embarrassed. Tears welled in his eyes as Henderson bent close to his ear and said, "Remember this asshole, because any more comments from you and I will put you in the fuckin' hospital."

The crowd thinned quickly as students headed for the front door, followed by the newest members of the student body and their first friend, Dominic Laina.

Reeves struggled to rise, receiving help from the few of his group remaining with Penelope and Rebecca watching from beside their SUV.

One of his friends offered encouragement with, "You can sue them Reeves. Get your dad to sue them. They can't get away with this."

"Fuckin' right I am going to sue those bitches, the school and that shit Laina. He will regret hitting me."

Penelope felt compelled. Casually walking the few steps to stand beside Reeves, speaking loudly so his friends could hear, she said, "Reeves, I suggest you chalk this up to a life experience. Maybe you learned something today. Maybe not. But either way, if you sue, or cause any difficulty for your fellow students, I personally will see to it that the video of your vulgarity will be on every California news channel which will block all roads to an Ivy League school and any hopes of ever being hired by a prestigious firm."

Rebecca was enjoying herself immensely, watching Penelope back the disgusting, privileged teen into a corner. Wanting to be part of the scene, she walked over to the group, pulled out her identification and flashed the Secret Service logo adding, "And I will be witness number two."

"Take the day off, get cleaned up and return tomorrow having learned to keep your mouth shut and your bigoted opinions to yourself."

Reeves' anger had not dissipated but it was evident he had heard them. It was expected that his friends would remind him that his future would be ruined if he didn't drop the issue immediately.

Rebecca and Penelope had planned on entering the school and mingling with the girls at their lockers before they headed to class, but considering recent events, they knew their presence would be superfluous.

The girls had a full lunch program paid for the school year and would be the topic of discussion in the cafeteria for days to come.

Rebecca and Pen made plans to have dinner with the girls the next night and hear what, if any, were the repercussions of the morning's occurrence.

"I'd like to know what prompted Vanessa's actions against the kid who tried to have the last word. That was a particularly vicious, albeit a well-executed tactic for a teenager. Maybe she will share voluntarily. Tomorrow night will be interesting, to say the least," offered Rebecca.

"No doubt. And I want to know who the kid with the swift foot and fist is," as she looped her arm through her partners and headed back to the SUV and to the office to sort out the day's assignments.

Chapter TWENTY-EIGHT

Jason and Jackson met Alane separately to discuss their individual federal retirement packages and set up an investment program which would divert monthly sums while leaving them a substantial cash flow.

As much as they enjoyed the company of each other, they knew it was time for separate accommodations and they requested Alane's assistance.

Neither agent owned a vehicle, or much of anything for that matter and would need considerable help in starting a residence. Jason suggested there might be vacancies in the complex next to *Marc Stucki's* within walking distance to the "J" Team Investigation's office.

Alane made a few phone calls and found two separate units, in the preferred location, which had been rented to professors both of whom moved back east to take similar positions with more of an interesting environment, apparently having become bored with Southern California's continuous sunshine.

Although there was a waiting list, Alane successfully argued in Jackson and Jason's favor and arranged for a deposit and the first month's rent to be transferred from each agent's account.

The agents were astounded with Alane's extensive influence. When retirement and housing arrangements were complete, he offered to connect them with his interior designer to work on their apartments. They accepted his offer, but it was the stipulation which brought laughter to Alane; Rebecca and Penelope were in charge.

Personal business completed, they thanked Alane profusely, then walked around the side of the building to join

Rebecca and Penelope in their office to tackle the growing business.

Jessica swung by the police station first thing in the morning to give the glasses to Detective Pelfini and ended up chatting over coffee in Elise's office. There were documents to sign attesting to the chain of evidence, then to log into Gutierrez's investigation database.

Jessica relayed the message regarding dinner for which Elise was more than ready to participate, she too having put in far more work hours without a break than was healthy.

Pelfini hadn't a clue of what to wear and had no desire to discuss the case, so they chatted about the availability of men in Santa Barbara, coming to the conclusion, there were none. Jessica high-fived her colleague and headed to Alane's to arrange her retirement portfolio, then to the office.

Rebecca and Penelope had just gotten into the swing of organizing their ongoing investigations and assigned several to each of the investigators when Rebecca's phone rang.

The high school principal.

She demanded Rebecca return to the school and, "explain the abhorrent behavior of her teenage wards, who appear to have been involved in a physical altercation."

Then she hung up.

"What a rude bitch?"

"Who was that?"

"The principal who apparently has a pickle up her ass about this morning. Let me go and talk to her while you get things rolling here. Fuck, this pisses me off."

Penelope stifled her mirth with a hand over her mouth. Momentarily regaining control, she offered, "How about I go and deal with this. We don't want the girls suspended the first day because you kicked the shit out of the principal." Not able to contain herself, she lost it, laughing at her own humor.

Rebecca stared at her partner, shook her head with a smile and said, "No kidding. Okay. You go. You are undoubtedly right. She reminds me of the asshole who kicked me out of junior high after I knocked the prick…grabbed my butt and the little shit had no punishment."

"I figured that was the driving force and I promise to solve the problem with sweet reason," replied Pen, laughing again at her own humor as she kissed Rebecca, then headed out the door.

"Every day we have opportunities to get angry but what you are doing is giving someone power over you. You can choose not to let little things upset you."

Joel Osteen

Penelope hadn't met the principal and had no idea what to expect. She did understand the school would undoubtedly have a *no tolerance* policy toward violence but how that policy manifested itself against the girls she would soon discover. They weren't involved…well except Vanessa.

Thinking of the teenager in her charge, she smiled, feeling good that the youngster had found the courage to speak up for herself, albeit a little on the rough side. But then again, boys and men like Reeves were too primed to objectify women to see them in any other light other than someone to control and dominate. Violence being the only means with which women and girls can stop the abuse.

My girls, she thought with a smile.

As she drove the short distance to the school, she decided to speak up for the unknown factor, the teenage boy who dropped Reeves. *I like this kid already*, she thought, as she pulled into the school's parking lot.

Exiting the SUV and locking it, she glanced around to see numerous students gathered in groups. Looking at her watch, she wondered why they were not in class at 9:30 am.

Walking quickly up the sidewalk and through weathered, wood doors with two small wire meshed windows, she was met by an unarmed security guard and a metal detector.

Stopping abruptly, she smiled at the grey- haired gentleman wearing a rumpled light blue shirt with 'security guard' patches on both sleeves and his name, Ralph, across the shirt pocket. His dark blue pants were baggy and too long, billowing over his black Hush Puppy shoes.

Feeling sorry for him, knowing he would be abused by students like Reeves, she smiled, turning on her charm as she reached into her back pocket for her identification.

"Good morning, Ralph. It is a gorgeous day out. I hope your day has begun cheerfully. I'm Dr. Penelope Barker. Ms. Hancock is expecting me," as she handed him her investigator's license and carry permit.

Standing right beside him, she anticipated his concern about her firearm and gently touched his right arm offering, "Ralph, if my being armed is a concern, I have no problem with you calling Chief Rodriguez who will happily verify my qualifications."

Ralph's face started to turn red. He gulped a couple of times, weighing the warm interpersonal experience he was enjoying against his responsibilities. There was a clear school district policy regarding the approval of armed law enforcement personnel and he quickly determined that the alluring woman beside him clearly fell into that category.

"That won't be necessary Dr. Barker. Please step around the machine," he offered, moving out of the way, allowing Penelope to pass. He continued, "Ms. Hancock is straight down the hall ahead and the first office on your right."

"Thank you, Ralph. I appreciate the courtesy," she replied, touching his arm one more time as she maneuvered around him, walked a few steps, turned back to him with a little wave.

Men. I feel bad about manipulating him. I've never had to or wanted to do that before. I suspect Rebecca used that ploy frequently in dealing with suspects, she thought, as she shook off her guilt and approached the office.

Entering the educational management portal, the décor was like a million other schools with a long five-foot counter, behind which were several female staffers were busy working computers.

The walls were a pale, aging green with posters attached haphazardly on every wall. Some advertising behavioral modification slogans and others reminding students that bullying was unacceptable. None warned of a zero-tolerance policy for violence.

Penelope walked up to the counter and had to clear her throat to be acknowledged. Momentarily, one of the keyboarders spoke from her desk. Pen figured she was advised by an efficiency expert to save steps.

"May I help you?"

"Yes, you may. I am Dr. Barker for Ms. Hancock."

"Certainly Ms. Barker. I will tell the principal you are here," she replied, picking up her phone and punching several numbers.

Penelope ignored the 'Ms.'

The staffer had hardly returned to her keyboarding when an office door opened and a woman stepped into the main office and walked aggressively toward Pen.

Ms. Amaryllis Hancock appeared to be in her mid to late forties, with severely bleached blonde, shoulder length hair. Attired in a dark blue suit with a white, button-down Oxford blouse and black patent leather, one inch singback heels, Penelope pegged her for a private girls' school administrator, not a public facility.

All business.

Her projected persona was not that of a teacher, more of a disciplinarian, fulfilling the archaic belief that teenagers needed obdurate discipline rather than understanding and guidance.

Penelope reached out with her hand just as Ms. Hancock turned and headed back to her office. The gesture?

Her command to follow.

Just as she crossed the threshold of the school's inner sanctum, she spotted the male teenager from this morning as he entered the main office and sat in a hardback chair facing the principal's office.

Hancock traversed a couch and table lamp to settle behind her eight-foot dark cherrywood desk with Victorian scrolling highlighting the perimeter.

Pen quickly scrutinized the office décor.

A stark contrast to the outer office, this was old private school interior with dark paneled walls, one of which housed a floor to ceiling, end to end bookcase resplendent in leather bound books of unknown genre. This couldn't have been created and paid for by the school district. She wondered why an employee would go to such expense to create an atmosphere so different from the environment she managed.

As Hancock sat, she waved a sweeping arm, gesturing for Penelope to sit.

Pen did.

She crossed her legs and clasped her hands on her lap and looked at Hancock, signaling she was ready.

"Ms. Barker," she began, but before she could continue, Pen interrupted.

"It is Dr. Barker. Please."

"Well. Yes. Fine. Dr. Barker," she adjusted herself in her black, high back chair and continued, "the reason I asked you to meet is regarding your sixteen charges' behavior this morning outside the school.

"I must say I was taken aback by their boorish actions on their first day back to school."

Pen leaned forward in the chair and raised her voice an octave above Hancock's, "Let me stop you right there Ms. Hancock so I can save us time and embarrassment for you and the school.

"My 'charges', as you've labeled them, were not the problem. My partner, retired Secret Service Agent, and I were there during the so-called altercation instigated by your unbridled and undisciplined male students.

"The filth spewing from their mouths was disgusting and disgraceful. A terrible display of the loose morality allowed to pervade this school.

"I sent you a video from this morning which you may peruse at your leisure. The words they used are so vile, I will not repeat them.

"Clean your own house, Ms. Hancock before you strike out at a group of fine young ladies who were forced into homelessness. They are back and they are going to flourish here at school and in life. Cleaning your own house can start with attendance. As I entered the school, I passed several boys congregating on the lawn smoking. Oblivious of the rules.

"There will be no disciplinary action against the girls, nor will there be any against Mr. Laina sitting in the outer office. He had the decency and courage to stand for what is right and stop the spewing of filth.

"If you choose to proceed with actions against either the girls or Mr. Laina, I will personally deliver the video to not only the local media but print and visual outlets in Santa Barbara and LA Country and the state of California school administrator disciplinary committee.

Penelope reeled in her aggression with, "I am a principal of the "J" Team Investigations along with Special Agent Simpson and two of our male colleagues, now retired. We hope you will come to see the girls for the lovely human beings they are and join us for dinner one evening at *Refugio Seguro.*"

Ignoring Hancock's astonished expression, she removed a business card from her slim identification case, slipped it on the desk, turned and left.

As she was leaving, once outside Hancock's office, she bent down next to Laina and spoke softly, "Mr. Laina, do you remember me from this morning?"

"Yes, ma'am, I do."

"Good. I just spoke with Ms. Hancock. There will be no disciplinary action against you now or in the future. I understand you are a successful student and athlete. I wish you all the success in both activities. Head back to class. You are done here."

"Really ma'am? I'm not going to be suspended? I can just get up and leave? Just like that?" He glanced around Pen to see if the office staff were watching.

They weren't.

"Yes. That is exactly what I am saying. But before you leave, I have one question. Where did you learn to fight like that?"

"My mom," he replied with a broad smile. "I guess it really works, huh?"

Laina got up off the bench, turned and almost skipped out of the office, wondering what just happened.

Penelope followed him out and headed back down the hallway to pass Ralph, making sure she thanked him profusely with a little arm touch.

Chapter TWENTY-NINE

The Blue Whale was awash in recessed exterior lighting, focusing on the arched entry to a private patio hidden by six-foot shrubs. The stone walkway leading from the street to the entry was lined with black scallop ajuga, luna red hibiscus and Sarah Bernhardt peonies set in weathered grey halved wine barrels.

Slightly behind the barrels, spaced four feet apart, were eight-foot-tall gas lights with brass shades.

The exterior replicated the barrels with burgundy trim and the front wall was floor to ceiling glass.

The interior held seating for eighty at polished pine tables with wrought iron legs and trim with the end to end bar identical in design. The chairs extended the iron design with weathered grey cushions.

Another patio projected out the back, repeating the wrought iron designed tables but with thick smoky plastic tops. Covering the patio was a pseudo gazebo with six by six by twelve posts carved to represent vines rising to support a smoky glass ceiling interspersed with twisted vines.

The Whale offered valet parking where staff welcomed diners in black slacks, button-down, long sleeve white shirts and grey vests matching the barrel colors. The guest's vehicles were then transported to a parking area guarded by a local security firm.

Rebecca and Penelope were the first to arrive, Pen dressed in a stunning white chiffon, short sleeve, calf length summer dress. It featured Alençon lace a front scoop neck and square back. She paired the outfit with mesh, one-inch heel taupe sandals. Rebecca wore a short sleeve maxi dress in a fall pattern of leaves, shells and hibiscus over a cream background.

Her open toe sandals with a one-inch heel and wrap around ankle strap were in a muted yellow which matched the leaves on her dress.

Both guests wore their Seecamp .25 around their middle with the dress pattern slightly altered to hide two snaps for quick access.

As Penelope handed the keys to the valet, Elise drove up behind them with Jessica waiting in the right-hand lane behind Elise, blinker flashing, waving at the others.

Elise slid out of her vehicle wearing an ankle length, strapless, red jump suit with white, turquoise, black, green and yellow wiggly vertical strips over an off-white background. As she rounded the car and handed the keys to the valet, she pulled up her pant leg to reveal a pair of Sam Edelman black pumps with a three-inch heel and singback strap.

Elise hugged Rebecca and Penelope just as Jessica slid out of her car in a red Rachel Parcell ruffle front tie dress and one-inch heel taupe open toe sandals with a wide ankle strap.

After greeting each other, Pen looked at her watch and glanced down the street wondering where Elisabeth could be, when Elise tapped her on the shoulder and pointed to the front entrance.

Elisabeth was leaning against one of the gas lampposts looking stunning in a short sleeve maxi-dress with a swirly pattern of yellow, turquoise, orange, black and cream. She had her arms spread as though to say, *what took you so long*?

Her friends, aka, colleagues, approached, shaking their heads, gave her a hug, then the entourage headed into the *Whale*.

They passed several diners who had chosen to sit in the front patio with the privacy bushes, but the night was slightly chilly by Santa Barbara standards, sixty-five, so the group was seated at an oblong table in a back corner, facing outward.

The maître d was about to offer them a wine list when Elisabeth interrupted with, “Excuse me, but rather than the list, might we have start with a bottle of Stone Winery’s Pinot Noir please?

“Certainly ma’am. I will have our sommelier here tout de suite.”

Before the maître d could depart, Penelope said, “Monsieur, est-ce que je détecte un accent québécois? (Sir, do I detect a Quebec accent?)”

The maître d replied, “Oh, madame, vous parlez ma langue. Délicieux. Je suis originaire de Gaspé, mais j'ai fréquenté une école de cuisine à Montréal. Je suis tombé amoureux de Santa Barbara et du roulement de tambour, je suis là.” (Oh, ma'am, you speak my language. Delicious. I come from Gaspé, but I went to a cooking school in Montreal. I fell in love with Santa Barbara and drum roll, I'm here.)

Pen replied, “Eh bien, monsieur, c'est un plaisir de vous rencontrer et de profiter de la générosité de votre beau restaurant. Je vous remercie.” (Well sir, it's a pleasure to meet you and enjoy the generosity of your beautiful restaurant. Thank you.)

“Mon plaisir madame,” he replied as he turned and made his way to the bar.

All eyes were on Penelope, so she responded with, “What?”

Rebecca interceded with, “Penelope speaks fluent French and times like this or when she is with Alane, are the only opportunities my love has a chance to parle français,” standing and offering a sweeping hand to Pen.

Penelope responded by standing, taking a little curtsy and offered a brief translation of her interaction with the maître d.

Penelope had just taken her seat when Francine, their sommelier, arrived with a bottle of the pinot noir on a tray with five long stem wine glasses. She welcomed her guests, introduced herself pronouncing her name with less of a French accent than her colleague, but still recognizable. She mentioned that there was another bottle waiting for them, courtesy of the manager, and would be brought over shortly.

Elisabeth, having ordered the wine, was asked to taste it. After Francine poured a small amount, Elisabeth held the glass to the light, swirled the wine several times, then placed the glass under her nose to experience the aroma. Satisfied, she took a sip, aerated the liquid with her lips, swirled the wine in her mouth, swallowed, then nodded her approval.

While Francine poured for the others, she commented, "Mademoiselle, je comprends que vous parlez français. Je viens de Montréal. Puis-je vous demander où vous avez appris notre langue?" (Miss, I understand that you speak French. I come from Montreal. May I ask, where did you learn our language?)

Penelope looked at the group wondering if she was overdoing her socializing in French. Receiving smiles and nods of approval, she replied, "Lorsque j'étudiais en médecine vétérinaire, j'ai eu l'occasion de terminer un semestre à la Faculté de médecine vétérinaire de l'Université de Montréal à Montréal. Une belle ville qui a conservé son charme du vieux monde. Je l'ai aimé là-bas." (When I was studying veterinary medicine, I had the opportunity to take a year at the Faculty of Veterinary Medicine at the Université de Montréal in

Montreal. A beautiful city that has retained its old-world charm. I loved it there.)

"Très bien. Je suis heureux que vous ayez apprécié votre scolarité et notre langue," (Very well. I'm glad you enjoyed your schooling and our language,) as she poured the last glass, turned and departed.

"Okay Ms. Linguist, what was that all about?" asked Elisabeth.

"She asked me where I learned my French and I replied that I completed a year at the University of Montreal's School of Veterinary Medicine. That's all. Enough French. Thank you for indulging me.

"How about a toast to us and "J" Team Investigations?"

"Here, here," responded the others in sync, raising their glasses and clinking.

Jessica opened the conversation with, "Rebecca and Penelope, tell us more about *Refugio Seguro* and how the girls are doing with their new home and returning to school?"

Penelope and Rebecca, now guardians to sixteen teen age girls, shared the last few weeks with the group, at times going into pantomime to share the girls' antics. Everyone knew of the attempted robbery and the outcome but were surprised that the teens were not critical of Rebecca and Penelope's actions.

The duo explained that the girls didn't have a strong female role model and they seemed delighted to be thrown, almost literally, into having two.

They chatted extensively about *Refugio Seguro,* the renovations, staff, the bus acquisition, Jackson and Jason's whereabouts and lastly, the incident at the high school.

Penelope was hilarious in her rendition of the interaction with Ms. Hancock, so much so, that other diners stopped eating to watch her in the aisle performing. Her friends were laughing unabashedly, which became infectious causing the staff to stop and engage in Pen's mirth.

Their jocularity ceased when Julian, their server, approached with menus. Introducing himself, the twenty-something, five-foot ten, one-seventy university student had apparently dealt with a table of celebrating women before and accepted their flirtatious overtones gracefully.

Julian explained the evening specials, refilled each glass with pinot from a second bottle, mentioned that he would return momentarily to take their order, bowed and departed.

After a brief debate, the officers decided to order a variety of dishes and share. They started with a garden salad; a variety of lettuces from local gardens with smoked blue cheese chunks, crisp lean bacon, radishes, dill and ginger. To accompany the greens, they chose the *Blue Whale's* Charcuterie (pronounced shaar·koo·tr·ee) consisting of Quebec brie, Wisconsin cheddar, Alabama goat cheese, succulent local berries and dates.

For their entrée, they decided on a Dungeness crab risotto with seared summer squash puree, spicy pancetta, Italian basil and topped with local cherry tomato halves.

Their second choice was an iron skillet roasted sea bass, or Branzino, with lime and ginger, roasted baby red potatoes and Brussels sprouts roasted in olive oil and garlic.

Their last entrée was deep sea scallops with cilantro, savory and marjoram and a Calabrian chile gastrique of vinegar and sugar infused with chilis.

Julian noticed they had placed their menus on the table and responded quickly to take their order. After submitting their requests to the kitchen, he returned with a third bottle of pinot, poured with one hand behind his back as Jessica surmised he was performing for them, then left abruptly, feeling somewhat uneasy with all five pairs of eyes examining and scanning his body.

While they were waiting for their meal, Elise shared that the National Crime Information Center had yet to respond regarding the fingerprints on the drinking glasses. Concerned that if the FBI was investigating their subject, any file may be classified and their enquiry would alert the federal agency to their investigation.

Elisabeth responded in a whisper and a smirk, "Pulease, there isn't an FBI data bank I can't get into. If you receive that or any other restricted information, text me on my personal phone with '*yes*' and I will get the info inside of an hour. No, make that thirty minutes," as she waved her right arm in a semi-circle indicating she had control.

The conversation hovered around various upcoming concerts in which each were interested, and which Hollywood bimbo was sleeping with which gym rat. All shared with high intensity laughter fueled by the pinot.

Their dinner arrived shortly with Julian spacing the numerous dishes evenly along the oblong table. Accompanying him was Francine with another bottle of pinot, "Courtesy of the maître d" as she stepped around Julian and poured for each of her guests.

All conversation ceased as the women plated from each of the dishes, some passing their plates for others to fill.

Twenty minutes and the platters were empty, even the garnish was eaten. Julian and the busser must have been hovering in the shadows because they seemed to arrive as soon as the last fork was set down.

Once the busser had removed the last of the dishes, Julian offered, "Ladies, might I suggest a digestif such as Ramazzotti Amaro Felsina? This delightful Italian bitters boasts rhubarb, cinnamon, oregano, sweet oranges from Sicily and bitter orange from Curaçao which dates back to 1815 in Milano, Italy."

Elisabeth, who seemed to be the alcohol chairperson, received nods from her friends and replied, "That would be perfect Julian. Thank you."

The university student was so confident in his suggestion, Francine appeared from behind him with a full bottle and five sniffers. As she finished pouring the last glass, Elisabeth asked her for two additional sniffers.

While Julian left to fetch the glassware, Francine chatted briefly with Penelope regarding the ladies' plans for the evening. Suddenly they were interrupted.

"Excuse us, ladies, but we couldn't help notice that you are enjoying the same drink that we are" pointing to a man standing beside him, "and we are wondering if you would join us on the patio to help us polish off ours. It seems a liter of Ramazzotti is a bit much for two.

Before the women could respond, his partner continued, "I am Jacques Ballentine," patting his suit jacket, "and my friend is Jerome Swanson," he offered with a slight French accent. "We couldn't help overhearing your discussion in French, my language of birth in Caen, France. It would be lovely if you could spare us a few moments of chat."

All five agents had turned at the first sound of a male intruding into their enjoyable evening, all expecting a couple of low lifers. They were so taken aback by what stood before them, they were momentarily speechless.

Penelope broke the awkward silence with, "Alors, messieurs, que pouvons-nous faire pour vous?" (So, gentlemen, what can we do for you?)

"Mademoiselle, quel plaisir d'entendre notre langue. Je suis ravi de le parler. Puis-je avoir l'audace de demander votre héritage?" (Miss, what a delight to hear our language. I am thrilled to speak it. May I be so bold as to ask your heritage?)

""Arrête-toi avec les jolies joues de la ligne de hussle. Je suis gay." ("Stop with the cute hustle sweet cheeks. I'm gay.")

Jacques was so taken aback by her bold rejection, he burst out laughing with his friend turning with a questioning facial expression as though to say, *What*?

The uninvited guests appeared to be in their mid to late thirties, one short dark hair, clean shaven with a blue pin-stripe business suit, pale blue button-down shirt and black ankle boots. Maybe one hundred and eighty pounds. Five-ten or so.

His partner was dressed similarly, except his choice was a chocolate brown herringbone suit with a brown and white-striped shirt open at the neck and two-tone brown wing-tips. He was slightly taller, possibly close to six feet and about the same weight with slightly longer blond hair worn in a messy casual manner reflecting the seventy-five-dollar style.

Every woman present had dealt with men hitting on them, usually inebriated creeps.

This was new.

So was the line. Wanting to speak French.

Sure.

The women looked at each other while the men stood there thinking maybe they should just leave after Penelope's embarrassing comment. They were preparing for rejection but hoping for acceptance.

Momentarily, Julian returned with the two glasses and Elisabeth rose, accepted the bottle from Francine, poured a half-inch in each sniffer and handed them to Francine and Julian.

Elisabeth turned to the two men standing like schoolboys waiting to enter the principal's office and said, "Hang a moment, gentlemen."

She turned to their servers as Jessica rose and offered a toast to the *Whale*, their delicious dinner and remarkable servers.

Francine and Julian took the accolades in stride, toasted with their guests, expressed their appreciation for the group patronizing the *Blue Whale*, turned and departed.

Jessica turned to the men and said, "Sit".

Rebecca caught Julian's attention, pointed to the men and the server understood. He retrieved the other bottle of Ramazzotti while colleagues brought over two additional chairs.

The men introduced themselves again to each of the women, shook hands and sat, Jacques at one end and Jerome at the other.

Penelope opened the conversation with, "So, what do you gentlemen do for a living?" as she reached over and kissed Rebecca's cheek which brought a smile from her friends and, to their amazement, a warmth from the men they had not anticipated. Rebecca turned, touched Penelope's shoulder, guiding her forward, kissing her on the lips, then looked straight at one of the men.

Julian was pouring the remainder of the men's Ramazzotti and as he passed Jerome, the latter answered, "We are accountants with the Anthony Henderson Agency here in Santa Barbara."

Fortunately, the men didn't notice the five women stifling their shock, all controlling their eyebrows not to rise, their mouths not to open and their eyes to not widen.

"It might be possible for things to work out sometimes. When you least expect it, life surprises you."

Susane Colasanti

Chapter THIRTY

Brian had become so complacent over the months of delivering cocaine that he figured he may as well be delivering milk for all the excitement he was experiencing. He had taken the temporary job, which quickly became permanent, for the adrenaline rush. He certainly didn't need the money.

It was late in the evening as he watched the last few minutes as Barcelona maintain a two-point lead against Liverpool FC in World Football.

As was his custom, he finished the evening with a round of drinks for him and his friends then headed home. Weaving in and out of the tables he managed to open the massive wood door and stumble down the street to his house, unaware of the two men watching in the shadows.

The Edmonton investigators followed at a considerable distance already knowing the location of Brian's house. Responding to him entering the front door, they detoured to the beach and approached the house in the dark, stopping several meters from the cascading light through the living room windows.

Fifteen minutes later, all the inside lights were extinguished.

The village being an hour ahead, and Brian no doubted passed out, they chose to wait until the morning to speak with him.

Confident he wouldn't leave during their brief absence, they walked to a small B&B they passed when tailing Sawyer.

They were the only guests and check-in was quick since they paid cash in Canadian currency. Dressed in Ripzone blue and yellow boardshorts, with one wearing a black T and the other yellow and both in baseball caps promoting the

Edmonton Eskimos and Oilers, they easily passed for Canadians spending a few days at Puerto Viejo de Talamanca surfing.

They took two separate rooms with single beds, dumped their backpacks on the floor, set their smartphones for an early wake-up and went to bed.

Inspector Wood had no idea when the massive shipment was to arrive and considering the mode of transportation, he was at a loss as how to proceed. He had received directions from Ottawa that the Force was not to arrest the crew or prevent the vessel from leaving, but to shadow the drug's transportation, keeping in touch with the Edmonton detectives.

He was further advised to use civilian vehicles and plain clothed officers, leap-frogging their surveillance.

This he knew.

Training and common sense to a Mountie.

What he needed help with was monitoring the canal and Barkley Sound. The deep-water channel and port made it impossible to know a particular landing site.

He texted Angie Taylor, the marina manager with whom he had touched base with previously about needing a meeting. He asked her to pick him up at the Harbour Quay. He would bring the coffee and donuts.

She replied immediately, agreeing to meet her friend, unaware that he was going to ask her to become involved in possibly the most dangerous activity of her life.

Within an hour Wood, dressed in jeans, pale blue Carhartt chambray shirt, black squall jacket, well-worn hiking boots and an Edmonton Oilers baseball cap, had stopped by the local coffee shop for two large coffees, two creams, no sugar and headed for the marina.

As he pulled into the parking lot in his personal SUV, he spotted Angie waiting for him in a 380 Super Sport Crossover boat. As Wood walked across the parking lot and down the gangway, he admired her choice in water rides. The vessel was an impressive thirty-eight foot, with a full-width cockpit, slept four, with two, two hundred horsepower Mercury outboard engines.

As he approached the sleek craft, Angie appeared from the cabin, waved and welcomed him aboard. The marina manager looked professional in jeans, blue golf shirt with the marina logo on the left front and Merrell Moab granite hiking boots.

Although Taylor's boat was an eye stopper, it had long ceased to attract local attention since she was out and about on the canal and sound frequently. Any bystander observing Wood approaching the boat wouldn't pay any attention to a man boarding with coffees.

Once aboard, Taylor invited him into the cabin while she removed the bow and stern dock lines, pushed away and then returned to the cabin.

Within minutes they were motoring at minimum speed out of the marina. Once clear, Angie opened-up the four-hundred horses and sped down the canal, her curiosity gaining momentum the longer Wood sat drinking his coffee, admiring the scenery…remaining silent.

Taylor continued down the canal for thirty minutes before pulling into a shallow inlet near Nahmint, home to some of the world's largest Douglas fir trees at 4.5 meters in diameter, an area hotly contested by international conservation groups opposing the British Columbia government.

Maneuvering out of the main channel and hidden from the curious, Angie dropped anchor, sat back in the captain's chair, put her feet on the dash, removed the lid from her coffee and waited for Wood to share what prompted this covert excursion.

Inspector Lorne Wood had been rethinking his decision to seek Taylor's assistance during the trip down the canal while she was busy navigating the double 200 Mercuries. His immediate supervisor was in Surrey at the provincial headquarters but his orders for this operation came from the commissioner herself, via the Edmonton deputy commissioner. If this operation failed due to his involving Angie, his career could be over. He didn't have approval and yet his experience told him asking permission was out of the question.

Musing his options, Wood thought about Rear Admiral Grace Hooper Ph.D. Mathematician, U.S. Navy and her philosophy of *better to ask for forgiveness than permission.*

There were no additional Mounties available to patrol the canal and if there were, its massive length with connecting coves and inlets made it an impossible task.

He was not authorized to proceed with Taylor.

But he did, taking Hooper's advice.

"Angie, I need your help and what I am about to ask you is RCMP confidential."

Taylor didn't flinch. Her facial expression remained unchanged.

She took a sip of her double cream coffee and waited.

"We are involved in an international drug interdiction with the Secret Service, LAPD and the Canadian Navy. I won't bore you with a lot of details. The main point is we expect a Colombian submarine to enter the Barkley Sound any day. It is carrying upwards of four hundred million in cocaine destined for Canadian consumers."

Angie was intrigued. She had assisted in other RCMP operations in the past, primarily spotting dealers selling at the marina and one case of a large boat being used as a brothel.

But this was different. Wood's words got her adrenaline going as she removed her feet from the dash and leaned forward, listening intently.

Wood needed to tell her as much as he could without violating his secrecy clearance so he skipped how the navy was able to track the submarine and said, "The navy has been following the submarine from Colombia and notes it has just passed Neah Bay on Washington's coast. The navy will keep me informed of its progress but as it passes the tip of the Pacific Rim National Park Reserve and enters the Sound by Bamfield, the navy destroyer will have to back off. This is where I need your help.

"We have no idea how long it will take for the sub to make its way from Bamfield to wherever it will dock. If it arrives at Bamfield during daylight, it will stay submerged there at the mouth and proceed to arrive in Port, probably around midnight.

We presume the docking and unloading will be at night. But without forewarning, we will miss it. I don't have the personnel to set up a watch every night. We can't include your boss…possibility of a leak is too great.

"When I hear from the navy that the sub has passed Bamfield, I need you to be working nights observing. I will have several Members prepared to follow the truck out of town, ostensibly headed for the ferry where surveillance will be passed on to others." He didn't need to tell her that CSIS agents would meet the ferry and follow the truck to its distribution location.

Angie thought for a minute, sitting back in the captain's chair, one leg over the other sipping her coffee, then said, "This is doable Lorne. I often take the night shift for the guards if one of them is ill. I also go out at night and check the lighting and ensure the marina kiosks are secure and lighted. When you call, I can be on the docks in minutes and let you know which facility they are using.

"May I share my opinion?"

"Please do Angie. I am in the dark here."

"I suspect they will use the mill's deep-water port. There are no personnel in the storage yard adjacent to the dock due to a strike. I doubt the smugglers would know that, but you never know."

"That makes sense Angie. I will have our Members spread throughout town so they can start tailing once the truck hits Redford."

"When this is over the media will remain ignorant. No mention to your boss or anyone else. If our local dealers get wind of this, we could have a war on our hands with them wanting this shipment. I can't tell you much more without breaking my own security clearance. I am probably walking a fine line sharing what I already have."

"I'm good Lorne. This conversation never happened," she replied with a smile.

"Perfect. Thanks Angie. I sincerely appreciate the help. So, we're good. It could be any day and we will be ready."

With that, Taylor raised the anchor, turned over the two Mercury engines, slowly exited the cove and opened the throttle wide heading back to Port, thrilled to be part of something this big, although not being able to share it was a bit of a bummer.

Chapter THIRTY-ONE

Marianna arrived home late after an exhausting day dealing with several irate clients dissatisfied with their sentencing hearing. She never understood her clientele, the majority had so much overwhelming evidence against them, it took all her skill to obtain a minimum sentence. *Then the bastards wanted to renegotiate her fee. Maybe it was time for me to retire*, she thought as she kicked off her heels at the door and hung her handbag and coat on the coat rack.

She moved slowly into the living room to the wine table tucked into the corner by the fireplace. Pouring a glass of Martini and Rossi Vermouth, she plunked herself down in the flowered chintz, ten-foot couch, activated the fireplace, put her feet on the coffee table, took a long sip, closed her eyes and savored the delicacy of M&R and the taste of tobacco, espresso and nutmeg.

She laid on the couch sipping her vermouth and reviewing her frustrating day. She finally pulled herself up, refilling her glass, put last night's leftover rigatoni with vodka sauce in the microwave and slogged up the stairs to check her encrypted messages and change.

She sat down in front of her computer, activated all systems, then sat back, sipped her vermouth, waiting the few seconds for the encryptions to be processed from Santiago Antunez.

The screen came to life with the message Marianna had dreaded. She sat her drink on the desk and leaned forward to read the screen. Although she was somewhat prepared, she wasn't, as the ramifications of what she read hit home. "Mother fucker. Son-of-a-bitch, these guys are screwing me royally," she screamed, slamming her fist down, almost knocking her drink over.

She pushed herself away from the desk and paced back and forth in front of it, turning occasionally to glance at the sun giving one last hug to the Pacific before dropping out of sight.

She slowed her pace, took several deep breaths, sighed, picked up her M&R, sipped and walked slowly into her bedroom, stripped, tossing her outfit on a corner accent chair, the pattern of which matched the chintz wall-to-wall drapes.

Slipping on a well-worn navy sweat suit with white arm and leg stripes, she picked up her drink and headed down to the kitchen. Removing her dinner from the microwave, she grabbed a fork, poured a glass of chilled chardonnay from the fridge, meandered into the living room while mulling over her options.

Sitting on the couch, enjoying her pasta and wine, she came to the conclusion that the news wasn't all that bad considering the magnitude of recent history.

Hermanos rejected her plea to regain the lost Los Angeles territory not wanting to go to war with the Mexican cartels, choosing instead to concentrate on the Western Canadian market. They paid the Colombians for the lost shipment and implied the responsibility for the bust was hers.

They indicated a payment had been made to the two Vancouver attorneys and accountant via the Caribbean account as an enticement. Loblinski was to pay Hermanos for the British Columbia delivery through the Caribbean account and he was responsible for collecting from his Vancouver dealers. He kept the balance.

Stan had a man in Port Alberni who would orchestrate the shipment's unloading and transportation via ferry to

Vancouver where Stan would meet the truck and supervise the distribution and currency collection.

So, that was that, she thought. Rather than concentrate on the lost revenue, she mentally prepared to prosper from the British Columbian profit.

As she finished her pasta and chardonnay, she pondered her earlier thought of retiring. She'd had an exciting and financially rewarding life and since she lost the Los Angeles sales and had zero interest in moving to Canada and freeze her butt off, maybe it was time to pull the plug and head to Vanuatu.

Hermanos de Wall Street had chosen these small islands off the coast of Australia decades previously as their safe haven from Canadian or American prosecution…no extradition treaty. With the tens of millions in the Caribbean to which she had ready access, even after paying her debt to Hermanos, leaving now might be a prudent decision.

Exiting with Hermanos' blessing would be mandatory and seeing the Canadian operation materialize profitably was the safest retirement plan.

Leaving the old me here in Santa Barbara will be cathartic, out with the old and in with the new, she thought. *Well not really. Out with the old and in with the old,* as she contemplated reviving her birth name. It didn't matter that Hermanos didn't know her other than Gutierrez. She would leave with that relationship intact. Having maintained her passport in her birth name and having it sent every ten years to a mailbox in a nearby strip mall she could leave without planning or notice…to anyone.

She regretted not having met Fukishura earlier, Jessica might have been able to convince Hermanos to fight for the LA territory.

Marianna felt at ease now that a decision had been made. She put her dishes in the dishwasher and headed to bed.

Prior to retiring she checked her communications one last time. The short three second burst from the Golden Girl off the Washington coast brought a smile as she sat at the desk and shared the information with Loblinski. His signal that delivery was eminent.

"Don't make money your goal. Instead pursue the things you love doing and then do them so well that people can't take their eyes off you."

Dr. Maya Angelou

Marianna disagreed with Dr. Angelou. She had made money her goal. Well, that and stumping prosecutors for decades. Now she would pursue the things she loved, relationships not being one of them.

Vanuatu had direct flights to Sydney, Australia and from there, the world.

Angie Taylor was having one of the busiest days of the year as she prepared for the community to receive the first of several scheduled cruise ships. Although the festivities would be primarily at the Harbour Quay with almost fifty vendors and entertainment, she was on the planning committee and had specific duties.

The cruise ships were scheduled to dock at eight am and leave the next morning at high tide. The Chica de Oro's captain was counting on inebriated youth, the outdoor enthusiasts to whom the cruise line were catering, wandering the streets at midnight engaging police to be a diversion.

Chapter THIRTY-TWO

The women and their unexpected guests finished the bottle of Ramazzotti and spent a little time chatting, the women getting the accountants to reveal that their boss had become unexpectedly disposed, leaving the firm somewhat rudderless.

Not wanting to appear too inquisitive, the investigators brought the evening to a close with Julian presenting each with their check. The women each placed one, one hundred-dollar bill and two twenty-dollar bills on the table while Jerome paid with his debit card, glancing down at the seven-hundred dollars and quickly calculating what an astronomical tip they just left and that he had to at least match it.

He couldn't figure it out in time as the women rose to leave.

He entered thirty percent and his passcode and returned the data machine to Julian.

All five thanked Julian again and left the restaurant to be met by the valets. Giving their tickets, they stood back from the street to wait for their vehicles, making small talk to fill the awkward silence.

The men stood with their backs to the street, while the women faced it. The officers immediately noticed three men approaching from the beach side of the *Blue Whale*. Their instincts kicked in and they were immediately in Level Orange, ready for whatever might occur.

As the three got within a few meters, they began shouting homophobic slurs, "Hey faggots, what are you doing hangin' with women, aren't there any boys around for you?" followed by laughter generated by intoxication.

They stopped immediately in front of Jacques and Jerome who had now turned to face the street. Taunting them, "So, faggots, what are you doing out so late? Aren't you supposed to have a curfew to keep you away from decent people?"

Elisabeth didn't move, but said, "Enough guys. How about you move on and let us enjoy our evening?"

"What? Are you some kind of a lesbo? You queer?"

That was all that Rebecca could handle. She had listened to men intimidate for decades and was not going to allow this to continue. She stepped forward and replied, "Yeah. I am a lesbian. What the fuck are you going to do about it, you ugly piece of shit?"

One of the intimidators sneered in her face. She didn't flinch in the nano second it took to head-butt him, her forehead breaking his nose, knee him in the groin and as his body dropped, she grabbed his head, held it steady and kneed his face, breaking his jaw and nose…again, spewing blood across the pavement.

As she dropped her intimidator, the other two prepared to move against Rebecca when Penelope said, "My turn, fuckers."

Elise touched her arm and said, "Let me." Kicking off her pumps she advanced quickly as the other two surrounded Rebecca who was taunting with, "What, you two assholes want to fight a lesbian?"

As one guy reached for Rebecca, Elise stepped around her, grabbed the guy's extended right hand as he attempted to punch Rebecca. Elise held his wrist with her right hand, then wrapped her left around and under his upper arm, grabbing onto her own arm, then spun on her right foot and twisted, pulling the captured arm to her midsection, dropping the attacker to the ground. Not satisfied she had him under control, she used the heel of her right bare foot to stomp his head, knocking him out. As a coup de grace, she bent the arm a little more and heard the elbow snap.

The third guy was not deterred by his fellow bigots laying on the ground and danced around Rebecca, exhibiting his mixed martial arts skills, a contender for the next Southern California fight in Los Angeles. Rebecca stood calm, motionless…waiting.

Jessica had been waiting for her opportunity to join in the fray and as the guy danced to Rebecca's right, Jessica flew out of the shadows and delivered a powerful jab to his face, using the heal of her closed fist.

The MMA contender wiped his nose with his right hand, looked at the blood and said, "Now you have had it, bitch. I am going to kick your queer ass all the way to Malibu," as he yelled, as he leaned back and spun on his right foot, bringing the other leg around preparing for a round-house kick to Jessica's head.

He wasn't prepared for her sliding forward on her left foot, crowding him. As the MMA contender's leg spun around, Jessica wrapped both arms around the extended leg locking it in the straight position, stepped forward with her left foot and dropped to the ground on one knee bringing her attacker down with her.

Once he was down, she stood and delivered a powerful heel smash to his groin, so viciously her colleagues could hear the sound of crushed flesh.

Jessica had been in dozens of fights and take-downs and had never done so in anger. Tonight was different. She too was tired of men being absolved from responsibility for their actions, so she stepped over the collapsed, barely conscious body with her left foot and delivered a heel stomp, cracking his sternum.

She didn't hit his head, but he was clearly out.

For the first time in her career, her heart rate hit 120.

Smiling broadly, she turned to see the other two were still unconscious, glanced across to her friends and said, "That was a wonderful conclusion to a great evening, wouldn't you say so boys?"

Jacques and Jerome stood speechless with Penelope and Elisabeth appearing somewhat rejected for not being able to participate.

Elise removed her phone from her pantsuit pocket, punch in the numbers for her office, spoke to the night dispatcher and hung up.

In less than a minute two patrol cars came screeching to a stop in front of the *Albatross*, just as the valets approached with their guests' vehicles.

An officer moved quickly out of each vehicle and approached the expanded crowd. One of the officers, Sgt. Alfonso, zeroed in on Rebecca and Penelope immediately and aggressively.

"What the hell is it with you two broads? Are you begging to be locked up for assault?"

He was so locked into the two investigators that he hadn't observed who else was present, figuring his partner would deal with whomever…until Detective Pelfini approached and offered, "I'd watch the language Sergeant, with so many phones videotaping your every word, the chief will not be happy to hear one of his senior officers using that language on the morning news."

"Awe fuck. What are you doing here Pelfini?"

"That's Detective Pelfini, Sergeant Alfonso and these women are my friends who were attacked by the men on the ground. I will attest to their need for self-defense. Now if you will excuse us, we wish to conclude our evening. We will be in the office tomorrow with our statements. Call an ambulance and video record the suspects in their present state. I will use that video and those of several bystanders to charge each with assault and a hate crime. You understand that morphing bigotry into violence is a crime, Sergeant?"

Alfonso didn't reply, his sneer and disdain for Pelfini palpable…all caught by numerous bystanders' phone.

Pelfini took several minutes to provide her business card and email address to several observant women to get access to their video of the incident.

She turned with a stern facial expression and nodded to her friends and the accountants to follow her up the street where the valets had their vehicles.

Jerome and Jacques were still speechless, neither ever having been involved in violence and never having seen women behave so aggressively. Jacques was first to respond as they approached their vehicles, "I don't know if I should thank you or run like hell from all of you. Who are you?" he asked with a forced smile.

Penelope, ignoring his question, answered for the "J" Team curtsying and saying, "You are most welcome gentlemen. Let's hope you never have to experience bigots like those two again."

"It's not just bigots who are rising from the swamps," offered Elisabeth. "I was riding an elevator in Omaha back to my room and a guy grabbed my butt. Security found him later, unconscious with several broken bones."

Neither man responded, both standing with their arms hanging, not sure of their next move.

Jessica chimed in as she approached her ride, "Guys, if it is any consolation, we are investigators here in Santa Barbara, the "J" Team," sticking out her arm in greeting.

Jacques stepped forward and shook her hand replying, "Really? All of you are investigators?"

Elise clarified, "They are Jacques. I am a detective with the police department," as she too stuck her hand out as an introduction.

She continued, "Do you guys get hassled much? I wasn't aware we had a homophobic problem to this extent in Santa Barbara."

"In our line of work we don't meet many like the guys you just put down," offered Jerome, "but they are here and we, I guess, are easy targets."

"Well, us and homeless kids, particularly the girls. They take a lot of crap from far too many people," added Jacques.

"Have you guys seen the remodeled motel up the street, *Refugio Seguro?* asked Rebecca?

"Yeah, we have. *Safe Shelter*, right?" asked Jerome.

"That is home to sixteen previously homeless girls," offered Penelope. "Come on by one day after work and we will show you around."

"We'd like that. Maybe we could help in some way," replied Jacques.

"Before we go, you guys being cops and everything, may we ask a question? If it isn't out of line?"

"Shoot," replied Elise with, "Sorry for the pun."

The women gave a nervous laugh knowing what the question would be.

They were right.

"Our boss, Anthony Henderson, hasn't been around for some time and we're getting into a bind with month end reports etc... on which he has to sign off. Any chance you could check and see what is up? I have called his home numerous times, left messages and no one returns my calls."

Elise responded, "Sure Jerome, I will drop by in the morning. How about ten?"

"We'd really appreciate that Detective. We just need some direction."

"Sounds good. See you at ten. And it's Elise," she offered with a smile.

Taking the invitation as a clue, everyone headed for their vehicles and left the area.

On the drive home, Rebecca said, "I doubt Elise knows about Vanessa. We know where her dad is, but I doubt her mom does. Maybe he was the problem and Vanessa can go home. What do you think?"

Pen replied, "Could be. I don't want to get in the middle of family situations. I have zero training for that. Also, I doubt Elise will locate Anthony. Let's talk to Jessica in the morning and see what she thinks. The company must have contingency plans if someone dies and maybe Mrs. Henderson is a partner and can step in."

"Sounds like a plan," replied Rebecca as she smiled and reached across the console and touched Pen's arm.

Chapter THIRTY-THREE

While the rest of the "J" Team were enjoying their girls' night out, including an epic meal and rubbing elbows with Gutierrez's incarcerated lieutenant's legitimate colleagues, Jackson and Jason were creating quite a stir at *Marc Stucki's*.

The agents left the ranch just after the women. and headed directly to *Marc's*. Marc had moved from StoneHead after President Bakus lost the election to his Republican rival. Marc was greeted by an overwhelming sense of appreciation from a group of movers and shakers...Democrats, who expressed their gratefulness for his eight years of service to the Oval Office by financing *Marc Stucki's*, providing a controlling interest in the business and building. His supporters added a two-bedroom condo fully furnished a few blocks from the beach and the restaurant.

In the short time Marc had been in Santa Barbara, *Marc Stucki's* had become THE place to enjoy a Wyoming, grass fed steak from former President Bakus' ranch surrounded by a railroad motif and prepared by a former presidential chef.

Jason and Jackson had become regulars, dining several times a week and were greeted as such by a staff member who showed them to a table between the massive gas fireplace and the small performing stage.

They started their evening with a pint each of Talon from the local craft brewery, Red Eagle. Talon was a heavy, lager which demanded a well-seasoned steak, for which the *Marc Stucki* was becoming legendary. Jackson chose their tenderloin medallion, medium, with garlic butter, baked potato and a green salad with house dressing (red wine, balsamic and herbs). Jason was ready for a change and ordered a sirloin, medium rare with shrimp, scallops and asparagus in a Béarnaise sauce.

Moments after their order was taken, Marc came to their table carrying his own pint of Talon, greeted the men and sat for a few moments, chatting about the business. Marc asked them how retirement was fitting, and they filled him in on the requirements before it became official.

Marc replied with, "When it is official, which I presume is for the entire Team, dinner is on me that night. Okay?"

"Sounds good Marc. We appreciate the generosity."

"Really? After what you guys have done for me, I owe you big time, for long time." He grinned at his attempt to mimic a line from his favorite sitcom, Two and a Half Men, then excused himself to deal with a staffing issue.

Jason took a swallow of his Talon and offered, "I feel incredibly blessed to have landed here in Santa Barbara working with my friends and to have fallen into this," he waved his beer around highlighting the incredibly warm and welcoming atmosphere, just as the local toy train made its way overhead.

"Agree completely," replied Jackson, and to think we were around Bakus' ranch for months and enjoyed many meals prepared by Marc never thinking he would become such an integral part of our lives."

They sat in silence for some time, enjoying their beer mesmerized by the numerous large screen televisions mounted next to the ceiling showing various views of Santa Barbara beaches, the wharf and the passing sailboats.

Just as their meal arrived, several men and two women passed their table carrying instrument cases. They set themselves up on the stage, stored their cases in the corner and created a quartet; sax, bass, piano and clarinet. One female on the bass, the other on piano with the guys playing the sax and clarinet.

The morning after the girls' night out, Elise was at the office at eight and finding Sergeant Alphonso MIA, so to speak, not available via radio and dispatch not knowing his location, Pelfini went directly to Chief O'Connor's office to give her statement.

His door was always open, so she knocked on the door jam. O'Connor looked from his computer screen, acknowledged the knocker with a broad smile and said, "Good morning Detective. I have your paperwork ready for your signature."

Elise entered the office not sure what was happening. Knowing her boss as she did, it was unlike him to become involved in a routine incident report…unless he considered this not routine.

"Good morning, Chief. What's up?"

"What's up Elise is that I saw Sergeant Alfonso's report from last night and I refused to accept it and told him so in an email. He is taking the day off, at my request.

"I've never been able to figure out the relationship you two have but reading his report, it dawned on me. It has to be successful women, or maybe women in general. The inflammatory comments he made about the two men from last night who, according to witnesses, were bystanders, were unacceptable. So, in addition to being a misogynist, he is a homophobic.

"As an addendum, he has it out for Rebecca and Penelope, even though he knows this office endorses them and the "J" Team."

Elise didn't know how to respond, so she didn't, figuring O'Connor would continue. She was not going to be drawn into speaking ill of a colleague, no matter how much of an asshole he was.

O'Connor did continue as he calmed down from his tirade, "I believe everything that happened last night is in this revised report I prepared," handing several sheets of paper to her.

Elise accepted the papers, perused them, signed, then slid them across the desk to her boss.

"Alfonso's comments were so inflammatory regarding Rebecca and Penelope that I disregarded them. I presume they will be in sometime today to give their statements?"

"They said they would be in this morning after they stop at their office and coordinate the day's assignments.

"Thank you Chief, I sincerely appreciate your handling this. I hate to think what these guys could have done to citizens unable to protect themselves," Pelfini concluded, rising from the chair.

"Me too, Elise. We have enough trouble controlling the never-ending stream of homeless without having to deal with this element.

"Oh, by the way, any chance of wrangling another party out of Penelope and Rebecca? I kinda liked that last one," he quipped as Elise turned, shaking her head and left his office.

Marc Stucki's was home to the thirty plus crowd; most being singles and couples, but with a number of families regularly. The cuisine, subdued ambiance, massive crab tank in the entry and the beach-monitoring flat screens cemented the demographic clientele to which the quartet was addressing their rendition of Brian McKnight's *Back At One.*

Jason and Jackson finished their meal and were each nursing a Talon beer, chatting about their retirement conditions, speculating when the current investigation would wrap up while the quartet played a series of Tony Bennett's hits, *It Had To Be You* with the pianist singing Carrie Underwood's part. They continued the set with *Fly Me To The Moon*, then segued into Michael Bublé's *Haven't Met You Yet* and *Home.*

They weren't in the loop. Jessica's plan to involve them in Gutierrez's Los Angeles business was scrapped, leaving them at loose ends.

Chief O'Connor had approved their private investigator and firearm's carry permits allowing them to engage with the "J" Team Investigators but officially they remained Secret Service Agents.

In limbo.

Alane had secured apartments in separate buildings at each end of the beach. Owned by two business associates who had removed them from the rental market for renovations, the agents accepted leases to commence when modifications were complete.

Jackson was watching the stage as Jason shared his insight on their gravitating to *locals* status. When the quartet completed the set, he turned to Jason and said, "I gotta do this," as he rose and walked over to the sax player.

Jason could see the animation between the men, hand shaking, then reading the sax guy's lips saying, "no way!", Jackson smiling, pointing back to Jason then accepting the sax as the player removed the mouthpiece, inserted another then walked over to Jason.

Jason stood, shook his hand, pulled a chair out as the sax player explained his conversation with Jackson.

"Cooper, I have worked with Jackson for a long time and never had the pleasure. I think retiring and settling in Santa Barbara had renewed his interest. I hope he remembers how to play."

"I am sure he will Jason," replied Cooper. "Playing is like other fine motor skills, they are never gone, just need tuning."

As the men chatted the quartet entered into *Saturday Night in the Park* by Chicago. Jackson thought he might have difficulty but after a few hiccups, he found his grove and as he glanced over at Jason, his smile was one his long-time friend and colleague had never seen; a warmth, an inner glow of joy.

Chicago segued into *Hello Dolly* from Louis Armstrong then *Dark Chocolate* by Gordon James. As they went into their last set before a break, Cooper excused himself and left the restaurant.

In a few minutes, Cooper returned carrying an instrument case, walked up to the stage just as the quartet finished Gordon James. Not saying a word, he opened the case and removed a sax, stood next to the pianist and started a Chris Botti's rendition of *I've Got You Under My Skin* with the base player singing Kathrine McPhee's segment, the two saxophones playing Botti's trumpet notes.

Jackson was beside himself with joy, to think this stranger thought so much of his playing that he did this. The more he played, the greater his animation and body movements became.

The quintet modified Botti's piece with each musician taking a turn at improvisation with the audience so into the presentation, they were clapping in time.

Jason was with the music as well, between sipping his Talon, unaware of an approaching woman, a slip that in any other setting might be his downfall.

But not this time.

"OMG! Jackson is amazing. I never knew he had that talent," offered Jessica as she pulled a chair out and sat.

Somewhat startled and embarrassed at his jumpy reaction to his boss' arrival, Jason regained his composure and responded with, "Hey, Jessica. Yeah, I can't believe it either. The other sax player is Cooper who loaned one of his saxophones to Jackson. He said playing an instrument is like any other fine motor skill. It is never lost.

"Look at Jackson's face. Look at his body language. Amazing."

"I've never seen him having so much fun," replied Jessica as she hailed a server and asked for two more of whatever Jason was drinking.

"So, that's Cooper on the other sax huh? Do you know if he is married?"

Jason was so taken aback, he snorted a swallow, sat his glass down, grabbed a napkin to wipe his face, laughing.

"What, I can't be interested? she replied with a smile.

"No, it's not that. I've just never seen you relax to the point of being interested in anything but work!"

"It's called retirement and I suspect you two are enjoying the same spiritual freedom," she added with a lift in her voice.

Their Talons arrived and they stopped chatting to listen to the next set, with Jackson showing no sign of confusion over the variety of music being played. The pianist began with Etta James' rendition of *At Last*, with the bass player joining in the lyrics and Cooper and the clarinet sliding in on the second verse. Jackson held back until the line, at *last the skies above are blue, my heart wrapped up in clover*, and he hit the keys with such conviction, many in the audience stood and clapped, not knowing he hadn't played in decades.

At the end of the set, the group announced they would take a thirty break, set their instruments aside and as they approached, Jason and Jessica, Jason waved them over to join their group.

Marc, never missing a beat, waved staff to bring additional chairs as he spoke softly to a server. Acknowledging her boss' request, she headed to the kitchen.

The chairs arrived immediately avoiding the quartet from an awkward wait. As everyone grabbed a seat, Jessica introduced herself and Jason to the quartet just as servers arrived with several large platters of potato skins with beer cheese and more pints of Talon.

Jessica was the first to try one of the skins and before Marc left, she asked, "Marc, these are amazing. What's in them, if you don't mind my asking?"

"Not at all Jessica. But of course, I can't tell you the exact amounts which is the key," he replied with a wide grin.

"About forty-five in the oven with the skins crunchy, then scoop out the pulp etc. and the secret is the crisp, thick bacon, sharp cheddar and," he leaned over and said softly, "a little dried mustard, cayenne and Worcestershire. But you didn't hear the last from me," he quipped as he turned to leave, offering, "Enjoy your evening folks. Let us know if we can get you anything else."

A person didn't have to be a restaurant critic to see the numerous reasons *Marc Stucki's* had become famous in such a short time.

The conversation was entirely concentrated on Jackson with everyone wanting to know where his talent came from and why had he been hiding it.

He shared that he had played in high school but missed a few years while in the service and picked it up again at Northern Michigan University playing at school functions and the campus pub.

The piano player asked, “How come we haven’t seen you around before Jackson?”

“I just moved here recently and am in the process of retiring.”

He glanced over at Jessica who was not happy but encouraged him to wing it.

“I am a teacher, just moved here thinking of getting on the substitution list but after tonight I’m thinking it is time for a career change,” he replied quickly, waving his arms excitedly.

“Well, I can see you might have found that second career, Jackson,” responded the pianist.

Cooper chimed in with, “We do this for fun on weekends Jackson, and I think I speak for the rest of the group, that you can join us any time. Marc donates whatever he would normally pay a group, to a local charity. We sometimes play at functions with the same remuneration agreement.”

“That would be great guys. I haven’t had this much fun in decades.”

Cooper was sitting next to Jessica and noticing the absence of a ring, asked, “Jessica, are you new to Santa Barbara as well?”

“I am, Cooper,” Jessica replied, setting her pint down. “Thanks for asking. I moved here recently from Washington,

DC and found a job the day after I arrived. I just moved into a rented house. How about you?"

"Every Californian has a story to tell of how and why they came to Southern Sun. Mine is probably no different than others. I finished an engineering degree and thought I'd try life in lotus land, chose Santa Barbara.

"I was very fortunate to find a job quickly exploring for oil reserves off the coast," putting his arms in the air, he added, "But I do not get involved in the politics of coastal oil drilling so please do not castigate me for my career choice," he concluded with a nervous smile.

Jessica laughed, an actual gut-wrenching burst, one that surprised her since honest expressions had been controlled for so long, then replied, "Cooper, I am an attorney," she said with her arms out to her side knowing the sax player got the message of the sometimes-social stigma of the legal profession.

While enjoying humor at each other's expense, the other musicians rose to return to the stage so Cooper offered, "We will be here next Friday night. Maybe you could stop by?"

"Definitely. It's a date," replied Jessica, immediately regretting her outburst, her face turning red, then added, "I'll be sure to stop by," knowing it was too little, too late, she had entered the realm of gender interaction, better known as dating.

Jason and Jessica stayed until the last set ended and had planned to thank the quartet, but the throng of fans made it impossible, so they caught Cooper and Jackson's attention, waved goodbye and headed out.

In the parking lot, Jason stopped and asked, "So, you guys getting together? You looked like you were hitting it off?"

"You are funny. No, nothing like that. I have to finish this case before I try to become a normal person. Hopefully soon though. You want to meet here next Friday night? Something tells me Jackson is going to make them a quintet."

"I hear ya, I have had the taste of a regular life and am ready too. Looks like Jackson got a jump on us," as he got in his car.

Jessica slapped the top of his vehicle, letting him know she was clear, then headed to her own, feeling a warmth and glow she hadn't experienced in decades.

"You can make more friends by becoming interested in them, than you can by trying to get them interested in you."

Dale Carnegie

Jessica had a great deal to learn regarding interpersonal relationships. She had spent her adult years being angry at the world which alienated her from her colleagues until her boss gave her some advice when he sent her to StoneHead Ranch in Wyoming, "Play nice," the essence of the message being, we can't afford you investigating solo or estranged agents.

The Christians for a Better America was such a massive organization which permeated every facet of American life and culture, she became stonewalled in her attempts to defang its leadership.

She knew she needed help and when she took Sorento's advice, her world changed over a lunch hour with the county sheriff and StoneHead police chief when they agreed to help.

The ensuing relationship was invaluable and she vowed she would maintain the new collegiality work disposition.

Chapter THIRTY-FOUR

Elise was at Anthony Henderson's office at ten the next morning where Jacques and Jerome were waiting for her in Jacque's office with croissants and coffee.

The staff wouldn't take her for law enforcement since, unlike her male counterparts, she didn't telegraph domination and control. Her persona could have been that of a client, in her powder-blue Irish, linen-cotton double-breasted jacket with notched lapels, convertible flap-welt waist pockets and fitted for her hip holstered nine-millimeter pistol. The matching ankle length wide-leg pants were set off by tan open-toe sandals with an ankle strap.

Ballentine and Swanson were looking particularly dapper in Ted Baker Italian wool suits. Jacques in a subtle grey plaid, a soft blue shirt and dark blue and white striped tie with tan lace-up shoes, while Jerome wore a Ted Baker charcoal black suit with a white button-down shirt and a black and white striped tie with black tassel loafers.

Accepting their greeting and hospitality, she poured a mug of coffee, broke a croissant in half, spread butter and sat between her hosts on cream leather accent chairs and engaged in small talk.

About last night's altercation.

She eased their concern by explaining that the issue was being handled by the department as a hate crime and they would not be required to testify; the four investigators and Elise testimony being more than sufficient evidence against the assailants.

Changing the subject, she asked the CPAs to recount their concerns regarding Anthony Henderson.

Elise was impressed with their presentation but didn't glean anything new about Henderson. They provided her with Mrs. Henderson's unlisted phone number and her home address, adding that they didn't feel comfortable calling her themselves.

Detective Pelfini assured the employees that she would let them know what she discovered as soon as she could.

Back in her unmarked, she quickly texted Penelope and asked for a quick meet at the beach parking lot. Pen was in the "J" Team office when she replied almost instantly, *on my way*.

Pen arrived first and parked facing the ocean at the empty end of the lot. Elise appeared moments later and backed into the slot beside Pen allowing the women to chat without getting out of their vehicles.

Pelfini related her conversation with Jacques and Jerome and that she was on her way to Mrs. Henderson's now and wanted Penelope to give her backup.

Pen agreed immediately and listened as Elise explained her desired questioning approach. Pelfini was entering an unknown investigative field; she didn't know where Anthony's wife fit into Gutierrez's drug cartel.

"What I'm looking for Pen is an additional pair of trained female eyes and ears when we listen to her explanation as to her husband's whereabouts."

"Got it. Rebecca and I stopped by your office this morning and Chief O'Connor was very pleasant about the entire incident, as though he had made up his mind before we arrived."

"Yeah, he kinda did. Oh, the other news I want to share, and I will include this in my CHAP posting, are you ready? Drum roll please."

Penelope's face lit up in expectation as she thumped her hands on her steering wheel.

"Gutierrez's real name is Cecilia Padilla. She worked for a San Francisco law firm several decades ago. Eight partners were charged with embezzling client funds and did six years each. They were disbarred upon conviction and have remained off social radar ever since.

"Padilla disappeared but we now know she changed her identity with new California Bar Association credentials."

"You suspect that Marianna was part of the scheme but wasn't implicated?"

"I don't know what to believe. The investigating officers have retired and the files are buried in the SFPD archives. I'd like to bounce this around with the "J" Team. The only safe place is the Ranch. Any chance of meeting later today? I'll bring wine and tacos," she asked with a broad smile.

"Consider it done. I'll text Rebecca. How about six-ish?"

"Done," Elise replied as she handed Henderson's address across the open windows.

Pen restarted her car and said, "See you there in five."

Elise nodded and drove off first while Penelope backed out and followed her, texting Rebecca using the vehicle's voice activated system.

The mini-sub's captain disconnected the tow line to the Chica de Oro, allowing the Golden Girl to enter Barkley Sound under her own propulsion.

The Canadian HMCS Toronto Naval ship detected the disconnect and propulsion commencement and signaled Elisabeth who in turn advised the Edmonton detachment.

Sergeant Richard Drought was in the detective squad room monitoring CHAP when Deputy Commissioner Benedetti arrived to bring him current and to direct him to gather his team and head to the Pacific Region Training Centre in Chilliwack. "I have arranged single accommodations for you and your team and the training facilities are yours. Hone your squad's skills Rick, everyone goes home unscathed.

"Also Rick, everyone wears body cams. We don't want any blowback when the suspects go to trial," offered Benedetti as she turned to leave the squad room.

Benedetti didn't need to remind Drought that all Members would carry the Colt C-8 carbine, a variation of Colt's well-known M-16. The weapon, manufactured in Ontario, was adopted by various Canadian troops and the RCMP, the latter choosing the three-round burst firing scheme over fully automatic.

Experience taught the Force that a thirty-round magazine on full auto, spraying the target, is less effectivc than finding and eliminating a target with the sites.

Stan received Marianna's communique late at night and due to the urgency, he immediately texted Larry Baird Sr. to have him ready his team to unload the Golden Girl scheduled to arrive shortly in Port Alberni.

Larry Sr. was not a seasoned criminal. He allowed himself to get caught in a financial web with no escape.

Stan's offer catapulted him to a level for which he had no experience. He was in survival mode, praying he could execute the operation, pay his drug debt, somehow help Loblinski Sr., then disappear and disconnect from Stan.

Baird Sr. felt sorry for Francesco Loblinski who worked hard all his adult life to provide his child with the best opportunities and now Stan was using his dad's work site to facilitate his cocaine business.

Hopefully the senior Loblinski will never discover the betrayal, thought Larry Sr. as he sent the group text to put his team on standby.

His last obligation was to text a Campbell River fisherman Stan had made arrangements with and have him prepared to execute.

RCMP Inspector Lorne Wood received the message from Benedetti through the Force's secure communique system. The plain-wrap, four-door rentals were gassed, hidden in the detachment's locked compound. The Members, two teams of male and female officers were in the detachment primed and ready to participate in what could be the greatest take-down of their careers. Anticipation, excitement and adrenaline were fueled by several cups of unpalatable detachment coffee.

Sgt. Major Curtis Leithead had spent more days fishing in the Strait of Georgia than any vacation he had taken in all his military years. He used the opportunity to leave America and her problems behind, accessing no US television or radio and associating with nobody from south of the Canadian border. Although he hadn't taken his blood pressure, he was positive it had to be as stable as it had ever been and his hip was feeling normal.

He had used the catch and release system, keeping just those he could process at the lodge, an after-fishing activity to which he had come to look forward; canning the fish plus several bottles of Phillips' Blue Buck, a heavy ale from Phillips brewery in Victoria.

Leithead planned to donate the cases of fish to local food banks, hoping the delicacy would be enjoyed by folks struggling to get by.

"Many men go fishing all of their lives without knowing that it is not fish they are after.

I went to the woods because I wished to live deliberately, to front only the essential facts of life, and see if I could not learn what it had to teach and not, when I came to die, discover that I had not lived."

Henry David Thoreau

Chapter THIRTY-FOUR

Rebecca arranged to be at *Refugio Seguro* when the students returned from school. The girls' post school activity had become routine, with Sabrina preparing healthy snacks the girls could take to their rooms while they did homework.

Rebecca gave them about thirty to settle in their rooms then knocked on Vanessa's door hoping she would be in a sharing mood.

The teenager opened the door and was taken aback to see her mentor dressed in tan shorts, a black over-blouse and a pair of Clarks Lexi Marigold black sandals with six straps across the instep and a heel strap.

"Rebecca. Hi. What's up?"

"Hi Vanessa. Do you have a minute?"

"Sure, come on in," replied the teen as she stepped to the side to allow Rebecca to enter.

Vanessa had changed from her school clothes into a pair of cut-off jeans and a short-sleeve, V neck, white beach T decorated with a girl catching a large wave, surfing.

Rebecca was pleased with the work the interior designer had performed.

Each girl had decorated uniquely with the help of a team from a local interior design firm. The rooms were quite large offering far more space than a university dormitory.

Vanessa had chosen antique white with brass knobs for her furniture choice. The headboard accessories matched the dresser and end table knobs. The double bed was highlighted by a cream chintz summer duvet dotted with a variety of sea creatures.

One corner was devoted to a small, round, four-legged, antique white coffee table creating a conversation area with three light green accent chairs. Between the seating area and the window which looked out over the gardens, was a desk also in the antique white but with brush strokes of the same pale green.

The drapes and valance were green and cream pattern of swirls reaching floor to ceiling.

Vanessa had her laptop open with homework assignments drawn up ready to complete.

Vanessa felt incredibly mature, hosting an adult for the first time in her room. She invited Rebecca to the seating area and after her guest sat, Vanessa chose the seat across from her and waited.

"I wanted you to know there will be no repercussions from the incident the other day at the school."

Before Rebecca could continue, Vanessa spoke, "I didn't understand any of what happened. One minute we were saying hi to you and Penelope and then two guys were fighting. What's with that guy Reeves anyway?"

"I think Reeves might be an adult version of his father from what I have discovered; narcistic, arrogant with zero social conscience.

"You probably have met many bigots in your life and undoubtedly more as you get older. They just keep coming out from under rocks and spill their venom. Reeves and his friends feel more successful when they can put someone down. Thankfully you and Dominic didn't allow that and left with your heads held high, destroying the hateful group's attempts at controlling.

"That sounds just like my dad, at least what he was like before he kicked me out."

Rebecca couldn't believe Vanessa had provided the opening to discussing her father. She replied, "You were homeless for a long time. Can you share with me what transpired that lead to your being on the street?"

"Sure, I don't mind Rebecca, although a month ago, I probably would not have shared. When I was a kid, he was just like other dads. He had his own accounting firm, still does I suspect, and we did stuff as a family like beach picnics and barbeques. I used to help him cut the grass on the weekends. It was a lot of fun.

"Then slowly things began to change. He and my mom began fighting regularly. Dad became moody and would yell at me for no reason. He told me one day that I dressed like a slut which made me cry because I was not dressed like that. Mom never stepped in to tell him to stop bullying me.

"Then he started to have strange men visit late at night. One time I was watching television by myself in my pajamas and some guy walked in, sat beside me and started pawing me. I told him to fuck off but he didn't. Dad came in and yelled at me for being so rude. I ran into my bedroom, locked the door and cried.

"One day, I couldn't take it anymore and told him to go fuck himself and I left. I have never been back."

Rebecca had been processing everything she said and figured the stranger was Henderson's lieutenant and bagman, Julio Fernández.

"I love to see a young girl go out and grab the world by the lapels. Life's a bitch. You've got to go out and kick ass."

Dr. Maya Angelou

"How do you feel about your mom?"

"Rebecca, honestly? I don't feel anything. For years my father treated me like shit. Sorry. But he did, and she did nothing to help. I have no desire to see her."

"Well, that is all in the past and Pen and I are delighted you grasped this opportunity to get your life back on track. Just think, there is absolutely nothing to hold you back and with the grades you used to get, and will again, you can attend a post-secondary school and have a career of your choice."

Vanessa got up slowly from the couch, tears in her eyes and stepped toward Rebecca who stood to give her a hug.

"I don't know how I can thank you enough for what you have done and are doing for me and the rest of the girls" she said, tears swelling. "We were at a dead-end and didn't know what to do. I know some of the girls were thinking of suicide."

Rebecca felt her body tense at the thought of teens being so destitute to consider taking their own lives while adults bickered about solutions.

She felt her throat swell up, caught herself and said, "I will let you get back to your homework and remember, if you or the others need something which Sabrina can't find, you call us."

Vanessa was wiping her tears with her sleeve but managed to reply, "Will do Rebecca." Regaining control, she continued, "I see you are not carrying a firearm."

"Yes I am."

"No! Is that what I felt when we hugged?"

"Shh!" Rebecca replied, putting her index finger to her mouth with a grin. Another hug, then she turned for the door, stopping once to smile, then was gone.

Brian Sawyer woke with a massive hangover, to which he had grown accustomed, albeit regrettably.

He stumbled out of his bedroom to prepare coffee and was so startled to find two men sitting in his kitchen that he grabbed the door jamb for stability.

Rubbing his face with both hands, he said, "I don't know what you two could possibly want from me. I have no money and there is nothing in this dump to steal."

One of the Samuel Jefferson agents replied, "We didn't come to steal from you Mr. Sawyer and we must say, this house is a far cry from a dump."

Agent Two chimed in with, "You see Mr. Sawyer, Mr. Loblinski wishes to speak to you and since you choose to live incognito, he sent us with a phone."

Agent One retrieved a simple flip phone from his pants pocket, opened it and prepared to dial. "Stan will make a request of you and we are here to ensure that you comply with his wishes," he concluded and dialed. When the connection was made, he spoke into the phone, "Mr. Loblinski, this is Samuel Jefferson Agency, I have Brian ready to speak with you."

He waited a few seconds listening to Stan, then said, "Certainly sir. Here he is," passing the phone to Brian.

As he accepted the phone, his hand started to shake. Agent Two held his wrist, then put the phone to Brian's ear and held it there.

Sawyer's face was red, either with embarrassment or fear, his guests couldn't determine which.

"Hi Stan." Then he listened. As the conversation continued Brian's facial expression changed as he heard the reason for the agents' travelling thousands of kilometers to give him a phone.

"Sorry Stan, when you told me to sanitize the operation and get lost, I never thought we'd be in touch again," Brian said, his face bright with anticipation.

"Sure, I can do that. I just need to speak with my neighbor for her to watch my place and I can be on the next flight.

"With these guys? Sure I can do that," he concluded and handed the phone to Agent Two.

"Yes sir. We will have him in Edmonton by tonight. Sure, we will meet you at the airport. Thank you, sir."

Agent Two put the phone away and said, "We are set to go. It seems your old boss can't do without you Mr. Sawyer. You are a very fortunate man. We'll wait while you pack this bag and speak with your neighbor. While you are doing that, we will make reservations for a flight out of San José this afternoon" as he handed him a used black duffle bag.

Stan packed quickly taking only the essentials for several days, his passport, locked the house, informed his neighbor and headed into the village with thc Albertans.

The drive to San José was uneventful for the agents with little or no conversation with Brian.

He, however, was beyond thrilled. He had thought the smuggling job he was doing would bring back the adrenaline rush.

It didn't.

He had spent all his free time drinking and eating far too much. He knew he was on a destructive path but didn't know how to regain control.

Now he did.

In a few hours he would be back in action.

Real action.

He hadn't seen Stan in years, ever since that first night at the party where he offered him the job of a lifetime and again a few months later exchanging information at an all-night market.

During the flight to Edmonton, he gathered his thoughts, stifled his enthusiasm and collected his demeanor to appear ready to participate in anything Loblinski offered.

The Golden Girl was navigating Barkley Sound under her own power, going solo since leaving the mouth of the inlet, and passing Nahmint, ignorant of the relevance of Nahmint to their operation.

Distance was gained slowly as the sub's sonar pinged off numerous sunken logs discarded from various logging operations which dated back decades. Some obstacles she could steer around while others brushed against her hull as she maneuver toward Alberni.

"There is a touch of the pirate about every man who wears the dolphins badge."

Jeff Tall

“I must confess that my imagination refuses to see any sort of submarine doing anything but suffocating its crew and floundering at sea.”

H.G. Wells

“He that will not sail till all dangers are over, must never put to sea.”

Thomas Fuller

Chapter THIRTY-FIVE

Rebecca had just entered her car after leaving the *Refugio Seguro* when she received a text from Penelope which had been sent some time ago. Starting the car, she texted back, adding a few smiley faces, telling her she would meet her at the Ranch then headed home.

Elise and Penelope met outside the Henderson home and headed up the sidewalk together. The house was far more than either investigator had anticipated. At least four-thousand square feet, the Spanish hacienda architecture was typical for the area but up a couple of hundred thousand in value.

The Italian tile curved walkway extended from the city sidewalk fifty feet to the house situated on the back section of an acre lot. The front garden was vacant of shrubs or grass but dotted with fifteen-foot eucalyptus trees, the ground covered with their fallen brown leaves.

The two story, white stucco home was asymmetrical with a gabled, dark tile roof and a ten-foot overhang. The entry, doors and windows were half arches with fashionable ornate tile and wrought iron work extensively exhibited across the front.

Elise knocked on the door and was taken aback by the forty something woman who answered. The shoulder length, auburn 'do with blonde highlights with long layers, front down with very few layers in the back. Mrs. Henderson work very little makeup, just eyeliner and a matte-nude lip gloss with a tanned, flawless complexion. Wearing white, high waisted, wide-leg linen pants, a cobalt blue, high collared, long sleeved silk blouse with her shoulders covered with a white linen shawl, she said, "Good morning, ladies. What can I do for you?"

Elise introduced herself and Penelope, each investigator showed her identification and extended their hands as a courtesy and explained the reason for their visit. The hand the woman offered was slightly tanned, with long, slender fingers highlighted with a light pink polish which highlighted a recent manicure.

Mrs. Henderson didn't impress the detectives as a grieving spouse as she invited them into a vestibule with a light, Italian avocado tile floor set at angles, on point. The walls were stucco, painted a darker avocado with mahogany stained wood accents.

She led them into a massive living room adorned with white leather couches set in four distinct seating arrangements, each with a six-foot, glass and wrought-iron coffee table. Every table was highlighted with dried flower arrangements.

Two of the seating arrangements faced six-foot wide, gas fireplaces with tile hearths matching the entry floor.

The twenty-foot cathedral ceiling was accented with six by six mahogany stained worm wood beams.

"Please, detectives, sit," she offered, waving her arm to nearest seating arrangement. "How might I help you?"

Elise shared the conversation she had with Henderson's husband's staff and their concerns for his safety as they had not heard from him in weeks.

"I don't know how I can help you detectives. I haven't seen or heard from Anthony in weeks myself."

"Is that normal behavior for Mr. Henderson, to be gone without sharing his whereabouts?" asked Penelope.

"No, not really, but he does leave on business trips without telling me his itinerary," replied Mrs. Henderson.

Penelope and Elise shared the same unspoken evaluation of the couple's relationship. Obviously, her access to money was not hampered by her husband's absence.

"We are concerned, as are your husband's employees. Apparently, there are numerous documents which can't move forward without his signature.

"May we have a look at his office to possibly ascertain his whereabouts and confirm for ourselves that he is not in harm's way? And may we have access to his computer?"

"Certainly. Please, this way," replied Mrs. Henderson as she rose from the impeccably clean surface and led them down a long hallway, passed several closed doors.

As Pen walked behind Mrs. Henderson, she noticed the right side of the woman's light-weight linen pants sag slightly.

Their host stopped at the last door.

Opening it, she stepped aside, allowing her guests to enter saying, "I really don't know what you might find here to allay your concerns. I am sure Anthony is fine. He has done this for years."

As Penelope passed Mrs. Henderson, Pen's left side brushed Henderson's right.

"I will be in the kitchen when you are through. Please let me know if I can assist with anything," she concluded, displaying a neutral facial expression while her stomach churned wondering what really prompted them to begin an investigation and wondering where Anthony really was. She fed them the bullshit story because her husband was never gone more than a few hours without texting his agenda and ETA for being home.

Mrs. Henderson hadn't paid attention to the family finances for decades. Finding joy in a steady supply of funds at her immediate disposal and knowing an accountant's record keeping would be too complex to understand, she savored the financial cornucopia.

Elise sat in the office chair, noticed the computer tower under the desk, reached down and turned it on. A few seconds later the screen was lighted and a prompt for a password. Turning to Penelope, she said, "Would you mind?"

"Not at all," replied Penelope. She retrieved a smartphone from her back pocket, tapped in a few numbers, saw that the message had been received, turned back to Elise and nodded.

Momentarily the screen command disappeared and a menu popped up. Perusing documents and spreadsheets, it was evident Henderson had kept the cartel's financial records on this hard drive. *Probably on a flash drive elsewhere and no doubt the cloud as well*, thought Elise.

Turning once again to Penelope who was observing over her shoulder, she nodded and Pen repeated her previous procedure with the phone. The next screen change took about a minute.

Elisabeth had obtained the Wi-Fi password from Penelope's phone which had cloned Mrs. Henderson's as their bodies touched slightly and their phones came in contact. The rest took seconds.

Mrs. Henderson was enjoying a cup of coffee, sitting at the kitchen counter, playing Candy Crush on her phone when she heard her unexpected and unwanted guests approaching. Kicking in her concerned demeanor, she turned to face the kitchen's entry as Elise and Penelope turned the corner.

"Were you able to find anything useful?"

"We were Mrs. Henderson. Thank you for your cooperation. We will be in touch," replied Elise as they let themselves out before Mrs. Henderson could respond.

As the women were walking back to their vehicles, Elise noticed Pen's quizzical expression and responded with, "I'll explain tonight," with a smile and mouthing, *we've got this.*

They entered their respective vehicles and headed to the Ranch.

Stan was enjoying a Caesar chorizo wrap and a coffee in the Edmonton International Airport lounge when the Costa Rica flight's arrival was announced. Quickly finishing his wrap and coffee, he took the bill to the cashier, paid by tapping his credit card on the debit machine and walked quickly to the international arrivals terminal to wait for the men to pass customs.

It didn't take long for the group to be accepted, the investigators providing their identification, Canadian passports and Brian his Costa Rican documents. When the Canadian Border Agent asked Sawyer where he would be located during his stay, the investigators provided the fake address Stan had provided.

Brian had never intended to return to Canada, had allowed his Canadian passport to lapse and had become a Costa Rican citizen.

He was a visitor to his native country.

A brief handshake, clap on the back and Stan ushered Brian out of the airport, thanking the agents for their invaluable assistance then headed to the parking lot.

Elise stopped by the wine store and picked up a case of Oregon's April Ridge's Chardonnay, figuring it was time for her to contribute more than a couple of bottles at a time.

She had called ahead to Taco Margarita so the twenty soft shell tacos, refried beans, guacamole and garden salads would be ready.

They were.

Arriving at the Ranch, she found everyone one glass of chardonnay ahead of her. Placing dinner in the oven with the setting on warm, she turned and found Rebecca holding a glass of cold wine, a hug and a warm welcome for the case of wine.

"This is fabulous Elise. A new winery! Let's get these in the wine fridge then join the others."

A conversation was in full swing as they entered the living room and sat together on the couch facing the fireplace.

"Hi Elise," offered Elisabeth. "I was just starting to explain how the investigation was progressing from my end."

For the benefit of the others, she recounted the interaction with Penelope and Elise a few hours earlier. "I have just started to analyze the hard drive but it looks like a prosecutor's gold mine. Jessica, do you want to scrutinize the data before I send it to Sorento and put it on CHAP?"

Jessica replied, "Send it encrypted to me and I will ensure it is packaged so Sorento can pass it to a prosecutor as is."

Rebecca shared her interaction with Vanessa. "She confirmed that Henderson had his lieutenant, Julio Fernández come to his house, presumably to drop off the currency from the Los Angeles street dealers.

"The currency confiscated from the earlier bust matches some of the serial numbers our Caribbean agent provided. I believe we can prove the money moves from the Los

Angeles drug sales, through Henderson but how does it get to the Caribbean?

"The most feasible method would be airplane. Someone would have to take it to LAX. Elisabeth, is there anything on Henderson's hard drive? Credit card receipts for travel? Anything?"

Elisabeth rose from the couch, placed her empty glass on the glass top, wrought iron coffee table, "Give me a few minutes and I will check. Will someone refill me please?" as she turned and jogged upstairs.

Elise looked around and seeing several empty bottles, went to the kitchen and returned with two of the April Ridge's Chardonnay and refilled everyone's glass.

The beauty of CHAP was that all agents were current on the investigation and while waiting for Elisabeth, they chatted in generalities about the various aspects of the case, starting with Sawyer.

"One of the things I am going to miss is our international connections. Maybe we can develop our own network," commented Jessica.

"The Costa Rican agents tailing Sawyer, watching him slide further and further into dissolution was like a recurring soap opera. The photos the agents took of the two guys looking for Brian were perfect for facial recognition to identify them. I have to hand it to Loblinski, that was a good move to get Brian back. What I don't understand is why reinstate Sawyer, doesn't Stan have anybody else?"

Elise added, "Maybe he just doesn't have someone he can trust. This is a massive operation and the first one for Loblinski. He and Brian have been together for decades. Well, not actually, but you know what I mean. That loyalty is hard to find."

Before anyone could add to the conversation, Elisabeth came bounding into the room with a Cheshire grin, sat down, took a sip of her white and said, "You are not going to fuckin' believe this. Henderson pays a monthly lease on a hangar at LAX for a ten-passenger jet."

"No shit!" exclaimed Penelope, pumping her right arm in the air.

"Hang on, there's more," offered Elisabeth maintaining her telltale grin, "Because the jet is costed out on a monthly basis, Henderson has a spreadsheet for the original value and the cost per trip…to the Caribbean.

Due to Jessica's involvement with Gutierrez while maintaining her cover with Katrina, Elisabeth continued to run the operation.

She was exuberant and said, "I'm sure we all agree, this is exciting news. Jason and Jackson, I suspect Fernández was the currency courier. Would you check out the hangar, view the CCT footage for evidence of him, probably carrying several large duffle bags into the hangar, possibly leaving with the collapsed bags? Interview the pilots too. I will see if Henderson breaks down the jet expense for the crew but we need to know their involvement."

"Got it. We'll head down there tomorrow," replied Jackson. "It won't be difficult to obtain the video but as an aside, what are we going to do when we can no longer flash our Secret Service shield?"

"Jessica has a plan for that which she will address."

"Elise and Penelope, do you think Mrs. Henderson was involved?" continued Elisabeth.

"No, we don't think so. She may have thought he was involved in something nefarious given Fernández's frequent visits, and their lifestyle, but we think she isn't that swift."

"I concur," offered Rebecca. "Vanessa's story is convincing and the way she describes her mother's lack of integrity for Vanessa's safety, her allowing Anthony to bully Vanessa, I'd also say no."

"Thanks Elisabeth," offered Jessica. "To your question regarding identification, Sorento has agreed to allow us to keep our shields as contract investigators. He says there has never been such a classification in the history of the Service and said it may get squashed at some point by the next director, but for now, our shields are ours in retirement.

"In reality, we will only be using the shield while investigating for the Service, so I don't see a problem."

Elisabeth picked up the conversation again, "A quick summary from CHAP. Brian Sawyer arrived in Edmonton and was met by Stan. The two private investigators are not involved. The RCMP will continue their surveillance. Karen, Kimberly and Tom are following the three Vancouver suspects. RCMP Inspector Lorne Wood has his team prepared to follow the cocaine once it is unloaded.

"Richard Drought, some of you remember from the cesium investigation. He is now a sergeant and heads up an assault team currently at the RCMP Pacific Training Centre in Chilliwack.

"Anything I'm missing?"

Penelope was about to burst with excitement and said, "Yes, Elise has news. Elise, you're on."

"Thanks Pen," and she proceeded to give the group an update on Gutierrez and her real background.

"It is all coming together," Elisabeth said excitedly. "I will let everyone know what I glean from Henderson's hard drive.

"I miss the action, the adrenaline rush. Man, that take-down in the vineyard was a classic and I suspect the Mounties will experience similar emotions.

"But, alas, I am probably getting too old for the fire-arms assaults and will have to stick to kicking ass here in Santa Barbara," she concluded mimicking a front kick to the groin.

"Here, here," shouted the others, raising their glasses.

"Now let's eat," said Rebecca.

Chapter THIRTY-SIX

When Inspector Wood was advised by Edmonton that the sub was in Barkley Sound. He texted Angie Taylor.

Larry Sr. had used his cell to notify his crew to park their vehicles in town, walk to the dock after dark and conceal themselves separately, have their phones on vibrate and be ready to unload.

Joint operations between Canadian and American agencies were often unnecessarily complicated, but Fukishura and Sorento's organizational plan avoided that confusion; the RCMP accepted CHAP.

Which was why Larry Sr.'s phone call was monitored by Elisabeth with that data being transmitted to Edmonton, Drought in Chilliwack and Wood in Port Alberni.

Jackson and Jason got in a thirty-minute run out the back of the ranch, skipped breakfast and dressed in jeans and multi-colored Ts. They headed to LAX allowing three hours travel time and arrived at the Executive Suite Private hangar on Imperial just as the maintenance staff was arriving.

The agents didn't have time to develop an undercover story so they made an aggressive appearance in front of the manager, presented him with their credentials and the federal warrant Elisabeth had printed and asked to be shown the jet, the specifics of which Elisabeth had noted on the federal document.

Whether it was the warrant or Jackson and Jason's forceful demeanor, the manager didn't hesitate. After glancing at the warrant and their ID, he said, "Right this way, gentlemen."

The sleek, four passenger jet was impressive. Their research gave the airliner a sixty-five million price tag, boasted a six-thousand-gallon fuel capacity with a distance of seven-thousand nautical miles. The Caymans were less than twenty-two hundred from LAX.

The manager preferred to leave but Jason took him aboard, into the restroom and handcuffed him to a custom, contemporary sink faucet. As the man began a tirade, Jason patted him down, looking for weapons and phones, put his finger to his lips with a facial expression…warning him. The agents didn't want the manager making any phone calls.

Both agents had done a great deal of flying, both personal and professional but they had never experienced anything like the inside of this private aircraft. Their first impression was the odor, it smelled of wealth. The thick pile, taupe carpet invited a person to remove their shoes, socks and wiggle their toes in its thickness. The interior walls were a combination of polished cream resin impregnated fiberglass, interspersed with polished teak accents. They familiarized themselves with the interior, walked down the aisle, passed four luxurious, off-white leather swivel chairs, each with a drop-down teak desktop and television screen. Extending the width at the rear was a couch in the same material and pattern as the swivel chairs. The galley was fully equipped to provide numerous hot meals during an extended flight while the cockpit for two pilots contained sufficient guidance systems to fly on autopilot through inclement weather.

The secret panels were not difficult to locate, albeit time consuming. It was presumed that Gutierrez's crew received preferential treatment in the Caymans which negated the Caribbean island customs from searching the plane.

The agents performed a slow, methodical search, videotaping every discovery. Their first unveiling was the couch. Lifting the cushions there was nothing there but the cloth covered springs, but upon closer inspection, there was more. With Jason filming, Jackson slipped his gloved hand around the perimeter, between the springs and frame. As his hand slid right to left, his other hand mirrored, both catching on a metal handle.

Pulling them simultaneously, the cushion popped out, leaving a deep, end to end cavern. Jackson turned to Jason and said, "This space would accommodate one-hundred thousand in twenties easily. But they are moving much more than that."

Examining the pulled-out section's frame, he found four latch assemblies, strike plates and key core. Someone in the Caymans had the key and left it unlocked. *Who had the key at this end*, he thought?

"Are you thinking what I'm thinking?"

"Definitely. Fernández would be thc key holder. We can check the video when we are done.

"One flight weekly from here, San Francisco and Vancouver, they could ship several million a week. That's almost fifty million a year. Not much. I'm thinking they are making more trips than once a week. The Vancouver law firm has, I don't know how many attorneys. This plane could be making almost daily trips for all we know. Let's have Elisabeth check Henderson's hard drive for maintenance records and flight information. We can also search the cabin to see if the pilots left their logbook."

"Sounds good. If the logbook isn't in the plane, the manager could have it locked up. Let's check the rest of the plane. I'm thinking there are numerous storage locations."

They spent the next hour or so, with periodic protesting from the hangar manager, seeking and finding numerous hidden compartments.

Below the contoured fiberglass walls were handcrafted leather panels. Jackson reached down, slipped his fingers under the panel and pulled.

Each panel could hold about a half of what the couch could. Jackson commented, “If they filled all available spaces it would be millions but getting it to the plane without raising suspicions would be a challenge.

“The surveillance video should reveal that aspect of their operation. We have to assume San Francisco and Vancouver are loaded similarly.

“They would then fly direct to the Cayman Islands, within range of all three cities.”

“That is it Jackson. That’s it exactly,” offered Jason with enthusiasm. “Let’s see those videos.”

When they entered the lavatory, the manager was leaning against the bulkhead, anger written all over his face. He began to protest, again, and Jason put his finger to his mouth, indicating to be quiet.

“Sir, we need to see all the hangar video for the past month. We will uncuff you to save you the embarrassment, but if you step out of line, they go back on. Do you understand.”

The manager was prepared to spout the profanity he felt but the left side of his brain, that’s responsible for analytical thinking, took over and he simply nodded.

Back in the office, the manager said, “Just so you know for the record, viewing the video of the hangar is violating our customer’s policy.”

“We understand that sir and will leave a copy of the federal warrant for your records,” replied Jackson. “Now if you would sit at that desk over there," pointing to one in the far corner where he wouldn't be able to see the screen, "we will be only a few more minutes and be out of your way."

As Jackson was booting the video system, Jason texted Elisabeth their location and request.

It took only a few minutes scrolling through the feed covering Gutierrez's plane to see Fernández entering from a side door with two large hockey duffle bags, one over each shoulder, obviously struggling under the weight.

Jackson continued the tape which showed Fernández exit the plane twenty later with the bags folded and held under one arm. Jackson stopped the tape while Jason texted Elisabeth.

Within seconds Jason's phone vibrated. The screen read, *Done*. No smiley face. Not permitted on government communications devices.

Jason put a hand on Jackson's shoulder. Jackson turned, looked at Jason's phone, smiled, rewound the tape, shut the system down, turned, thanked the manager then joined Jason and left the office.

Chapter THIRTY-SIX

Joe Palermo had been a commercial fisherman out of Campbell River for as long as he could remember. He started with his dad and grandfather washing dishes aboard the twenty-eight-foot *Fish Haven*. In elementary school, he worked weekends, baiting hooks for the salmon run and was always on the water during spring break. By the time Palermo was a teen, he was part of the paid crew.

His grandfather retired first, then his dad, leaving him the *Fish Haven*. Joe had fond memories of his time with his two role models and had followed their techniques for decades and now as he faced his own retirement, he found the fishing industry in free-fall. The yearly salmon run had dropped so drastically that he and most of his fisher friends could no longer sustain their lifestyle.

With the industry's decline, the value of the *Fish Haven* had dropped from two hundred thousand, to less than fifty.

It was during a Federal Fisheries symposium on sustainable fishing off the British Columbia coast that Joe ran into Larry Baird Sr., a friendship he had developed during the nineties' Clayoquot Sound logging protests. Eight hundred and fifty environmentalists were arrested save he and Baird. They had kept in touch over the years and now shared a few beers at their mutual hotel post-conference.

Palermo was lamenting the loss of his livelihood when Baird threw him a lifeline with a payday that, combined with his government pension, the sale of the *Fish Haven* and his home paid for, would provide him with a comfortable retirement.

Joe had no idea what to expect from his old friend but he was desperate. He was not going to ask his wife of forty years to get a job along with himself in order to survive.

He was in.

Baird Sr. texted him outlining the plan, verifying that Palermo had a valid insurance policy on the *Fish Haven.*

Inspector Wood had gambled and lost. He didn't have sufficient personnel to monitor the cruise line's intoxicated passengers whooping it up on Third Ave and Argyle. Although no arrests were made, several fights were broken up at one of the seedy bars while other Mounties walked the streets, reminiscent of military shore patrols of yore.

Leaving those Members to deal control the tourists, he called Angie who left work immediately to grab a few hours of sleep. Before she left, she verified that all the CCTV cameras were functioning and recording.

Larry Sr. was secluded, along with several old friends including another Clayoquot Sound protester, Robert Billings, within the lumber piles next to the dock. Workers had been off the job for weeks as a result of a labor dispute. They had the place to themselves.

Larry Sr. checked the time on his phone then hit T911-Send, which immediately went through his VPN data base. Once connected to the emergency call center, he texted that there was a bomb on a fishing boat.

Simple. Direct. And a perfect diversion.

Untraceable.

So he thought.

Sgt. Major Curtis Leithead had finished canning his day's catch late into the night and now sat on his deck, sipping a much-deserved Sleeman's Honey Brown Lager. The Strait was pitch black; the empty canvas framed by Campbell River's city lights.

Leithead had experienced numerous pivotal, life changing incidents during his vacation, or what he liked to call, *my pre-retirement planning holiday*. There was no turning back after this glorious time in British Columbia. He would accept the offered medical retirement with full benefits and since he was unattached, he just might apply for Canadian immigration. Canadians sound like him, well, almost, but that is the only similarity and he liked the difference.

He was musing his next step when he dropped his feet to the deck, jumped up and watched in shock as something exploded in the Strait.

Using his phone, he dialed 9-1-1 to report the incident, then sat back to watch the event unfold, hoping whoever was aboard escaped unharmed. He had seen enough death to last an eternity. No more.

Unknown to Leithead, the Campbell River RCMP had received a bomb threat just moments before the explosion and now was in the process of deploying their Marine Unit along with the Comox Valley Marine Rescue, a civilian vessel forty-five minutes south.

The Campbell River detachment commander initiated their emergency plan requesting two Members from Comox Valley and two from Port Alberni to aid in dealing with the 9-1-1 text, no longer a threat.

Curtis watched in amazement as the two vessels converged upon the burning…whatever.

Observing, fearfully, from an alcove across from the marina and away from CCTV cameras, Joe returned his phone to his pocket and headed home. He would visit the marina in the morning, ostensibly to check his boat. Finding it missing he would report it stolen to the RCMP.

Inspector Wood was monitoring the evening's patrol events when the request arrived for two of his officers. *A bomb threat. No coincidence* thought Lorne.

He immediately removed two officers from foot patrol at Third and Argyle, leaving two officers monitoring the drinkers.

The five-ton enclosed truck Robert Billings provided had its tailgate down, and a forklift was standing by.

Midnight.

The Chica de Oro surfaced like a mythical sea creature; silent and impressive in its futuristic design.

Water continued to drip off the bulkhead as the forward hatch opened and a ramp was extended to the dock. Several men emerged holding Israeli Tavor X95 assault rifles. They stepped aside and guarded the unloading. Larry Sr. ignored the overt threat. He and the crew fastened the fore and aft with deck ropes and immediately began piling the ten kilo packages on pallets.

Angie Taylor couldn't be seen from the Golden Girl dressed in jeans, blue polo shirt with the marina logo and a medium weight navy blue bomber jacket. As she stood in the dark, her phone light was covered by her open coat as she quickly texted Wood.

Time was of the essence. The crews worked expertly. The first pallet was removed by the forklift, placed on the tail-gate. Load raised. Pallet jack transferred the load to the front.

Considering his depleted staff, Wood was counting on none of his officers noticing the activity at the lumber dock. With so much attention on the cruise ships and their passengers milling around in the bright lights, it was unlikely.

He hoped.

Two members were stationed along Redford Street in a non-descript vehicle, the other car was waiting about ten minutes out of town, to begin surveillance of the five ton.

Three thousand, ten kilo packages unloaded quickly, and fifteen minutes after surfacing, the hatch was closed and the Chica de Oro dropped silently into the darkness.

Baird Sr. hopped into the truck with Billings driving. The truck moved slowly into the lumber stacks and stopped. Several pallets of cedar six by six by eight posts were loaded behind the multi-million-dollar cargo.

The tailgate rose, self-locked, the forklift returned to its previous location and the unloading team dispersed.

"Deception may give us what we want for the present, but it will always take it away in the end."

Rachel Hawthorne

Chapter THIRTY-SEVEN

Wood arrived soon after receiving Taylor's text. He stood at the peninsula where the Somas River enters the Alberni inlet and utilizing a pair of high-powered binoculars, watched millions disappearing.

With so many moving pieces, trusting in others to complete their segment was difficult. It took all his concentration to watch and not act.

He became transfixed by the gunmetal grey vessel, all but invisible save for the movement; humans attired in overalls matching the sub's color.

When the transfer was complete and the sub sunk to blend with its murky surroundings, he swung the glasses and noticed Angie moving through the shadows, probably home to ponder the evening's events; lifechanging and yet forever a secret.

Intellectually he understood the decision to allow the sub to return to Colombia and make another delivery, but all his training and instinct told him that it was wrong. And yet he knew if he had orchestrated the takedown of the sub and its crew, another would spring up out of Colombia or other drug producing country and society would be no further ahead.

This way, he convinced himself, thirty tons of poison would never make it to the streets.

He was right, and wrong.

Wood texted Edmonton, then returned to his unmarked and headed home, to work with Angie in the morning to download the CTV footage from the evening. He was confident he would have proof of Larry Sr.'s involvement as well as that of his crew.

After meeting Brian Sawyer at the Edmonton airport, Stan and Brian headed to the parking lot to Stan's four-door pick-up. Once in the vehicle, Stan went over the plan, how he arranged with several Lower Mainland, BC street dealers to leave their current supplier and sell for him.

"Might this start a turf war with the established gangs?" asked Brian.

"It might. But I chose dealers from the smaller gangs. They each have their own territory and believe they can get a higher price for our more pure, safer product and a guaranteed supply than what they are currently selling. Plus, I offered them a much greater share of the profits than they are currently receiving.

"I don't anticipate any problems. The primary gangs have no idea that we are bringing in choice Colombian or the quantity.

"We're good. Get some rest Lieutenant. I am going to need all your savvy and expertise in a few hours when we meet the truck in Mission."

Sawyer smiled. *I am back*, he thought, as he leaned against the door and closed his eyes.

RCMP Deputy Commissioner Benedetti called Sgt. Drought directly on the Force's encrypted system relaying the movement of the truck.

"Rick, four Members are leap-frogging the five ton," she explained, meaning there were two or more surveillance vehicles, where the drivers change places with the passenger, alter their appearance and alternate road positions with the other police vehicle, making it difficult for the suspect to detect their presence.

"They will follow it to the Duke Point Ferry Terminal in Nanaimo and to wherever on the mainland. Your team has a challenging task, which is why I am calling.

"We don't know the final destination of the cargo. The Members tailing Stan texted that he picked up Sawyer at the airport and they are headed west.

We assume he has turned several Lower Mainland small-time dealers to sell for him. Their previous suppliers and the gangs are not going to accept this when they find out.

"We are counting on them not discovering the influx until the delivery is complete and we have the shipment. Then there is no conflict. No rivalry. We have the shipment.

"But we can't count on that. We have no idea what to expect other than what Inspector Wood has discovered. We need your interdiction team to be prepared to engage those transporting the drugs, the new dealers who will be at the drop to accept their delivery and possibly shooters from any number of gangs.

"Use a minimum of two Cougars and I want you to work with the ERT supervisor and coordinate the hit on the drop. Make sure the assault team has the maximum carry of thirty-round magazines for the Colt C-8 Carbine. You are not taking any chances.

"Everyone comes home from this operation Rick," she concluded somewhat emotionally. She had seen far too many fellow officers killed in the line of duty, to not be prepared.

"Yes, ma'am. Got it. We are gearing up now and I will call the ERT team leader. They will be here within the hour."

"Good. Oh, one more thing. Make sure the entry team uses the Level 1V Body Armor which includes ceramic plates covering vital organs.

"Also, Karen Winthrop, Tom Hortonn and Kimberly Breyman are tailing the Vancouver suspects. If we work this correctly, we will have all players in custody with sufficient evidence for convictions, millions in currency and the same value in Colombian cocaine.

"The Secret Service assured us they will have the California connection behind bars within hours of our arrests."

She concluded with, "Be safe Rick. Everyone comes home," and she hung up.

Sgt. Major Leithead was fascinated with the operation unfolding before him in the dark. He wished he had a pair of binoculars to get a closer look. What he could determine was that two vessels were circling the still burning boat with search lights spanning the open waters, presumably seeking survivors.

They would find none for there never was someone aboard, save Joe's initial presence. Timing was essential with precise vessel placement before he swam to shore and slipped into the shadows.

Joe sat alone in his dark kitchen sipping a tall Jack Daniels. Not having second thoughts, there was no turning back, but wondering if he performed the so-called "terrorist act" with sufficient precision as to not implicate himself.

The old rayon sweater he left beside the white gas stove in the galley with his discarded cell phone beside it had sufficient static electricity to be the accelerant. Joe called the old phone creating the spark. The plan was for the boat to burn all evidence and sink one hundred and sixty meters to the bottom.

He waited.

The marina surveillance cameras would have his image but it would not reveal his identity, just a man of his height in a black, non-descript hoody, jeans and common black work boots.

Investigators would certainly be looking at him given his current financial dilemma, but that was insufficient evidence for them to evaluate him further. It could only develop into a catch-22 if Larry Sr. was caught.

Robert and Larry Sr. found nothing to chat about as they headed up Redford Street and onto the Port Alberni Highway heading over *The Hump,* an elevation of four-hundred and eleven meters, and onto Parksville and Nanaimo. The steady rain created limited visibility making driving treacherous. They knew that an accident would result in the RCMP traffic services member asking for the vehicle's cargo papers.

There were none.

Numerous recent fatalities had added to their cautious driving.

The first leap for the RCMP tailing vehicles occurred at Cathedral Grove, British Columbia's heritage to the eight-hundred-year-old Douglas fir trees measuring seventy-five meters in height and nine meters in circumference.

The first surveillance vehicle pulled off into the parking area while the second car waited for two vehicles to pass, then pulled into traffic.

The first team quickly changed appearances; different shirts, a floppy tan, wide-brim hat and the other with a neck scarf. They changed drivers then pulled into traffic and quickly caught up to their colleagues, staying well out of sight and several vehicles behind.

The process continued every ten kilometers until they reached Duke Point Ferry Terminal with one surveillance vehicle entering the adjoining lane but well behind their subject and their colleagues several lanes away.

Loading the product, plus the cedar and the slow grind up and over *The Hump* and to Nanaimo took almost four hours, allowing the three vehicles to arrive the required thirty minutes before sailing.

As the five-ton pulled up to the window for payment, Larry Sr. pulled out a wad of twenties, peeled off twelve and handed them to Robert.

Once confirmed their cargo was not classified as dangerous with no propane or explosives, they drove ahead to the staging area.

The two surveillance vehicle occupants did likewise, not wanting to draw attention to their status by using a government credit card.

Six people.

None exited their vehicles.

Thirty-minute wait to load.

Once aboard, the subjects and their surveillance team left their vehicles, a BC Ferries' requirement, and walked up to the cafeteria for breakfast.

Robert finished his corned beef hash and eggs, then excused himself for the washroom.

Instead, he walked out the first exit beyond Larry Sr.'s view and made a phone call.

Ten seconds, then he went to the washroom.

The member following him observed the call but had no way of knowing with whom he spoke. Finished in the bathroom, he exited an opposite door, walked onto the deck, stood behind a life raft and made a call.

Chapter THIRTY-EIGHT

Stan and Brian stopped in Hope, British Columbia, the entrance to the province's Lower Mainland for fuel, then a drive-thru for sandwiches and coffee.

They were forty-minutes from their destination.

Their law enforcement surveillance team pulled into another gas station allowing them a full view of the suspects, refueled and were within a few vehicles as the pick-up pulled onto the highway.

Just as Sgt. Drought closed his phone after taking an emergency call from Benedetti, it rang again. It was Stan's surveillance team advising their ETA to Drought was thirty-minutes.

Rick conversed with the ERT supervisor who brought both teams together to advise the heavily armed officers to expect a firefight and confirm strategy.

They loaded into the Cougars, left the Pacific Training Centre, headed west, on Highway Seven to parallel the suspects' vehicle traveling west on Highway One.

Kimberly, Tom and Karen were exhausted, having tailed their suspects non-stop for days without a break. Fortunately, Elisabeth's tracking the subjects' vehicles allowed the officers sleep time.

The call from Kopas was exciting; they saw an end in sight. The three were traveling on different highways, following their respective assignments, heading east. Regrettably, they didn't have sufficient personnel to perform the preferred leap-frog system, so they changed lanes frequently, moving in and out of the heavy traffic to prevent being spotted.

Robert and Larry Sr. made good time after leaving the ferry terminal, beating the morning rush hour traffic. Turning north on Highway 11 it was a short distance to the Blueberry Hill Chicken farm on the right where Stan and Brian were waiting by the side of the road.

Common to criminal gangs the world over, greed destroys any chance for peace. According to the Combined Forces Special Enforcement Unit, there were an estimated one-hundred and eighty-eight competing gangs. Production, price and distribution drove the economy of the drug trade.

The Octopoda were renown to guard their territory with such violence, neighboring gangs gave them a wide birth. Targeted shootings in the Lower Mainland were usually attributed to the Octopoda assassins. Octopoda was named for the octopus, which uses camouflage and threats against its enemies, quick mobility and ability to hide.

What the genesis group ignored was the species' short lifespan.

When their leaders heard about an Alberta gang, led by Loblinski, planning to introduce a huge quantity of Colombian cocaine at a ridiculously low price to the Lower Mainland, they were enraged. They had controlled their competition for years with intimidation and violence and now outsiders were attempting to undo years of market development.

No.

When they received the phone call, they rallied their shooters, armed with M4-A1 (a shorter and lighter version of the jungle warfare M-16) automatic rifles, smuggled in from

Washington State, previously stolen from a California National Guard Amory, and used the timing of the ferry landing, provided by Robert and caught up with the five ton just as it turned north on Highway Eleven.

Stan viewed the five ton's approach in the side-mirrors and drove ahead and into the farm's driveway which wound through fifty-year old evergreens blocking all sight of the barn at the rear of the twenty acres, blocking all sight from the main road.

He flashed his lights once and two twenty-foot tall doors slid open through which he and the five-ton entered.

Following the five ton down the road were three vehicles which had met at the intersection of Highway One and Eleven. Brosman and Snow would be well represented as would the accounting firm of Kuznetsov Chartered Accountants.

Karen, Tom and Kimberly were close behind their suspects, saw them enter the driveway and pulled to the side of the road to be available if the assault team needed assistance during the operation.

The barn door closed behind the five ton, leaving the two vehicles dimly lit in an area reserved for thirty-six thousand chickens in the forty by five-hundred foot, twenty-thousand square foot barn.

The men exited their vehicles and were met by a caravan of small, white cargo vans with a cartoon character of an Orca whale emblazoned on each side and rear. Above the whale read, *Orca Dry Cleaners*.

Stan smiled as he approached the former Albertan who had arranged the fleet and organized the dealers into the drug delivery system.

Brief greetings between Stan, his dealers and the British Columbia financial wing were exchanged, all sharing in the happiness at succeeding in the complex and profitable operation.

Each *Orca Dry Cleaning* vehicle was equipped with a GPS system which was programmed from a main unit housed in the *Orca Dry Cleaning* manager's office.

The concept had been attempted previously by other drug entrepreneurs such as Dial-a-dope with some success until they were inevitably caught. Stan's concept was slightly different with roving vans, no cell phone usage and delivery instructions sent from the office to the GPS units. Sales would be generated through the Dark Web. Customers paid electronically, so drivers didn't accept payment. The vans' mobility made them less susceptible to being raided by rival gangs.

Stan had arranged financial accounts for each street dealer allowing them to pay monthly with their internet accounts. Marianna had financed the Colombian shipment and Loblinski had several months of a grace period before he had to start paying her.

When Stan pulled to the side of the road on Highway Eleven, the surveillance team did likewise some distance behind and called Drought.

As the officer closed his phone from speaking to the Sergeant, two identical, non-descript vans passed. Instinct told him the opposition had arrived.

Quickly calling Drought back, he said, "They're here."

Drought closed his phone, placed it in his tactical vest pocket and gripped his Colt 8, telling the driver, "Now".

Stan and his dealers had just completed dividing the cocaine when a side-door opened and six men, all wearing black balaclavas rushed in, setting off a bevy of automatic fire.

"Okay mother fuckers, on the ground," shouted one intruder.

Robert and Larry Sr. had moved into the barn's shadows during the shipment's allocation.

Robert looked at Larry Sr. and whispered, "What the fuck? Move behind those boxes before we get killed," as he grabbed Larry Sr. and pulled him down, immediately regretting the phone call.

They quietly maneuvered further into the shadows just as several of the Orca dealers opened fire on the *Octopoda* shooters who immediately ran for cover and returned fire.

Stan momentarily froze. He couldn't believe he had been betrayed. Brian was nowhere in sight.

While the opposition concentrated on their shootout with his dealers, he ran to the pickup, retrieved an APS-95 assault rifle, with a thirty-five- round magazine, manufactured in Croatia, smuggled into Italy by relatives and shipped to Stan in Canada.

Spinning away from the truck, he searched for the Octopoda shooters, trying to distinguish them from his dealers.

The dim light he specifically created to keep a low profile, now hampered his defense. Dropping behind several stacks of chicken hauling crates, he opened fire at the shooters' entry.

The RCMP assault teams cut their lights as they entered the long driveway and one Cougar sped around the barn's perimeter to the rear.

Perfectly timed, Members launched flash grenades through front and back barn windows, immediately disorientating everyone in the building with a blinding light and a deafening bang, greater than one hundred and seventy decibels.

All shooters were instantly confused, looking around, their eyes seeing nothing, during which time both Cougars crashed through the barn doors, lit the interior with flood lights as black balaclava officers exited the armored vehicles, splitting into teams left and right, yelling, "Federal officers. Down, down, down," as they fired numerous rounds into the air while rushing the shooters.

Several of Stan's dealers turned their attention to the officers, so unhinged by the blast, they fired wildly in the general direction of the blinding light.

The skilled officers cut them down instantly. Other Members concentrated on the Octopoda shooters, eliminating everyone as they popped up from hiding trying for a shot at the heavily armed and armored officers.

Stan was dedicated to his financial success and wisely decided to live to deal another day, dropped his rifle and hit the ground with his arms spread.

Brosman and Snow attorneys and Kuznetsov dropped immediately, covering their heads when the shooting began, each praying they would survive. Stan had promised their physical involvement would be minimum and that he was taking all the chances. Greed and the desire to see the result of their multi-million-dollar investment led to their downfall.

Brian having no idea how to react, fearing for his life and regretting ever accepting Stan's offer, chose to stay under the pickup until the shooting stopped.

Larry Sr. and Robert were too frightened to move and remained prone in the chicken excrement.

Their ears still rang and their vision was limited when they were both hauled upright by two ERT Members and dragged in front of a Cougar where officers bound their wrists behind their backs, zip tied their ankles, then forced them to lie flat in the chicken waste.

The officers didn't speak and Larry Sr. and Robert were smart enough to keep quiet.

Brian remained under Stan's truck with his hands over his head and elbows tucked into his ears. He was unaware the shooting had stopped until he was forcefully grabbed by the ankles and dragged from under the truck and over to the Cougar.

Other officers were less gentle with Stan, who had fired at them. Although he remained prone, breathing in the putrid air, officers pounced on him, putting a knee in his lower back and one on his head, forcing dust into his eyes and chicken shit into his mouth.

The officer closest to his butt cuffed his wrists behind his back, then hauled him by the wrists across the filthy floor, dropped him by the others, then zip tied his ankles.

Stan obviously knew what had happened but he was too scared to look up to see the three Vancouver financiers being treated similarly.

Stan lifted his head somewhat, staring at Brian, wondering whether he was the traitor. Loblinski figured that unlikely. It couldn't be Larry Sr. they went back too far. The informer had to be the guy Larry Sr. recruited.

He would deal with him later, right now Stan had to survive.

Five criminals survived. Stan's dealers would be identified later as being low level street operatives for other gangs while the Octopoda shooters were top level members, assassins, well-known to police across the Lower Mainland.

Once the shooting ceased, Karen, Kimberly and Tom entered the barn, firearms holstered, holding their neck chained Buffalos above their heads. They introduced themselves to the officers guarding the smashed barn door, then proceeded inside.

Not knowing these Members either, they circulated, introducing themselves, gratified that weeks of scrutinizing their three subjects had resulted in arrests with a few less cocaine pushers feeding poison.

The cocaine was cataloged, loaded into the five ton while each of the Orca vans was searched. Officers found several hundred thousand dollars, presumably good faith money for Stan. Certainly not the amount Benedetti anticipated. It was all tagged, bagged with officers signing evidence documents attesting to the total.

All of the Orca's windows were shattered, tires destroyed and panels riddled with bullet holes. They would all be towed to the RCMP evidence yard where a forensics team would dismantle each to ensure there weren't hidden compartments, then match fingerprints with the deceased dealers.

Seeing that the post raid was progressing as planned, Sgt. Drought leaned against one of the Cougars and called his boss.

"Drought here, ma'am. All clear. No injuries for us. Loblinski's dealers dead. Octopoda dealers dead. Five in custody."

He listened briefly to his commander, then closed the phone, spoke with the ERT leader who nodded, then turned at the sound of approaching sirens.

The Golden Girl left Barkley Sound and was met by and connected to the min-sub one hundred kilometers south of the Pacific Rim National Park Reserve peninsula. An automatic coupling system designed by Adrian Achterberg but actually copied from Alexander de Seversky's invention in 1923, simplified the task.

The Coalition Forces which flew over the Middle East during several skirmishes used the system for mid-air refueling. Achterberg changed the metal compound to withstand saltwater but otherwise the coupling and the boom were identical.

The Golden Girl shut down her power and was towed to its Colombian fiord.

The HMSC Toronto had monitored the Chica de Oro through the Sound and would follow her back to Colombia. The Canadian warship would maintain that assignment until relieved at some future date by either another Canadian or American ship.

The Chica would be monitored 24/7 for the foreseeable future.

As soon as Benedetti closed her conversation with Drought, she called Inspector Wood.

The prisoners were taken to the Surrey Pre-Trial Detention Centre where they were housed in isolation until an interrogation team arrived. The cocaine and half a million in currency were taken to the Surrey Detachment and locked in their evidence locker. Both would be kept until trial then the drugs would be destroyed and the money forfeited to the government.

A warrant was obtained for each of Stan's dealers and Stan's Edmonton condo and his vehicle.

"Juvenile crime is not naturally born in the boy but is largely due either to the spirit of adventure that is in him, to his own stupidity or to his lack of discipline, according the nature of the individual."

Robert Baden Powell

Stan beginning his criminality as a high school student while being raised by loving, disciplining parents, would, according to Baden-Powell, leave either stupidity or a larcenous spirit to explain his behavior.

"My father kept me busy from dawn to dusk when I was a kid. When I wasn't pitching hay, hauling corn or running a tractor, I was heaving a baseball into his mitt behind the barn. If all parents followed his rule, juvenile delinquency would be cut in half in a year's time."

Robert Feller

Stan had the opportunity to which Feller referred, working at the mill while in high school. Loblinski was not stupid, evidenced by his entrepreneurial endeavors, leaving many to wonder where he obtained his criminal gene.

Chapter THIRTY-NINE

Curtis Leithead went to bed after watching the burning boat pass into the somber darkness. The next morning, after coffee on the deck, he showered, dressed and headed down to breakfast hoping to hear the local chatter about the vessel fire.

He took an empty booth facing the water and within moments, Noah, a high school student, appeared with a menu and coffee. "Good morning Sgt. Major. How was the fishing yesterday?"

"Good morning, Noah. It was fabulous as usual. You and your fellow British Columbians have convinced me I need to retire here.

"Any news on all the commotion last night with the burning boat or how it started?"

Ignoring the compliment, Noah replied, "Not a lot so far. Probably more as the day progresses. The Mounties can't investigate in this small community without everyone knowing. The rumor is someone called in a bomb threat. Plus Joe Palermo, a local fisherman, his boat is missing."

"That's too bad. What would prompt someone to eliminate a man's livelihood like that. You wouldn't think a fisherman would have enemies. I wonder if the theft and explosion was random? Hopefully investigators will know soon.

"Thanks for the update Noah. Seeing the blaze last night, it sure didn't look like there would be anything left.

"Anyway, Sgt. Major what can I get for your breakfast?"

Leithead was used to folks making a big deal about his rank. And it was a big deal, his rank was the highest for a non-commissioned officer. He appreciated the respect but quickly moved on, ordering the farmer sausage and scrambled eggs skillet.

Noah left to place his order while Curtis watched the numerous boats in the general area of the fire, presumably attempting to gather evidence.

He suspected what debris there might have been was long gone, having been swept out by the tide.

There were few diners and his breakfast arrived quickly. He enjoyed his meal but didn't spend much time eating as he had a busy morning schedule.

Karen, Tom and Kimberly hung around chatting the case with their colleagues until supervisors from the "E" Division arrived.

Not wanting to get caught up in answering questions from the RCMP when they were under orders from CSIS, they quickly slipped out the battered door as the bureaucracy began organizing the area for the crime scene investigators.

Walking back to their respective rentals, they shared how weird it was that the subjects of their surveillance for weeks had no clue they were being followed, photographed or had tracking devices affixed to their vehicles.

Kimberly quipped about the proximity of the Matsqui prison almost within sight and if the suspects would "Go to jail, go directly to jail, do not pass 'go' and do not collect your cocaine money".

She got a laugh from her colleagues with Karen replying, "Good one, Kimberly. I wonder how many years the survivors will get?"

"Probably not as stiff a sentence as they should. I wonder if the courts will hand out additional years for the use of a firearm or shooting at officers," offered Tom rhetorically.

They gave each other high-fives, made arrangements to take the day off and meet the next morning at the UBC detachment.

Sergeant Major Leithead met the food bank director at her office, adjacent to the food storeroom.

He had borrowed a pick-up to transport the canned salmon and with the help of a volunteer, unloaded and stacked the boxes on a large cart.

Several other volunteers joined them, opening the boxes and stacking the cans on shelves.

It took thirty-minutes to empty all the containers. When the task was complete the director appeared with a camera and took a photo of the team, including Curtis.

The group had coffee, then as Curtis was about to leave, he handed the director one-thousand dollars in traveler's checks endorsed to the food bank.

The director and volunteers were so taken aback by his generosity they were momentarily speechless. The food bank found it difficult at the best of times to marshal support and here was an American tourist donating thousands of dollars in quality fish and currency.

Hugs all around and as Leithead reached the door, he turned to wave and the director said, "We hope to see you back here soon, Sgt. Major."

"You will ma'am, very soon," Curtis replied with a wide grin.

As he headed to the borrowed pick-up, he wondered how long it would take for Canada to process his paperwork.

When Deputy Commissioner Benedetti finished speaking with Drought to ensure he procured a valid currency and product count, she called the Commissioner, requesting permission to speak directly to David Kopas.

She got it and was speaking with him within minutes of closing the conversation with the head of the RCMP.

Chapter FORTY

Inspector Wood met Angie at the marina and retrieved copies of the CCTV footage from the previous night and was in his office at six am reviewing the evidence when his phone buzzed.

"Wood here," he answered in his customary tone when interrupted.

"Lorne, Samantha. How is the footage looking?"

"Ma'am. Good morning. I am just now getting into it. From the various angles, we have enough for Crown to proceed.

"Ma'am, you have to see this submarine. It is like nothing I have ever come across before. There isn't a conning tower. With all the diversions and the cruise ships, it went unnoticed. When it broke the surface right next to the dock, the only thing visible was one hatch. Two guys popped out carrying automatic rifles, then several other crew members appeared and started unloading immediately.

"It was difficult to allow it to leave."

Samantha agreed saying, "It would be interesting to talk to the two members of the Joint Task Force who were involved. But that is for another day," she replied with urgency in her voice. "Lorne, I need you in Surrey today to interrogate Loblinski, the Vancouver Three and the two from Port. You are familiar with the operation and I think you can get the most from the suspects."

"Will do, ma'am. I should be there late this afternoon."

"Good. Keep me informed," replied Samantha, just before the line went dead.

The two Costa Rican agents had watched Brian Sawyer as he was escorted from his house to the airport and onto a plane destined for Edmonton.

They had not been informed that CSIS or the RCMP were sanctioned to remove a Costa Rican citizen but had no authority to detain the two men escorting Brian.

Unbeknown to the Costa Rican agents, Loblinski's private detectives were tailed from Edmonton by a CSIS agent who called Kopas once Sawyer was airborne. David in turn placed a courtesy call to the Costa Rican security forces apologizing for not informing them but ensuring the agency that it was not the Canadian government which ushered Sawyer back to Edmonton, but two private detectives.

Kopas and Benedetti knew that if they told the Costa Rica agents they suspected millions in American currency were hidden in Sawyer's house, Canada would not receive any of it.

Since it was the Force which took down the Colombian cocaine operation, Benedetti convinced Kopas to a joint operation; a visit to Sawyer's Costa Rica house and search for what they believe was currency from the Southern Alberta Cannabis operation. Brian shipped the product into Idaho and then to Wyoming to be sold, to finance the Christians for a Better America.

Sawyer's nefarious actions having crossed an international border, Kopas assigned the JTF2 to a covert operation.

The Canadian warship, the HMCS Yellowknife was currently serving in the Atlantic, three hundred nautical miles east of Martinique, monitoring communications in and out of politically troubled Argentina. They were combat ready with a JTF2 Team on board.

Kopas spoke directly with the unit commander via encrypted radio aboard the Yellowknife, providing all the necessary details for the covert operation then confirming them with an encrypted email.

The Yellowknife sailed undetected between the southern tip of the British Virgin Islands and the northern coast of Montserrat in the eastern Caribbean and within two hundred nautical miles of the Costa Rican coast, timing their arrival for just after dark.

Two teams of six agents covered the distance between the warship and the coast in inflatable boats with rigid hulls propelled by twenty horse outboard motors. They cut their motors one kilometer from the beach and swam the remaining distance, pulling the boats behind them.

Team One set up a security perimeter while Team Two advanced on Sawyer's house. Wearing night goggles, the team was able to enter the structure without creating light and spent several hours quietly tearing the interior apart. In addition to the currency, the JTF2 Team discovered seven bricks of cocaine. It appeared Brian was stealing from the Colombian cartel instead of taking the entire shipment to the Limón docks.

The final count was ten million in American currency, the fruit of Brian's years of growing high- level cannabis for Stan.

It took the agents several trips to load and transport the cash in duffle bags to the beach. They reversed their procedure, swam out from the beach one kilometer, climbed aboard, cranked the engines and motored back to the Yellowknife.

Once aboard the warship and debriefed, the commander called Kopas with the news, which David immediately shared with Deputy Commissioner Benedetti.

Wood spent the next hour perusing CHAP, making notes on Stan's involvement, his relationship with Marianna Gutierrez, Brian Sawyer, the texts back and forth from Bronson and Snow and Kuznetsov and Loblinski's financial connection to Gutierrez.

Experience taught him to keep a fresh uniform and personals in his locker, which he grabbed while heading out of the detachment, when he heard the RCMP helicopter land in the parking lot. Benedetti wanted him in Surrey now, not spending valuable time driving.

He used the thirty-minute airtime perusing his notes and developing an approach. The five suspects fell into different prosecutorial categories and his interrogation technique would be specific for each of the apprehended.

Karen, Tom and Kimberly met at the UBC detachment at 8 the next morning as planned not knowing what to expect of the day.

They had just settled at their respective desks and were straightening files when Karen's phone vibrated.

Answering immediately she said, "Winthrop."

Looking at her inquisitive colleagues she mouthed, *Kopas.*

"Yes sir. We will head there right now," she replied, made a note and closed her phone.

Before Kimberly or Tom could enquire, she offered, "Kimberly and I are ordered to the Surrey detachment to meet with an Inspector Wood who is conducting the interrogation of the suspects. They are being transported from the detention center. David said, 'You guys did the work, gathered the information, now I want you to learn to interrogate on an international level.'"

"David also said Wood has an impressive track record and that the Secret Service, LAPD and Santa Barbara Police Department are expecting us to bring them evidence to produce indictments against Gutierrez and her organization."

Tom appeared confused, offering, "Did he say what I'm supposed to do?"

"He didn't say, except that he wanted a woman's approach to the suspects' interviews," Karen replied, turning from Tom so she wouldn't burst out laughing.

Kimberly couldn't stifle a grin, which Tom caught and said, "Okay, okay, I get it. Now, seriously. What did David say?"

"What, you don't believe me Tom?" Karen asked, tilting her head to one side, arms outstretched.

"No, I don't. Now give," he replied with a huge grin, acknowledging his colleagues were playing him. "I don't want to be stuck here counting paper clips."

"Okay, fair enough. David said he had another job for you and to meet him later this morning at his office."

"Great. Where is his office?"

"I have no idea and he didn't say other than for you to use your department phone, punch in this code," she handed him a piece of paper, "and follow the directions."

Tom looked at the paper, then said, "Man, he is starting to get really clandestine."

"Starting? Do you remember Costa Rica?" Karen replied with a grin, referring to their operation in the Central American country, uploading data, to a CSIS satellite, while they were parked on the roadside. "Anyway, we will see you later. Come on Agent Kimberly, we have a class to catch," as she held the door open.

Kimberly smiled and said, "Sounds good. Who's driving?"

Karen looked at Kimberly, grinning and replied, "I'll flip you for it," both laughing as they headed out the door with Tom on their heels, pulling out his phone, not sure if their levity was at his expense.

"Women have been trained to speak softly and carry lipstick. Those days are over."

Bella Abzug

Chapter FORTY-ONE

Deputy Commissioner Benedetti was pleased with the money JTF2 had retrieved and although it was gratifying to get the seventy kilos of cocaine out of Costa Rica, there was zero cash value to the Force. Although Alberta's "K" Division wouldn't reap the benefits directly, the money would assist the tight national budget and hopefully the Commissioner would use part of it to complete equipping all Members with Colt Carbines.

She smiled to herself, pushing her chair away from her desk, placing one leg over the other, clasping her hands behind her head and thought, *sure beats the hell out of the measly bust BC's Project Ester bragged about,* referring to a recent operation which netted two million in currency and cocaine.

Continuing her musing, *that haul of the Secret Service in California was unprecedented. I am glad I'm not having to deal with sharing the four hundred million. The DEA's confiscation of the seventy-seven million at the Port of New York earlier this year plus the thirty-eight million from the Port of Philadelphia last month would be nice though.*

DEA's investigation discovered that the two American ports were the last in a series of cocaine drops, including Chili and Panama where fishing boats downloaded large bundles of shrink-wrapped cocaine.

The Canadian warship airlifted the cocaine and ten million dollars to the roof of the Canadian High Commission office in Bridgetown, Barbados, guarded by the JTF2 assault team dressed in civilian attire; chocolate colored slacks, tan and cream patterned Tommy Bahama shirts, untucked to conceal their handguns and off-white linen, lace-up shoes.

The HMCS Yellowknife's commander had no difficulty in receiving approval for the Canadian helicopter gunship to enter Barbados airspace.

Canadian Military Police personnel in full battle gear met the helicopter as it landed on the consulate roof, surrounding it facing outwards. The JTF2 agents disembarked quickly and were immediately surrounded by MPs who marched the group into the building as two MPs guarded the roof door.

The embassy was ready for the delivery. The duffels were placed in the massive document and currency safe, signed for and the agents reversed their movements and were airlifted back to the warship.

The money and cocaine would leave Barbados for Toronto the next day aboard a military jet, guarded by four MPs. The detail would continue their journey to RCMP Headquarters in Ottawa where the product would be tested, the currency counted and all locked in an evidence locker.

The RCMP "E" Division helicopter landed easily at the rear of their Surry headquarters. While the rotors continued, Lorne exited the airship, ducked his head and jogged into the building and was met by "E" Division's commanding officer, Deputy Commissioner Barbara Halloway.

Although Lorne knew the way from previous visits, Halloway walked alongside briefing Wood on the location of each of the five suspects, and the video and digital scribing system. Not only would each interview be recorded, but the spoken word would be captured and transcribed ready for the suspects' signatures once Wood verified the data.

He was impressed. The technology would reduce his labor immensely.

Halloway showed the inspector to the AV observation room. Closing the door behind her, Halloway said, "Inspector Wood, I'd like you to meet Karen Winthrop and Kimberly Breyman, Members seconded to CSIS. They are here to observe and may have questions regarding your interviewing techniques. I told them you were the master," she concluding with a grin.

Lorne extended a hand to each of his colleagues and replied, "Thank you for the compliment Deputy Commissioner, let's see if I measure up," as he turned and left Karen and Kimberly to watch the interview on the monitor.

He chose Larry Baird Sr. for his first interview and would work his way up the criminal management chain, expecting each of the lesser conspirators to provide evidence against Loblinski.

The interview room, although small, was designed to elicit information, not intimidate, although Lorne often thought a little of that aura might prove effective.

The small room held a three-foot, almost a meter long and two-feet wide flat surface attached to a wall. Upholstered office chairs, one each for the officer and interviewee and two additional if needed, was the extent of the furnishings.

The environment was modern; light grey walls with overhead florescent lighting, creating a mood, if not comfortable, better than the cell from which Baird had been transferred.

Lorne entered with a laptop under his arm, a notebook, yellow legal pad and a small calculator. Baird raised his head from the platform, showing visible signs of emotional distress. Often Wood would use his stature, six-foot three and over two hundred pounds to his advantage, but he immediately saw this would not be necessary. *This may be easier than I expect,* thought Wood.

"Good day, Mr. Baird. I am Inspector Wood with some questions, the answers to which may set the course of your life for the foreseeable future, as he pulled out a chair and sat across from the suspect.

"I'm going to show you a video. There isn't sound, but the visual will be easy to identify."

Lorne opened the laptop, turned it to Baird and hit play. The silence was golden as Wood watched with a mixture of sadness and pleasure as Baird's face turned pale. The long time Vancouver Island resident put his hands over his face and dropped his head to the platform.

"Mr. Baird, I need you to look at me please."

Larry Sr. lifted his head with a ghost-like expression but said nothing.

"Mr. Baird, the Crown prosecutor is preparing terrorism charges against you for your part in the thirty tons of cocaine smuggled in from Colombia."

Baird stuttered, ran his hands over his face and through his hair. He replied in a muted voice, "I am not a terrorist," emphasizing the not. "I am an honorable and proud Canadian."

"No, you aren't sir. The cocaine was destined for Lower Mainland drug dealers, all of whom are dead. The money from the dealers' customers was to be funneled to a domestic terrorist group in the US. This group was responsible for the destruction of the Marina del Rey Convention Center and the attempt to destroy a Mahalo Airlines plane as it landed at LAX, forcing it into the Pacific Ocean."

Baird stared but said nothing.

"The video clearly shows you loading the submarine's cargo into the five-ton truck. You were followed by four Mounties from Port Alberni to your destination.

"Sir, you are lucky to be alive. All the dealers are dead. We found you huddled behind boxes in that barn with Robert.

"What are you going to say at your trial? Not guilty?"

Baird appeared as though in shock but said nothing.

"The US Attorney General has filed terrorist charges against you as well and wants you extradited immediately," Lorne lied.

Lorne sat back giving Baird a chance to absorb the information, then he read him his legal right to representation.

Larry Sr. waved his right to legal counsel, feeling that adding that process to already downward spiraling circumstances would be disastrous and prolong the agony. With the video, there wasn't anything to say, but he mustered a question.

Asking meekly, "What do you want from me?"

"The Crown prosecutor will want to know your motive. What would prompt an otherwise upstanding citizen to become a criminal?"

Still with a blank face, Baird responded, "That is where you are wrong sir. I have not been an upstanding citizen for several decades. I just got caught," running both hands over his face.

"I don't follow, Mr. Baird. Are you saying you have a criminal history?"

"Yes. There is no point in hiding anything now. I first met Stan when he was in grade ten at Alberni Secondary School. He worked part-time for the lumber company cleaning up after school. I caught him loading gas into jerrycans in his pick-up. He sold it for half the cost at the pump and over time bought a newer pick-up.

I don't know what got into me. Instead of turning him in, I blackmailed him to split the sale of the gas. Pretty soon we were stealing chain saws and other expensive equipment.

"Then he graduated and I didn't think anything of it until he called recently and told me my share in this would be seven hundred thousand."

Larry wasn't about to tell his interrogator about Joe; the bomb scare or that Joe would receive half of the seven hundred.

"Greed got to me I guess or maybe I am predisposed to be crooked. I don't know. I thought the money would buy me things my retirement income couldn't."

He seemed spent and put his head down on the platform again.

"Mr. Baird. Look at me, please."

Baird raised his head again, propped up by his hands, elbows on the platform.

"You are leaving out valuable information Mr. Baird. Explain your relationship with Stan's father. Mounties are searching your Port Alberni home as we speak and if what you are telling me is true, then there may be some hope if the officers find nothing incriminating."

Wood already knew the answer to his question. Before leaving his detachment, he assigned several officers to question the senior Loblinski. The fully recovered longshoreman, albeit opioid addict, suspected the quantity of drugs Baird Sr. was providing him was not being obtained through the largess of his union, but were illegal. He apologized profusely to the Mounties, feeling guilty for possibly pushing Larry Sr. into criminal activity to pay for his habit.

The inspector sat looking at Baird, waiting for a reply, "Mr. Baird. Tell me about your relationship with longshoreman Loblinski."

Larry Sr. had his head between his arms on the desk. He had been considering a way to continue the ruse that he had somehow swung from being a law-abiding citizen to a criminal. He didn't want to get the senior Loblinski involved. He knew after Stan graduated and left town that it had been a mistake to join the scores of other employees stealing from the company and had resolved the issue with his conscience by giving the ill-gotten cash to Francesco.

Baird Sr. leaned back in his chair pushing his head toward the ceiling, having arrived at a conclusion. He leaned forward, placed his forearms on the table and told Wood the entire story, the entire truth.

"Thank you for your honesty, Mr. Baird. Your situation can be resolved quickly and smoothly. I can have the terrorism and trafficking charges dropped if we find you are not more involved than you claim and provided you testify against Stan Loblinski."

Wood was expecting the ubiquitous hue and cry but he received none. Baird simply stared ahead as though he was in a trance.

"Mr. Baird, do you understand what I am offering?"

"Yes, I think. You want me to testify against Stan. I don't know if I can do that. He and I go way back and he has done nothing to me, nothing to hurt me. He certainly isn't responsible for my being here."

Lorne knew he had to pull Baird back to the moment, the time right now where the case against Loblinski could become more complex. He needed Baird's testimony.

"Larry. Do you mind if I call you Larry?"

"Sure. No, I don't mind," he replied, slouching in the seat, folding his arms and hugging his body.

"Okay, Larry. You are mistaken. Stan implicated you unnecessarily. He chose you as the easiest target for his criminality. I suspect he blackmailed you based on your previous larceny.

"Stan is responsible for a lot of death and destruction over a long period of time. The man he was with when you were arrested is Brian Sawyer. He has been living a luxurious lifestyle in Costa Rica since escaping prosecution in Alberta a number of years ago. We retrieved ten million dollars from his Central American house and seventy kilos of cocaine.

"The cocaine you smuggled is one hundred percent pure, with a Vancouver street value of thirty-five thousand dollars a kilo. There were thirty thousand kilos in that van, Larry. Do the math.

"Brian was well rewarded by Stan for years of growing powerful cannabis which he sold to the Christians for a Better America in Wyoming. They retailed it across the US and made millions which was used to finance their agenda.

"Brian is as guilty as Stan. Are you as guilty as they are Larry?"

That got his attention. He jolted awake, almost knocking the chair backwards and saying, "What do you mean? I didn't do any of those things?"

Without replying Lorne took a page from the notebook, a pen and the calculator and slid them across the platform to Larry.

"Let's do the math together Larry. You smuggled 30 tons of pure Colombian cocaine. There are one thousand kilos per ton," he said, writing them down on the paper.

"That is thirty thousand kilos Larry. Now multiply that by thirty-five thousand dollars and what do you get?"

Larry did the math and Lorne watched his jaw drop, then said, "That is no mistake Larry. The drugs you smuggled are worth 1.5 billion on the streets of Vancouver.

"Do you understand now the magnitude of trouble you are in? Crown could easily jail you for the rest of your life. You would never see your family, your grandchildren.

"I can still contact an attorney for you and you can discuss it with her or him. I am okay with that. It will slow the process down but if that works for you, it does for me. Probably six months or more to work out the details and of course you will be detained for that time."

Wood saw that Baird was thinking through his options. After about a minute, Wood continued, "Or, you sign a statement to how Loblinski implicated you in the smuggling, explain your relationship with him and I will discuss it with Crown.

"I believe I can get the prosecutor to agree to your release until your trial wearing an ankle bracelet and living with your son Larry Jr. in Calgary."

That last statement caught Larry by surprise and he blurted out, "How do you know my son?"

"Larry, we have been tailing Stan for months when he and your son met at an Edmonton pub, watched some football and enjoyed a meal and a few beers. It turns out they attended the same high school in Port Alberni. We have been monitoring your son ever since."

"Oh my God, this is getting worse and worse. I was hoping he wouldn't find out."

"Kind of difficult for him not to find out Larry. Over a billion dollars? When the media gets a hold of the details?" he concluded, raising his eyebrows and his voice highlighting the question.

Larry paused for a few moments, sat straight in the chair and replied, “Okay. I agree. But you have to let me talk to my son on the phone before I leave here. I don’t want to cause him any more pain than what he is going to endure.”

“That is a wise decision Larry,” Lorne said as he slid a yellow legal tablet across the platform and continued, “Write out every detail of your relationship with Loblinski, how you met, your dealings when he was in high school and how you became involved in the smuggling. Also, I want the names of the others who helped you load the truck in Port Alberni. As an aside Larry, the shooters who opened fire on you and the others in the barn were Octopoda, notified by Robert. You might ask yourself why your long-time friend turned on you.”

That last sentence shocked Larry…again. He wondered if the inspector knew about Joe in Campbell River. His heart sank as he thought of all the years he had known the men who helped and now he was giving them up to the police.

“Just knock on the door when you are finished. I will have it transcribed for your signature,” Lorne concluded as he picked up the laptop and calculator, keyed in a code at the door and left.

Baird Sr. would not be allowed a phone call to his son. Wood had all the information he needed on Larry Jr. He knew there wouldn’t be a rejection and he wanted to put Larry Sr. on the spot, similar to restorative justice - where the offender explains his actions to those he had hurt.

Chapter FORTY-TWO

Karen and Kimberly rose from the monitor when he entered the media room and were ready when he asked, "Any questions?"

Kimberly asked, "Sir, did you teach interrogation at Depot?" with an inquisitive smile.

"No. But thanks for the compliment," Lorne replied with a grin. "When he has finished his statement, might you have it transcribed and attach the digital print-out of the interview dialog? We can get the package to Crown and have Mr. Baird back in lock-up for dinner," he concluded.

"Yes sir. We will take care of it. Do you want us to observe the other interviews?" asked Karen.

"Certainly. I suspect the attorneys and accountant will be quick, then I want to do Brian, Robert and leave Loblinski for the last," Lorne replied as he headed out the door.

His years of experience proved his analysis correct. The three suits demanded an attorney, rejecting Wood's offer to share the Crown's evidence against them.

Lorne had seen this many times with the result always the same; a long drawn out process, thousands spent on legal fees with any plea agreement disappearing. A deal could offer a shorter sentence; in exchange for incriminating other participants, financials etc.

They each contacted their respective legal counsel and were returned to lock-up. Lorne anticipated the outrage; they expected to be released on their own recognizance, but instead, exchanged their business attire for burnt orange jump suits, the judge rejecting release believing they were flight risks.

Wood returned to the media room seeking progress and found Kimberly and Karen waiting. Karen offered, "Sir, the transcripts are completed and Baird is ready to return to lock-up," as Kimberly extended a folder.

"Terrific. Thanks. The suits are holding out for attorneys and are heading back to lock-up as well. Make sure they are transported separately from each other and from Baird."

Kimberly asked, "Sir, even in light of the evidence against them, they wanted an attorney before proceeding?"

"Exactly. None wanted to hear the evidence.

"Okay. Are you ready for Sawyer? It will be interesting to see if he knows he can be sent to Costa Rica for trial," Lorne commented, a slight smile gracing his face as he headed to the door.

"Good day, Mr. Sawyer. I'm Inspector Wood here to discuss the recent events which landed you in our office."

Brian stopped pacing, looked at Lorne.

Said nothing.

Returned to pacing and muttering.

Lorne placed the laptop on the platform, pulled out the chair, then quickly lifted it, slammed in down on the floor and yelled, "Brian!"

Sawyer jumped and turned to Wood, fear on his face as though seeing Lorne for the first time, his whereabouts confusing.

Lorne responded quietly, pulling out the other chair saying, "Brian, please have a seat."

Sawyer walked unsteadily to the platform and sat.

Lorne took the chair across from him and offered, "Mr. Sawyer, may I call you Brian?"

Sawyer looked exhausted slouched in the chair with his arms across his chest in a classic psychological defensive move, and replied, “Whatever.”

Wood read him his right to legal counsel to which Brian repeated his previous reply, shrugging his shoulders, “Whatever.”

Lorne opened the laptop, hit play and watched Brian’s reaction.

There was none.

Wood continued, “Brian, do you recognize the details in this video?”

“No.”

“You should. What you are seeing is from the barn from which you were arrested and the unloading of Colombian cocaine with a street value of a billion dollars. This is the cocaine with which we found you, Stan, your dealers and the Octopoda assassination team, all of whom are dead by the way. Only Stan, the two attorneys, the accountant and you are alive.” Lorne purposely didn’t tell him about Larry Sr. or Robert.

“Big fuckin’ deal. You can’t prove I had anything to do with those drugs. You cops shot everyone, not me. I got nothing to do with none of that,” Brian replied, gaining an arrogance and steeliness he was unaware he had in him…driven by fear.

“I’m not here to argue with you Brian but to share information and make you an offer.”

No reaction except a cold stare.

The inspector always found it fascinating in an educational manner, how some suspects have the audacity to feign ignorance as though the police hadn’t a clue. But it was also very gratifying to back them into a corner and elicit a confession, saving the Crown and taxpayers the cost of a trial.

"I have another video which you may recognize," Lorne said as he hit another laptop button revealing a visual from the JTF2 team's body cameras.

The scene showed the team rise from the beach and advance on a house.

Brian sat up and stared at the screen, his eyes wild with confusion, pointing at the screen. He said, "That, that, that's my house. What are those guys doing?"

"That's right, Brian. Your house. Watch."

Brian was mesmerized by the sight of four heavily armed men with night goggles enter his house and begin tearing the walls apart.

"What the fuck are they doing?" Brian yelled as he jumped up for the chair. "They have no right to destroy my house like that? What the fuck is going on? I'm going to sue your ass," raising his voice to a scream, anger generating sputum as he yelled.

Lorne didn't reply as the screen showed agents pulling American currency out of the walls.

Sawyer appeared in shock as he saw years of labor disappear into large, black duffle bags.

"You have no fuckin' right to take my money. Who the fuck are those guys anyway? I'm going to sue your ass. That is my money," he yelled at a manic level.

Lorne answered quietly, "The concept of right or wrong never came up Brian. The total is ten million plus of course the seventy kilos of cocaine also hidden within the walls worth another two and a half million.

"This is what we intend to prove Brian; you grew high grade cannabis for Stan at a farm in Southern Alberta, shipped the product via CP Rail into Idaho where it was transported into Wyoming and sold to finance a terrorist group, Citizens for a Better America.

"That group was responsible for the downing of a Mahalo Airline jet into the Pacific off the coast of LAX and the destruction of the Marina del Rey Convention Center.

"You are being charged with terrorism and attempted murder of the two hundred plus politicians on the flight and for fleeing prosecution.

"The Americans want you extradited for terrorism. They have a slam-dunk case, as do we, but if the Americans prosecute, you will live the rest of your life in Guantanamo Bay, better known as Gitmo.

"Also Brian, you are a Costa Rican citizen. They want you extradited for drug trafficking. And of course the Colombian drug cartel from whom you stole the seventy kilos wants you dead.

"It would take very little effort on our part to communicate with them that you are in the Surrey Detention Center. How long do you think you would stay alive Brian?"

Lorne was lying. He had no idea how to contact the cartel. CSIS would for sure, but he didn't have a clue.

"You have to decide Brian; America, Costa Rica, Canada or the Colombians?"

Lorne waited for a reply. Getting none, he rose and said, "I think you need an attorney Brian. None of this is sinking in," as he grabbed the laptop and left before Sawyer could respond.

Wood entered the media room and joined Karen and Kimberly sitting in front of the monitor, his frustration obvious.

“Sir, may I make a suggestion?” offered Karen as Lorne took a seat by the monitor.

“What?” Lorne replied curtly, exhibiting frustration in his voice.

“Tom Hortonn and I found Sawyer in Costa Rica and spent considerable time with him. May I have a go at him?”

Lorne thought for a moment, “Sure. Show me what you’ve got,” he replied with a grin.

Karen rose quickly, grabbed the laptop and headed through the door before the Inspector could change his mind.

“Good day, Brian,” she said after closing the door behind her.

Brian was so shocked, he jumped up and stammered, “You!”

“Yes, Brian. Me. Welcome back to Canada. It appears you didn’t keep our agreement not to engage in the drug business,” Karen responded quietly while setting up the laptop.

She logged into her CSIS account, hit a button, then turned the computer towards Brian.

Hitting play, she said, “We have you on video retrieving the cocaine from the small cove south of your house, taking it to the docks and loading it with the banana shipment to Europe.

“You have been under surveillance twenty-four-seven since I left.”

Having Sawyer’s attention, Karen wanted to press the advantage but wasn’t sure the Inspector would approve.

What the fuck she thought. *I can’t make things any worse* as she moved on.

"In the end, the best victory is the one that looks like a defeat."

Neel Burton

Glancing at the camera, knowing Wood was watching, she waited a moment for a door knock. Not hearing one she said, "Here is the deal Brian. You have four choices. A: We ship you to Costa Rica to stand trial and live the rest of your life in their prison system. B: We send you back to the Surrey Pre-Trial Center and notify the cartel of your location. C: We ship you to the United States to stand trial for terrorism and life at Guantanamo Bay for the rest of your life. D: You testify against Loblinski, accept a ten-year Canadian sentence and have a chance for a life. Your choice," she concluded as she gathered the laptop and headed for the door.

As she keyed in her code, Brian spoke softly and said, "D".

Karen repressed a smile, turned back to Sawyer, laying a yellow legal tablet and pen in front of him and said, "Explain your relationship with Loblinski: when your relationship began, the Alberta cannabis operation, how you delivered the product, how you were paid by Stan, how you transported the cash to Costa Rica, how you transported the cartel's product in Costa Rica and any other details you feel will persuade the Crown prosecutor's sentencing recommendations. The questions are at the top of the tablet."

"Take all the time you need Brian. You want to get this correct the first time. Knock on the door when you are finished and we will have your statement transcribed for your signature.

“You made the right choice Brian. This will enable you to have a life. I would suggest you lose the attitude if you want leniency.” she concluded as she moved to the door, keyed in a code and left.

“To have been a criminal is no disgrace. To remain a criminal is the disgrace.”

Malcolm X

Winthrop walked the short distance down the hall, with a lightness in her step she found exhilarating. Karen had many successes as a Mountie but this was big, at least she thought it was. Now to see if the inspector agreed.

She walked into the media room as Kimberly and Wood stood, both nodding their approval accompanied by warm smiles. “Nice job Sgt. Winthrop, nice job indeed. Now to Loblinski, the kingpin of this incredibly complicated operation,” offered Lorne.

“It was the wont of the immortal gods sometimes to grant prosperity and long impunity to men whose crimes they were minded to punish.”

Julius Caesar

As Inspector Wood headed to the next interview room, he mused Caesar’s take on criminals and hoped fate would be delivered to Loblinski whose criminality dated back decades.

Chapter FORTY-THREE

Working two hundred and fifty meters/eight-hundred feet above ground, creating the city's next landmark, had its own stress, even if you were born to the job. But as a Calgary Iron Worker, Larry Baird Jr. had a system to help him decompress, particularly on the weekend; sweatpants, a BC Lion's Jersey, lunch and Lion's football…with a glass of Jack Daniels and a shot of water with Patrón.

Baird had just finished his nachos and Jack when half-time was announced. Taking his dishes into the kitchen, he was interrupted by knocking at the front door.

Placing the dishes in the sink, Larry made his way to the door and looked through the peep hole just as another knocking rattled the entry startling him, his face jolting backwards instinctively.

Putting his eye to the door a second time, his head careened backward again, this time from what he saw, his brain unable to calculate.

Outside his front door, in the middle of a Saturday afternoon, stood two sheriff deputies, one on each side…of his dad…in handcuffs.

Lorne entered the interview room, shut the door and said, "Good day, Mr. Loblinski. I am Inspector Wood with a few questions regarding the circumstances surrounding recent events. You have the right to counsel and the right not to answer my questions. I understand you are a terrorist."

Stan jumped up, somewhat restricted by his handcuffs chained to the platform and yelled, "What the fuck are you talking about. I'm not a fuckin' terrorist. Are you fuckin' crazy? You can't say I'm a terrorist. Shit, I will never get out of here."

"That is about right, Mr. Loblinski, you may never get out of jail. In fact, the United States wants to extradite you to stand trial on terrorism charges."

"No, no," yelled Stan. "You have this all wrong. I am not a terrorist. And what does the United States have to do with anything?"

Lorne felt good that he had Loblinski on the defensive so quickly. Now to manipulate him.

"Sir, surely you are aware that the stolen cesium was used to down a Mahalo Airline off the coast of LAX and the funds generated by the cannabis Mr. Sawyer grew for you was used by the domestic terrorist group, Christians for a Better America. They blew up the Mariana del Rey Convention Center using the drug money to purchase the explosives."

Loblinski jumped up again, pulling on the chains, kicking his chair out of the way yelling, "No, no. I didn't have anything to do with any of that. And who is Sawyer?"

Wood always enjoyed these moments when suspects lied so easily, diving into the hole they dug for themselves.

"Mr. Loblinski, yes you do. Not only do we have Sawyer's signed confession but we have been following you for over a year. We have recorded text messages between you and Sawyer as well as a slew of communications you instigated to your Vancouver connections.

"We also have a direct connection between you and Marianna Gutierrez in Santa Barbara and a link with Caribbean banks to you, the attorneys and accountant.

"Mounties watched you pick up Brian at the Edmonton Airport. The Edmonton private detectives have given statements detailing your instructions in finding Sawyer and we have the phone conversation between you and Brian from Costa Rica.

"What else. Let me see." He consulted his notes and continued, "Oh, yes, Mounties followed you to the Mission barn where we caught you with the one billion dollars in cocaine. Baird will testify that you hired him to transport it from Port Alberni to the Lower Mainland."

Stan remained standing and replied, "That is all such bullshit. And there is no way there was a billion dollars. I'm not answering any of your questions. You can't prove any of that. I want an attorney."

"Good decision, Mr. Loblinski. You have that right. When you are properly represented, we will provide your attorney with the evidence against you. The right to counsel is Canadian, not American, and therefore I can't guarantee you will be here to meet with your attorney when the U.S. Marshalls arrive with their extradition warrant," he lied.

Loblinski glared at him venomously.

"What I do know for certain," Lorne continued, stifling his enthusiasm for getting to the suspect, "is that the Americans will have all of the same evidence we have and your conviction is almost a guarantee. When that happens, you will spend the rest of your life at their detention center for terrorists at Guantanamo Bay. You may have heard of it as Gitmo.

"And let's not forget, you owe the Colombians the four hundred million for the cocaine. Gutierrez and her band of thieves won't be available to help with the finances, but I suspect the cartel will be in touch."

Lorne could see Stan thinking through the last bit of information, his body sagging somewhat.

Wood rose from the platform and retrieved the chair Stan had kicked and placed it behind him.

Loblinski sat, his head down, indicating the conversation was over.

Wood was satisfied with the interview and figured either with or without an attorney, Loblinski would confess, leaving the remaining four. *Attorneys and accountants,* he thought, *was it bravado that prevented them from seeing the obvious? Robert will be slam-dunk,* he concluded.

"Personal, private, solitary pain is more terrifying than what anyone else can inflict."

Jim Morrison

Larry opened the door and said, "Dad, what the hell?"

"Mr. Baird, may we come in sir?" asked the deputy with sergeant's stripes.

"Yeah. Sure. I guess. What's this all about? Dad, what's going on?" he repeated nervously.

"I'm sure Mr. Baird will provide the details in his own time sir. Our instructions are to deliver him to you. Here is a letter from the British Columbia Attorney General explaining the situation," he said, handing a letter to Larry.

"The crux of this is that Mr. Baird is under house arrest here in Calgary, away from British Columbia influences. No one knows his whereabouts other than law enforcement and we need to keep it that way. The leg monitor, or bracelet, is configured for this house. He is not permitted to leave for any reason. We will notify you when we will be picking him up for his court appearance."

His dad remained standing between the two deputies. Silent. Embarrassed. Humiliated.

"Do you understand the requirements for Mr. Baird to remain here with you sir?"

Larry replied, still confused, "Yes, I do."

"Fine. Then please sign at the bottom," the sergeant said, opening a binder and offering it to Larry with a pen, "and we will be out of your way."

Larry signed without reading, still in a stupor, handed it back to the sergeant and almost collapsed in a hall chair.

The officers removed Baird's handcuffs and body chain, checked the bracelet, turned and left.

Larry rose unsteadily, limped toward his dad, gave him a hug, then stepped back and said, "What the hell is going on, dad?"

The inspector returned to the media room and reviewed what Kimberly and Karen had observed, answered their questions, then told them to call it a day. Lorne would see that Sawyer's testimony was signed and returned to lock-up. He figured Robert would take fifteen minutes, if that. Loblinski would be held at the detachment with the hope that he would accept Crown's offer once his attorney explained his options. The last three suspects could be weeks away from making a deal with the prosecution. Robert would do time, minimal but he would be incarcerated, probably on the Island. Loren promised to call Kimberly and Karen if he thought they could gain from observing.

He concluded his summary by explaining what he intended to recommend to Crown for Baird, Robert, Sawyer and Loblinski, shook their hands and left the media room, figuring Karen and Kimberly could find their way out.

Larry Baird Sr., offered the horrifying details of his activity which brought him to his son's door, adding, "If there is any consolation for my stupidity, it may be in my agreeing to be a confidential informant for the RCMP in Port Alberni. I accepted their offer which includes testifying against the guy who got me into this, no jail time and ten years' probation."

Larry had a slew of questions which his dad humbly answered, apologizing profusely for involving him. Larry accepted the answers figuring there was no point in adding to his dad's pain with his own scorn. The exception was when Larry asked the identity of whom he was testifying against.

It was just like his dad to help his fellow longshoreman when the system failed. And Larry could appreciate how the altruism spiraled and how his dad was overwhelmed with debt. The blackmail by Stan was what pissed him off more than anything. He and his dad were tight and to be used in that way angered him to such a degree he wanted to break Stan in two.

Not too much shocked Larry Jr. at this point in his life and he could see how everything came full circle. Larry shared with his dad his encounter with Stan at the *Highway Men* and understood how the deputies knew how to find him.

Both men appreciated the inspector arranging for Larry Sr. not to be held anywhere near the other prisoners fearing retaliation from the cartel.

Larry's spare bedroom was always ready for a visitor so he showed his Dad the way, hugged him goodnight and told him he would be with him through the process.

The parental visit would be a short two weeks, before the deputies arrived to take Larry Sr. back to Vancouver to have his testimony accepted by a judge who had already approved Loblinski's confession.

Stan received ten years in a federal penitentiary and with good behavior could be paroled in six.

Brian was sentenced to eighteen months in a British Columbia minimum security prison, as was Robert. Brian's time would be spent accompanying paramedics responding to opiate overdoses, supervised by a Restorative Justice Facilitator. Robert would do the total eighteen months at a facility in Nanaimo.

The attorneys and accountant intended to ride the accusations out to the end, their trial expected to be heard the following year.

When the judge was presented with evidence of the massive financial backing available to the three accused, she didn't hesitate to reject all bail requests, the last being a million-dollar bond.

The threesome's bravado disappeared after two weeks in the Surrey Detention Centre, eating, bathing and interacting with murderers, thieves and pedophiles, they chose to end their hold-out status.

The Inspector made a deal with Aleksander Kuznetsov first. Alek turned on the Brosman and Snow. The accountants received a five-year sentence each to be served at the Williams Head minimum security prison near Victoria, BC

The attorneys were unaware that Kuznetsov had provided all the evidence Crown needed to prosecute them. When Wood met with the two back at the detachment interrogation center, he was not surprised that they maintained their haughty attitude and he took delight in slowly introducing the evidence against them, leaving Kuznetsov's confession and implications to the end.

The two were so angry that their longtime business colleague had turned on them, Lorne thought for sure he would have to bring in restraints.

Wood convinced the two that ditching the attitude would go a long way in convincing a judge to accept their plea.

He was going to add that their present arrogance could land them in the infirmary as prisoners retaliated against a common enemy; attorneys.

Chapter FORTY-FOUR

Anastasia Zinkton had been kept apprised of the RCMP's case and, utilizing all their evidence, filed charges against Marianna Gutierrez, aka Cecila Padilla and the members of Hermanos de Wall Street.

Warrants were issued for the San Francisco group while Detectives Jenny Wong and Teresa Vasquez joined Detective Elise Pelfini in Santa Barbara to arrest Padilla.

The three officers, with back-up from two patrol units, descended upon the beach house at dawn only to find the house empty. A patrol unit sent to Marianna's office was told that Ms. Gutierrez had not been in for several days and had not been in touch.

There appeared to be nothing missing in the house; her suitcases were in a hall closet, clothes were in her bedroom closet and dresser, toiletries in the bathroom and the fridge had several prepared dishes.

Did Gutierrez/Padilla and the Hermanos have a falling out? A warrant had already been issued for her arrest with a BOLO, Be On The Lookout throughout the western states.

With no time to deal with LAX or Santa Barbara Airport surveillance personnel, Pelfini enlisted Elisabeth's aid. Within minutes of hacking both institutions' data files, Elisabeth found a visual of Gutierrez exiting security two days previously.. Checking flight manifests she found Cecelia Padilla had boarded a flight to Heathrow. The UK airport surveillance picked up Gutierrez as she disembarked, and her disappearance, swollen by the crowd.

Subsequent investigations discovered Marianna had fled to Vanuatu, a small nation lying between Fiji and the

Solomon Islands in the South Pacific, a country lacking an extradition treaty with either America or Canada.

Zinkton would be notified later in the day that the Hermanos suspects had also fled to Vanuatu with their families, leaving everything behind.

Bank accounts had been emptied weeks previously causing Zinkton self-criticism for not attempting to seize their assets, knowing full well there was insufficient evidence until just the last few days for such legal action.

The Central California Maintenance Company CEO had been monitored since their participation in money laundering had become evident. Elisabeth was positive they were involved but couldn't find any bank transfers from the Caribbean accounts to CCMP. She stepped to the side of the money issue and hacked the California Department of Transportation's records and found all the contracts awarded to CCMP.

Next, she compared the approved costs, including any cost overrides, to the company's bank records and found a massive discrepancy.

Sufficient evidence for the state to close the business and arrest the owner and several principals was obtained through Elise and Penelope's interview with Anthony Henderson's wife when the detectives provided Elisabeth the means to hack Henderson's home computer.

Henderson personally delivered cash to CCRM and that fact, coupled with the bank records and the state's contract system proved the company laundered cartel money by inflating projects' costs and supplementing with Henderson's delivery.

Little attention was given to the recipient of Marianna's largess, Jeremy Addington, the Orange County mover and shaker, because no direct link could be made between him and the Citizens for a Better America. It was believed that Addington gave the money directly to right wing candidates from his personal account to which Gutierrez deposited from the untraceable Caribbean account.

Detective Pelfini planned to pursue that investigation jointly with the Orange County Sheriff, in conjunction with the Anaheim, Irvine, Huntington Beach and Santa Ana Police Departments. Pelfini was working on the assumption that the county residents, known for their conservative politics, would be scattered throughout the southern California political enclave.

When Jessica and the "J" Team learned of their suspects fleeing American jurisdiction, they took solace in the fact that Gutierrez's Southern California cocaine operation had been terminated, the tons of cocaine wouldn't hit the streets and the Christians for a Better America had their financial support curtailed, albeit temporarily.

The day after Pelfini and the LAPD detectives discovered Gutierrez had vanished, Fukishura met with Katrina and shared the secret kept far too long.

Jessica arrived before Katrina or staff, poured a coffee from her thermos, arranged the day's activities and reviewed her speech one last time.

Thirty later, Barbados stuck her head into Jessica's office as she walked by, "Good morning early bird. Getting a jump start on your day. Do you have time for coffee?"

Jessica couldn't believe her good fortune with Katrina's opening. Grabbing her mug and several papers, she swiveled out of her chair, followed Barbados, took a seat on the couch and waited for her boss to hang her coat and prepare a mug of black.

Coffee in hand, Katrina sat across from Jessica in an armchair, slipped one leg over the other, held her coffee in both hands, took a sip, then asked, "What is the latest on Marianna's case?"

The segue couldn't have been planned, it was so perfect Jessica thought as she replied, "I've run off my billing statement for her," handing the sheet across to her boss. "There is a check in the mail to cover the total."

Jessica didn't mention that the check was from the United States government.

Katrina looked at the account which included air transportation to and from Los Angeles as well as sundry of other items incurred over the course of their representation. Satisfied that it was inclusive, Barbados asked the obvious, "Has she terminated our services? Did the DA decide not to press charges?"

"No. Zinkton has charged Marianna and three detectives attempted to arrest her at her home yesterday but she is gone. Apparently, she left several days ago and has taken residence in Vanuatu."

"Where the hell is Vanuatu? And why would she leave without fighting the charges?"

"It is kind of a long story which is also long overdue in my sharing."

"I don't understand Jessica. What are you trying to say? What the hell is going on," she concluded, her voice edging toward irritation.

"For openers, I am a Secret Service Agent."

Katrina laughed, leaned forward slightly and said, "Yeah, right. You just graduated from law school. Come on Jessica. Out with it."

And out it came.

Several times Barbados interrupted for clarification, then allowed Jessica to continue.

Jessica concluded with, "I hope you understand that I was following orders. My boss enlisted the help of a Washington friend for the recommendation, the educational and employment records."

"I don't know how to feel Jessica. You are one hell of an attorney, there is no doubt about that. The story about an abusive ex was part of the cover?"

"Yes. I have been an agent since graduating from Berkeley. The people you met at Rebecca's party are all agents sent here to take Marianna down. I am their supervisor.

"But we all retired as of yesterday," she offered, explaining the "J" Team Investigations.

"The Team would like your firm to handle their legal business, are prepared to submit a retainer and I would like to remain an employee."

The last comment caught Katrina off guard. She leaned forward, quickly placing her mug on the coffee table and covered her face as she snorted the last sip of black.

"You gotta be fuckin' kidding me. I don't know whether to be honored, pissed off or both. I get duped for who the hell knows how long, and now you want to work for me? Like legitimately?"

"Yes. I love working for you, albeit not so much representing the drug cartel, but yes. I think we get along well, I can earn the company a great deal of money and since I am retired, everyone will know you have a retired Secret Service agent on staff," she smiled, "and I suspect the "J" Team will be a profitable account.

"I am truly sorry Katrina. I didn't know you when I was assigned to Santa Barbara. Marianna was operating a massive cartel, funneling millions to a far-right political group and needed to be stopped."

She left what she felt was her best-selling argument for now, "Do you remember the Mahalo Airline crash and the destruction of the Marina del Rey Convention Center? That was organized by the Christians for a Better America which received funding through Gutierrez. Marianna also financed a Canadian cartel which the RCMP just broke, confiscating Colombian cocaine with a street value of over a billion dollars."

Seeing no reaction from Katrina, Jessica continued.

"I am good at my job, very good, and if you give me a chance, as me, Jessica Fukishura, attorney at law, I promise the deception is over."

"Wait a minute. Are you saying that you and those I met, Jason, Jackson, Elisabeth and Rebecca were responsible for catching the bombers?"

"Yes ma'am.

Katrina laughed again, this time with warmth and replied, "Son of a bitch. I read about the airplane going down off the coast and the bombing of the center. Your team was involved in all of that. I'll be damned. Will the surprises never end? So when we had dinner at your new place with Marianna, she was a suspect then?"

"Yes."

"What about the DA not filing charges during your meeting in LA? That was a set-up too?

"Yes. Sorry Katrina, but I needed Marianna to believe she was in the clear. And it worked. We dismantled Gutierrez's cocaine cartel. She is gone, never to be prosecuted but we removed thousands of kilos of poison from the street.

"Oh, and as an aside, her real name is Cecilia Padilla and is a key partner in the Hermanos de Wall Street, a corrupt group of disbarred California attorneys. They took the fall years ago for embezzlement while she came here, established a false identity and the cocaine cartel."

"Shit Jessica. What the hell else? You obviously went to law school. Was Berkeley a lie as well?"

"No, I graduated from there decades ago, passed the bar exam and have maintained my license. We knew Hermanos would do a background check so it all had to be legit. Before the Canadians broke their case with the Colombian shipment delivery to Vancouver Island, I had made it into her inner circle and was to be her lieutenant in charge of her LA dealers. My boss arranged with Google to remove me from their data base until the operation was over."

Katrina was exhausted hearing all that had occurred without her knowledge but she recouped and said, "There is no doubt you are an excellent attorney. One hell of a liar too, which is a court room asset.

"What the hell, why not. I can't stay pissed at you for long but the deal includes being invited frequently for drinks and dinner at your new home," she concluded with a genuine smile.

"Fuck," she said as she grabbed her coffee off the table and rose from the chair. "I can't believe I was duped for so many months and I just hired a Secret Service agent…again. Wow," she concluded shaking her head…but smiling.

"You are undoubtedly right about my clients being thrilled to be represented by a former Secret Service Agent."

Jessica had gotten up from the couch simultaneously and reached out to shake her boss' hand, but Katrina knew she had to make the first move. She put her coffee down and hugged Jessica.

Jessica smiled to herself, enjoying the warmth of another human being, genuine warmth with neither expecting nor needing anything from the other.

I'm going to enjoy this new life, she thought as she disengaged the hug and left Katrina's office.

Later that week, Alane emailed her with the news that the owners of the beach property in which she was living had agreed to apply all rental payments to a down payment. He attached the legal documents for which she only had to sign, scan and return to Alane and the house was hers, furnishings included.

Jessica thought Alane's suggestion was a stretch but she was unaware that Alane had collaborated with Katrina who called the owners. Once the couple heard who their renter was, they made the offer without Katrina asking. They also agreed to carry the mortgage at two percent interest, an absurdly low rate.

Jessica was beyond elated, never believing someone would exhibit such kindness.

Patriots.

Knowing she had to pay it forward, she called Jason and told him about the unit attached to her house and offered it to his mom, rent free, utilities included.

Jason asked a slew of questions and said that his mom would never accept rent free but if Jessica wanted to charge her a nominal amount and donate it to a charity of his mom's choice, without telling her, he could make it work.

Jessica agreed to the thoughtful conspiracy and invited Jason to join her that night at *Marc Stucki's.*

Lastly, she arranged for a cleaning company, recommended by Rebecca, to come weekly, including Mrs. Spencer's unit, then sent an email to her former landlord asking her to arrange for Jessica's furniture and personal belongings to be shipped to Santa Barbara. Sorento would transport her Gecko Green Volkswagen bug.

Refugio Seguro residents all graduated with high enough grades to be accepted to various colleges and universities, a monumental application process simplified by the school counseling staff. The majority would be attending UC Santa Barbara and continue to live in residence while a few were accepted into specialized programs in other states. All their costs were covered by Rebecca, Penelope and their philanthropist friends.

During a progress meeting with Alane and their supporters, it was decided to remodel twenty more rooms this year, bringing the total to forty-five with the remaining twenty to be completed the following year.

The selection process for the twenty new girls wasn't as confrontational as the genesis group due to *Refugio's* positive reputation. The women's resource center staff handled most of the screening, with all the girls following the same system as the others with clothes shopping, hair and makeup etc. and of course returning to school that fall.

Mrs. Henderson was persuaded to sell the accounting firm to the employees, a group led by Jacques and Jerome and after selling her house, had sufficient funds, managed by her former accounting firm, to enjoy a high standard of living in a condo by the beach.

Larry woke the next morning and readied for work, allowing his dad to sleep in. He was mortified that his dad, the man to whom he had sought guidance all these years, could become so lost that he would get caught up in a criminal activity. He felt sorry for Stan's dad who hadn't seen or spoken to his son in over twenty years. For obvious reasons it appeared.

Larry decided he had to do something for Mr. Loblinski and during his lunch break he called the person whose signature was on the legal papers.

After a lengthy argument he convinced the department of corrections to give the Bairds seventy-two hours to travel to and from Port Alberni for the express purpose of making amends.

The trip was cathartic for both men, sharing emotions they never thought would be of interest to the other. The meeting with Mr. Loblinski was difficult for both he and Larry Sr., the latter confessing to being part of Stan's larcenist beginnings.

The Bairds left the senior Loblinski with sorrowful apologies and a promise to appeal to the RCMP to have Stan serve his sentence in British Columbia's Williams Head minimum security prison so Francesco could visit.

They also arranged for Mr. Loblinski to enter a rehab program in Nanaimo.

Larry Sr. received no jail time, ten-years' probation and became an RCMP Confidential Informant, responsible to Inspector Wood, much to Wood's delight.

Kimberly and Karen needed to celebrate and chose the Aqua Marine restaurant…right on the shores of English Bay. They parked their vehicles at Karen's hotel, taxied to the Aqua and celebrated until seven. They hailed a taxi back to Karen's where she invited Kimberly to binge watch Netflix, spend the night and head home in the morning.

As the cab descended upon the hotel, Karen's phone vibrated. Reading the text from Tom, she smiled and passed the phone to Kimberly, *"We three have a new assignment. Will be in Vancouver by tomorrow afternoon. You guys available for lunch and I will reveal?"*

Kimberly gave the phone back to Karen and high fived her as the taxi pulled into their hotel. Karen texted Tom with a thumbs up emoji.

This down time would give the women an opportunity to ditch work conversation, catch up on their friendship and speculate on what Kopas had assigned.

Jessica was at *Marc Stucki's* for dinner and an evening of jazz on Friday night.

It turned out to be an impromptu retirement party with the "J" Team, Alane, Katrina and several *Refugio Seguro* supporters, who, when they discovered the "J" Team's identity, had to participate and cover all costs.

Marc outdid himself once again with StoneHead, Black Angus fillet, salty, herb smashed red potatoes and mixed local vegetables with several bottles of Talon beer and cabernet sauvignon red wine.

The meal arrived just as the set finished and the band broke. To ensure Cooper sat next to her, Jessica rose as he approached the table, walked over to him, shook his hand expressing her appreciation for the talent and invited him to sit beside her.

A little confused at the overt hospitality, Cooper accepted Jessica's invitation, sat, took a sip of the Talon and turned to Jessica…who was looking right at him.

Before enjoying their meal, Jessica had to do this. It had been far too long. She had missed far too many opportunities for happiness and love due to her frankness, but she couldn't not tell dates who she was at the outset. Something told her this man was different.

Cooper had women interested in him over the years and he had done his share of dating, but well into his thirties, he had given up on seeking dates, choosing instead to enjoy his leisure with his sax and firearms competitive shooting.

"Cooper, I have two tickets to see Boney James, Jeffery Osborne and Chris Botti at the Dolby Theater tomorrow night with dinner at Skanks beforehand." She was hoping the opportunity for Cooper to listen to famed saxophonists and trumpeter to be too enticing to reject, but also felt the need for full disclosure, so she added, "I am recently retired from the Secret Service; I carry a nine-millimeter firearm twenty-four seven and led the operation which investigated the Marina del Rey Convention Center and Mahalo Airline's downing. I am an attorney for Ms. Barbados sitting across from us," she nodded in Katrina's direction. "Would you like to go to the concert and dinner?

"And, I hope you like cats," she added, more for her benefit than his as she planned to go to the animal shelter the next week and adopt some kittens. Having enjoyed the litter at StoneHead Ranch which had complete access of the several thousand square foot ranch house, she was determined to have several more heartbeats in her home, other than her own.

Cooper was not as taken aback by her assertiveness as she would have expected. Instead he sat through her nervous diatribe with one leg over the other, facing her with a slight grin, holding his chin with one hand.

"I am delighted you are a firearm's enthusiast as I am a competitive shooter with the USPSA and yes, I would love to have dinner and attend the concert with you. Yes, I like cats and I presume you are driving."

"Oh, okay," she replied, with a voice uplift, unexpectedly pleased, anticipating the usual rejection. Regaining her composure she said, "Terrific. I will pick you up tomorrow afternoon at four. From where?"

Cooper couldn't contain his smirk as he pulled out a pen and wrote his address and phone number on a napkin and slid it across to Jessica.

Seeing his grin, she asked, "What is so funny?"

"Nothing Jessica. I just have never met a woman with your effervescent personality and I am delighted by the new experience."

Magical words that are absent, thought Jessica, referring to the lack of negative comments regarding her career choice or firearms.

"When love beckons to you, follow him.
And when he speaks to you believe in him,
Though his voice may shatter your dreams as the north wind lays waste the garden."

Kahlil Gibran

Acknowledgements

Barkley Sound Secrets is dedicated to First Responders for their compassion toward sexual and domestic assault survivors and their expertise and professionalism in providing the necessary assistance.

It is also dedicated to survivors. May you gain courage, direction and enthusiasm for the next step in your journey. We hope Jessica, Rebecca, Penelope, Elisabeth, Elise Kimberly and Karen inspired and have set an example of who and what you can be.

My sincere appreciation to Elise Laina for the use of her maiden name for Detective Elise Pelfini and her fashion and cuisine guidance.

Thank you Elise also for your hours of editing, assisting with the intricacies of travel times as well as the scope of each character's abilities and limitations. Your dedication produced a better novel than I could have done on my own. And of course to Gus, for his hours of snuggles on the couch during your editing.

My appreciation to James Laina for the cover design and his computer expertise.

My gratitude to Les Wiseman of Royal Roads University for starting me on the "J" Team journey and for his support, encouragement and direction through *Wyoming Secrets*, *30,000 Secrets*, *Barkley Sound Secrets* and book five, *Vancouver Secrets*.

To Cst. Roy Davidson, RCMP retired, for his guidance on law enforcement issues and the name *The Horseman.*

To Cst. Richard Drought, RCMP retired, for assault tactics, firearms choices and for educating me on law enforcement management. May the National Police Federation grow strong supporting Members in their trying and challenging times.

My appreciation to RCMP Staff Sgt. Lorne Wood for the use of your name. Sgt. Wood portrays himself and offered support and enthusiasm throughout the process.

To RCMP Cst. Kimberly Breyman (real last name omitted per her request) for your support of the "J" Team Series and for joining them in *Barkley Sound Secrets* and in *Vancouver Secrets* debuting 2021.

I am indebted to Kasteen Beltowski RN, for her medical expertise, and support through the character development and writing process.

Our thanks to Jim Seredick for his assistance with the technical details of the Somas River and Barkley Sound.

Lt. Col. Dave Grossman, U.S. Army (Ret) is honored in each of my novels for his tremendous support and the impact he has had on my life. I had the pleasure of attending the Colonel's law enforcement seminar, *Sheepdogs*, the content of which is shared often throughout my novels.

My martial arts expertise is credited to Tenth Degree Black Belt Bradley Steiner of the American Academy of Self Defense in Seattle and the former Washington State Director of the American Society of Law Enforcement Trainers who provided the instructional atmosphere for me to teach Seattle Police Department officers and King County Sheriff Deputies defensive tactics.

My appreciation to the countless counsellors with women's resource centers and support groups in every country where women are assigned an inferior social role, for their assistance in moving women beyond that category so they know there is more to life.

Kelowna, British Columbia's Chef Marc Stucki added his expertise in cuisine development and plating, creating the numerous opportunities for the characters to socialize and experience new delights. My sincere appreciation Marc. I look forward to the dining excitement you create in *Vancouver Secrets*.

Thank you Dominic Laina for your kind words of encouragement and the use of your name. I appreciate your folk's support and hope I have done justice to the Laina name.

Our sincere appreciation to Larry Baird and his Dad for the use of their names and to Larry Jr. for the invaluable information on Edmonton's social life.

Angie Taylor, Curtis Leithead and Paul Manhas, my sincere gratitude for your enthusiasm and willingness to participate by sharing your names and expertise. Angie for educating me on navigating the Sound and Paul for your medical expertise in treating Loblinski Sr.

Grizzly Bear Brewery authorized the use of their name for *The Horseman* for which I and Larry Jr. are appreciative.

Thanks also goes to *Spirit Eagle Coffee* in Coquitlam, British Columbia for the use of their name and excellent products. The elegance of your brew helped Karen and Tom navigate those raining, dreary Vancouver mornings.

Thanks also to British Columbia's *Kicking Horse Coffee* for the use of their brand and their support of the "J" Team.

We appreciate *Hello Toast* in Kamloops, British Columbia for sharing their name and menu to the delight of Rebecca, Penelope and Gabriella.

Janis Joseph, your contribution paired perfectly with the inspiration we offered here. We appreciate sharing your epiphany and life's new direction.

My continuing and deepest appreciation to my spouse for her editing skills and patience during the months of writing, ignoring my waking at one am to write, having dreamed the scene I needed.

Although *Barkley Sound Secrets* doesn't involve classroom management scenes per se, Secret Service Agent Elisabeth Peltowski's contribution to the detection, surveillance and apprehension of the cocaine cartel has its background in a junior high classroom where her teaching acumen was honed by Dr. Barrie Bennett, retired education professor at the University of Toronto from whom I took many classes in Cooperative Learning.

Jonathanmccormick.com/blog receives many comments and contributions regarding domestic violence and sexual assault supporting the elimination of violence against women. We encourage readers to subscribe to the blog and receive notification of new posts.

We appreciate all who share their ideas and stories, that working together we can make a difference.

To Domestic Shelters and Shelter Safe for their continuous support and direction for violence survivors.

Vancouver Secrets

A

"J" Team Novel

by

Jonathan McCormick

For

Women's resource and rape survivor counsellors, women's shelter staff and all those who support an end to violence against women.

We honor these women through this work of fiction, drawing attention to the fact that society has made little progress in thirty years in ending violence against women.

Vancouver Secrets is a work of fiction. Characters are the author's creation. Names, characters and incidents are of my imagination or used with the permission of the owner. Any resemblance to actual events, or persons, living or dead is co-incidental.

Vancouver Secrets embraces mystery, suspense, love, sex, martial arts, fashion and cuisine while the officers investigate plot of money laundering in Canada and the United States.

The agents enjoy fine dining and shopping in boutiques in Southern California and British Columbia

Vancouver Secrets portrays educated, articulate and driven women living in an age of *Me To* and *Times Up* movements. Jessica, Rebecca and Elisabeth are retired Secret Service Agents, Kimberly, Karen are RCMP Members seconded to Canada's spy agency, CSIS while Anne-Marie Carter is seconded to CSIS from British Columbia's Combined Forces Special Enforcement Unit. These officers work with Santa Barbara, California private detective, Dr. Penelope Barker and Santa Barbara Police Detective Elise Pelfini.

As individuals, they long ago gave up on the concept of marriage and family, deciding instead to forgo having to care for a man incapable of managing his own life, albeit Jessica, Kimberly and Karen begin to deviate from that concept.

Jessica spent years disliking men, an attitude which stems from her mother sharing the atrocity of the 1989 massacre of fourteen women at Montreal's École Polytechnique and the fact that men left the women to die.

Two protagonists are gay, having found their relationship while working together in StoneHead, Wyoming. Several are obsessed with catching and prosecuting antagonists.

All their careers flourish while encountering, overcoming and in many instances, destroying workplace harassment, misogyny and sexual assault.

The female characters are supported by retired Secret Service agents, Jason Spencer and Jackson Pennington. Spencer was recruited to Jessica Fukishura's "J" Team from a unit in North Africa tasked with tracking al Qaeda operatives while Pennington had retired from Delta Force and obtained his teaching degree in Michigan when Fukishura tagged him for her team.

The characters encourage readers; to leave abusive situations, to change their environment and to accomplish their goals and dreams.

Along with their male law enforcement partners, the women inspire readers to find encouragement, support and reject violence and control as givens.

"I love to see a young girl go out and grab the world by the lapels. Life's a bitch. You've got to go out and kick ass." Dr. Maya Angelou

Books
by
Jonathan McCormick

Wyoming Secrets
30,000 Secrets
Santa Barbara Secrets
Barkley Sound Secrets
Vancouver Secrets (2021)

Introduction

Forty-seven billion dollars.

One year.

2018.

Canada.

"It is difficult to figure out how much money is being laundered. Money laundering is a big problem globally and can have a huge effect on local economies," Patrice Poiteven, former RCMP anticorruption investigator.

British Columbia has been the epicenter for such transactions for years, resulting in the purchase of multi-million-dollar properties in Vancouver, high end vehicles, insurance policies with the proceeds of crime; most often currency from drug sales.

Purchasing high-end vehicles; Bugatti La Voiture Noire, twelve million, Lamborghini Veneno, five million, Mercedes-Maybach Exelero, eight million and Rolls-Royce Sweptail, thirteen million with bags of currency was not uncommon. The criminals would later sell the vehicles and their illicit cash would be laundered.

A Vancouver based RCMP investigation, E-Pirate Inquiry, involved forty officers, a budget of millions and several years which resulted in a solid prospect of conviction. Regrettably the case was dismissed in the fall of 2019 when the required disclosure documentation was sent to the defense team along with information regarding the informants. The RCMP and prosecutors could not take the chance of the suspects identifying those who shared their criminal secrets and dropped the charges.

It seems inconceivable today with controlling legislation introduced in 2018, but the province had a history of the various activities mentioned above. One laundering source saw suspects exchanging millions at casinos for chips, playing briefly, then cashing out with a casino check. Crime proceeds cleaned in less than an hour.

By the end of 2019 the curtailing legislation had reduced casino cash flow considerably, so much so that politicians pointed to the previous government, accusing them of allowing the criminal activity to flourish, not wanting to lose the casino tax revenue.

Today, realtors, investors, insurance companies and car dealers will not conduct a transaction in cash over ten thousand dollars and are required to inform law enforcement of any suspicious cash transactions.

Nationally, the 2019 election left the country with a minority/coalition government which does not have money laundering as a high priority.

"Our government's message is simple; criminals, domestic and foreign, should not be able to hide their illegal money in Canada. Our government is committed to detect, stop and prosecute money laundering." June 2019 (edited for space)

Bill Morneau Canada's Minister of Finance

"As a police officer for four decades, I have seen the harmful effects of money laundering. Our 2019 budget made significant investments in the RCMP. FINRAC (Financial Transactions and Reports Analysis Centre) and CRA (Canada Revenue Agency) to meet evolving threats." June 2019 (edited for space)

Bill Blair, Canada's Minister of Organized Crime Reduction

Such was not the case. The E-Pirate Inquiry was short-handed during much of their investigation and the unit has since had their personnel reduced significantly.

"Our weak anti-money-laundering laws protect money launderers from detection and prosecution."

Keven Comeau

America has a ten-thousand-dollar rule for every bank which has prompted syndicated criminals to ship their cash to Canada for laundering, a service for which cartels charge a hefty fee. Smaller criminal groups laundering lesser amounts bribe casino employees.

Prologue

Octopoda was the most vicious drug cartel in British Columbia's Lower Mainland. Their objective was to control every niche of the drug trade from Hope to the Pacific, a goal they were achieving through intimidation and assassination, as noted by the numerous killings in Surrey and surrounding communities where aspiring gangs had the audacity to challenge the Octopoda.

So fervent to maintain their territories and consume those of competitive gangs, they had attempted to steal three thousand kilos of Colombian cocaine smuggled into Port Alberni on Vancouver Island, then transported to Mission, just east of Vancouver.

Octopoda sent six assassins to the distribution location, a poultry grower facility in rural Mission. Thinking they could take the Alberta drug lords by surprise; they were not prepared for the assault by the RCMP's Emergency Response Team (ERT).

All six were killed in the shoot-out, several hundred million dollars in cocaine was confiscated, Albertan Stan Loblinski was convicted of drug trafficking as was his lieutenant, Brian Sawyer, brought back to Canada from Costa Rica for the operation.

The British Columbia drug cartel had lost members and currency before and took the mishap as the cost of doing business and moved on, but this was different.

The Octopoda was not greedy, having learned early on in their entrepreneurship, that financial gluttony would quickly terminate their business and their lives.

Their primary concern was how the Albertan was able to mastermind the shipment of a billion dollars (street value) in Colombian cocaine. They knew all the cartels in western Canada and Loblinski never popped on their radar.

Was he a loner or did he have an operation which could make another attempt at their lower mainland territory? They needed that information to shore up their defenses. The shooters would be difficult to replace and without a strong enforcement barricade the cartel could be in for a bloody and costly turf war.

Presumably Loblinski wouldn't give up the information voluntarily and they had nothing with which to bargain. Using violence in a prison would be an irresponsible move. Octopoda needed his information. A face to face. But with all prison communications monitored and mail screened, they were left with one choice.

"When a man is denied the right to live the life he believes in, he has no choice but to become an outlaw."

Nelson Mandel

CHAPTER ONE

The winds from Strait of Georgia were absent this cold and damp Richmond, BC morning. The fog embraced the community early, creating a bone-chilling discomfort, closing residents and business off from the rest of the Lower Mainland.

Benoît Caron left the Octopoda, (named for the octopus which uses camouflage and threats against its enemies with quick mobility an ability to hide) safehouse before the hectic morning commute with a busy schedule ahead of him. His first task was to deposit the cash from the weekend drug sales to their Richmond bank and get on with his day.

His sleek, metallic black BMW M5 Sedan made good time leaving Mission, BC on Highway Eleven, to the Number One heading into Vancouver. He could see a wisp of fog hanging over the city's downtown as he reached Surrey and switched to Highway 17 for a direct route into Richmond.

As he passed New Westminster across the Fraser River, the density increased to envelop his low six figure ride as traffic increased and his speed was reduced to a crawl across Annacis Island as he entered Richmond.

The metallic silver BMW M5 cloaked him in comfort as he shivered unconsciously. He was enraptured by the twin-turbocharged 4.4-liter V8, 617 horsepower engine which drove effortlessly. He stroked the light grey leather console as he steered with his left hand, musing the reality of his entrepreneurial success.

Caron was hyper conscious of his driving skills knowing any law enforcement stop could prove fatal for his freedom and Octopoda's finances.

He continued on highway 17 until it changed to 91, providing a direct route to the Richmond Town Square several blocks from the Strait, in an upscale neighborhood. The parking lot was empty at this early hour which always worked in his favor…no curious observers.

Benoît pulled in front of the Marseille Bank, parked, exited, removed two large black duffle bags from the Sedan's trunk and headed for the front door.

Glancing over his right shoulder, Caron was pleased to see his security team parked in a powder blue van with blacked out windows. Inside were six Octopoda shooters armed with fully automatic rifles.

Benoît had the utmost confidence in his new security team, all of whom were former members of the Canadian Special Forces with decades of combat missions in the Middle East and North Africa.

Caron turned his attention back to his mission. Each bag weighed approximately ten kilos/twenty-two pounds making his task effortless. He dropped one bag to key in his five-digit code, then perused his surroundings as the door opened automatically. He picked up the dropped bag, entered, turned to ensure the automatic door locked and walked forward.

He was unconcerned that someone could exercise their curiosity to look into the bank's windows. They were murals of French landscapes making it impossible to see inside. The site was so gorgeous to admire a passerby didn't question the fact that no one ever saw a business being conducted there.

The interior lighted automatically as he proceeded to the back of the room, stopping at a reinforced steel door imbedded into a structure of steel beams, crisscrossed with welded five-centimeter steel bars. Setting the one bag down again, he entered another five-digit number into a security panel, heard a click, grabbed a recessed handle, pulled and entered what appeared to be a high-end law firm office.

The door closed automatically behind him. He waited to hear the magnetic cylinders complete the action of the impregnable entry.

Along the furthest wall to his right was a tan, leather couch and square oak end tables with chrome U shaped legs. In front of the seating area and about three meters in front of Benoît was a four-meter oak table matching those beside the couch. Three walls were a light coffee color with the fourth a deep chocolate which paired attractively with the thick pile cream carpet.

Several large landscapes of the Canadian Rockies adorned the walls to his left and right while facing him was a simulated bay window with a moving scene of valleys, cliffs and rivers, the flora and fauna filmed from a helicopter. He could hear the rush of the river as it meandered through a meadow, the bellowing of a bull moose and a grizzly bear raised on his hind feet scratching a tree.

"Morning," said a male; mid-thirties, dark complexion, black shoulder length hair parted in the middle and falling over his ears. Edmé wore an impeccably fitting blue, pinstriped suit, light blue, button down shirt with a white and navy-blue striped tie. He paired the suit with tan laced oxford shoes.

"Good morning to you cousin. We had a good weekend," replied Benoît as he advanced to the table and placed the two bags on the extended surface.

Edmé had been enjoying a morning cup of coffee behind a three-meter desk. Setting down his drink, he joined his relative at the counting table and the two proceeded to empty the bags, placing the packages of twenty-dollar bills neatly on top of one another.

The empty bags were folded neatly and laid on the floor as the men began the laborious task of machine counting each stack. Each dealer was required to submit a machine verified account of their currency but Octopoda trusted no one and always performed their own count prior to making the bank deposit.

This delivery?

Two million.

When the count was complete, the total would be sent via a secure, encrypted laptop to a server at the Mission safehouse. There would be no paper trail or account which could be hacked and exploited by law enforcement.

The two million would join the other millions in the massive safe hidden behind the bay window. The wall was controlled electronically and slid open with the pressing of two hidden buttons, simultaneously located at either end of the office.

The currency would remain hidden and secure until it totaled four hundred and fifty…million, at which point it would be shipped.

"It's true I have a lot of friends in politics, but they wouldn't be so friendly if they knew my business was drugs instead of gambling, which they consider a harmless vice. But drugs, that's a dirty business."

Marlon Brando

The irony was, Octopoda had numerous political friends in Victoria, Ottawa and Washington, who, although they acknowledged the cartel laundered millions through casinos, were not ignorant to the source of that money.

"One way to make sure crime doesn't pay would be to let the government run it."

Ronald Reagan

Criminals count on governments to cloud issues with their incompetency. The cartels are often unaware of or choose to ignore the reality of law enforcement agencies which reject bureaucratic ineptness, choosing instead to interface their agencies world-wide and particularly in North America.

Canada, The United States and several European Union countries contribute on-going investigative data to CHAP, an integrated communication system designed by U.S. Navy Seal, Commander Cheryl Chapman, at the request of, then, President James Bakus. The system was credited with interagency destruction of drug cartels, confiscation of millions of kilos of cocaine and the arrest of key personnel in various criminal syndicates in Canada, the United States and the United Kingdom.

Chapman was a SEAL, the U.S. Navy's special operations force (Sea, Air and Land). The United States Navy did not have female SEALs. That was the rule, not the policy. The rule. No women.

Debunking that public policy, Chapman was a decorated Navy SEAL along with several platoons of other accomplished strong female sailors who were trained secretly thousands of miles from the male SEAL's training center in California.

The President had tired of law enforcement agency infighting which had allowed the infiltration of terrorists and the spread of sex slavery/drug trafficking.

Her task was to create a department answerable only to him and a supportive software program. The objective was to tie every law enforcement agency across the country to one system, CHAP, allowing each department to post their investigative details, sharing specifics and receiving support from other agencies.

The system was successful immediately, allowing the Secret Service, FBI, Homeland Security, RCMP, CSIS and the Drug Enforcement Agency and numerous state and local law enforcement officers to stop the murder of several hundred American Democrat politicians on a Mahalo Airline flight from Minnesota to Los Angeles.

Previously, numerous agencies were duplicating their efforts unnecessarily. Using CHAP, the RCMP, Secret Service, FBI and Denver Police detectives worked together to take down the leader of the Christians for a Better America who orchestrated the bombing of the Mahalo Airline…a United States Senator.

CHAP was instrumental in the infiltration of a Southern California drug cartel which operated in Costa Rica, Canada and the United Kingdom.

Through the shared software, Scotland Yard intercepted thousands of kilos of Colombian cocaine shipped with Costa Rican bananas.

The LAPD Drug Squad was similarly successful collaborating with the Secret Service and Santa Barbara Police Department in intercepting several hundred millions dollars of Colombian cocaine, the millions buyers had brought to the exchange and arresting cartel lieutenants.

Made in the USA
Monee, IL
05 February 2020